"This fiction can become reality. Our reality."
—*USA Today*

"Totally believable!"
—*Kirkus Reviews*

"A real page-turner."
—*World Entertainment*

I0662365

"A perfect adventure."
—*Tulsa World*

"Truly frightening material."
—*Huntsville Times*

"Scary and mind-expanding."
—*Fredrickson & Friends*

"Joseph Massucci does an excellent job in combining New-Age literature with an action thriller."
—*Ron Callari, Editor, y-two-k.com*

"A good read, with plenty of bang for your Millennium buck."
—*Kevin Rittner, The Herald Tribune*

"Massucci blends imagination with a potentially devastating computer crisis to create the industry's best millennium thriller."
—*Howard Miller, Huntsville Times*

ALSO BY JOSEPH MASSUCCI

EXTINCTION
THE MILLENNIUM PROJECT
THE RESURRECTION OF ANDREW FINSBURY

JOSEPH MASSUCCI

GORGON

JOSEPH MASSUCCI

GORGON

GORGON

JOSEPH MASSUCCI

Safari Multimedia, LLC

Published by Safari Multimedia, LLC.

For information: contact@safarimultimedia.com

www.massucci.com

This novel was adapted from Joseph Massucci's "CODE: ALPHA" originally published in 1997 by Dorchester Publishing Co., Inc.

ISBN-13: 978-0615644998
ISBN-10: 0615644996

Artwork by Adina Nani, Vassiliy Mikhailin and Dejan Novakov (Dreamstime.com)
Book design by Safari Multimedia, LLC

To my Father

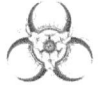

ABORT

Afghanistan (Pakistan border)
Monday, April 25
0200 hours

"Sir, we've got a problem," said Warrant Officer John Barron. One of the Navy's most experienced Black Hawk pilots, Barron wouldn't voice a concern for the safety of his aircraft unless he was certain of trouble.

Special Forces Maj. Joseph Marshall unbuckled himself from the forward observer seat and peered over the pilot's shoulder at the gunship's multi-function display. The major's intense dark eyes followed the green dot moving ahead and away from the flight group in patterns that could hardly be called regulation military flying. *The British NATO AH-64 Apache attack helicopter pilot is a mother fucking barnstormer,* he thought.

"His princely highness of Wales is getting cocky," Barron said.

Marshall's jaw tensed when the pilot switched his monitor to lowlight level to reveal the rolling mountain terrain a heart-stopping 400 feet below them. The low clouds had virtually blinded them.

"We're too damned low for royal heroics," Marshall said.

The former Seal knew this joint NATO assault mission was a mistake even if the Brit pilot weaving in front of them managed to fire the avenging shot at the mastermind of the 2005 London underground bombings. *He wins, we die getting him there.*

The major glanced at the copilot, Capt. David Johnson, whose calm and deft hands commanded the fastest and nimblest military chopper in the world. The Black Hawk's high-speed, low-altitude penetration made it ideal for stealth night missions across sovereign borders.

"What's our ETA?" Marshall asked.

"Twenty four minutes."

Don't grow impatient and careless, Marshall silently advised the royal pilot – *not with bin Laden so close.*

"He's broke formation again," Barron said, watching the British gunship maneuver heedlessly into harm's way. The strain was audible in his voice. "He's ahead of us now." A wind gust buffeted the Black Hawk. "He's dropped from our radar. I can't see through this shit."

Marshall knew damn well what the Brits were doing. *They weren't taking any chances with a ground assault – they intended to level bin Laden's compound with every missile their two gunships could lob at it.*

Marshall placed a hand on Captain Barron's shoulder. "Let this weather cover us, not kill us, son. Don't make me call a safety-of-flight abort."

"Yes sir."

Marshall returned to the Black Hawk's troop compartment and scanned the eight commandos sitting shoulder-to-shoulder on drop seats, their gear strapped to the fuselage. Each wore identical dark camouflage suits, and each carried the weapon of his choice – everything from modified Ingrams machine pistols to Franchi SPAS-12 semiautomatic military shotguns. No one spoke. No one moved about. The troops remained within themselves under the compartment's dim red lights, anticipating the assault landing.

"Hang on, ladies," Marshall said, making his way aft. "ETA in 23 minutes."

"What's up, sir?" This from Gunnery M.Sg. J. C. Williams, Marshall's right-hand man. The powerfully built black man from Mississippi had taught each of Marshall's troops to shoot three consecutive rounds from a Remington 40XB sniper rifle through a one-inch washer at two hundred yards.

Marshall eased himself against the fuselage beside the sergeant. "Our British friends are singing from different sheet music," he said. "His highness is going in first to claim the prize. I suspect they'll flatten bin Laden's camp with their two gunships."

Williams, his brow deeply furrowed, drawled, "The Brits wouldn't settle for no ground support duty. We're freaks to them. Air strikes, hard and bloody. That's what they know. They'll let their machines do their talking—"

The chopper gave a sudden yaw to starboard as the APR 39 warning voice announced, "ACQUIRED."

"Missile lock," the pilot shouted over the intercom. "Dropping."

The pilot increased power and pitched the aircraft's nose down to the left to break the missile's radar lock. A gut-wrenching concussion to the aircraft's lower fuselage nearly tore the ship in two.

There was an outburst from the men. "Christ!" Williams yelled.

Marshall was on his feet in an instant, scrambling into the cockpit. "Barron ... talk to me."

There was a flash and detonation ahead of them. Marshall's hands shielded his face instinctively as the windshield exploded into a blizzard of Plexiglas. A terrible wind ripped through the cockpit, masking the sound of a dozen simultaneous instrument alarms. The chopper lurched violently, sputtering and spinning from the sky like a wounded falcon. Captain Barron slumped, his head bouncing grotesquely. The copilot, his face a bloody river, groped for the control column, valiantly failing to control the chopper's descent.

Marshall clawed forward. In one wild motion he struck the pilot's buckle release and yanked Barron from the armored seat. An instant later the major was wrestling with the cyclic, ignoring the blast of wind and sand pouring into his face through the shattered windscreen.

The cockpit lights were out. Only the glow of the warning indicators, lit up like Christmas, told the major what he already knew – the aircraft wouldn't be in the air much longer. They were out of the game. A second U.S. Black Hawk *whumped* overhead to continue the mission.

Copilot Johnson grasped at the controls. "I can get her down."

"Take your hands off!" Marshall ordered.

The copilot sank senselessly back into his seat. "Ground-launched missiles. The British Apache flew right into our path when we took standard evasive action. Flew right into our *fucking* path. Couldn't maneuver. Two surface-to-air missiles detonated in our chaff. Get us down, major. For God's sake, get us down."

That was exactly what Marshall intended to do. The Black Hawk, swinging and side-slipping, spun toward the ground. He allowed his eyes a quick scan of the instrument panel. Hydraulics ... multi-function display ... TV monitor – everything gone. The cockpit display told Marshall he didn't stand a chance in hell of landing the chopper in one piece. *Two hundred feet ... one hundred seventy ... one hundred forty ...* Even for an aircraft in perfect working condition, a landing in mountain terrain would be difficult. *Do something!*

Marshall's face, streaked with sweat, reflected a mixture of determination and desperation. The lives of eight of the Navy's finest SEALS depended on his next move. He knew he could never bring the aircraft to a hover. *Auto-rotate it down – control the crash.*

"Impact positions," he shouted into the intercom.

One hundred ... fifty ...

The chopper's airspeed was still much too high. Marshall pulled up hard on the collective. The vibration threatened to break his knuckles and tear apart the control column. The twin turbo engines screamed a final desperate cry. The chopper dipped sharply as it hit the ground, then skidded sideways, ten tons of momentum pushing it down a ridge. Disintegrating rotors sheared off half the cockpit's roof.

Somehow the Black Hawk's cargo area remained intact. The aircraft came to a jarring halt on its side. Marshall cut the ignition, killed the main electrics and activated the aircraft's fire-control system. There was stunned silence while the emergency fire lights silently warned him to hustle ass.

Williams called in to him, "You okay, Joe?"

A shower of blood rained down on Marshall from the injured copilot dangling above him. "I got wounded in here," he shouted over his shoulder.

Marshall unbuckled the copilot and pulled him into the troop compartment. The others had already evacuated through the partially opened rear ramp door. The night was cold. He dragged the injured airman through the shattered fuselage into the face of a miserable mountain storm. Several pairs of hands carried their wounded comrade to safety.

Williams held a transceiver to his ear. "The op's officially aborted." His words spat out in short puffs of vapor.

Marshall forced a nod, his expression dour.

"I don't like when you get that look in your eyes, major."

"My pilot's dead. We didn't get bin Laden."

Williams shook Marshall's shoulder. "Not tonight, Joe. But we'll get him – and soon."

PART ONE

The Winds of Death

"Acquiring [chemical and nuclear] weapons
for the defense of Muslims is a religious duty."

—Osama bin Laden

"In modern war... you will die like a dog
for no good reason."

—Ernest Hemingway

Maximum Containment
Biohazard Level 4

Infectious Area
—Crash Door—
No Entrance

BIRTH

U.S. Army BL-4 Biological Laboratory
Fort Detrick, Maryland
Monday, 0720 hours

"We've got a breach!"

A horn blared in the high-security lab's staging area in sync with a flashing red alarm light. The lab's two technicians jumped to their feet and began jabbing rows of touch screens on the tactical console.

"Do we have contamination?"

"Checking."

There came a high-pitched whine, followed by a metallic click.

"Auto-lock complete."

"Jesus, he's sealed inside."

Burns, the center's chief engineer, spun around to one of the computer monitors while pushing his wire-frame glasses up the bridge of his nose. "Talk to me, Ricky. What's the situation in there?"

Ricky, the youngest technician assigned to Fort Detrick's maximum containment laboratory, punched one reset button after another while checking and rechecking the readouts. "I'm not getting anything."

Burns switched on the scanner. "Air particulates?"

"Zero. The air's clean."

"Must've torn his suit – hit the manual alarm." On the video monitor Burns saw Dr. David French inside the BL-4 "hot suite" hunched over a lab bench. He appeared to cradle his arm, but Burns couldn't be sure from the camera's angle. He hit the intercom. "Doctor, talk to me."

No answer.

"Jesus," Ricky said, "he isn't moving."

"Get the colonel down here – fast."

There was genuine fear in Ricky's eyes.

"*GO!*" Burns shouted.

Ricky bolted from the lab's staging area, his desperate footsteps echoing down the cinderblock corridor.

Burns nearly ripped the cord out of the wall when he pulled the receiver to his ear. "Security, we have a Code Seventeen SIGMA alarm in BL-4. Repeat, a Code Seventeen SIGMA alarm in BL-4. Auto-containment completed."

Burns could hear a thin voice on the other end asking questions, but the siren obscured the words. He put a finger into his left ear and shouted, "We have a Code Seventeen down here. Dr. French needs help, for chrissake. He may have breached his suit." Burns glanced up at the lab's closed-circuit monitor. He could no longer see Dr. French. *Where'd he go?* "Get Colonel Westbrook down here now!"

Julie Martinelli burst into the staging area, her white lab coat flowing behind her like a cape, her rubber-soled shoes punching the grated flooring. "What happened?" she shouted over the siren. "Where's Dr. French?"

"Inside," Burns said. "He's locked inside."

Julie's deep brown eyes scanned the monitors with practiced, professional detachment, checking for anomalous readings. "No air contamination."

"French hit the alarm," Burns shouted over the din.

"I can't hear a *fucking* thing." Julie slammed a console button to silence the siren. The red alarm light continued flashing.

"I don't see him." Julie panned the lab's two cameras first one way, then the other. "Where the hell is he?"

Burns shrugged. "At his lab bench a second ago."

Julie hit the intercom. "David? Answer me please."

Nothing.

Julie zoomed the camera on Dr. French's lab bench. She could see the active gamma radiation unit ... the beakers ... the vials labeled GROUP A STREPTOCOCCAL VIRUS....

"David, you stupid—" Julie removed her lab coat and opened a suit locker with a bang.

Burns reeled away from the console. "What may I ask are you doing?"

She already had one foot inside the one-piece, full-body polyurethane laboratory suit – a second skin the technicians called a prophylactic overcoat – and pulled it up to her waist.

"Going inside."

"The hell you are," Burns said. "Only the colonel can reset that door. Sit tight. Security's on its way."

"I'm not waiting."

Burns stood defiantly in her way. "You don't have much—"

Julie pushed past him with more force than she intended and took a seat at one of three computer workstations. She brought up the lab's security interface.

ACCESS CONTROL CODE?

"Don't even think about it," Burns said. "The colonel doesn't like grad students decompiling his security code."

"Then he shouldn't have left the network's remote access port wide open." She began typing, then entering, typing, entering.

LAB ACCESS DENIED

More typing.

MACRO COMPILED. PROCEED?

"Yes," she prompted the screen, then jabbed the enter key.

PLEASE WAIT

Burns couldn't take his eyes off of her. "You're making me very nervous."

MACRO COMPLETED

"Take a Xanax," she said, then entered a final command.

AUTHORIZED

"Yes!"

"You're a very dangerous woman," Burns said.

Julie pulled the lab suit over her shoulders and thrust her arms into the sleeves, fumbling to push each finger into the proper glove digit. Finished, she put on the hood and sealed it. She spun the releasing wheel on the vault-like door until it pulled forward with a loud hiss. "Tell the colonel he's got a huge problem on his hands."

"Are you going to clue me in—?"

Julie closed the fourteen-inch, two-ton steel door behind her with a mechanical click that echoed hollowly inside the airlock. Once inside the lab, she attached her suit to one of the spring-coiled air hoses hanging from the ceiling. The air supply hissed in her ears, and the magnified view through her face shield distorted objects beyond arm's length.

She took a deep breath and proceeded inside, her eyes scanning the lab.

The maximum containment laboratory was a claustrophobic compartment of centrifuges, incubators, freezers, benches and computing workstations. Cluttered, but very high-tech. She saw no trace of Dr. French.

"David?"

No response. Julie stepped to the lab bench. Her eyes followed the bench's row of culture dishes, beakers, the active gamma radiation unit ... the used syringe ... the rack of vials labeled GROUP A STREPTOCOCCAL VIRUS and a second labeled TETRODOTOXIN.

The sweat inside her suit chilled. "No way—"

"My ... head hurts."

Julie whirled with a start. *Where in hell did he come from?* She recognized Dr. French's features behind his face shield – his shaved head, his magnificent handlebar mustache. Something was terribly wrong. She could see his contorted expression beneath a magnifying face shield that made his eyes look like a pair of poached eggs.

Her anger swelled. "You son of a bitch. You did it, didn't you?"

She expected him to begin reciting one of his cliché philosophical lectures about stretching the limits of the scientific envelope. But he said nothing.

"David, you made me a promise...."

She froze. A drop of blood beaded atop the fingertip of French's white polyurethane glove. Was he even aware, she wondered? "Your finger..."

He held out his hand to her as though it belonged to a powerless lab animal. "Stupid ... so stupid ... a small distraction ... I never felt the needle."

Julie noted the sweat flowing down his face inside his suit. She touched his shoulder. "I'll take you into decontamination...."

Dr. French shook his head repeatedly. "Too late ... too late. An army of red ants ... burrowing through my brain."

He doubled over in agony.

"David?"

When he raised his head, she could see his lower lip quivering. "Julie ... the pain—"

A cough exploded from his lips, speckling his face shield with blood-laden mucus. He grasped at a row of bottles on the table with trembling and twitching fingers. Before he could touch the bottles, his arm began undulating in an unholy dance. Julie realized he'd lost all muscular control.

"Gancic ... gancic ... gancic ..." He couldn't form the word.

Julie grabbed the doctor firmly by his shoulders and tried to ease him back onto a lab stool. "What are you trying to say?"

He lashed out at her with a violent energy, catching her Plexiglas face shield at the chin. The blow drove her backward onto one of the lab's two scanning tunneling microscopes, rocking the seven-hundred-pound instrument.

French collapsed into a heap, his face a grimacing mask of agony, his arms and legs flailing and thrashing. He grabbed his suit at the neck and clawed at its collar, tearing the material. "The heat ... the awful heat..."

Julie watched, incredulous, as within seconds radical dehydration shrank the biochemist into a wizened caricature of his former self. Capillaries, rupturing en masse, mottled his skin with black-and-blue swirls, which exploded with high-speed devastation.

Julie inched backwards.

Finally Dr. French grew still. His remains lay heaped in a twisted pile, the airflow from the ceiling-mounted hose still animating his suit with the illusion of life. Red and yellow sap oozed where he had ripped open his suit, forming a puddle around him.

Julie knelt down and, breathing deeply, peered through the face shield at what was left of the doctor's face.

His eyes flared open and stared up at her.

She gasped in horror. *Those eyes ... they're not human!*

His face – a visage bubbling with secretions – forfeited any claim to humanity. *God ... he had literally melted inside his suit,* Julie thought.

His rubber hand grabbed her wrist with fingers that still possessed surprising strength. The ravaged flesh beneath his limp mustache tried to form words, but his tongue had become an engorged mass. The foul moan that erupted from his throat sounded like the last breath of a dying wolf.

No sound penetrated the lab's fourteen-inch-thick metal walls.

GORGON

Barlar Settlement, Afghanistan
Monday, April 25, dawn

Five miles outside the remote settlement, two Jeep travelers spotted the first signs of an unfolding nightmare. The gritty haze barely veiled a procession of old men, motherless children, fear-crazed drivers and other stragglers fleeing from a once-vibrant village into the forbidding desert. Some of them wept bitterly. Most simply walked in stunned disbelief.

Tarra passed a row of defeated soldiers, their rifles hanging in limp salute to the unseen enemy still lurking inside the town. Finally her Jeep swept past the tribal elders squatting helplessly around the perimeter. A lifetime of clan warfare and skirmishes with the superpowers did nothing to prepare them from this invasion.

But this was not war. It was a test.

Tarra barreled fearlessly around the trail's curves, chasing knots of dazed refugees into the ditches. She laughed at them all. Some men found her attractive – and so she was, with seductive features, short black hair and deep green eyes that could impale you. However, her vicious contempt for men was legend, her feline beauty hinting at the untamable beast within.

Tarra jerked the Jeep to a halt at the edge of the settlement of meager huts hastily cordoned off with thick spools of barbed wire and splashes of red paint warning not to proceed.

Tarra turned to the lone passenger in the rear seat and smiled, her piercing eyes alert and eager for more. For this one man she harbored no contempt, only unyielding loyalty and an insatiable longing. He was a giant, intimidating to look at, dressed in a tailored silk suit and a civil red tie that set apart a dark face bloated by hatred. He responded to her mischievous smile with detached frigidity.

The man stood, peeled off his aviator-style sunglasses and raised a pair of high-powered binoculars to his dark, distant eyes. He could hear wailing in the distance, a far-off echo of mourning, but could not discern whether the sound was human or animal. He scanned the settlement, coolly assessing the extent of this disaster. At first he could see nothing but neglected wood-and-straw structures that had fought a generation-long war against the encroaching desert. Scores of huts, undamaged, stood empty. He saw no people, no activity of any kind.

He focused on the dirt road that cut the settlement in two and saw the bodies. Dozens of them. Women huddled in doorways clutching their children, men draped across the road reaching futilely to help them. Carcasses of mules and dogs lay scattered along the roads. Barlar had become an appalling settlement of corpses.

He removed the binoculars and let his war-trained mind consider how this could have happened. Poisoned water? No – death had come too quickly. An air strike? There were no craters.

The north road.

He focused the binoculars on a stretch of open road atop the far ridge three hundred yards upwind of the settlement. Through the distant curtain of dust he could see the outline of an overturned tank truck for transporting hazardous liquids, its lethal contents emptied. *Well done.* The people of Barlar were the unlucky participants in a lethal experiment. Their homes stood in the path of a wind that carried with it a death far more effective than an advancing army. He grinned, amused by the experiment's deadly outcome.

"Abdul Banna!" a voice called out to him.

Banna whirled to see who had shouted his name so brazenly. Several soldiers dressed in strange suits with gas-mask snouts and large glass eyes that allowed them to fight in a contaminated environment approached him along the barbed-wire barricade. Their suits, thick and bulky with gloves and boots to match, included an armband with the subtle markings only a very few would recognize as al-Qaeda extremists.

The lead soldier ordered the others to halt, while he alone approached the Jeep. The soldier removed his mask to reveal a face doused with sweat. It promised to be a long day. The heavy suit had consumed what little of his energy remained.

Banna knew this soldier. His name was Wafiq Sabri, al-Qaeda's deputy operations chief.

"You are a desperate man, Sabri," Banna called to him in Arabic. "Is this pathetic demonstration your best plan for another attack on the West?"

Sabri climbed into the back of the Jeep and plopped heavily beside Banna, displacing a cloud of dust from the leather seat. He curtly ordered the woman behind the wheel to leave.

Tarra, sneering, didn't move.

"She will stay," Banna said.

Sabri, uncomfortable in the presence of a woman, nodded wearily. "Tonight this settlement will be buried and with it all that happened here today."

Banna shrugged. "Is he ready to pay?"

"The Lion will pay what you ask. He wants Operation Harness done just as you planned. Allah has given us a unique opportunity. You are to begin immediately."

Banna smirked. "I admire bin Laden's conviction. He finally concedes that his field operatives are mere children in his war."

"Your plan has given him new hope," Sabri said. "The West closes in. He is convinced they will find him. He cannot fight the infidels that attack him from the sky or by sea. These murderers strike again, this time destroying our laboratories, which cannot yield enough uranium to power a clock. But you –" he thrust a finger at Banna– "you are his secret weapon. You can do what an army of our cadres cannot. And may Allah praise your name."

"I am only interested in bin Laden's payment."

Sabri nodded. "In two days, the first eighty million pounds will be deposited into the London branch of the Bank of Credit and Commerce International, just as you requested. You will report to me—"

"I report to no one. I work with my own people. The plan is mine, as is its execution. I shall divulge the details of Harness to no one, least of all to you. Once I leave here, you will not hear from me again. I shall become invisible. Tell the Lion he will soon have his greatest victory."

Banna could sense the dread swelling within Sabri as the soldier considered how the world would soon change because of the man seated next to him.

"Then let it be done," Sabri said. "May Allah be willing."

Banna scoffed at the soldier's prayer and wiped his forehead with a silk handkerchief. This was not Allah's affair. This was simple economics. The desert Lion cannot defeat the alliance of force the superpowers have rallied against him. The next strike must be done another way – Banna's way.

"There is one more item that is not for negotiation," Banna said. "You are never to utter my name again."

Sabri nodded. From this day Abdul Banna would cease to exist. "How will you be known?"

"I have a passion for Greek mythology." Banna replaced his aviator sunglasses and touched the chin of his charming Tarra. "Men dare not look her into her face, except by degrees: they mistake her for a Gorgon, instead of understanding she is Athena."

She smiled coolly at her master.

"I will be Gorgon."

ABDUCTION

Anne Arundel County, Maryland
Monday, 2302 hours

Dr. Reinhard Sterling hailed the next available cab in the line of yellow outside Baltimore/Washington International Airport, tossed his carry-on travel bag and satchel into the backseat and climbed in after them. Never before had he been so happy to greet a world-weary cabbie. He wanted to get far away from airports, a sentiment shared by fellow travelers on Lufthansa Flight 407 from Frankfurt. The flight had arrived three and a half hours late in the wake of a bomb threat at the German airport. Now he had to find his way to the U.S. capital at midnight and, worse, function coherently at a 7:30 A.M. meeting with a United States senator.

"Please take me to Washington," Dr. Sterling instructed the driver in his German accent, still thick after three decades as a naturalized U.S. citizen. "The Sutton House."

The affable driver, an old black man with a winning smile of gold, nodded and pulled his cab away from the terminal. Sterling could sense him making a mental tally of tonight's fares. *Jackpot!* This trip would net him a very good night indeed.

"Pretty late to be gettin' into town." the cabby called back to his fare.

"Yes, very," Sterling said, his sixty-four-year-old face revealing the strain of the last twenty-four hours. The biochemist was not in a conversational mood, something the cabby quickly picked up on. The cab pulled onto the Baltimore/ Washington

Expressway and headed southwest toward D.C. The traffic this time of night was sparse, allowing them to make good time.

Sterling closed his eyes and relaxed for the first time since leaving Geneva. Sleep had been elusive ever since he received the phone call last night. In fact, the whole tenor of his trip changed following the hasty summons by Senator Baker. What began as a business visit and a brief speech at a conference of fellow molecular biologists at Fort Detrick now included an unwelcome high-level meeting at the capitol. *All because of a lab researcher's stupid blunder.* Sterling first learned of the Fort Detrick incident in a news report along with everyone else. The military may have pitched an unholy war against humanity and won. *Idiots!* The day of reckoning was at hand.

Soon the late-night traffic thinned to a few specks of red taillights well ahead. The cabby tuned in an all-night talk station, one of the many devoting its programming exclusively to the possibility of another war in the Middle East, this time with Libya.

"Do ya think he has it?" the cabby offered over his shoulder. "The bomb, that is. Do you think he'll nuke the Jews?"

Sterling didn't answer. He was trying to sleep, the gentle drone of the road providing a sedative for his frayed nerves. The cabby turned the radio low.

Sterling's nap was short-lived. A flashing blue light blinked on behind them, filling the vehicle. His eyes flared open, and he heard the cabby utter, "Shit."

Disoriented, Sterling glanced out the rear window and saw another car approaching rapidly from behind, blue dashboard lights flashing. The car pulled so close to their rear bumper that its headlights disappeared below the cab's trunk. "Slow down before he kills us."

The cabby glanced at his speedometer. "Six miles over the speed limit – a lousy six miles!"

His smile long vanished, the cabby pulled onto the soft shoulder of the highway with a thump, gravel raging against the undercarriage. So much for his jackpot night.

"Damn cop," the cabby muttered, lowering his window.

Sterling twisted his neck and peered through the rear window. All he could see was the backlit silhouette of a hefty uniformed man wearing a state-trooper's hat.

"Please come with me," the officer ordered the cabby through the open window. It was a command, neither a polite nor routine request.

"Yes, sir." The cabby slid from the front seat.

Sterling listened to the retreating gravel footsteps. He glanced at his watch, and then closed his eyes and scratched his closely cropped beard in frustration. Would he ever get to a bed tonight?

Suddenly the cab doors flew open and three people slid neatly inside. A powerful-looking woman with short black hair pushed Sterling roughly to the center of the backseat and jammed hard metal into his ribs. He was too stunned to flinch.

"What is this?" Sterling said. "Who are you people? What are you doing?" No one answered him. He appealed to the woman for an answer, but her stern look of contempt terrified him.

The man behind the wheel, a dark, grisly brute with a squashed nose like a trained fighter's, put the cab in gear and pulled back onto the highway. The doctor's worst fears were realized when the unmarked patrol car passed them quickly by. He could see the uniformed officer with his round-brimmed hat, but no one else. What had happened to his cabby? And who were these people? *For God's sake, what is happening?*

The woman passed Sterling's travel bag and satchel to a distinguished-looking man in the front passenger seat. The man could have passed for Sterling's twin brother. Like Sterling, the man exuded an academic aura. He was of medium height, mid-sixties, enjoyed a healthy head of silver hair, a large frame with a notable paunch and even the same inquiring scientific eyes. The doppelganger opened Sterling's well-traveled satchel, snapped on a pencil-thin flashlight and began a meticulous search of its contents.

Sterling watched him carefully with his practiced, academic calmness. "Someone please tell me what this is about."

The woman slipped an arm over Sterling's shoulders and applied pressure as a warning. "Do not ask questions." She spoke with a clipped, refined British accent. He smelled the strangest scent of sun bleached sand and musk.

"Let him speak, Tarra," ordered the man with his coach satchel. He, too, had an accent, which Sterling recognized as German. The man's careful and deliberate phrasing suggested he was a student of languages.

Tarra poked Sterling cruelly in the ribs with a Walther. "Speak to him."

Sterling's mouth was too dry, his tongue too heavy for speech.

"My name is Dr. Carl Wynett," said Sterling's counterpart in front. "My associates call me 'the Businessman' – now you will tell me something about yourself."

Tarra poked Sterling harder. "Speak!"

"Where ... are you taking me?"

Businessman demanded, "More," without looking up from his exploration of the doctor's satchel.

Another vicious stab to the ribs.

"You can have my money ... everything. I am carrying one thousand dollars."

Tarra laughed wickedly. "We do not need your money—"

"Be quiet," the Businessman shouted. He looked severely at Sterling. "More."

Sterling's breathing became more labored. He felt dizzy. This was insane. Why hijack a cab carrying a faceless academic? He shuddered. "Please. I do not want trouble. I am a doctor – a biochemist. I am to address a conference tomorrow in Maryland."

"I do not want trouble," the Businessman echoed. The timbre and tone of his voice now perfectly matched that of his captive. "I am a doctor – a biochemist." He mimicked Sterling's facial expressions as he spoke, even scratching nervously at his beard. Hours of practiced skill were evident in this masquerade. "Tomorrow I will address my colleagues at a conference of the American Society of Microbiology convening at Fort Detrick."

Sterling gaped. The imitation was remarkable.

"You have him," the driver affirmed with a grin. Tarra agreed.

The Businessman closed the satchel. "I see the text of your speech and a working draft of an as yet-untitled paper on enzymes. Still, there is something missing. Your secretary confirmed for me your seven-thirty appointment tomorrow morning at the capitol, yet I see no correspondence here related to that meeting. Surely you would bring it with you."

Sterling, still trying to make sense of the situation, said nothing.

"Surely you brought it with you," the Businessman repeated tersely.

Tarra grabbed Sterling by the lapels and felt inside his suit. She retrieved a black leather billfold and passed it to the front. Sterling sat passively. These people would take what they wanted, with or without his cooperation. The Businessman rifled through airline tickets, a membership card for the National Academy of Science, a travel itinerary that included a hotel confirmation at the Sutton House, an employee ID for GenTech Laboratories. Then he found an email printout, which he read with particular interest.

"I have it," he said, directing his penlight's beam at the paper. "A personal invitation to meet with Senator Michael Baker tomorrow at seven-thirty A.M. to discuss a laboratory incident, it says. There are no details." He shone his piercing penlight into Sterling's face. "Please elaborate for me, doctor. Perhaps this meeting is about an unlawful gene-splicing experiment?"

These people intend to kill me, Sterling realized, stunned.

The Businessman nodded imperceptibly at Tarra. She delivered two quick, hard elbow blows to Sterling's ribs, cracking two of them.

He cried in pain, surprised by her strength. Tarra poised her arm for another blow, but Sterling, winded and grimacing, waved her off. "I know only what was in the newspapers. No one has yet briefed me."

"You are lying."

"One mile," the driver warned, turning on the cab's inside dome light. They were out of time.

The Businessman stuffed Sterling's billfold inside his own suit coat, then appraised the doctor's features like a plastic surgeon scrutinizing his work. "What have we missed?"

"His eyeglasses are different," Tarra noted.

"Give them to me."

Tarra removed his glasses and passed them to the front.

Sterling squinted helplessly as the inside of the car became a blur.

"His beard is thinner and has more white hairs," said the driver, scrutinizing the doctor in the rearview mirror.

"Yes, yes, I will take care of it. What else?"

"His ring and watch," Tarra said. These, too, she roughly removed and gave to the Businessman.

The cab pulled into a well-lit rest area and jerked to a stop beside a black Ford Expedition. There were no other passenger vehicles parked this time of night, just a couple of rigs idling in the outer lot. The cab had barely stopped when the Businessman exited, taking Sterling's travel bag and satchel with him. He leant through the opened window. "Are you absolutely clear on your instructions?"

Tarra nodded, her feline features exuding a cool look of confidence. "No one will find his remains."

"I can get you money," Sterling pleaded. "As much as you want. My employer will give you whatever you want. Anything."

No one paid him the slightest notice. The condemned scientist looked despairingly at the faces of his abductors, searching for signs of compassion, a willingness to deal. But he saw only the hard, professional expressions of ruthless people who knew what they wanted and how to get it.

Tarra let mucus drip from her mouth onto on his trousers and smiled.

The Businessman vanished from the window and climbed behind the wheel of the Expedition. Less than a minute later, both cars were gone.

GOLDEN KEY

Washington, D. C.
Tuesday, April 26, 0738 hours

"Dr. Sterling, it's a pleasure to finally meet you," said Sen. Michael Baker, offering a sincere handshake to the man with Dr. Reinhard Sterling's appearance and identification papers.

The senator led his guest to a plush couch in the center of a room that looked more like a university library than the office of a statesman. The room smelled of leather. The high ceiling allowed ample room for two walls of oak bookcases filled with sanitized leather-bound volumes. The senator obviously loved his books, the Businessman noted – not for the ideas they contained, but for the image they conveyed about their owner.

Senator Baker, a jovial, rotund politician on the long end of his sixties, tried to conceal a manila folder tucked under his left arm. He wasn't successful. The Businessman spotted it immediately and surmised its contents were the reason for Dr. Sterling's summons.

"I know you have a full day up at the institute, and my day's a mess," the white-haired senator told his guest. "So I'll keep this short and sweet."

The two sank comfortably into the deep leather couch, like old friends about to enjoy a couple of scotches. The Businessman knew the senator could be quite affable when he wanted something, and today he wanted a lot from Dr. Sterling. Baker opened the manila folder and put on a pair of old-fashioned, half-lens reading glasses that made him look like a flushed-cheek Ben Franklin.

35

"Dr. Sterling, I hope you will help me in what I pray won't become a major national embarrassment."

"Certainly ... if I can."

"When it comes to microbes and viruses, my experience is limited to an annual bout of the flu – at least the kind we understand so far." He chuckled. "But you are one of the few people outside the military qualified to distinguish the natural from the man-made when it comes to microorganisms."

The Businessman gave Senator Baker a professional nod with a hint of a smile.

"Last week," the senator continued, his eyes inside the folder, "the U.S. Army's chief biological engineer died in a freak accident at Fort Detrick. Perhaps you heard about it?"

The Businessman nodded. "Yes, I read the news account. It was Dr. David French. Very unfortunate. He and I dinned together a year ago in Geneva."

"What hasn't been reported yet – and I implore you to keep this in strictest confidence – is that a Stanford doctoral candidate interning at Fort Detrick, a young woman named Julie Martinelli, made some serious allegations about that accident. In her note to me, Ms. Martinelli claims that Dr. French synthesized a virus just prior to his death."

"May I know the nature of this organism?" the Businessman asked.

The senator dug deeper into the folder and produced another document. "Does this help?"

The Businessman took the lab report and scanned it. "Most interesting. I was aware of Dr. French's pioneer work on a gamma radiation mutagenesis technique that would allow him to splice protein around the RNA strand of a virus. A remarkable achievement, if he was successful."

The senator peeled off his reading glasses and thrust them toward his guest. "If the virus French created was part of an offensive tactical weapon, it would be in gross violation of the 1972 Biological and Toxic Weapons Convention and the 1925 Geneva Protocol. Ms. Martinelli was with Dr. French when he died. But she has since been denied clearance to gather hard evidence to support her charges. So she has appealed to me to look into the matter. Now I am appealing to you."

The Businessman sank back into the overstuffed couch with feigned astonishment. "Interesting. How may I help you?"

Senator Baker presented him with the woman's letter and a one-page biography of Julie Martinelli. "Ms. Martinelli mentioned you by name. She knows you, or at least knows your work, and sent me this letter after learning you would take part in the conference at the fort today. She says you can gain the clearance to access Detrick's maximum containment labs and that you would be able to determine the nature of Dr. French's work."

The Businessman scanned the letter and then perused her biography. He suppressed a smile. *Beautiful.* Martinelli was handing him a golden key to the city – a city of corpses. "Why doesn't she take her charge to the Defense Department? Or go to the press, if she feels this strongly?"

"Because of this." He passed the Businessman another sheet of paper, a research synopsis. "She attached that to her letter. French can't claim credit for his creation. The idea belongs to her, and she is not at all comfortable about her complicity in French's creation."

"I am not following."

"Ms. Martinelli believes her original thesis proposal could have spawned the incident that led to Dr. French's death. In that paper she proposes to genetically engineer a microorganism that could well prove useful as a biological weapon."

"A graduate student?" the Businessman said, rapidly digesting the sheet's information. "According to this, she proposed to splice tetrodotoxin protein – the most potent neurotoxin known – around the RNA strand of a Group A streptococcal virus that causes rheumatic fever. Her goal was to create an airborne virus four hundred times as lethal as conventional neurotoxins, with characteristics that would make it ideal for covert tactical biological warfare."

Senator Baker raised a halting hand. "She had no intention of going through with the experiment. The technology didn't even exist – or at least that's what she thought. She believes Dr. French's gene-splicing technique allowed him to create this new life-form, and the experiment caused his death. If her suspicions are correct, she fears she might be indirectly responsible for creating the potential for a terrible plague."

"According to the autopsy report," the Businessman said, reading another page, "it appears as though he succeeded. Brilliantly so."

Senator Baker rubbed his brow wearily, then looked at the Businessman with genuine pleading in his eyes. "Dr. Sterling, I need to ask you to do me a very large favor. Before I can take Ms. Martinelli's charges seriously and begin a formal investigation, I need to know the facts. Can I ask you to put one more item on your agenda today? I need a military outsider to ask the right people at Fort Detrick the right questions and, more important, to know when he hears the right answers. I will bow to your expertise to phrase those questions."

A fleeting smile animated the Businessman's features, an unspoken agreement between gentlemen. "Senator Baker, I trust in our new friendship and would be only too happy to inquire on your behalf. And I promise to exercise the utmost discretion." *And thank you, Senator – and most of all you, Ms. Martinelli – for making my trip here so immensely profitable.*

FORT DETRICK

Fort Detrick, Maryland
Tuesday, 1004 hours

A Bell Ranger jet helicopter *whumped* over Fort Detrick's one-story barracks-style buildings and settled on a helipad inside the main gate. A gray sedan, its engine idling, sat waiting. The chopper's skids had hardly touched the tarmac when a uniformed young man with spit-polished shoes and a buzz haircut bolted from the car and crossed the pad to greet it. The helicopter's twin turbine engines throttled back to idle and a door opened behind the cockpit. The Businessman leapt to the ground, Dr. Sterling's well-traveled satchel tucked securely under his arm.

The uniformed soldier, a clean-cut American boy with a sincere grin, ducked under the blades and extended his hand to the visitor. "Dr. Sterling, I'm Lieutenant McPherson. I'll take you over to the conference."

The Businessman accepted the proffered hand with a forced grin. "I must ask you to make a detour. Please take me to see Colonel Westbrook immediately. He should be expecting me."

The lieutenant returned a puzzled expression. "Sir, your presentation is scheduled to begin in 15 minutes."

"Do as I ask, lieutenant. And may we please hurry? I do not wish our chat to result in any more needless deaths."

Lieutenant McPherson delivered his guest to the compound's newest building, a three-story bunker made of institutional, sand-colored concrete. The Businessman paused before the building's entrance, the home of the United States Army Medical Research Institute of Infectious Disease, or USAMRIID. A tangle of smokestacks and pipes lining the roof offered telltale clues to the institute's hazardous aerosol research. The Businessman smiled, inwardly bowing to this monument to mankind's never-ending quest for new and exotic ways to kill its own. Although there had been a notable attempt to make the building appear singularly uninteresting, he knew that in the event of a mishap, this concrete structure could help safeguard the state against the biological equivalent of a nuclear meltdown.

The lieutenant escorted his guest through a set of double glass doors to the guard's station. There the Businessman forged an entry in the register and stood by impatiently while a security woman with serious blue eyes verified his appointment and prepared an ID tag.

He clipped the tag to his lapel and turned to Lieutenant McPherson. "Please show me the way."

The guard buzzed the two through to the building's administration area, where they disappeared down the sterile hallway.

The lieutenant rapped his knuckles hard three times on the door's metal frame, which opened into a large corner office.

"Enter," Colonel James Westbrook snapped in his curt physician's voice.

Lieutenant McPherson marched into the colonel's office, jerked to attention before the huge desk, fixed his gaze on a point just above his superior's head and announced, "Dr. Reinhard Sterling to see you on behalf of Senator Michael Baker, sir."

Dr. Westbrook glanced up from a *Baltimore Sun* article about the gory dismemberment of a Maryland cabdriver. "So I've been informed. But no one's told me yet what the fuck he wants?"

"Forgive the short notice, colonel," the Businessman said from the doorway, "but we need to talk."

Westbrook flashed the lieutenant a frown. "Call Senator Baker's office and make sure this guy's business is legit."

The lieutenant saluted, turned and vanished.

The Businessman took the lieutenant's place before the colonel's gray metal desk, which reminded him of an aircraft carrier, and offered his hand. The center's commander stood and accepted the Businessman's firm grip, returning an expression as rigid as his uniform.

"I'm well aware of your work," Westbrook said in his Texas drawl. "Hell, everyone here is."

He waved the doctor into one of three leather chairs facing his desk and stuck an ugly blue pipe into his mouth. Westbrook obviously enjoyed pipes and disliked tooth whiteners, facts betrayed by his worn and discolored teeth.

"I've read your work on biotechnology and genetic engineering. Impressive." Obligatory plaudits aside, the colonel's tone became as serious as a bowl of boiled cauliflower. "I understand you're here today to help figure out what al-Qaeda can do with an arsenal of chemical and biological weapons, if we give them a chance." He glanced at his watch with raised eyebrows. "You're late for the conference."

The Businessman took a seat in the center chair. The office trappings, like the medals on the colonel's jacket, existed to impress visitors with the officer's experience abroad – a framed parchment from Egypt, bone carvings from China and countless wall masks from Africa. Westbrook, he concluded, was a well-traveled warrior who worried too much about making general.

The Businessman pulled an envelope from his satchel and pushed it to the center of the colonel's desk. "The conference will wait." He pointed to the envelope. "This must take priority."

The colonel gave his visitor a scowl. "What is this shit?"

"Senator Baker assured me you would cooperate. I have taken him at his word. I came here to investigate the death of Dr. David French. You could help matters immensely by keeping the tone of this meeting professional. Perhaps we can work together to dissuade the senator from conducting a full Senate hearing on this affair."

The colonel sat rigid and stared at the man on the subservient side of his desk. Westbrook started to cross his legs, then began merely fidgeting a bit. The Businessman suppressed a grin over the martinet's discomfiture. The colonel must have known it was only a matter of time before Washington stuck its thick nose into this ugly business, the Businessman thought. *Your day of reckoning is here, sir.*

"Our investigation's closed," the colonel said, choosing his words carefully. "Dr. French's death was an unfortunate accident. Poor bastard stuck himself with a contaminated needle. I'll get you a copy of the report."

"May I ask the nature of Dr. French's work?"

"Bolivian hemorrhagic fever."

"We must be honest with each other, Colonel Westbrook. You will find among those papers an autopsy summary. The facts do not support death by hemorrhagic fever. An infection of that sort would not deplete a one-hundred-and-seventy-six-pound man of forty percent of his body fluids in 30 minutes. Nor am I aware of any virus that would."

The colonel banged his pipe gavel-like into a heavy glass ashtray. "Are you some sort of detective, doctor? A fucking Sherlock Holmes wannabe?"

"I am a defense consultant – biogenetics. Senator Baker asked me to verify the facts of this case, a straightforward request, unless someone is hiding something. In which case I will simply turn the investigation over to the senator."

Colonel Westbrook slumped back into his padded chair, propped a foot up on his desk, removed the envelope's contents and unfolded the stack of papers. The top page was a letter to him from Senator Baker, chairman of the Defense Department Investigation Subcommittee, asking him as a personal favor to give Dr. Sterling his full cooperation. The text outlined the possibility of a Senate hearing. Next was the autopsy report, the details of which the colonel had probably censored himself. The more the colonel read, the harder he sucked on his empty pipe.

The Businessman knew that even the most careful cover-up attempt could backfire, and the colonel would be the first scapegoat if the real reason for Dr. French's death became public. There was still too much information in these documents, details from which a man with Sterling's credentials could glean volumes.

The colonel pulled a thin appointment book out of his shirt pocket, opened it to today's date and made a note. He no doubt intended to investigate everyone who had access to this information. Someone's head would roll for this.

"If I didn't know better, I'd say the senator is trying to sandbag me," the colonel said at last. "What's your take?"

Before the Businessman could answer, there came another three hard knocks on the door's frame. The colonel glanced up at the lieutenant, who gave him a thumbs-up signal. "He checks out with Senator Baker."

The Businessman said, "I would now like to meet someone."

"Who?"

"Julie Martinelli."

Westbrook's head jerked up from his appointment book. The Businessman knew he had just provided the colonel with the source of this leak.

The colonel shook his head, scowling. "She's a nobody. A student working here thanks to the influence of her daddy, an army colonel. She can't tell you jack shit."

The Businessman withdrew a one-page biography the senator included in the file. "Ms. Martinelli is a Stanford graduate student six credits short of her Ph.D. in molecular biochemistry. She was a computer prodigy. At the age of five she could navigate through a mainframe system. At seven she could program in three machine languages. Along the way Ms. Martinelli mastered algebra, geometry and calculus, all on her own. She entered Stanford at sixteen on the basis of a scientific visualization program to display cosmic string interaction, which she developed as a high school science project. Then she turned her talents to biology – molecular bioengineering, to be

43

specific. She developed seventeen revolutionary gene-mapping visualization programs, and is chairing a team to develop one of the most extensive genetic databases in the world. Her research paper proposing the use of chemical units of DNA as computing symbols has researchers in awe. She describes a memory bank constructed from a pound of DNA molecules suspended in a tank of fluid one meter square. The DNA molecules are synthesized with a chemical structure that represents numerical information. The vast amount of number-crunching that could be done in parallel as the reaction proceeds could potentially create the world's fastest supercomputer and store more information than all the memories of all the computers ever made. Everyone from computer scientists to physicists to molecular biologists is intrigued. I would very much like to meet your *nobody*, colonel."

Westbrook's cheeks flushed with anger. "You're on a wild-goose chase, for chrissake."

"Allow me to decide."

Colonel Westbrook let out a huff of cynical laughter and jabbed the mouthpiece end of his pipe at the Businessman. "Sterling, the work we do here at Detrick is vital to national security. We're looking at all sorts of crap taken from terrorists all over the world that could potentially be loaded into a missile warhead. I can't allow a goddamn geek get in the way of our nation's business."

The Businessman shrugged innocently. "I am only asking to interview a graduate student – a nobody, you said. Please introduce me to Ms. Martinelli. Or should I advise Senator Baker for congressional oversight?"

USAMRIID

The walk from Colonel Westbrook's office down spotlessly drab hallways to the research area of USAMRIID impressed the Businessman. Electric eyes scanned the visitors and activated double doors that swung open, admitting them into a red-painted cinder block-and-concrete corridor, where white-coat technicians pushed carts of test tubes that clinked and echoed. Thick, bitter odors of nutrient broth and lab animals permeated the building's prisonlike atmosphere, smells the Businessman found invigorating.

Westbrook led the way through a second set of electric doors and down a stark, battleship-gray corridor that ran the length of the USAMRIID building. On either side of the corridor, windows and doors offered tantalizing glimpses inside labs where scientists and researchers were working. Above one door sealed from ceiling to floor with duct tape, a sign read: INFECTIOUS AREA – CRASH DOOR – NO ENTRANCE. Access to any one of these labs could have suited the Businessman's needs, but he revealed no outward signs of impatience. He fully intended to play his masquerade for the highest payoff – access to a maximum-containment BL-4 lab.

The pair reached a partially open door devoid of identification and entered unannounced. The Businessman noted the large, windowless room was actually a common academic office, devoid of the test tubes and lab equipment that were the staples of Detrick. In their place, arranged neatly between file cabinets and book-laden metal desks, sat three computers: a

Sun scientific workstation, an Apollo microcomputer, and a Macintosh desktop.

A striking woman in her twenties, with gorgeous black hair flowing over her shoulders and a figure that would turn heads, worked the keyboard of the Mac. She was dressed for a hike in a pair of khaki slacks and a tan T-shirt. The Businessman concluded she was too preoccupied with her appearance to be an effective biochemist. She radiated a self-confidence disconcerting – conceited – in one so young. Nevertheless, he could readily see that she also radiated a genuine intelligence. Gifted? He intended to find out.

"Martinelli," Colonel Westbrook said, "this gentleman wants a word with you."

Startled, the woman spun around in her chair, her penetrating brown eyes riveted on her visitor. There was a flicker of recognition.

"This is Dr. Reinhard Sterling," Westbrook said. "Says you and he have something to discuss."

There followed an awkward silence. Julie stared at the Businessman as though he were a homicide detective with an arrest warrant. She probably had been dreading this moment ever since sending Senator Baker that email, the Businessman guessed. And now that he was here, there was no turning back.

Suddenly aware of her hesitation, she stood, offered her hand and bequeathed a forced, if splendid, smile. "A pleasure, Dr. Sterling. We've met before."

The Businessman wrapped her hand in both of his and answered in measured cadences. "Have we now?"

"Yes, in Geneva, at last year's National Academy of Science conference. You were arguing against regulations limiting the field of biotechnology. We spoke together briefly at a reception after your lecture." She smiled. "I told you that you reminded me of Captain Nemo from *Mysterious Island*."

The Businessman let out a huff of relieved laughter and patted her hand affectionately. "Forgive me, Miss Martinelli, I meet so many students."

She giggled infectiously. "No, forgive me. I hardly recognized you. Shame on you for putting on weight."

"I must do something to reverse this," he said, touching his paunch. "Too many late dinners in hotel dining rooms." The two exchange ice-breaking laughs.

"Are you on a social, Dr. Sterling," Westbrook interrupted, "or are you here to ask some serious questions?"

"Of course," the Businessman said. "My dear, you could humor an old professor by explaining what so lovely a biochemist is doing here at Fort Detrick."

Julie smiled. "I'm a theoretical biochemist," she corrected him, then glanced warily at the colonel. "I can do better than explain. Please sit down."

She seated herself in front of the Sun workstation before grabbing her shoulder with a grimace of pain. "I ran this morning to help ward off a muscle spasm in my back, but I only managed two miles instead my usual five before my legs cramped." She rolled her shoulders then dragged a palm-sized optical mouse across a mirrorlike pad and clicked on an icon. The sparkle in her congenial eyes focused on an impressive color graphic now displayed on the high-resolution monitor.

The Businessman wheeled a chair next to hers while a three-dimensional visualization of a protein molecule appeared on the screen. The image reminded him of a bag of mixed-size colored balls suspended in a black void.

"The army allowed me use of one of its Crays to construct a theoretical model of the enzyme triosephosphate isomerase," she explained. "I used the center's Alliant mini-supercomputer to create this visualization. I'm in the process of animating it in realtime. I'm mapping its theoretical structure down to the genetic level."

The Businessman frowned. Her voice faded while he studied the computer-generated image. "This is not right," he finally muttered. He wheeled around in his chair and glared at Westbrook with cold, dark eyes. "You needn't stay, colonel." He might as well have told Westbrook to fuck off.

Westbrook's jaw tightened. He scowled at Martinelli and said, "I want to see you in my office when you're through here." He slammed the door on his way out.

"Young lady," the Businessman said, his kind, fatherly tone now a terse monotone. "This is not what Senator Baker nor I care to see. Please tell me about your plan to splice tetrodotoxin protein onto a Group A streptococcal virus."

Julie's lovely features withered and she shook her head. "I apologize for getting you into this. When I learned you were coming here, I knew you were one of the few people who could help me. But this has become a nightmare. I'm genuinely frightened about what's happened here."

The Businessman dismissed her apology. "You were correct to involve me. Rest assured I will keep our conversation in strictest confidence. Please tell me everything – from the beginning."

She sighed, rolling her head and shoulders as though attempting to loosen her stress-tightened muscles. "For my original thesis," she began, "I proposed creating a genetically reconstructed virus using neurotoxin protein. That's why Dr. French was so eager to sponsor my internship here. The army wanted to know if tetrodotoxin would be synthesized by the virus and, if so, could it live outside a test tube. The experiment had the potential to radically enhance the potency of the toxin and move the virus into the category of a T_4 supertoxin."

The Businessman sat absolutely still, careful not to reveal the excitement swelling inside him.

"But I never carried out the experiment," she said. "My thesis adviser – Dr. Nancy Shaw – convinced me of the hazard if an anomaly of that sort somehow escaped this center." She gestured to the screen. "So I chose another project – something much more useful."

"Safe and mundane," he said. "Now you suspect that Dr. French went ahead with the experiment. Why?"

She shrugged. "It all fits – his symptoms, the rapid rate of infestation. Everything. Of course he did it."

"I must see it. Take me to his lab."

Julie shook her head. "It's in maximum containment – a level-four hot suite. Only Colonel Westbrook can authorize entry."

The Businessman removed his glasses and rubbed his eyes. "My dear Julie, we must have proof. Senator Baker suspects you are overreacting. If we do not do something, and without delay, the army will quickly and quietly bury this incident. And most likely you with it."

"You must convince the senator that splitting the gene is far more hazardous than splitting an atom," she said, her voice raised. "Whatever Dr. French created must be destroyed. I don't want to become the person who helped create a virus that could potentially wipe out the Eastern seaboard."

The Businessman sank back into the cheap fabric chair. "My dear Julie, it appears you already have."

SAINT VITUS

USAMRIID
Maximum Containment BL-4 Laboratory

Colonel Westbrook escorted the Businessman down a concrete tunnel beneath the USAMRIID building to a massive vaultlike door. Theirs was the only foot traffic down the dead-end corridor. The colonel, his face a permanent scowl, did not like what he was about to do. He disliked visiting this lab, its entry authorized strictly on a need-to-know basis. Worse, he hated divulging its secrets to anyone, least of all to a goddamn civilian. And he hated to be near what was inside.

What choice did he have?

Thanks to Julie Martinelli, Dr. Sterling knew everything about French's blunder, and no doubt the world soon would know too. She had placed him in an unconscionable situation. Westbrook decided to discharge French's pet intern this afternoon, effectively ending her career in military biochemistry. Fuck her lieutenant colonel father. He had no choice now but to show Sterling the virus and pray he had the brains to appreciate its strategic value to United States security. It was imperative that Senator Baker keep his fucking mouth shut. The alternative was to endure a full-scale Senate investigation into this ugly affair, which could reduce Detrick's charter to cancer research. If that happened, he would lose his lab and with it his shot of becoming a general. Westbrook barely tolerated civilians, and hated politicians.

"Ready?" Westbrook snapped.

The Businessman nodded.

The colonel punched his ID code into a keypad next to the door. A green pin light blinked on. There was a soft buzz and a mechanical click. He pulled open the stainless-steel door. "There's a step," he warned.

They stepped over the eight-inch sill and entered the lab's staging area, a cylindrical control center with grated floors and walls lined with pipes. The door locked automatically behind them. They passed several panels of instrumentation that controlled the lab's environment down to subtle shifts in air density. All automatic indicators glowed a comforting green.

"This isn't the usual BL-4 configuration," the Businessman remarked. "You've done an extensive retrofit. Keeping something secure inside, colonel?"

"Don't touch anything."

One wall was lined with lockers, like a fire-station dressing room, containing full-bodied polyurethane suits. Without a word of instruction Westbrook removed his jacket and began pulling a polymer suit over his shirt and trousers. The Businessman selected one of the largest suits on the rack and also began dressing.

The Businessman stood, clad in full environmental gear. He knew very well the routine of entering a highly contagious pathogen research area. The inside of his suit quickly grew stuffy. He needed the lab's air supply.

The Businessman followed Westbrook to a narrow door not unlike a bulkhead hatch on a freighter. Westbrook spun the releasing wheel. The airtight door opened with a loud hiss. A rush of air sucked past them into the lab – negative pressure. The Businessman's inquisitive eyes scanned the laboratory splendidly outfitted with expensive centrifuges, incubators, freezers and computing workstations. At the opposite end of the lab, sandwiched between two electron microscopes, sat a DNA synthesizer. He allowed a grin. *A glorious sight.*

They were not alone inside the lab. A figure, also dressed in a polyurethane suit, sat hunched over a lab bench that rose like a pedestal under a complicated exhaust hood that filtered away hazardous aerosols. The technician was inserting a micropipette into a beaker, touching nothing and letting nothing touch him. The Businessman could see the frown behind his face shield. Visitors obviously were not welcome here. They were a dangerous distraction in a lab where researchers routinely handled the most hazardous and least understood bacteria and viruses in the world. These laboratory warriors were on the frontline of the next world war and hated to be disturbed.

Westbrook and his guest attached their air hoses to the central manifold and moved awkwardly into the lab, like deep sea divers tethered to a surface ship. When they approached the lab bench, the technician put down the pipette and stood from the stool.

"You could have warned me, colonel," the technician said, his voice oddly amplified by a special cylinder mounted in his face shield over his mouth.

"Blame him," Westbrook said, raising a gloved hand toward his guest. "This is Dr. Reinhard Sterling."

The technician's hand shot out automatically, a cordial smile forming beneath his hood. Realizing his safety error, the technician withdrew his hand. "It's an honor, Dr. Sterling. My name is DeMarco. David DeMarco."

"A pleasure."

"You and I are the only ones who know Sterling's down here," Westbrook informed the technician. "Let's keep it that way. Understand?"

"Yes, sir."

"Now kindly retrieve French's pathogen for us," Westbrook instructed.

The technician's grin faded beneath his face shield. "Sir?"

"Save it. Sterling's on official Defense Department business for Senator Baker. I've agreed to show him the virus in return for his and the senator's word to keep French's work in strictest confidence. Now get me that specimen."

"Yes, sir."

DeMarco opened a lab freezer, releasing a nitrogen-coolant mist that sank to the floor. The Businessman stepped closer. Inside, arranged in neat rows on metal racks, sat several hundred tiny vials with plastic caps. Frozen within each glass container was a tiny sphere of plasma containing billions of viruses and bacteria, some exceedingly rare, each named after the exotic, faraway places from which they had originated: Lassa, Ebola-Marburg, Junin, Machupo, Congo-Crimean Hemorrhagic Fever, West Nile encephalitis, and countless others unknown to the general scientific community.

DeMarco selected a vial from the doomsday collection of pathogens. He handed it to Westbrook, who, in turn, passed it to his guest.

"Here's what all the fuss is about," Westbrook said. "A sample of Dr. French's blood."

The Businessman held the unassuming vial close to his face shield. Scrawled across the label in barely legible handwriting was the name *Saint Vitus*.

The Businessman looked questioningly at Westbrook. "Why a saint?"

"It was my idea," DeMarco volunteered. "Thanks to French's infection, we know some of the symptoms include a sensation of burning in the extremities caused by contraction of the veins and arteries. As the disease progresses it causes convulsions, hallucinations and purging of bodily fluids wherever the tissues burst."

"I fail to see the connection."

"A fungal poison called ergot wiped out a third of Europe during the Dark Ages. Ingestion of tainted bread caused victims to collapse, convulsing in the streets. Others went insane. Some of those stricken fled to the shrine of Saint Vitus. This pilgrimage didn't do a thing for them, of course, but their trip at least took the victims away from the source of tainted grain. Some survived simply by changing their diet."

The Businessman stared. DeMarco added defensively, "We needed a code name. So I named it after the patron saint of epileptic convulsions."

"Indeed." The Businessman turned to the electron micro-scope. "May I see it?"

DeMarco reached into an incubator and carefully removed a glass slide from a slowly revolving tray. He had been working with the pathogen. The technician positioned the slide under the microscope's probe and fine-tuned the focus. Satisfied, he stepped aside.

The Businessman's face shield precluded a full view of the sample beneath the microscope. Nevertheless, he could see the cytoplasm of French's blood cells deformed to alarming proportions. "How long have you incubated this tissue specimen?"

DeMarco glanced up at the lab's clock. "Seven minutes."

The Businessman stepped back from the screen and let them see his deliberately incredulous features beneath the face shield. "Unbelievable. The cell's nucleus already is distorted beyond even the most formidable agents. Your pathogen is incredibly prolific. Dr. French has created a very interesting new life-form."

"You might also find this interesting," DeMarco said. He retrieved a plastic container from the workbench and presented it to his guest. "What do you see?"

The Businessman peered into it. At the bottom lay a lab rat jerking as though in the final stages of a grand mal seizure.

"I see that soon you will be minus one lab rodent."

"This specimen is already dead," DeMarco said.

The Businessman stared at the lab technician, genuinely surprised. "I do not understand."

"I killed this rat with chloroform an hour ago, then injected the virus directly into its brain. It's been convulsing ever since, though its movements are growing increasingly fainter."

"Are you claiming to have raised this animal from the dead?"

"Hardly." DeMarco raised the container closer to the Businessman's face shield. "The synthesized virus is feeding on the dopamine in its brain and is producing electrical charges as a by-product. We're observing the aftermath as muscle spasms.

The result is an uncanny simulation of life. Extraordinary, isn't it?"

The Businessman waved it away. "It is the stuff of nightmares."

"Seen enough?" Westbrook snapped.

"More than enough." The Businessman couldn't believe his incredible fortune. He had counted on obtaining one of the two known samples of the dreaded African Ebola virus. But the vial in his hand contained something extraordinary, something much more dangerous. *God help us all.* He decided at that moment to double his fee to Gorgon.

"I assume you are aware, colonel, that Dr. French's exploitation of molecular biology for military purposes is a criminal act."

"I beg your pardon?" Westbrook said.

"It was French's duty to preserve life. Instead he betrayed and perverted his oath to science and medicine by deliberately effecting the opposite." The Businessman held up the vial. "He created an agent of mass destruction that will guarantee his name a place on the list above the doctors at Auschwitz."

"Sterling, you're talking bullshit. That organism will never leave this lab."

"Colonel" – the Businessman stepped to the freezer and opened the stainless-steel door – "what else do you keep hidden in your house of horrors? A bug that does not kill, but simply puts its host into a lifelong coma? Or makes him violently ill after smelling a rose? Do you have something that can change the mental capacity of an entire city? Or suppresses a soldier's will to fight? I would wager you have all of that in here, and more."

Westbrook's face flushed with anger. "Mister, the purpose of this center is to defend the United States against a biological attack. Any crazy group with a kitchen and a couple of dollars' worth of specimens bought through a mail-order catalog can brew enough plague to assault our cities. Al-Qaeda is recruiting experts from around the world to combine supertoxins for maximum killing effect, maximum speed and action. We know they intended to put botulinum toxins, enterotoxins and mycotoxins in their Scud warheads and fire them at our ground troops. We must have deterrents. We must find antidotes!"

The Businessman grew weary inside his suit. He wanted out of it, and quickly. He gestured DeMarco forward. "Close up your circus from hell."

DeMarco slipped past the Businessman to secure the freezer door. His gloved hand clasped the latch, but his muscles froze. He looked questioningly at the Businessman, who observed him with clinical curiosity, making no effort to conceal a small needlelike object in his palm. The lab technician looked down at the puncture in his suit just below his right shoulder. He tried to speak, perhaps to raise an accusation, but his tongue made only a lame sucking noise in the back of his throat. He clutched his shoulder to stem the leak. DeMarco's eyes rolled backward inside his head as he stumbled and collapsed with a crash between two lab benches.

"Jesus Christ!" Westbrook knelt quickly at the technician's side. "Press the security alarm ... it's the red button by the crash door—"

The Businessman drove his huge rubber boot hard into Westbrook's face shield. It had all his weight behind it. The mask shattered, and the colonel spilled backward. He was out cold.

The Businessman slipped the Saint Vitus vial in his suit's deep utility pocket, then reached into the freezer and withdrew a random vial labeled OROPOUCHE FEVER and hurled it on the metal floor beside the colonel. The glass vial shattered and sprayed Westbrook's suit with its ice contents.

The Businessman returned to the freezer and withdrew several more vials. He backed away and began hurling them one at a time at the colonel. Some of the vials bounced off the colonel's plastic suit with a muted pop, while others shattered on the metal floor and cabinets, scattering their lethal contents over half the lab.

When the colonel opened his eyes, his shattered face shield was covered with shards of contaminated ice crystals. His head spun, and he knew he could not stand. Stunned, he tried to brush the mixture of ice and blood from his exposed face, but his gloves could not reach beneath his shattered face shield. Another vial exploded on the floor by his feet. Then another. Westbrook stared at the blurry visage of the Businessman, but he was unable to focus his eyes.

"What in God's name are you doing?" His brushing actions became frantic, bordering on panic.

The Businessman, his eyes cold and calculating, offered no explanation while he hurled still more vials.

"*You fuck!*" Westbrook struggled to rise but finally sank back, his breath short and labored. The melting ice flooded the lab with billions of lethal viruses and bacteria.

"You fuck ... you fuck..."

The Businessman disconnected his air hose from the manifold and walked to the lab's door as quickly as the suit would allow. He closed the hatch behind him with a thud, spun the wheel and gave it a secure tug at the end of its threads. He entered a shower stall and doused his suit with phenolic disinfectant. Only when the timer had counted to zero did the automatic door admit him to the staging area. He went to work with practiced mastery. In fifteen seconds he had shut down the lab's communications, lights, electronics, ventilation and life-support systems. Rows of pin lights blinked from green to red. The computer displays, centrifuges, freezers – everything – systematically turned off. Only the overhead emergency lights inside the lab remained lit. He stepped to a console marked EMERGENCY and turned a final key. The console went dead, as did the lab's emergency lights. He stripped off the environment suit and put on his jacket, carefully placing the Saint Vitus vial into a thermal canister inside his coat pocket.

The Businessman exited the lab and closed the outer door behind him with a solid click, sealing the colonel inside his tomb. The concrete hallway stood empty. There was no indication that anyone was aware that one of the center's labs was now "hot." He rode the elevator to the main level and walked into Westbrook's office to retrieve his satchel. The thermal canister would keep its contents frozen for seven hours. He would need less than half that time to smuggle Saint Vitus out of the country.

"Did you see it?"

The Businessman whipped around. Julie Martinelli, her eyes anxious, looked questioningly at him from the threshold.

"My dear Julie," he said slowly, "I did not expect—"

"Did French do it?"

The Businessman hugged the satchel close to his chest. Besides the thermal container, the satchel contained a Browning 9mm automatic. "You are a most persistent young woman."

"If you know, please tell me."

"Yes, your intuition was correct. I saw it. You needn't concern yourself any further. I will take this matter up with Senator Baker. Please forgive me, my dear Julie, but I have already kept the conference waiting too long."

"Where's Colonel Westbrook? He wanted to see me."

"He ... was detained. Something to do with an indicator in the lab's staging area. I expect he will return directly." The Businessman felt her curious eyes boring into the back of his neck as he swept past her into the corridor.

The Businessman's performance was over and now it was time to collect his second payment. He made a quick mental calculation and smiled. He was now a very wealthy man.

The Businessman returned his ID tag to the reception guard, exited through the center's double glass doors and climbed into a waiting car – a black Thunderbird, a visitor's pass displayed beneath the windshield.

Tarra drove the car uneventfully across the parade grounds and through the Fort's main gate.

Colonel Westbrook grabbed the lab door's releasing wheel and pulled himself up to his knees. Not even the emergency lights remained lit. The disorientation caused by sudden and complete absence of light summoned images of indescribable horrors closing in an inescapable circle. Mustering all his strength, he tried to move the wheel. But it would not budge. Fighting a concussion-induced dizziness, he felt for the emergency button and punched it repeatedly. But the lab was dead.

He sank wearily back to the floor, staring at eternal darkness. He listened to the slow, sinking sound of the lab's expensive equipment winding to a halt. Then silence. There was no one and nothing, only absolute, terrifying blackness. For the first time in the colonel's career, he was scared shitless.

Westbrook's face burned terribly and his extremities felt heavy and unresponsive. His lungs were congesting, and he could feel the onset of a peculiar headache. This was no illusion. His body temperature was rapidly melting the ice crystals. Billions of unseen organisms already infested the lab, with billions more awakening with each passing moment. Most of them had no known cure. He knew he was a dead man. The fight was finished. He had lost.

The air within the lab grew increasingly foul. *Good. Let me suffocate. Better to die that way than to face the alternative.*

"DeMarco," he shouted, his voice phlegmy.

There was no sound of movement from the darkness.

His thoughts returned to Sterling. Clever bastard. Very clever bastard. He had guaranteed that no one would ever touch his corpse. Like a radioactive spill, it would take months of decontamination, perhaps years, before a team could enter the lab and determine what Sterling – or whatever the fuck his name was – had stolen. He had gone to a lot of trouble to steal French's supertoxin. Why? He expelled a hoarse laugh at the absurdity that he had simply handed it to him. Only he and DeMarco knew what French had created, and only he knew the enormous ramifications of what Sterling had taken.

No – there was Julie Martinelli. How much did she really know?

The colonel pulled off his gloves and reached inside his torn polyurethane suit until he found his trouser pocket. One final mission in his less-than-glorious military career. He retrieved his appointment book and pen. Feverishly, in absolute darkness, he began writing.

SUMMONS

Bagram Airfield, Afghanistan
Tuesday, 1600 hours (local time)

Special Forces Maj. Joseph Marshall watched his gunnery sergeant rush toward him with a portable ComSat receiver.

"You got a call," Williams said, thrusting the receiver at him. "It's patched through to a General Medlock in Washington. Top priority." He added in a whisper, "He sounds pissed."

General Medlock? He'd heard of the general, but never met the man.

The major grabbed the receiver. "Marshall here."

"I understand you've had a real bad night crossing the border," a gravel voice said over the secured satellite channel. "The task force is regrouping to launch another assault."

"I respectfully suggest the next op be DEVGRU only—"

"You won't be involved," Medlock said. "I want you on a Mach-One transport to Fort Bragg within the hour. We'll pick you up there. You're to be at Bragg no later than tomorrow at twenty two hundred hours."

Marshall glanced at his mountain watch. *No way!* "Sir, I need more details."

"Right now you don't need to know shit. I don't want to hear excuses. Just get your ass moving."

"How many troops should I deploy? I've got two units mobilized—"

"One," Medlock said.

"One unit?"

"One man."

The general wasn't making sense. Marshall looked quizzically at Williams and shook his head. "Sir, I've got men on the ground here who can take down this bastard—"

"One man," General Medlock repeated.

"Who?" Marshall snapped, letting the general hear his irritation.

"Bring along your best."

TAMPICO

The hills of Tampico, Mexico
Tuesday, 1903 hours

The Businessman made his way through the gathering dusk down an overgrown path to what once had been a cabin. The years had been unkind. Time had reduced the structure to little more than a ramshackle hut, its timber severely sagging, its moss-covered walls leaning at frightful angles. The Businessman put his shoulder to the warped cabin door and wrestled it open. He passed inside.

The cabin's single filthy room offered few furnishings – a small table supporting an ancient oil lamp that gave off more smoke than light. The Businessman wasn't alone. He could sense more than see the three figures watching him, mere shadows beyond the lantern's pale glow. They were killers of the worst sort. Friends.

"Sit," ordered a deep, menacing voice that cut through the gloom like a foghorn.

The Businessman sat on one of the table's chairs, which sagged and cracked under his weight. He scratched his closely cropped silver beard, anxious to consummate a deal with his comrades.

The glow of a cigarette pierced the gloom to his left, followed by a stream of smoke that reeked of heavy Russian tobacco. As the Businessman's eyes adjusted to the dimness, he could see Tarra, his escape driver and Gorgon's first lieutenant. The Businessman's eyes shifted to the figure seated next to her, a man with a black beard and a squashed nose, the Arabian driver who had also helped in Sterling's abduction.

But it was the man seated aloof in the corner, a huge shadow fondling a curved Bedouin dagger, who demanded his undivided attention. Gorgon sat there observing the Businessman intently, studying him like a hawk eyeing its prey.

"I cannot see you," Gorgon said, his accent a hybrid of Middle Eastern dialects.

The Businessman leaned forward, allowing the lamp's scant illumination to bathe his face, revealing his altered features.

Gorgon laughed. "Well done. Your new face improves you."

Gorgon's grin vanished and the dark folds of his forehead deepened when he looked into the Businessman's eyes. He didn't trust him. "Do you have the specimen, Herr Wynett?"

The Businessman dropped the serious academic gaze. His hooded eyes narrowed in warning. "Yes."

Gorgon did not blink. "Show it to me."

"Impossible. It must remain frozen."

Gorgon seemed to accept that. "You had no difficulty?"

"None. Detrick's security is pathetically lax. In two days you will command a formidable plague."

Gorgon stared coldly. "Very good. Then let us hasten to Mazatlan—"

The Businessman raised his hand in a halting gesture. "First we will discuss payment."

There came stifled laughter from the other two, followed by another waft of heavy cigarette smoke. Gorgon eased back in his chair, and when he spoke there was benign superiority in his voice. "No advance compensation. I do not trust you. Most men would simply abscond with my generous down payment and live comfortably for the remainder of their years. You would do the same, I am certain."

The Businessman's eyes grew dark and angry. "I gave you my word I will deliver—"

"You brought me no proof. I will pay you after I have the tanks ... nothing before. I have decided."

The Businessman forced out a laugh. "Then go to Mazatlan alone."

Gorgon pointed his dagger at him like an accusing finger. "You will do as I order."

"No, sir. I will synthesize the organism without your muddling interference. When I have incubated the virus in the quantity you require, I will allow you to purchase it. Your cost will be ten million American dollars – two million for each tank."

Gorgon rose to his feet. "You are mad to come here and demand new terms."

"A service fee, my friend. My price has doubled. What I have is worth far more than I am asking."

The others, stilled by the Businessman's brazen demands, watched Gorgon mutely. The giant said slowly, "You will not leave this room alive, Herr Wynett."

"Then you will have nothing," the Businessman said. "Your plan will be finished. If this is about money, then you place a very low value on the Lion's future. The price of a thermonuclear device, even if a reliable one could be assembled and purchased, would be one hundred times what I am asking. I am offering you a weapon far more effective and far easier to deploy. If you cannot acquire the sum, then tell the Lion he must go back to plotting his war on a small scale with amateurs."

Gorgon stepped into the light, revealing piercing eyes that glinted as ferociously in the light as the dagger in his hand. Gorgon drove the curved blade into the table's splintered top between the Businessman's left index finger and thumb. His guest didn't flinch.

"I do not care what it costs," Gorgon shouted. "I will defeat the evil enemy and crush their arrogance. I have but one weakness – you, my Achilles' heel. I will not tolerate treachery. I will show you."

Gorgon plucked the dagger from the table and, with startling swiftness, spun dancelike on his heels and hurled it at the Arabian driver. There came a dull thud as the blade struck bone, followed by the guttural gasp of a man expelling his final breath. The driver died instantly, his head pinned to the wall, his brutish face contorted in an incredulous look of horror. Only the hilt of Gorgon's dagger still protruded from what had once been his left eye. Tarra gave a throaty chuckle, amused by the noisy evacuation of the corpse's bowels and bladder.

"Remove his brain," Gorgon said to her, "and send it as a warning to those who paid him to betray me."

Tarra gave the Arab driver a lingering kiss on his still trembling lips before wrenching the dagger from his eye and driving the blade into his skull with a sickening crack. The Businessman winced.

Gorgon said in a voice that sent a cold warning, "For money he revealed my name to my enemies. *For money!* I should have killed him slowly, but I am in haste. What proof will you offer that you will not betray me?"

The Businessman had negotiated shrewdly, leveraging his advantages and sealing the deal under his own terms. "You have my word. And that, my friend, is all I will give you until my work is finished."

Frederick, Maryland
Wednesday, April 28, 1203 hours

There came a severe knock on Julie's apartment door, and a deep, resonant voice of authority called in to her, "Ms. Martinelli?"

Julie swung away from her Mac computer and drew in a sharp breath at the sight of the two men – a black man in a suit, the second an army security officer – standing on her threshold. She had expected intimidating-looking men with unnerving stares to show up on her doorstep. And they did not disappoint.

"You are Ms. Martinelli?" the black man asked again, stepping into her apartment. He was tall, with broad shoulders and sharp, intelligent eyes that moved about the room, professionally absorbing its clutter of computer peripherals and books.

"Who are you?" Julie asked. "How did you get in here?"

"The door was open ... ajar, actually," he said. "You should be more careful. Your ID please."

"First, I want to see *your* ID."

"Ms. Martinelli, there isn't time. We're 22 minutes late."

"Your ID – now!"

He maneuvered around the pillars of books stacked across the floor. He reached inside his coat pocket, produced a shiny black wallet and flashed it in her face: STONY ROBINSON, CIA.

Oh shit. Julie leaned back into her cheap wicker chair, unable to think clearly. The CIA was taking her into custody! All because of a stupid letter. Where were the handcuffs? What were the charges? High treason and violating countless international treaties, for starters – who knew what else she'd overlooked in her self-righteous quest to protect humanity. No Ph.D. No residency. No future. Her career was over, her life in ruins. *Don't panic ... think this through logically.*

Had she made the right decision sending Senator Baker that detailed letter, which she now realized was full of vague suspicions? And no proof. She was certain Dr. French had created a dreadful new organism – a creature she undeniably dreamt up – but there was no way to prove she wasn't intimately involved with his project, or even in league with the man masquerading as Dr. Sterling. With no tangible defense she would go to prison as an accessory. Maybe there would even be a murder charge thrown in.

"Your ID, please," Robinson repeated.

Julie held up the Detrick identification tag still clipped to her camel sweater. He put his nose to within inches of the tag and scrutinized it with intense, narrowly focused eyes that seemed to record every detail.

"Your Stanford ID," he said.

Julie found her backpack, fished out a plastic, slightly bent university ID card and offered it to him. He looked hard at it before nodding slightly at the security officer, who spoke into a handheld radio. "Command, three-eight. We have her. ETA in three minutes."

The radio crackled an acknowledgment.

"Ms. Martinelli," Robinson said, "please collect your things and come with us."

"Let me finish sending a note to my adviser," she said, her fingers hovering over the keyboard.

"There isn't time."

"Then a phone call. I want to call my father."

"No time."

"He's a lieutenant colonel in the army."

"I know, Ms. Martinelli. We have a vehicle waiting."

"I'll need to power down the equipment."

"It will be taken care of."

Julie nodded numbly and picked up her blue leather jacket and purse. The security officer's fingers tightened around her arm. He led her – not too gently, she thought – into the hallway. *We have her.* On her way out she shot a sideways glance at her cat, Tad, sitting rigid on the chair by the door, his acute hazel eyes watching her leave, his ears pinned back in disapproval. Tad was her one true friend, the only creature that seemed to care what happened to her. *See ya later, Tad – maybe.*

A third security officer stood just outside her door. Several neighbors were huddled in a small group, talking in hushed tones that stopped abruptly when Julie emerged from her apartment. The door across the hallway opened and a young couple – he wearing a terry-cloth robe that barely covered the tops of his thighs, she wearing only a T-shirt – watched her with suspicious looks. The boyfriend pushed her gently behind him, protecting her. Julie wondered, envious, what it felt like to have a kind man always looking out for her. Now she might never know.

She was intelligent, independent – and selfish. Traits no good man with generous qualities she desired would ever be interested in. Sure, men looked approvingly at her body, and there was never a shortage of suitors as long as she left her brains and independence back in the lab. She intimidated her dates, or so many of them claimed. She had an obsessive need to control, mandatory to succeed in the male-dominated field of biochemistry. She was resigned to a life of textbooks, computer programs, arcane databases and microscopes, studying life at the molecular level, instead of living it.

Julie pulled out her keys.

"Leave it open," Robinson said. "Sergeant Ryan will power down your equipment. Whatever else you need will be provided."

I won't need much in jail. "I've got a cat."

"We'll take care of it, Ms. Martinelli."

"There's coffee on a hot plate—"

"We'll turn it off."

Agent Robinson led her out through the building's main entrance, where a Ford Excursion sat idling, waiting for them. Julie realized she was shaking. *Hang in there ... maintain control – and some dignity.* She always found it easy to numb out her feelings.

"Let me take your coat," Robinson said, opening the rear door. He helped her inside, then slid in next to her, while the security officer climbed in front with the driver. The truck shrieked out of the apartment complex.

Julie's mind raced to formulate a defense for the ugly interrogation she imaged would come next. Not until the vehicle pulled onto the Washington National Pike leading to D.C. did Julie have the nerve to ask, "Are you taking me to the State Department?"

Without looking at her, Robinson said, "State Department? No, ma'am – Dulles International."

The airport? She tried unsuccessfully to mask her deepening fear. "Why? Where are you people taking me?"

Robinson stared emotionlessly out the window. "Dulles, ma'am. That's where they usually keep airplanes. Your father has a transport waiting for us."

"My father? He doesn't know anything. Don't drag him into this."

Stony Robinson snapped his head around and looked at her – for the first time he really seemed to look at her. "He has communicated with you, hasn't he?"

She shook her head, more confused than ever. "Not since this whole thing started."

Robinson threw a sharp look at the security officer in front. "He was supposed to communicate with her. He told me this morning he would call her."

The officer just shrugged.

Julie realized that the computer in her apartment had been linked to Stanford's mainframe via a special DSL modem since six-thirty that morning, tying up her phone line. She pulled her cell phone from her kakis and realized she'd never turned it on today. No one could get through to her. "Communicate what? Where are you taking me? Someone please tell me what's going on."

Robinson's poker face melted. He looked genuinely embarrassed. "I've spent one *fucked* morning in Pentagon briefings – I'm in no mood."

He shed his military demeanor and said to her apologetically, "Your father was supposed to brief you. As a personal favor, he asked me to pick you up on my way to Kirtland Air Force Base. He's taking you with us to Brazil."

STONECUTTERS
GARDEN

Mato Grosso, Brazil
The Amazon Basin
Wednesday, April 27, 1647 hours

The Businessman called his plantation Stonecutters Garden, a name he had chosen to remind him of his days in bleak London. He arrived at dusk, alone, emerging on foot from the rain-spawned mist that hung like great cobwebs from the jungle's thick foliage. He had made quick work of the two-mile hike from the road, a path with a pair of tire tracks rutted into clinging moss. There he had abandoned his truck and continued on foot, a cautious hand always on the rucksack draped carefully over his shoulder.

Finally the overgrown path with its immense canopy of trees gave way to high stalks of sugarcane. The crop belonged to him. Though the soil of this region yielded poor results, the Businessman smiled every time he inspected his harvest. Only an utter fool would break his back tending this cleared acreage that fought a never-ending battle against the invading jungle. He knew of more lucrative ways to earn a living off this wilderness.

The Businessman emerged from the last row of stalks and watched a man on horseback, partially silhouetted against the estate's high pole lamps, ride toward him. The rider wore a huge straw hat, boots, a garment that looked like a leather dress instead of pants and a white shirt opened wide to show off a broad and woolly chest. He carried an automatic rifle, and an enormous holstered revolver hung loosely from his hip.

"The beard distinguishes you, *chefe*," the rider greeted him in Portuguese. The dark cavalier dismounted, and the two men patted each other spiritedly, the usual welcome of the region.

"Come inside, doctor," the rider said to his employer. He gestured toward the farmhouse, a grand English manor worth far more than the land on which it sat would ever earn. "I will round up the others and we will drink to your return."

"Later, Tucco," the Businessman said in the rider's native Portuguese. "First I must inspect the barn."

"The barn?" Tucco teased. "Your bed is too soft?"

The Businessman was not in a whimsical mood after a hard eighteen-hour trip. "First we will work. Then we will drink."

Tucco led the way through a gate in the twelve-foot chain-link fence topped with barbed wire, which surrounded the estate. Each stout support pole, buried deep inside slabs of granite, could withstand a tank assault. They left behind the jungle and rows of cane and crossed landscaped grounds accented with marigolds and edged by several acres of closely cropped sod. The lovely grounds were as tame as the jungle was wild. The two made their way to an impressive stone barn, which housed feed, trucks and farm equipment. They passed inside.

The Businessman rarely visited the barn. On its best day the storehouse reeked of an offensive mixture of manure and oil, which he refused to inhale, however briefly. But he knew few places would serve him as well. "The cellar, Tucco," he said.

The rider removed his straw hat and wiped his already perspiring brow. "So late, doctor? First we sleep—"

"Now," the Businessman demanded.

A resigned Tucco lit an oil lamp and led the way to the back of the barn. He raised the light over a slab of stone, half hidden by the straw, and passed the lantern to the old man. Tucco found a pick and, hissing and grunting, pried the slab upwards and finally tilted it over with a bang. Damp and fetid air wafted up from below, driving Tucco back with a scowl. No one had gone beneath the barn in more than a year. The Businessman extended the lantern over the black opening and peered into it. A wooden staircase, half rotted from unchecked moisture, descended into the gloom.

The Businessman said to Tucco, "There is equipment on my truck. Take ten men and bring it down here. Be certain they are careful with it. Then you will clean and paint the cellar to make it habitable."

Tucco cocked his head at the strange request. "Whatever you say, *chefe*."

"There is one more item you must initiate immediately." The Businessman's eyes grew dark and firm. "We will need more men who can use guns. Many more. I have a formidable client, Tucco. And we must be strong when he comes here for his merchandise."

Tucco's grin vanished. "I do not like this new customer of yours."

"He is a strong man. An extraordinary man. In twenty-four hours I want at least ten more men with guns on my payroll. Now please hurry."

Tucco vanished to wake his roustabouts.

The Businessman stepped into the hole and, with one hand on the wall for support, carefully tested each twisted plank before applying his full weight. His first visit to the barn's basement would be a short one. A year of fungus and mildew had rendered the air beneath the barn unbreathable. A handkerchief over his mouth, the Businessman lifted the lamp high to let its light touch every corner. The cellar reminded him of a catacomb, a place of death and decay. Squat wooden arches supported the low ceiling, and niter and moss had all but covered the cinderblock walls. But soon it would become a nursery of sorts, a place where new life would grow.

The Businessman hugged his rucksack like a good father. He had brought his adopted children home. Now he would use this place to nurture them and make them multiply.

Tarra lay spread-eagle in a patch of tall grass directly across from the compound's main gate. Concealed by the tall blades, she watched the Businessman's estate through a pair of low-light binoculars.

Her arrival at dusk that afternoon – three hours before the Businessman – afforded ample time to study the movements of the farm's workers and their families. She took meticulous notes. She recorded Wynett's interest in the stone barn behind the house and watched a contingent of roustabouts march single file into the jungle, most likely to retrieve his equipment. He intends to keep it in the barn, she concluded.

Tarra stared through the binoculars and watched.

And waited.

PART TWO

Containment

"The emerging gene synthesis industry is making genetic material more widely available ... (which) could potentially be used to assemble the components of a deadly organism."

—US Secretary of State Hillary Clinton
Global Biological Weapons Convention, Geneva, Switzerland

"Mankind already carries in its own hands too many of the seeds of its own destruction."

—President Richard M. Nixon, abolishing the United States' biological weapons program November 25, 1969

STARLIFTER

Fort Bragg, North Carolina
Wednesday, 2305 hours

Maj. Joseph Marshall heard it before he saw it, four massive turbofan engines powering up, the telltale sound of a military transport about to taxi. The Jeep's driver, a young corporal named Boyd, accelerated toward the huge hangar at the end of the airstrip. The major and Gunnery M.Sg. Williams each reached for a handhold, bracing for the sudden turn that threatened to throw them headlong onto the tarmac.

Thanks to a stiff Atlantic headwind, their aircraft arrived at Fort Bragg 20 minutes behind schedule. General Medlock's strict orders didn't allow Marshall and Williams time to shower at Bragg's "stockade" quarters. Nor, to their objections, were they permitted to secure additional gear. Each would have to make do with a single duffel bag, which contained a shaving kit and a change of clothes, and another, longer case, limiting them to one weapon each.

"A lot of folks are up late," Williams observed. "An op's under way."

Marshall acknowledged him with raised eyebrows.

The Jeep rounded the hangar and jerked to a halt beside an aircraft that had just finished refueling, a red tank truck unhooking from its wing. The aerial beast, easily the size of a city block, was a Lockheed C- 141 Starlifter, a cargo transport capable of moving entire battalions, including tanks and choppers.

"Word around here says the Starlifter's from Kirtland Air Force Base," Corporal Boyd said, "but there's no record of the aircraft scheduled to land here."

"Nor is there likely to be," Marshall said, then added unkindly, "Where I come from, corporals don't pump officers for information."

Boyd's expression fell. "Yes, sir."

A soldier wearing combat fatigues and a serious frown beckoned Marshall and Williams out of the Jeep with a wave of his M-16.

Boyd screwed his neck around and said to the two, "Hey, good luck, guys." His tone suggested genuine concern for their safety.

Marshall stepped down onto the runway and returned a halfhearted salute. The corporal seemed to know a lot more about what was going on here tonight than he did.

Marshall and Williams started to brush past the no-nonsense guard, who stopped them with a quick snap to attention.

"Your IDs," the soldier ordered. He was a young man with a narrow face sculpted by drill sergeants who knew a thing or two about crawling up asses. The C-141's engines surged to taxi power, making it difficult to hear. "*Quickly.*"

The two fished through their fatigues, then flashed him their cards. The guard scrutinized the IDs under the light of a hammer-sized flashlight, then directed its beam into their faces. Satisfied, he presented the two with a rigid parade-ground salute.

Marshall bolted up the staircase that had been rolled to the transport. Someone called down to them, "Move your ass, Joe."

The voice belonged to a man in camouflage fatigues standing backlit in the forward doorway of the Starlifter. Marshall recognized that voice. He stopped midstride. "Tony?"

The man stepped onto the landing with a hoot and extended his hand. "You bet your nuts. Your butt's mine now, Joe."

Marshall accepted the sincere handshake. Col. Anthony Martinelli, salt-and-pepper-haired and about to find out what it was like to turn fifty, offered Marshall – twelve years his junior – a congenial smile and enthusiastic eyes. Age hadn't sapped the colonel's energy level. In fact he looked younger than Marshall remembered, solidly built and ready for action of any kind, the tougher the better. Martinelli had pulled the right strings to get Marshall into the Special Forces. He had been his mentor, a military father figure. But they had lost touch over the past year – a special assignment had swallowed the colonel whole.

Colonel Martinelli acknowledged the gunnery sergeant with a casual salute. "Glad you're still taking care of my man. How's your aim these days?"

"Never better, sir," Williams grinned.

"Good. We may need your unique talent." Then he looked at Marshall, his eyes serious. "I heard you had a rough night in Afghanistan."

Marshall waved away the incident. "I'll fill you in later. I never thought I'd see you again at Bragg. Why aren't you spending the army's retirement money in the Colorado Rockies?"

"What Rockies?" the colonel said, leading the way back into the transport. "I'm running the most interesting op of my career. Which is why I insisted you be part of the team I'm putting together. I wanted you in on this, Joe."

Marshall stopped him cold. "Tony, I left a lot of good men in Afghanistan, some of them hurt bad. We were very close to bin Laden."

"Is Abdul Banna important enough to haul your butt over here on short notice?"

Marshall's hardened expression affirmed that it was.

"We're going to nail both of them," Martinelli said. "I'll have you back at Bragg within the week."

Marshall gave his mentor a curt nod. They had no sooner set foot inside the Starlifter than the ground crew pushed the steps quickly away. The transport rolled down the taxiway.

"Get cozy," Martinelli shouted over the throttling engines, pulling the door shut behind them. "There'll be a briefing as soon as we're airborne. When this is over we'll all retire on our reward money." He gave the two a reassuring thumbs-up before disappearing into the flight deck.

Marshall took one look around the inside of the Starlifter and nearly dropped his duffel bag. This was no cargo aircraft. The Starlifter had become a flying command center, complete with sophisticated surveillance electronics and overhead displays. And people – Marshall estimated at least fifteen, plus crew – scrambling like traders in the soybeans pit around the converted aircraft. What was going on here?

"You're late," a steel-chisel voice barked at the two. The voice belonged to an older man dressed in common khakis and a short-sleeved shirt minus any indication of rank. He wore a holstered military-issue .45 under his left armpit. He reminded Marshall of a peregrine falcon, lean and tough, his movements quick and constant. General Medlock?

Before Marshall could introduce himself, the falcon pointed to a pair of fold-down seats along the fuselage. "Strap in." Then he shouted into the flight deck, "Let's get this circus in the air."

Marshall and Williams stowed their gear under the seats, buckled in and settled back for takeoff. Men in uniforms stashed maps and charts, technicians in white overalls strapped themselves in before banks of electronic equipment racked in high metal cabinets, and a couple of civilians buckled themselves into cushioned seats around a conference table.

At the far end of the crowded cabin, a dozen tough-looking soldiers, most black or Hispanic, raced through a sliding hatchway into the Starlifter's rear compartment. Marshall caught a glimpse of a squat, black, disassembled chopper before the last soldier pulled shut a bulkhead door behind him.

Incredible.

The turbofan engines roared to full power. Eighty thousand-plus pounds of combined thrust pushed Marshall and Williams sideways in their seats. The aircraft began swaying and bumping along the runway, gathering speed. With a final bump the aircraft was airborne, banking right, steadily gaining speed and altitude.

At 20,000 feet, Marshall decided he had waited long enough to find the head. He unbuckled and headed aft.

"No one gave you permission to move around in here," spat the peregrine falcon with the .45. Marshall noted that the man wore the frayed look of a leader in the midst of a battle he feared he couldn't win.

"We haven't met, sir," Marshall said, softening his features with a winning smile. "I'm Major—"

"I'm General Medlock," he snapped, his eyes narrow and intense. "This is my operation."

Bing ... bing ...

The C-141 leveled off at 25,000 feet with a signal from the pilot that it was safe to move around the cabin. There followed a rush of activity as the passengers resumed their preparations – for what, though, Marshall hadn't a clue. Several men descended on the general, demanding his immediate attention. Marshall was quickly forgotten.

The tough-looking soldiers returned to the main cabin. Huddled together, they exchanged rowdy banter while checking an arsenal of automatic weapons and strapping intimidating knives to interesting hiding places on their bodies. Commandos, Marshall concluded, and well equipped.

"Stay clear of the general," Williams advised. "Whatever this is all about, it's his big show. And he doesn't seem too happy about how things are going."

"It would behoove you to take your friend's advice," came a female voice behind them.

Marshall whirled and peered into the most striking pair of brown eyes he had ever seen. She squinted back at him as though uncomfortable around soldiers who looked like they had just stepped off a battlefield. She wore her long, black hair pulled back in a ponytail, her perfect body stuffed into a pair of tight overalls. No makeup. He noted her face was perfectly angled, with high cheekbones and an elegant nose, but it was those hypnotizing dark eyes that held his undivided attention. Why hadn't he noticed her before?

"This is the worst possible time to get in the way," she warned. "I suggest you either make yourself useful or find a corner and hide there."

Her voice had just the right intonation to put a professional edge on a thoroughly feminine quality. The academic type, Marshall figured. *Nice.* He smiled at her, a cynical grin softening the hard lines around his equally piercing brown eyes. "And how do you suggest I make myself useful around here?"

She scrutinized his solid, eternally serious face, then let her eyes run down his sooted six-foot-three frame. "Depends. You're the special forces major, right?"

"At your service."

"You could always covertly kill somebody."

And feisty, too. He liked that. "I have a softer side you might like to get to know. I studied philosophy in college – existentialism."

Her eyes brightened. "Ooo ... perfect. Then strap your macho ass into a seat and contemplate Kierkegaard and your army boots."

Marshall, smiling, bowed slightly. "Yes, ma'am."

"I've got a better idea," she said, brushing briskly past him, her perfectly angled nose wrinkled. "Find a shower stall and knock yourself out." She whispered to Williams, "Tell your commander he stinks."

Williams's stone features melted into a broad grin. "Right away, ma'am."

Marshall, basking in a sudden wave of self-consciousness, began buttoning his well-traveled shirt. "I don't even know your name," he called after her.

"Martinelli," she said, taking a seat beside the white-frocked technician. The two quickly became engrossed in some technical discussion.

Tony's daughter. Marshall hadn't recognized her. He had met Julie once, and then only briefly, perhaps ten years ago when she was still in high school. What was she doing here?

"You look like you just swallowed a turd you thought was a Reese's cup." Colonel Martinelli laughed, slapping Marshall hard on his shoulder. He gestured to his daughter. "Don't look so surprised. She's quite capable."

Marshall didn't doubt that for a moment. "Since when did the brass start allowing relatives in the same combat unit?"

"I got approval from the joint chiefs to put this team together any way I want. It's that damned important."

"Did she enlist?"

"Nope. Julie's interning at Detrick to finish her Ph.D. She's already one of the best biochemists in her field. In fact, she's the reason we're here." He was quite the proud papa, Marshall noted. Not a good sign.

"What field, Tony?"

"Genetic engineering."

"Ten minutes to briefing, people," General Medlock announced to the group, then beckoned the colonel to follow him aft.

Marshall grabbed his mentor's arm before he could rush away. "Where can I wash up?"

Colonel Martinelli gestured forward. "The head's behind the flight deck, Joe. And while you're in there, flush that shirt of yours out of this aircraft."

CONTAINMENT

The Starlifter

Marshall emerged from the C-141's wash stall clean shaven and scrubbed as thoroughly as the telephone booth-sized head would allow. His hair was toweled and slicked back, and his fresh, untucked shirt agreed with the group's lax dress code. He wondered if anybody thought to bring along a couple of sandwiches.

"Let's get started," General Medlock shouted, igniting the cabin's already eager atmosphere.

Marshall ignored his protesting stomach and joined Williams on the fold-down seats away from the conference table around which the rest of the group was gathering. Finding supper would need to wait.

"The name of this highly classified operation is *Containment,*" the general began, raising his scratchy, nail-hard voice. "Some of you got to know each other over the past two days. For the benefit of the newcomers we'll introduce ourselves. I'm General John Medlock, a member of the Biochem Advisory Council, chairman of BERT and commander of this task force. I'll be monitoring this operation from Washington. The man to my right is Colonel Anthony Martinelli, deputy commander of the Alpha Special Forces Unit. He'll be in command once this transport touches down."

Marshall shot a sideways glance at Williams. What the hell was *Alpha?*

"Colonel Martinelli brings with him a wealth of experience from several Special Forces units, including Delta, the Green Berets and a stint with the British SAS," Medlock continued. "He's stationed at Fort Detrick and is the army's premier troubleshooter when it comes to bioterrorism. Alpha is his baby. And you people are the Alpha unit."

Some of those in the room – notably the military types – didn't blink at the news, while the civilians exchanged puzzled looks.

"Alpha is the code name for BERT – Biological Emergency Response Team," Medlock continued. "BERT is a small, fast-reaction team of scientists, military officers and specially selected antiterrorism commandos. Martinelli, please introduce your team."

"Yes, sir." The colonel stood before his captive audience, sporting an eager grin. "The gentleman to my right is Stony Robinson, the best damn deputy squad leader ever to wear an army uniform."

A black man in civilian khakis stood next to the colonel and bowed smartly before the group. Stony was sturdily built, tall, with keen eyes that exuded confidence he was fully capable of taking care of himself and a whole lot of others when the need arose.

"The CIA recruited Stony from engineering at Fort Sherman," Martinelli said. "We borrowed him from the CIA. His training system is the best the army has ever produced – hell, it's the best anywhere in the world. And he's used that system to train the most able commandos I've ever had the pleasure to inspect. We are indeed lucky to have his services."

Colonel Martinelli acknowledged Stony's men – eight soldiers standing along the aft fuselage. Far from the spit-polished professionals typical of Special Forces units, they looked more like ex-cons than the army's elite, Marshall noted. Some wore beards and mustaches, none was clean shaven, and their hair varied from ponytails to bald. Very unmilitary. He assumed they, too, were CIA.

"These commandos are Alpha's muscles," Stony said in a resonant voice that reminded Marshall of Lou Rawls. "We recruited these men from the administration's covert strike force for drug trafficking, and I've taken them through nine months of special commando training. They can speak Spanish, Portuguese and English without an accent. We handpicked each man on his ability to infiltrate and operate covertly in what we consider to be hot spots on continental North and South America."

So far Marshall wasn't impressed. He was prepared to pit his Seals hand-to-hand against these pukes anytime.

"Next is Telecommunications Lieutenant Dennis 'DOS' Spangler, who is one of the best satellite reconnaissance analysts in the business," Martinelli said, indicating a balding, thin-faced man in his mid-thirties, wearing a white technician's smock and owl-like, metal-rimmed glasses. "Spangler will use a newly developed ComSat transceiver to make sure every finger knows what the hand is doing. He'll monitor every broadcast frequency within 800 miles of our staging area. Spangler's job will be to keep surprises to a minimum. By the way, don't even think about turning on a cell phone in the area."

Lieutenant Spangler absently shuffled several computer memory sticks in his hand like toy cars. Marshall pegged him as the nerdy sort, long on brains, handy with electronics, short on everything else. And nervous too.

"Next is our special-op pilot Captain David Youngblood from Task Force One-Sixty, night reconnaissance flying in Iraq."

A blond-haired jet jockey dressed in jeans and a Georgia Bulldogs sweatshirt, sat comfortably with his right snakeskin cowboy boot resting on the conference table. He acknowledged the colonel with a raised fist. A macho ladies-man type, Marshall noted, the antithesis of Spangler. Youngblood riveted his women-charming blue eyes on Julie and settled into a smug grin. When she spotted him looking at her, she returned an awkward smile.

"Youngblood will be flying a heavily modified Black Hawk with stealth technology, which is stowed in back."

Marshall gave Williams a raised-eyebrow nod of approval. "The team's molecular biochemist is Julie Martinelli," the colonel said with a special note of pride. "I don't have to tell anybody by now that she's my daughter. Her field is theoretical biochemistry, specializing in molecular bioengineering. One day we're going to read about how she engineered a vaccine for the common cold."

The colonel's introduction drew polite laughter, prompting Julie to give her father a scolding pout that quickly melted into a charming smile. Still, Marshall preferred the beauty of her more serious academic look. Youngblood appeared smitten too.

"And, finally, meet Major Joseph Marshall and Gunnery Master Sergeant J. C. Williams on loan from the Naval Special Warfare Command," the colonel added. "The major and his sergeant are part of an elite commando unit operating in Iraq and Afghanistan. They handled many of the riskiest, most covert jobs in the war: deception operations in Afghanistan, reconnaissance and rescue missions inside Iraq. They'll be riding shotgun for us. We'll rely on their broad experience of staying alive in hostile territory to defend our staging area. We're singularly fortunate to have them on our team."

Marshall fidgeted uncomfortably in his fold-down seat, unsure of what to make of his role as a peripheral observer. *We're goddamn baby-sitters.*

"Lady and gentlemen," Colonel Martinelli concluded, "welcome to Alpha unit. I needn't point out that some members of this team are not connected with the military. If it wasn't so damned important, we wouldn't be asking civilians to participate. There simply wasn't time to go through regular channels. We needed the best and got clearances to recruit each of you for this operation."

Marshall resisted the urge to fidget some more. He hadn't left his men in Afghanistan and flown 10,000 miles at Mach 2 to listen to pep talks. He was pumped for action.

"One more thing, people," Colonel Martinelli added. "While aboard this transport, the general and I need to know what you all think. We don't have time to coddle behind military politics. So there will be no rank distinctions until we land. We expect candor – frequent and relevant."

That's all Marshall needed to hear. "Tony," he called to the front, "where is this aircraft going?"

General Medlock spat, "Antarctica."

There were puzzled looks around the cabin.

Medlock looked directly at Marshall and said, "This is a medical transport. It's on its way to provide hospital services to a NATO meteorological research team on Britain's South Shetland Islands on the Antarctica Peninsula, something this transport has done each month without fail for the past three years. This month, however, a mechanical problem will force it to make a brief unscheduled landing at an abandoned airstrip 30 miles outside of Sinope, in Brazil's Amazon basin. Texaco built the airstrip to shuttle in seismic trucks and drilling rigs. It's huge. Hasn't been used in two years, though. The runway is serviceable. Our people have made repairs. That's where most of you will get off. That airstrip will be Alpha's staging area, and you'll direct surveillance from the field's single hangar. The structure has a sagging roof and no utilities, but otherwise it's intact. Colonel?"

Colonel Martinelli withdrew a page from a folder and laid it upon the conference table. "What I'm about to tell you is highly classified. This priority-one State Department cable was issued two days ago. It says the U.S. government has information that bin Laden has ordered terrorist attacks against the United States mainland. And I quote, 'We believe these attacks will be deliberately designed to cause U.S. fatalities and/or destruction to U.S. facilities. We consider the Southeast as the most likely target, although no region can be completely precluded.' End quote. This warning has been sent to all U.S. military bases, international airlines, U.S. energy companies and other multinational businesses. Our State Department analysts issued the warning because of growing tensions over the U.S. and NATO involvement in Libya. But that's not the real reason. This is."

Martinelli picked up a palm-sized remote-control unit. Someone dimmed the cabin's lights, and an overhead projection TV snapped on. An image of a corpse-lined street filled the large screen. An infant wearing a nightgown, its face eerily placid as though it were a doll, lay in the foreground.

"This is the Afghan settlement of Barlar, about 200 miles west of Al Kufra," Martinelli said.

The next picture made even Marshall wince. It was a closeup of a young man's face, an expression of convulsive terror. His beard and coat were smeared with crusted vomit, his dried eyes sunken into his skull.

"On Monday," the colonel said, "a deadly nerve gas swept through Barlar and killed one hundred and three men, women and children. Unofficially, Afghanistan accused the United States of killing the people of Barlar during a military transport accident. There is no substance to this charge, of course. Israeli intelligence suspects that the incident was the result of a deliberate spill from an Afghan tank car en route from a terminal in Rabta. We believe bin Laden was involved. However, we can't prove that. All traces of the accident and the settlement are now gone. In any event, neither side has taken the issue public."

"Why don't we just order another full-scale air assault on every known al-Qaeda camp?" It was chopper pilot David Youngblood, speaking in his Georgia drawl.

"Because of this man," the colonel said.

The next image was a long shot of a huge, sinister-looking man with narrow eyes and dressed in a combat trench outfit. No one would deny that even from a distance he was frightening to look at. Marshall leaned intently forward. This wasn't the first time he had seen this rare photograph.

"Meet Abdul Banna," the colonel said, "better known to the terrorist underground these days as *Gorgon*."

Marshall, for one, needed no introduction. Banna was the reason his squad had been on nearly continuous alert for the past two years. A half dozen of his men were dead because of him.

Colonel Martinelli noted Marshall's keen attention. "I thought you'd be interested, Joe. This isn't your ordinary terrorist, people. Gorgon is a freelance mercenary. Very good. Very lethal. He isn't driven by religious fanaticism – only money. Believing he's operating out of either Afghanistan or Pakistan, the Italian government has sentenced him to death in absentia for the hijacking of the cruise ship *Ameno* and the murder of her crew. He is being sought by antiterrorist officials on three continents for hijacking, assassination and political violence. Israeli intelligence now estimates he has more than three hundred mercenary soldiers scattered among covert bases throughout the Middle East. However, we believe his network is much broader and includes an infrastructure in the United States. For the past eighteen months the CIA has been working to develop sources, identify Banna's associates and day-to-day movements, and devise a plan to intercept him.

"Two days ago, the U.S Embassy in Cairo received information from a reliable Arab informant," Martinelli said. "The caller – a well-paid Lebanese national who has worked for Banna for the past two years – said bin Laden hired Gorgon to carry out a terror assault on the U.S. mainland. Israel has confirmed this information. We have reason to believe Gorgon will attack using a highly lethal organism."

Unsettled murmurs swept through the cabin.

"What organism?" Marshall probed.

"Indulge me for one moment, please, Joe. There is one more man I want all of you to meet." Colonel Martinelli raised the remote control and another face filled the screen. This one was a passport photo of an older man with a weight problem. "Meet Dr. Carl Wynett, a former biochemical engineer with Friedrich Chemical Company of Gronau, West Germany. In the underground he is known as 'the Businessman,' and for a good reason. Wynett has made a fortune selling arms to al-Qaeda, Iraq and now Iran. During the past four years he has sold at least seventy tons of arms to bin Laden's terrorists."

The screen dissolved into another face – a distinguished-looking gentleman in his sixties, a pair of spectacles perched on his nose above a neat, silver beard. The quality of the image was not as good as that of the first.

"A surveillance camera at Detrick took this picture," the colonel said. "This also is Dr. Carl Wynett. Only the name on his Detrick ID tag yesterday said Dr. Reinhard Sterling."

The next screen showed two faces: on the right the distinguished image of Wynett, and beside it a head-and-shoulder portrait of a man who bore an uncanny resemblance to Wynett's altered image. The new face was studious, decisive, utterly self-assured.

"The man on the right is the real Dr. Sterling, one of the world's leading experts in bioengineering." The colonel paused, and for a moment there was only the steady drone of the Starlifter's engines. "Sterling was scheduled to take part in a conference at Detrick sponsored by the American Society of Microbiologists. Wynett showed up instead. His masquerade was clever enough to con Senator Michael Baker, chairman of a special Senate investigation subcommittee, and gain him access to a specially retrofitted BL-4 lab at Detrick."

"Has there been any word from Dr. Sterling?" Julie asked.

"His wife confirms dropping him off at the Frankfort Airport," the colonel said. "We're not sure when Wynett took his place. But there's been no word from Sterling after he boarded his flight. A police search is still under way in both countries."

"What in God's name was Wynett after?" Lieutenant Spangler asked.

"Something to sell to Gorgon. Something very rare and very potent. Something brewed up by the United States military." Colonel Martinelli passed the remote control to his daughter. "I'll defer the specifics of that question to my expert."

Julie passed a memory stick to telecommunications officer Spangler, who inserted it into the unit attached to the overhead monitor. She stood before the group, her eyes fixed on the remote control in her palm. This was not the confident, self-assertive woman Marshall had met earlier, he noted. She appeared deeply troubled about something. When she spoke there was controlled anger in her voice.

"Wynett stole a vial containing a genetically engineered T_4 supertoxin," she began. "It was a hybrid. A Detrick researcher found a way to splice tetrodotoxin into a Group A streptococcal pathogen. He created an airborne virus at least four hundred times as lethal as conventional neurotoxins. Wynett now has it."

Marshall's empty stomach suddenly felt queasy. He glanced at Williams, who shook his head in disgust.

Julie punched a number on the remote control, and a black-and-white image of a laboratory filled the screen. "This is Detrick's BL-4 lab following Wynett's visit."

The next image showed what used to be a man, half clad in a shredded environment suit, contorted like driftwood on the lab's floor, his features no longer recognizable.

"This is what's left of Colonel James Westbrook, commander of the United States Army Medical Research Institute of Infectious Disease," Julie said. "Wynett sealed Westbrook and a technician inside the lab after opening dozens of vials containing the world's most lethal viruses and bacteria. He then turned off all life-support systems."

She zoomed in on a pocket-size notebook opened beside the corpse to enlarge barely legible scribbling. It was a list of sorts, each line more erratically written than the previous.

"Before he died," Julie said, "Westbrook wrote the name 'Saint Vitus' seven times in his calendar notebook. This was no prayer. Saint Vitus is the code name for the synthesized supertoxin—"

"Please note," General Medlock cut in, "that the name itself is highly classified."

"Of course," Julie allowed. "Although it may be months before anyone can enter the lab to be certain, we're assuming Westbrook was trying to tell us what Wynett had taken."

"Ms. Martinelli," Spangler asked, "just how dangerous is this pathogen?"

"When tetrodotoxin protein was successfully introduced into the virus, a highly lethal new organism was born," she said. "Tetrodotoxin is found naturally in the skin, ovaries, liver and intestines of the blowfish or puffer fish. It's one of the most poisonous substances known. Laboratory analysis has demonstrated that it is more than one hundred and fifty thousand times more potent than cocaine. I would conservatively rate it five hundred times stronger than cyanide.

"The army was interested in the new organism because of the speed with which it attacks its host's central nervous system. It's extraordinarily communicable, requiring only several hundred particles to produce an infection, compared to influenza, which requires several million. And unlike nerve gas, which can dissipate rapidly in poor weather conditions, an organism can breed and spread. An outbreak of Saint Vitus could produce a localized plague for which there is no antidote. However, the organism can survive only in an environment of pure oxygen. Once contaminated by carbon dioxide, succeeding generations mutate rapidly into less volatile strains, which is useful to the military from a tactical standpoint – after a few hours soldiers can occupy the contaminated area. Specific data are not available. The only remaining sample is now in Wynett's possession."

"And you think Wynett intends to sell this ... this bug to Gorgon?" Youngblood drawled, more a conclusion than a question.

"Absolutely," interjected the colonel, standing. "In fact, we're certain Gorgon hired Wynett for the theft. Our informant was working with Wynett at the time of the Detrick theft. Apparently Gorgon got wise to him. Our spy turned up dead in an abandoned shack in Tampico, Mexico. His brain had been removed and mailed to the State Department via pouch mail as a warning. Gorgon was fucking with us. However, it did tell us he had left Afghanistan, which bought us some time."

"But only one vial?" Spangler said. "How much of a threat can one vial pose?"

"It's an unprecedented threat, DOS," Julie said. "Wynett can incubate as much of the organism as he wants. They have no lab data about the specimen. Wynett knows it's terribly lethal, but little else. He has no way of knowing that if a gallon of Saint Vitus was aerated over New York City, the organism would seek and kill ninety-six percent of the population in less than one hour. Assuming Wynett knows advanced molecular biochemistry, in a week he could produce enough virus to infect the airspace between New York to San Diego."

The men around the table sat rigid, their expressions suggesting they were visualizing corpse-strewn streets in their own neighborhoods far more gruesome than the image of the Afghan settlement of Barlar.

Colonel Martinelli broke the uneasy quiet. "Perhaps you now can appreciate what bin Laden is up to," he said. "What better way to promote his cause around the world than to reveal in such a dramatic fashion what the U.S. Army is brewing in its own labs? He wants to hoist us with our own petard."

Marshall's mind reeled while he digested the flood of information and tried to grasp all its ramifications. "Total candor?"

Colonel Martinelli nodded.

"Why was Detrick messing with this stuff in the first place?" he asked. "I thought we were out of the offensive biological weapons business."

"Detrick is a defensive research facility," Medlock interjected, his firm voice doing its best to convince. "This situation is an unintended consequence of that research."

"I agree with the major," Spangler said, standing. "This is going to feed a new-age biological weapons race whose end could become the most efficient way to exterminate man from this planet."

"The man who dreamed up this poison should be up here risking his neck with us," Youngblood shouted, fueling the objections. "I want to know the fucker's name!"

"*I did it,*" Julie shouted.

The cabin fell abruptly quiet, and all eyes shifted to her.

"Saint Vitus was my *fucking* idea."

Julie dropped into her seat and locked eyes with Youngblood. He was too surprised to do anything but stare back at her. Marshall looked away. For a few awkward moments no one spoke – no one knew how to react to the news. The revelation that the colonel's own daughter was responsible, however indirectly, hung over the team like another unfathomable toxin.

"What my daughter means," began Colonel Martinelli, his tone apologetic, "is that she originally proposed a theory for the new organism as part of her doctoral thesis. But it was just an idea. She declined to pursue it. The notion was purely theoretical – she had no technological means to pull it off. Unfortunately Detrick's experimental gene-splicing technique is much more advanced than anything the universities have. Dr. David French, an army biochemist, created the new strain without approval or authorization. And he paid for it with his life."

"No one is happy about this, least of all me," General Medlock rasped. "Nevertheless, the people of the United States have a very big problem. We can't allow Gorgon to get his hands on this toxin – goddamnit, we can't let him or his minions set foot in the United States. Now that you've all asked your questions, it's time we do something about this fiasco."

Medlock glared into the somber faces around the cabin as though looking for dissension. He found none.

"Good," he said. "Martinelli?"

The colonel coolly surveyed his team, his infectious grin gone, his sparkly eyes now a pair of dark spheres. "This team is the last defense against mass murder on a scale unimaginable until French came along. Hell, the world's not coming to an end, people. We're going to get back our bug and Gorgon with it. Wynett owns a plantation in Mato Grosso in Brazil's Amazon basin about 60 miles east of the airstrip where we'll be staging. He calls the place Stonecutters Garden. It's a front for his gun-running business in South America and a damn good hideout. Our recon satellites are monitoring activity on the plantation, and word's out he's recruiting men who can handle guns to strengthen his already formidable security force. We believe Wynett's on his way to the farm with Saint Vitus. Officially the U.S. can't touch him there. That's where we come in."

"So we enter a sovereign state illegally and assault the plantation," Marshall said. "How does that get us Gorgon?"

"By letting Wynett brew his poison," the colonel said.

Unsettled murmurs throughout the cabin confirmed that no one liked the idea.

"Keep in mind, people, that al-Qaeda is no doubt paying Gorgon a great deal," the colonel said. "If he doesn't get his hands on this supertoxin, he'll find another bug to carry out bin Laden's attack. That's why we're going to let Saint Vitus bring Gorgon out in the open where we can deal with him permanently. The next time Gorgon and Wynett meet, we'll take down both of them. Very quietly, very efficiently. We are not, I repeat, *not* interested in making arrests. Our first task will be to get as many of Stony's men as possible onto the plantation as hired guns. Those of Stony's men who aren't recruited to beef up Wynett's security force will work in the fields as roustabouts, picking sugar. Once inside they'll be our reconnaissance and will make damn certain the vial Wynett stole doesn't leave that plantation. And when I give the order, they'll be our firepower."

"Too risky," Marshall said. "The price of failure is too high."

Colonel Martinelli, his eyes coming alive again, said, "There's no risk of Gorgon getting his hands on Saint Vitus. Wynett's incubated pathogen will be worthless."

More quizzical looks. "I don't get it, sir," Spangler said. "If the vial he stole from Detrick is the real thing, what's stopping him from producing more?"

"As a chemical engineer," Colonel Martinelli said, "Wynett lacks the expertise to incubate a synthetic neurotoxin. He's going to need help from a molecular biochemist. We know he's used such a specialist at least twice before, a professor on the staff of the biochemistry department at the University of Sao Paulo. The man's got a lot of problems, drinking only one of them, but he knows his science and Wynett trusts him. He's under our surveillance right now. If Wynett contacts him to assist, one of our people will attempt to take his place. If successful, our man will make sure the culture medium Wynett uses in the incubation process is toxic to the organism. Wynett will deliver to Gorgon a harmless stew."

"Suppose Wynett doesn't go for it?" Youngblood asked. "What if you can't get a man next to him?"

"That's a very real possibility," the colonel said. "In that event Stony's men will simply eliminate Wynett and return what he stole to Fort Detrick. Under no circumstances can we allow Wynett to incubate a lethal strain of Saint Vitus in any quantity."

He intends to send his own daughter to Wynett's plantation, Marshall thought. *What the fuck?* She wasn't trained for a covert sting operation. What if she panicked? He shook his head, appalled by the idea.

"Sir," Marshall said. "No disrespect intended, but Julie won't last 10 minutes inside Wynett's camp. He'll cut her throat before she can open a notebook."

The colonel looked astonished. "Are you suggesting I send in my own daughter to work with Wynett?"

Marshall scanned the faces in the cabin and saw no other likely candidate. "Who else do you have in mind?"

Colonel Martinelli leveled a shrewd gaze at Marshall.

"Me."

STAGING

Sao Paulo, Brazil
Thursday, April 28, 0804 hours

Dr. Jorge da Silva welcomed his drunken stupor. The alcohol's sedation numbed the deep cut above his right eye and the pain of four broken teeth. He didn't look much like a member of the University of Sao Paulo's prestigious biochemistry department. He had been foolish to resist the two goons, each twice his weight, who pushed their way into his apartment two hours earlier. Since then, they waited for a phone call. Dr. da Silva sat rigid during that time, staring through fogged vision at the two men, and tried to speculate about their identity. American FBI agents or some other U.S. government agency that specialized in torture.

When his cell phone finally rang, the anemic doctor gasped in surprise, then winced at the pain in his chest from a collapsed lung. He needed another drink to further numb his pain and his fear. But nothing was offered. One of the goons squeezed a piece into his ear and instructed the doctor to answer. Dr. da Silva was no hero. He did exactly as he was told.

"Dr. da Silva," he said into the phone, trying not to slur his words.

"I need you again." It was his business associate Carl Wynett. The plantation's satellite link sounded remarkably clear. "I can give you one week's work. Please be ready by eight tonight at our usual rendezvous."

Dr. da Silva looked at his captors glaring at him with dark expressions, then chose his words carefully.

"Sorry, Carl," da Silva said, echoing the speech the special agents had rehearsed with him. "I have a collapsed lung of all my dumb luck. A spontaneous thing. I was just leaving for St. Luke's Hospital." Dr. da Silva coughed and felt a peculiar ache in his chest. His captors made sure his excuse rang true.

A lengthy pause. Da Silva feared Wynett had hung up on him. *Steady.*

Finally Wynett said, "I am sorry to hear about your health. Nevertheless, this leaves me in a bind. And I am in haste. I am prepared to pay you double."

He is up to something big – and that means cash, da Silva thought. *Too bad I won't be part of it.* "I am in too much pain, Carl," da Silva said, then added slowly, "Why not use Armstrong this time?"

"Who?"

"Dr. Henry Armstrong, the department's new American instructor I told you about," he lied. He'd never uttered the name before. "We are good friends. He teaches biology, but his field is molecular biochemistry in medical research. He is very good."

"I do not recall you mentioning a Dr. Armstrong." Another pause, then, "Can I trust him?"

"He has his faults." Dr. da Silva shot a sideways glance at the goons and ad-libbed, "several outstanding felony child molestation charges in the States. He needs cash. He will jump at a chance for freelance work."

Another long pause. "Describe him to me."

One of the men held a 5 X 7-inch photo of Col. Anthony Martinelli in front of the doctor's face, almost too close for da Silva's bloodshot eyes to focus properly.

"He is older than I by ten years, and stockier. He wears his hair short, and it has much gray in it. He is clean shaven and has a medium build." He leaned back to focus on the photo. "Nothing spectacular."

One of da Silva's guards signaled him to end the conversation. The longer he talked to Wynett, the greater the chance of him blowing this. "Carl, I have to go to St. Luke's. I am coughing blood."

"No," Wynett snapped. "I must speak with your Dr. Armstrong immediately."

One of his captors nodded.

"You can contact him through my secretary at the university. He should be there now."

"Thank you, Dr. da Silva. I will miss our chess games. Does Armstrong play?"

Dr. da Silva looked questioningly at his captors, whose expressions remained blank. They were unprepared for the question.

"Yes, sir," da Silva volunteered with a mischievous smirk. He would repay the men who had beaten him. "We play regularly. The man is a pro."

"Very good. Again, I am sorry about your health."

One of the goons snatched the cell phone and disconnected it. Dr. da Silva expelling a long, relieved sigh, prompting another bout of chest pain. He looked expectantly at his captors, but neither man's dark face provided any feedback about his performance.

One of the gorillas produced a bottle of Canadian Club and passed it to da Silva. The doctor downed a quarter of its contents in two impressive swallows. His captors traded amused glances. Da Silva exploded a cough, spraying the front of his shirt with whiskey. *The goons had spiked the liquor.* In minutes he would most likely be in a coma-like sleep. And only God knew where he would wake up with a demonic hangover.

New York
0815 hours

No one in the biology department of the University of Sao Paulo heard Dr. da Silva's office phone ring. Not surprising, considering it had been replaced with a device that looked like a telephone but, in fact, had a far different function – ringing not one of them. The simple switching device transferred all incoming calls from Dr. da Silva's office via satellite to a small office in New York City leased by the United States Central Intelligence Agency.

Two people worked the office. One of them was Mrs. Hilda Gonzales, a heavy middle-aged woman with six children and more than twenty years of experience as a linguistic communications specialist with AT&T. Each time her console buzzed with an incoming call, she switched on a recording of keyboards clicking in the background before answering. She had a stack of messages for da Silva. Her routine this time was no different.

"Chemistry department," she said in Portuguese.

"I need a reference regarding a Dr. Henry Armstrong," Wynett said.

"One moment please. I will transfer you to his office."

"Madam, first I would like to speak to his superior."

"The dean will not be in today," she said, "but I can let you talk to the dean's assistant."

"Very good."

Mrs. Gonzales put the caller on hold, switched off the recording and looked at her boss for a cue. The dark man wearing a darker suit, a headset pressed to his ear, gave her a nod. She connected the call.

"This is Dr. Ribera," the agent said, also in Portuguese. "How may I help you?"

"My name is Ernst Stenger from the Bianco Nacional Bank of Sao Paulo," Wynett said. "I need a loan reference for a Henry Armstrong. Is he employed by the University?"

"Yes, Mr. Stenger. He teaches biology."

"May I ask how long he has been employed there?"

"About four months."

"Would you be kind enough to give me a personal reference regarding his loan application?"

The CIA agent sighed for effect. "Mr. Stenger, I can vouch for Dr. Armstrong's integrity as a teacher – he is very good at what he does. But I will have to decline comment about his personal affairs."

"I understand. Thank you, Dr. Ribera. You have been very helpful."

"May I transfer you to his office?" The special agent held his breath. Go for it, bastard.

"I would appreciate that very much, Dr. Ribera. Thank you."

The special agent nodded to Mrs. Gonzales, who redirected the call through the satellite system to Sinope, Brazil. He replaced the receiver and, sighing deeply, gave her a relieved nod of gratitude.

Sinope, Brazil

Ten minutes after the Starlifter touched down on the abandoned airstrip in the jungles of Sinope, the flight crew had unloaded half its equipment and supplies and stacked them along the runway. The transport's engines idled at twenty-five percent. It would be airborne in another 10 minutes.

Stony rushed across the tarmac to the colonel, cradling a suppressed M-16 rifle. "We got company ... a couple men barricaded in the hangar. Four, we think, and armed. They know we're here – one took a shot at us. Another bolted into the jungle. Four of my men surrounded the structure. The others are searching the brush."

"Goddamnit," General Medlock spat. "This place was supposed to be secure."

"Who are they?" Julie asked, stepping next to them.

"Most likely guerrillas and cocaine traffickers," Colonel Martinelli said. He wiped his sweat-soaked brow with the back of his camouflage cap. "These valleys are a source of most of the world's coco leaf. The jungle is full of illegal airstrips and drug labs. When our people repaired this runway, a drug lord probably secured this airstrip for his own use."

"Nice," Julie said.

Marshall pushed in beside the colonel. The plan's already *fucked*. "So what are we going to do about it?"

"Colonel, secure that hangar," Medlock said, "and fast." He glanced at his watch. "I'm out of here in eight minutes."

"Get your men inside that hangar, captain," the colonel ordered Stony. "Take prisoners, if you can. But I want that hangar cleared in three minutes."

Stony nodded and disappeared.

Colonel Martinelli looked severely at Lieutenant Spangler and said, "I want your ear glued to that radio. If you get the call from New York, give it to me. I don't care what I'm doing, you come get me. You understand?"

A pallid Spangler nodded. "Yes, sir."

Marshall positioned himself in a ditch across from the hangar, which was little more than a ramshackle barracks overgrown with jungle. Stony's men positioned themselves along its side. Stony jammed his boot solidly against the door. The planks shattered in a blizzard of mildew and rot. It was dim inside the hangar, too dark to make out specifics, but Marshall heard ratlike scuffles and saw vague figures rushing into the shadows, taking up positions.

"*Go!*" Stony shouted.

His commandos followed him inside, their suppressed weapons popping single rounds into the shadows. Marshall heard men screaming and kicking at the planks in a desperate bid to flee. A lone shotgun blast from one of the inhabitants blew a hole in the hangar's roof. A quiet followed. Stony's men had secured the hangar.

Marshall followed Colonel Martinelli inside the hangar and inventoried the dead. Four men lay scattered across the floor, their bodies riddled with bullets, their dusty faces soaked in red.

"I want light in here," the colonel demanded.

Outside, Williams pushed a curious Julie away from the hangar's doorway and kept his Galil rifle pointed at the underbrush along the runway, scanning for movement.

Inside the hangar, Marshall shouldered his Franchi shotgun and towered over one of the casualties. His jaw tightened. The luckless man was at least sixty, with thin white hair and worn-out clothing, his hands callused from hard work. At his side lay an antique shotgun. The corpse stared vacantly out the ravaged door as though he had some particular destination in mind. Neither he nor his companions were going anywhere.

"Looks like you saved us from some formidable villains," Marshall mocked.

Stony whirled from one of the dead and glared at Marshall. "Sorry to mess up your day, major. We're not going to blow this operation over a couple of vagrants."

The colonel extinguished a still-lit cigarette with his boot. "We have work to do. Get these bodies out of here."

Spangler bolted into the hangar, a yellow light flashing on his portable satellite transceiver. "It's the New York link, sir," he yelled, slipping on headphones to monitor the call.

"I want it quiet in here," Colonel Martinelli's voice boomed into every corner of the hangar. Julie watched from the doorway.

The colonel put on a headset attached to Spangler's transceiver. "Armstrong here."

"Dr. Armstrong?" asked a voice on the other end, an older gentleman with a German accent.

The colonel allowed himself an inaudible sigh. "That's what I said."

"I was told you could help me."

The colonel gave Marshall a serious nod. "Who are you?"

"My name is Dr. Carl Wynett. I am a research scientist. Dr. da Silva assured me that I can trust you. I will pay you ten thousand American dollars cash for one week of lab work as my assistant. Can you accommodate me?"

Martinelli paused several heartbeats for effect. Marshall yanked the headphones off Spangler's head and placed them over his own ears so he could monitor the call.

"What kind of lab work?" the colonel asked slowly.

"Routine. How soon can you be ready?"

Marshall glanced at Captain Youngblood in the doorway. He knew it would take at least three hours to prep the Black Hawk chopper.

"First thing in the morning," the colonel said. "If I'm still interested."

"Sir, if you want the job, you will tell me so immediately, then meet outside the currency exchange office on Iguatemi Street at eight tonight."

One thousand miles to Sao Paulo in less than twelve hours in a chopper that's still needs prepped, Marshall thought. *That's cutting it fucking close, pal.*

"Ten thousand cash?" the colonel asked.

"Yes."

"How will I know you?"

"I will find you – assuming you are on Iguatemi Street at eight tonight."

Martinelli allowed another pregnant pause. "Sure, why not?"

"Very good. By the way, your friend assured me I can count on you for a good game of chess."

Martinelli paused again, this time uncertain how to respond. Marshall knew he wasn't a player.

"I can hold my own," he allowed.

"Good. Tonight at eight then."

The line went dead. Colonel Martinelli removed his headset and looked into the questioning faces of his team. "It's a go." He looked at his watch and scowled. "I've got less than twelve hours to get to Sao Paulo." He yelled at Youngblood, "I want that chopper ready ASAP. Joe, I want you and your sergeant to help him. Goddamnit, I want this place looking like an op staging area, not a drug-infested latrine."

The pilot and the gunnery sergeant vanished from the doorway, but Marshall stayed behind.

"Get your men into town *now,*" The colonel ordered Stony.

"Yes, sir."

Marshall watched the ungroomed commandos follow Stony single file into the jungle. The *town* was a farming community of drifters who hung around drinking and waiting for work, preferably as Wynett's farmhands or mercenaries. Mostly they drank. With luck, Stony's troops would be in Wynett's employ within twenty-four hours.

The colonel said to Marshall, "Your job is to take care of my people while I'm gone." He grabbed Julie's hand. "Take care of my daughter."

"I can take care of myself, thank you very much," Julie scoffed. "I don't need one of your grunts standing guard over me."

Marshall grimaced.

"You'll do exactly as Joe says," the colonel said, curtly.

"There are too many 'ifs' in this plan of yours, Tony," Marshall said. "Are you sure you can pull off this masquerade?"

Colonel Martinelli scowled. "For the past year I've been eating, drinking and living this material at Detrick."

"He knows biochemistry very well," Julie said.

"Relax, Joe." The colonel turned to Spangler still holding his transceiver. "I heard you can play a mean game of chess."

Spangler gawked at him through his owllike spectacles and nodded. "I can beat my computer ... one out of three games."

"Good. You have one hour to teach me."

La Strata Air Base
Cuzco, Peru

Peruvian Air Force Capt. Laszlo Valachi found himself in the middle of an uncommonly busy day. He spent the morning honoring a Peruvian Defense Council request to monitor and record all transmissions originating from a remote Brazilian rain forest. The order at first seemed routine – another snooping session on the local drug traffickers. But this morning's events proved most interesting. Over the past four hours the air base's surveillance equipment had recorded scrambled satellite relay signals transmitting on a frequency usually reserved for high-speed data links. Captain Valachi wasn't a telecommunications expert, but he knew this was no drug trafficker with a shortwave set.

The second incident occurred just before noon. Valachi monitored a distress call to the Brazilian Air Force Command Center in Cuiaba from a NATO transport plane requesting permission for an emergency landing at an abandoned airstrip outside of Sinope. The airstrip was less than 60 miles from the source of the satellite transmission. Thirty minutes later, the pilot reported a critical oil leak was repaired and that the transport had resumed its flight plan to Antarctica.

Coincidence? Probably. Nevertheless, the captain reported the activity to the Defense Council and then ordered his tiny but powerful air-force squadron – two Russian-made MiG-23s and a Hind MiL gunship – on alert.

INFILTRATOR

Sao Paulo, Brazil
Thursday, 2007 hours

Colonel Martinelli waited outside the neon-lit currency exchange office on Iguatemi Street. *What a piece of shit part of town.* He rubbed his two-day-old beard, then glanced at his watch again. *Damn – seven minutes late.*

After flying at full throttle for more than eight hours at treetop level, Captain Youngblood delivered him to the outskirts of Sao Paulo an uncomfortably close 30 minutes ago. Still, he wasn't at his appointed rendezvous. He had to jog nearly two miles down dark, narrow side streets before finding a driver willing to take him into the worst part of the city after dark. Not an easy task, he quickly learned. His fingers curled with relief around his custom-made Beretta in a back holster under his sweat-soaked shirt. He breathed easier.

Martinelli's duffel bag was stuffed with toiletries and spare magazine clips sewn into the lining. While he waited, his mind swirled with facts and tables from the crash course in microbiology his daughter had given him, tutoring sessions he likened to taking sips from a fire hose.

He glanced again at his watch. Where was Wynett? Maybe he suspected something and backed off. Maybe Operation Containment was already over, only he just didn't know it.

"Good evening, Dr. Armstrong," a voice with a thick Portuguese accent greeted him from behind.

Martinelli turned. A man, his face obscured by a large straw hat, lit a fat cigar, revealing grizzled cheeks and heavy lidded eyes.

"You *are* Dr. Armstrong?" the man asked in choppy English. Martinelli nodded.

"I am Tucco," he said. "You are late." He pulled at the colonel's sweat-soaked shirt. "You have been running?"

"I couldn't get a cab," Martinelli said.

Tucco made a circling gesture. "Turn around, *faz favor.*"

Martinelli complied. Tucco frisked the colonel and removed his Beretta.

"An odd possession for a schoolteacher," Tucco said, scrutinizing the handgun with professional detachment.

"As long as I'm in this country, it goes where I go," Martinelli said.

Tucco removed the magazine and returned the weapon to the colonel. "You cannot come armed."

A quick inspection of Martinelli's duffel bag yielded nothing that seemed to interest him. Then he scrutinized the colonel's appearance.

"You must shave before we arrive. He does not care about the farmers. But those who work close to him must groom."

Martinelli grunted. *An eccentric bastard, this Wynett.*

With a jerk of his thumb Tucco directed the colonel into the front seat of a waiting car. The colonel slid into the vehicle next to the driver, a Brazilian not much more than a boy. Tucco squeezed the colonel to the middle. The driver headed south toward the airport. Sandwiched tightly between the two, Martinelli winced at the powerful odor of sweat and the brim of Tucco's straw hat tickling his temples.

"Care to tell me where we're going?" Martinelli said. "I thought this was a local job."

"You thought wrong, *amigo*," Tucco said, drawing deeply on his cigar, filling the car with thick, acrid smoke. "I hope you enjoy helicopter rides."

Sinope, Brazil
Friday, April 30, 0530 hours

Julie writhed in agony from the severe pain spreading through every muscle of her body. She knew what it felt like to be terribly ill – she once had an acute case of salmonella that put her in a hospital for two days. But this wasn't food poisoning. She touched her right arm and contorted in agony. The bloated appendage had become a black, throbbing stump that threatened to rupture in a pool of rancid blood if she dared rub it.

Saint Vitus...

She was infected. The virus had reduced her body to an obscene mockery of its former splendor. Every organ, muscle and tissue ravaged beyond any conceivable hope of repair.

She whisked off the sheet and gaped in horror at two appalling bags of yellow sap that had once been an enviable pair of legs.

"Ganciclovir!" she shouted, but the sound from her throat sounded like the hiss of a crushed snake....

Julie clung desperately to her soaked sheet. *Another damned nightmare.* Trembling, she slid from under the mosquito net and placed a socked foot next to a Cane toad, which she first mistook for a round, squat teapot. She and the unblinking amphibian stared impersonally before the odd creature hopped under the frame of her cot. *Marvelous.* Better to find vermin that hopped, she reassured herself, than ones that slithered.

Neither the climate nor the early hour agreed with Julie. Unending nightmares and the thunder of a heavy rain exploding like firecrackers on the hangar's corrugated iron roof exhausted her. Her dreams alternated between seeing a Satan-like virus under a microscope to finding her father's decomposing remains. By morning Julie felt like the old hangar looked – worn and undesirable. The heat, even for dawn, was oppressive. Pulling a sweat-drenched T-shirt down past her waist, she trudged across the rotted and warped planks toward the bathroom before she remembered there wasn't one. Nor was there any running water.

"You sure can pick them, dad," she muttered to no one. The other members of Alpha appeared to fare better this morning. Youngblood was still stretched out on his cot, sleeping off the effects of nightlong, low-level flying. Lt. Dennis Spangler sat behind his computer terminal, headphones over his ears.

Marshall stifled a belch that tasted of his sardine breakfast and began his predawn regimen of push-ups, stomach crunches and deep-knee squats. He actually enjoyed the old hangar. On more than a few occasions he had paid to sleep in rooms worse than this.

He didn't envy Tony, didn't envy his role in this whole ugly affair. However, he did admire the colonel's courage. One mistake would cost him his life – and those of many others as well. Sure, there was a brilliant daring in the mission, and maybe just enough serendipity to make it work. The risks were high, but the reward was far greater – Gorgon. He just hated the waiting.

Marshall saw Julie steal a glance at him before she headed to the water bin to wash up. Too bad she wasn't more sociable. He really wanted to get to know her better. But that would need to wait. Maybe this old hangar had gotten to her. No –he suspected she felt guilty for putting her father in danger, a situation he did not envy her.

He grabbed his Franchi shotgun and jogged into the jungle to relieve himself.

The old Brazilian trapper noted that the trespassers were awake. He saw fleeting movement through the hangar's glassless window and heard voices. But it was the sudden appearance of a woman in the crooked doorway that softened the cracks around his dull, tired eyes. What he saw riveted his attention as no other sight in the jungle ever had. Stretching her arms above her head, she inadvertently thrust her ample breasts boldly toward him. The *gringa* was the most beautiful woman he had ever seen. He stared at her, his eyes wider than his mouth, and allowed her image to burn into his mind, where he hoped it would linger forever.

The old man jabbed a skinny hand through a mane of pure white hair, then replaced his yellow baseball cap and stroked his enormous drooping mustache. There. He was presentable. What a fine wife she would make for his son, Roberto. He damn well intended to make a good first impression on the woman, his future daughter-in-law. He thought of his own wife. He had last slept with her twelve years ago, two years before she died of tuberculosis. Loneliness had made him a bold and foolish man.

"Move and you're a dead man," said a cold voice behind him. "Understand? Just nod if you do."

The trapper's hand reached for his archaic double-barreled shotgun, only to find a black military boot on it. He chanced a look over his shoulder and stared into the business end of an exquisitely machined paramilitary shotgun. He did not doubt that the tall, sturdy soldier in camouflage pants and a sleeveless T-shirt, would use it to blow his head apart. He heard a sharp click to his right. A powerfully built black man, standing naked to the waist in the underbrush, watched him through the scope of a high-powered rifle.

"I asked you a question," the soldier with the shotgun repeated.

The trapper shrugged.

"Who is he?" the black man called.

"Damned if I know." The soldier said to the trapper in poor Portuguese, "*Que vos?*"

"This is my camp," the old man answered in equally poor English. "You make me sleep in the rain with the turtles."

The soldier raised his weapon into a more civil position, but kept his boot on the trapper's shotgun. "Says he lives here," he said to his partner. "He looks like part of the clan Stony's boys shot up yesterday. He's lucky to be alive."

The black man kept his rifle pointed at the trapper. "Careful, major. He might be looking to get even. He might have more family around here."

"He could be useful." The soldier said to the old, "Tell me your name."

"Jose."

"My name is Major Joe Marshall. I'll make a deal with you, Jose. Let us stay at your camp for a few days and I'll pay you in bolivars what it would take you ten years to earn off the jungle." Marshall sealed the deal by adding, "And I'll leave you twenty cases of sardines."

The old trapper scrambled to his feet with a smile, revealing a rotted set of teeth. "The woman," he asked. "Is she your wife?"

"Julie?" Marshall laughed. "She's not my type – she's nobody's type."

The old trapper's smile widened. First he would eat sardines. Then he would arrange for the woman to marry his son. This was a good day, a very good day.

Marshall picked up the trapper's shotgun, its wooden stock half eaten by fungus, and led the way back to the hangar. The trapper followed, flapping behind in his sandals.

Lieutenant Spangler's announcement shot through the hangar like a gun blast. "The colonel's in!"

Julie peered over the telecommunications officer's shoulder at a thirty-two inch monitor. Marshall tossed the trapper's shotgun to Williams and pushed his way between Spangler and Julie, leaving the old man standing wide-eyed and alone in the doorway.

"The computer-enhanced satellite images of Wynett's Brazilian estate came a few minutes ago, courtesy of General Medlock," Spangler said.

"The detail is extraordinary," Julie said.

"The conditions were good," Spangler said, studying the monitor's image with a magnifier. "The rain ended early and there was a break in the clouds. No haze, low-morning-sun angle."

Marshall leaned toward the monitor and scrutinized the aerial image. "When were these taken?"

Spangler checked the image's time mark. "The first was taken 48 minutes ago, sir. The others are one minute apart. Wynett's got one heck of a spread." He tapped his pencil's eraser on the image's features. "This is the main house – looks big enough for about twenty rooms – and the structure behind it looks like a stable. The estate is surrounded by a tall fence, and these look like guard towers on the east and west corners. The spheres behind the house are satellite dishes." The lieutenant's pencil slid to a cluster of houses behind the estate. "These structures probably house the farmhands. I don't see any roads leading in, though."

"Nice going, DOS," Julie said, moving around Marshall and sliding next to the lieutenant. "How do you know my father's in there?"

Spangler tried to ignore the breasts pressed against his right arm. "Simple – there's a helipad in the middle of this unharvested field of sugarcane," he said, tapping his eraser in the image's upper right corner. "See the chopper's main rotor blades?"

"Yeah, but there's no way to tell if the colonel was aboard." It was Williams, peering over Julie's shoulder.

"There's more detail on the second image." Spangler scrolled to a second image, a close-up of the area between the helipad and the estate's main gate. "Two men are walking toward the house. Another man with a rifle, probably a guard, is following about ten paces behind them."

"So you think one of the first two is my father?" Julie asked.

"Does this help?" He brought up a third image. The close-up showed two men, one wearing a large straw hat and white shirt, the other a shorter man with salt-and-pepper hair, carrying a bag. "The man on the right is the colonel. That's his duffel bag."

Marshall nodded.

Julie moved closer to the monitor. "He doesn't look like he's being coerced."

"Just the usual precautions," Spangler said.

"What do we do now?" Julie asked. "How can we help him?"

Marshall shrugged. "We do just what the colonel ordered – nothing. Tony's a resourceful man who managed to get himself right where he wants to be. Now he's about to find out just how much he knows about biochemistry."

Stonecutters Garden

Tucco led Colonel Martinelli from the sugarcane fields into the magnificent grounds of Wynett's estate. The view astounded Martinelli. The lawn, a hardy green carpet unblemished by weeds, flowed neatly around cobblestone paths that wound between pruned shrubbery and trees of every variety and color. Wynett obviously appreciated horticulture artistry and indulged that passion with impressive results. But the real treasure was an English Tudor house dominating the grounds like a grand castle. Its massive irregular granite blocks gave it the solidity of a fortress. Martinelli wondered how many guns Wynett had sold to transform this part of the Amazon rain forest into a posh European countryside.

As they stepped inside the fence, an iron-grilled gate closed automatically behind them. *"Claro!"* someone shouted in Portuguese. A loud crack echoed across the estate followed by an electric generator whining to life.

Martinelli assumed they would go into the house straight-away to unpack. He assumed wrong. Tucco led them along an ornate cobblestone walkway, then across an acre of sod leading to a stone barn. Between the two structures sat a cluster of satellite dishes and hefty gas storage tanks surrounded by a high barbed-wire fence. A dozen men with tools worked in and around the barn. A few carried rifles and looked as though they knew how to use them. Martinelli scanned each farmhand's face. He released his breath slowly when he spotted one of

Alpha's men, a shovel slung over his shoulder, walking toward the barn. How many more of Stony's men had made it in?

A black man in stiff overalls emerged from the barn and walked straight toward them. Martinelli's expression tightened. It was Stony, sweating profusely, his disinterested gaze fixed well past them. He carried a shovel, evidence the special-op captain was unable to convince Wynett he could be trusted with a rifle. As he passed, Stony's right hand batted an imaginary mosquito away from his ear – a signal they needed to talk.

The sound of kids screaming focused Martinelli's attention back to the barn. Several black boys, running and pushing each other, raced inside just ahead of a black woman chasing and scolding them. Martinelli's brow furled with disapproval. Women and children complicated the plan. How many more were in here?

Tucco noticed the colonel's expression. "You like watching the boys, yes, doctor?"

"Say what?"

Tucco grinned. "*Chefe* has told me about your problem in America."

"Yeah? You'll have to fill me in sometime."

The two entered the barn. Its darkened interior was a welcome respite from the heat of the early-morning sun. Inside, two workers grooming a magnificent equine shooed away the spirited boys darting underfoot. Tucco led Martinelli to the back of the barn, where another of Stony's men – a commando nicknamed Buckshot – guarded a hole in the floor with a Kalashnikov automatic rifle. *Nice going, Buckshot.*

Tucco said something to Buckshot in Portuguese, and the soldier allowed the two to pass. There was no eye contact. Tucco stepped into the blackness and carefully descended a flight of twisted steps reinforced with solid hardwood planks. Martinelli followed. The climate-controlled basement was much brighter than the barn above, thanks to a dozen fluorescent fixtures suspended from the ceiling's twisted rafters. Two heavy-duty ventilation units attached to makeshift aluminum ductwork did their best to pump out the cellar's mildew, with only moderate success. The walls had been recently scrubbed and whitewashed, and the paint fumes helped mask the musty odor. A Mozart concerto from an unseen sound system provided lovely working music.

Martinelli didn't like what he saw. Wynett had transformed the cellar into an advanced molecular biology laboratory, complete with lab benches, test tubes, beakers and diagnostic equipment. The cellar's most interesting features were two stainless-steel fermentation units, which resembled old-fashioned diving bells enclosed in steel pedestals. A myriad of pipes protruded from each unit, and a lone porthole on each domed top provided the only glimpse of their interiors.

Martinelli was intimately familiar with these apparatuses. At Fort Detrick he had worked with similar units engineered to grow cultures for biochemical products used in pharmacies and hospitals. The microorganisms from these modified units, however, most likely were intended for warheads. The colonel hadn't counted on Wynett's ability to procure such sophisticated equipment, let alone two fermentation units. Wynett could work much faster than they had estimated.

At the far corner of the cellar, half hidden in an overstuffed chair before a computing workstation, sat Dr. Carl Wynett. Wynett's appearance surprised Martinelli. The old man looked more like Dr. Sterling than even Sterling. He looked tired and worn, the deep lines on his aged face evidence of an ambitious work schedule of a man pushed to the max. Wynett pulled himself from the stuffed chair and offered his hand to the colonel.

"Welcome to my little garden in the forest, Dr. Armstrong," Wynett said. "My employees call me the Businessman, a name I rather enjoy. You may call me Carl. I trust your trip here was not too uncomfortable?"

Martinelli accepted his host's firm grip. *Spending the last fourteen hours aboard two different helicopters, first rushing to Sao Paulo, then back again, isn't my idea of a comfortable weekend, pal.* "Not at all."

Wynett regarded Martinelli curiously. Perhaps he expected someone like Dr. da Silva, prematurely aged by alcohol and drugs. Instead, Martinelli obviously took his health seriously and looked more like forty than fifty. But his hands were not those of a scholar. They were athletic hands with strong, thick fingers and callused palms.

Tucco stood behind the colonel, watching him.

"Let us begin our business," Wynett said, waving Martinelli into the folding chair next to his. "It is critical that I get this laboratory operational this morning. Later we will have time to chat so I can learn everything about you. I trust you are familiar with the fermentation process?"

"Fermentation?" Martinelli feigned a surprised look. "Since when do you ferment cocaine?"

It was Wynett's turn to look surprised, though his expression was genuine. "You believe I asked you here to help me refine drugs?"

"I assumed—"

"Do not assume anything while in this laboratory," Wynett ordered curtly. "It could prove very costly to us both."

Martinelli nodded in apology, afraid he had overplayed his naiveté act. "Of course."

Wynett's deep facial lines softened. "Excuse my impatience this morning. I spent the night unpacking this laboratory. I have very little energy left. I am not a drug dealer, I assure you, Dr. Armstrong. You must first understand that I asked you here simply to consult with me. I forbid you to touch this equipment. Any adjustments will be my responsibility alone. If you believe a parameter should be changed, you will immediately inform me and, if I agree, I will adjust the process. Is that absolutely clear?"

Jesus. "Consult about what?"

"A culture medium. Its maintenance is tedious work. I cannot allow my fatigue to introduce errors. That is why I will pay you a large sum simply to be my watchdog."

"May I ask the nature of the microorganism?"

"A synthetic T_4 neurotoxin."

Martinelli let out a low whistle, a reaction Wynett did not seem to like.

"Is there a problem, Dr. Armstrong?"

The colonel offered Wynett his best embarrassed shrug, reminding himself about the first rule of cover stories: never make promises about yourself you can't keep. He intended to cover his ass. "I've never worked on a synthetic neurotoxin before. But, hell, I'm willing to learn."

"No one has worked with this organism before. That is why we must exercise extreme care. Because the organism's precise growth-factor requirements are unknown, I have chosen a complex synthetic medium. I am concerned that if the medium is too rich, the nutrients may become toxic. I would like your opinion on the construction of that medium."

"Of course."

Wynett punched several keys on the computer, and a table of numbers scrolled down the display. "I have analyzed the cells in the blood specimen and refactored the requirements based on the growth results I require. Study this list carefully. If I have overlooked anything, you will please bring it to my attention. My notes are in this journal. Please familiarize yourself with them."

Martinelli opened the notebook to a random section with the heading *Viral Pathology*.

He studied the screen ruefully.

Water	*1 liter*
Energy source:	
Glucose	*25 g*
Nitrogen source:	
NH4Cl	*3 g*
Minerals:	
KH_2PO_4	*600 g*
$FeSO_4 \bullet 7H2O$	*10 mg*

K2HPO$_4$	600 mg
MnSO, • 4H2O	20 mg
MgSO, • 7HHO	200 mg

Organic acid:

Sodium acetate	20 g

Amino acids:

DL-Alanine	200 mg
L-Lysine	250 mg
L-Arginine	242 mg
L-Methion	200 mg
L-Asparagin	400 mg
DL-Phenyl	100 mg
L-Proline	100 mg
L-Cysteine	50 mg
DL-Serine	50 mg
L-glutam. acid	300 mg
DL-Threonine	200 mg
Glycine	100 mg
DL-Tryptoph.	40 mg
L-Hist. • HCl	62 mg
L-Tyrosine	100 mg
DL-Isoleucine	250 mg
DL-Valine	250 mg
DL-Leucine	250 mg

Purines and pyrimidines:

Adn. sulf • H$_2$O	10 mg
Uracil	10 mg
Guan. • 2H$_2$0	10 mg
Xanth. • HCl	10 mg

Vitamins:

Thiamine • HC1	1 mg
Riboflavin	5 mg
Pyridoxine • HCl	1 mg

Nicotin. Acid	1 mg
Pyridoxamine	3 mg
p-Aminobenz	1 mg
Pyridoxal • HC1	3 mg
Biotin	1 mg
Cal. pantothenate	5 mg
Folic acid	1 mg

Jesus Christ, he's way ahead of me. "Interesting."

"Oxygen is crucial to the organism's growth. How do you suggest I accomplish that?" The old man was testing him, Martinelli knew.

"Continuously aerate the synthetic medium with pure oxygen. What about phosphate contamination?" It was the colonel's turn to test him.

"I am considering adding insoluble carbonates to the medium to prevent excessive changes in hydrogen ion concentration. The timing of that introduction may prove critical. We will need to work out a schedule."

Martinelli couldn't take his eyes from the screen. *Bastard isn't going to be tricked by me or anyone else.* "And temperature?"

"Incubation will be carried out at elevated temperatures for precise periods. The culture collection will be transferred at regular intervals to ten-liter tanks, where they will be frozen in a vacuum. I have written a script that will regulate the incubation temperatures. The tank transfer also will be automatic."

While Wynett talked, Martinelli realized he could not sabotage the incubation process. *He doesn't need anybody's help, and he knows it.* Wynett could readily produce large, potent batches of Saint Vitus. The colonel would need to work out a new plan to thwart the incubation. How? "Let me look this over and make some notes. Can we take this up in a couple of hours?"

Wynett looked exhausted. "Take the remainder of the morning and be accurate. Meanwhile I must lie down. After lunch, we will begin."

INCUBATION

Sinope
Friday, 1532 hours

Julie stepped to the hangar's glassless window. The others sat outside below the window, backs against the wall. She watched Williams show Jose the trapper how to hand-load ammunition, while the major cleaned his disassembled shotgun. She forced an expression that could pass for an amiable smile, but said nothing.

"So tell me why you want this crazy woman for a daughter-in-law?" Marshall asked the trapper.

The grizzled old man held out his hands palms-up. "She is *magnifico.*"

Marshall laughed at him. "What if she disappoints you and your son, Jose? What if she doesn't satisfy him? What if she can't cook?"

The old man shook his head fiercely. "She would not disappoint. She would give me many grandsons." The trapper's arms surrounded a large, imaginary family. "I can see that it is her nature to please a man."

Julie snorted.

"Well, I wouldn't know anything about that," Marshall said.

Williams laughed genially. "Joe, you sound like a man who hasn't been laid in months and knows he ain't gonna get any down here."

"This can't be happening!" Lieutenant Spangler shouted from inside the hangar. "This can't fucking be happening!"

Julie reeled away from the window with a start.

GORGON

Marshall bolted back inside the hangar. "What is it, Spangler?"

The lieutenant handed him the unscrambled telex. "It's from General Medlock, a priority-one message."

083100Z ******** JHW047
TOPSECRET ****** PRI-1
FROM: MEDLOCK-ZJHM0I—BAC
TO: ALPHA-ZJCM0I

RE. OP CONTAINMENT
SHORTWAVE TRANSMISSIONS ORIGINATING IN YOUR AREA HAVE BEEN DECODED * SOURCE GORGON * REPEAT * SOURCE GORGON * PROCEED WITH EXTREME CAUTION.

A CODE RED HAS BEEN ORDERED * ALERT COLONEL MARTINELLI TO TERMINATE ORGANISM IMMEDIATELY * REPEAT * TERMINATE ORGANISM IMMEDIATELY* WYNETT AND GORGON SECOND PRIORITY

NEXT COMMUNIQUE: 1600

END   MESSAGE
083214Z
BREAK

Julie noted anxious creases on Marshall's forehead as he read the communiqué, which triggered waves of dread in the pit of her stomach. "What's wrong? What does it say?"

"Gorgon's arrived early for his merchandise," Marshall said, passing the telex to his sergeant.

"What's this fucking shit?" Williams said, scanning the message.

"Gorgon's here," Spangler said. "Medlock suspects he may move now."

"That's his style," Marshall said. "He'll never follow anyone else's schedule. Doesn't say how many men he has with him, though."

Youngblood, alerted by the shouting, emerged from his work area on the opposite side of the hangar. The old trapper followed, stroking his long, white mustache.

Julie appealed to Lieutenant Spangler. "Get word to my father right now."

"Do as the lady says, DOS," Marshall ordered.

"Can't, major," the lieutenant said. "Wynett's jamming signal is ingeniously layered. Nothing has been getting in or out of that compound unless it's on his private satellite channel. I'm having a hell of a time trying to crack it."

"Then contact Stony's men in Sinope," Marshall said. "The next one in can brief the colonel."

Spangler's perspiring brow threatened to slide the wire-rimmed glasses off his nose. "Too late. The last of his team went in two hours ago. Wynett's hard up for men."

"That's fucking great," Marshall spat.

Julie grabbed Marshall's arm. "One of us must warn him ... go inside."

Marshall riveted a hard stare at Youngblood. "Can you drop me five miles from Wynett's compound without anyone knowing about it?"

The pilot shrugged. "Probably, but—"

"Jose," Marshall said to the trapper, "I'm enlisting you into Team Alpha. You're going to lead me through the jungle right up to Wynett's compound."

The old trapper drew himself up a full two inches taller than his normal five-foot frame and stood at attention. He shouldered his ancient shotgun. "I get you there."

"Lose that weapon first," Williams barked. "I'll issue you an Uzi."

Spangler wouldn't stop shaking his head. "Sir, the colonel's orders state that you're to guard this staging area. General Medlock's orders—"

"Screw Medlock's orders," Julie said. "There's not going to be an Alpha unit if we don't warn my father."

"Use your goddamn heads, people," Youngblood said. "Barging in there now will blow their cover and probably get a lot of people killed. Stony's men can take care of themselves. Stay put, major. This is an upscale party and you're not invited."

Marshall dismissed him with a curt wave. "I'm not waiting here until the fighting's over. Get your chopper ready. Or do I fly there myself?"

Stonecutters Garden
Friday, 1840 hours

"We got problems," Stony whispered, falling into stride beside Colonel Martinelli.

"Guns?" Martinelli asked, his eyes alert for other foot traffic.

"Yeah, guns."

"How many have you secured?"

Stony shifted the shovel to his left shoulder to conceal his face. "Only two of my men are part of Wynett's armed security force. The rest are picking goddamn sugarcane. Getting our hands on weapons isn't going to be easy."

"Do it," Martinelli snapped. "I don't care how, just do it. We're taking out Wynett tonight."

"What about Gorgon?"

"Fuck him. We're putting Wynett out of business."

Stony scowled. "That's not good enough."

"It has to be good enough," Martinelli said.

Stony stopped midstride. "Sweet momma ... it's the bug, isn't it?"

Martinelli nodded. "Wynett didn't take my bait. I couldn't convince him to change the culture medium. He's creating incredibly potent strains of the virus and securing them in tanks that are practically indestructible. And he's way ahead of schedule – only seven hours for each batch. The bug is amazingly prolific when it amplifies. He already has five tanks – he wants seven. Tomorrow I get paid and he ships me out."

"You're scaring the shit out of me, colonel. Slow him down."

Martinelli shook his head. "Can't do it. He won't let me near the equipment, and he's got his best men defending the lab. Even if I could smuggle a charge down there, an explosion would rupture the incubators and release the organism. We're taking him down tonight."

A husky female voice from the cobblestone path ahead said, "I'm looking for strong men with dry throats."

Wynett's housekeeper, Renee, an attractive middle-aged black woman educated in the States, stood watching them, her hands on her hips. Renee had done a splendid job turning Wynett's jungle retreat into a civilized country home. His better judgment notwithstanding, the colonel genuinely liked the woman for her amiable but firm manner.

"Well, are you men thirsty or not?" she repeated, her generous smile broadening.

"You're a godsend, Renee," Martinelli said, returning her cordial grin.

Renee gave Stony a handsome smile that suggested more than an offer for refreshments. If she thought it strange that these two were sharing company, she kept her suspicions to herself.

"Evening, ma'am." Stony rubbed the back of his scaly, fly-bitten neck. Martinelli could smell of manure venting off his filthy overalls.

"The boss man's in a very good mood tonight," she said. "He put a keg of beer on the patio for everyone to share. It's all the way from Germany. And I'll be putting salmon on the grill directly."

"Delightful, Renee," Martinelli said. "Tell the doctor I'll be there after I log the latest readings."

But Renee was looking at Stony. "How 'bout you, handsome?"

The special-op commander bowed politely. "Wouldn't miss it for anything."

Another charming smile. "Good. That's very good. I'll see you both on the patio."

Renee continued toward the house, and Martinelli resumed his walk toward the barn, wary of others on the cobblestone path ahead and behind them. His expression turned cold. "How do we protect them, Stony? I don't even know how many families are in this compound."

"Six families – about twenty-three men, women and children who aren't part of this. I'll be damned if Wynett isn't trying to make a go of this farm. He's playing fucking Lawrence of Arabia way out here where he thinks no one can touch him. He's only succeeded in building a prison for himself and his people trapped inside."

"What about that fence?"

"Twenty-five hundred volts from a propane-fired generator behind the barn. Wynett's banking on it to keep out trouble. He's putting all his defense eggs in one basket. If that fence is breached, he's shit out of luck."

"What else?"

"Our radios are useless thanks to Wynett's jamming station. It's one hell of a setup. He's a paranoid son of a bitch."

"So we're effectively out of touch with the others."

"Exactly."

"Bloody wonderful. Get your men near some guns, and fast. I don't care how you arrange it."

"What about you?"

"I've got my Beretta and two magazines. I'll take down Wynett and as many hired guns near that tank as I can."

When they reached the barn, Martinelli broke abruptly from Stony and proceeded to the back of the barn. He nodded brusquely at Buckshot, still guarding the cellar steps, the Kalashnikov slung over his shoulder. Martinelli descended the wooden steps into the laboratory.

Outside, Tucco emerged from the deep shadow of a spruce tree and stuck a fat cigar in his mouth. He lit it and savored the heavy smoke, pondering the tantalizing snippets of conversation he had just overheard. He exhaled the smoke, considering the odd camaraderie between a newly hired farmhand and Wynett's shady lab scientist.

La Strata Air Base Peru
Friday, 2000 hours

Air Force Captain Laszlo Valachi met the AC-130 troop chopper as it touched down on the Peruvian air base's helipad. Three men in British air force uniforms, toting hefty gear bags, climbed from the chopper's troop compartment and marched toward him. After a curt salute, the lead soldier said to Valachi, "I am Colonel Grainger. You are aware of my orders?"

The Peruvian captain nodded. This morning's Defense Council communiqué instructed him to give full support to three British *SAS* special forces officers en route from Afghanistan – a high-priority mission involving terrorists. The soldiers had made good time – they weren't expecting them until morning.

Colonel Granger presented the captain with a brown envelope. "This is your new directive. Your gunship and its pilot are now under my command."

Valachi frowned. "What is so important that I should give them to you?"

"I'm making a brief trip across the border. I intend to kill a terrorist who enjoys setting off explosives in London tube trains with children aboard."

DARKNESS

Stonecutters Garden
Friday, 2118 hours

A shadow emerged from the gloom of the jungle. A shade blacker than the enveloping darkness, the figure moved with stealth and purpose among the tall stalks of sugarcane. The figure stayed well away from the harvested field where a great bonfire blazed. A half dozen farm workers stood in a semicircle around the blaze, feeding its flames with armfuls of dried stalks.

Tarra didn't look at the fire, careful not to destroy her night vision. The flames briefly lit her feral features as she moved quickly through the tall rows of unharvested cane. She stopped beneath Wynett's electric fence, its powerful electromagnetic field rippling over her flesh like a swirl of gnats. Crouching, she opened the rucksack and removed its contents, arranging the items on the ground with meticulous precision. She anchored a spool of uninsulated twelve-gauge Beldon wire to the ground and hooked its free end to a steel arrow seated in a large cocked crossbow almost too heavy for her slender frame. She raised the formidable weapon against her shoulder, angled it and pulled the trigger. With a muffled snap, the steel projectile shot high into the night, propelled by gas from a CO_2 canister. Countless meters of wire hissed rapidly through the spool. One second ... two ... three ... four ... The arrow landed tip-first inside the compound with a solid thump, plunging deeply into the sod. Its long wire tail dropped onto the electrified coils of barbed wire atop the fence.

Crack!

The compound's lights sputtered out, plunging Wynett's Amazon estate into darkness.

The sudden loss of power to the barn prompted startled outbursts from the roustabouts working inside. Most of the men bolted outside. Buckshot, however, didn't abandon his post by the cellar's entrance. The special-op commando flung his Kalashnikov off his shoulder and pointed its muzzle at the barn's huge door, the only way in and out. The open cellar door at his feet provided modest illumination from the lab's emergency lights. No one would get near the fermentation tanks on his watch.

Only one other worker remained inside the barn with Buckshot – a wiry old stable hand with a fistful of horseshoes. Unfazed by the darkness, the old man set down his tools, lit a lantern and hung it high on a stall beam. Buckshot gave him a quick nod of thanks.

The barn door creaked open. Buckshot raised his weapon at another roustabout leading a horse inside. He saw the old stable hand move in his peripheral. He whirled toward him. The old man held a Browning automatic, a suppresser fastened to its barrel. A 9mm slug caught Buckshot hard in the chest just under his rib cage and toppled him against the barn wall.

Tucco was the first to arrive at the smoking generators, two hefty diesel-powered machines enclosed in a huge steel cage. The air was heavy with the smell of burned wire but, luckily, there was no fire. The compound's only illumination came from Wynett's manor. Lit up in grand style, the house was unaffected by the blackout, thanks to the house's dedicated generator.

A group of men, some carrying flashlights, others guns, gathered around the generator cage. Even the armed men looked spooked. Tucco scoffed at their petty fears of the dark. He needed muscle and support, not a legion of children.

"Darkness comes and everyone believes we have ghosts," he murmured. *"Idiots."*

Tucco unlocked the generator cage and found his way to the breaker panel by the uneven beam of his flashlight. He located the main breaker, grabbed the handle and pushed it back into place. Another loud snap with a frightening flurry of sparks. He frowned. A second try failed as well. The circuit wouldn't close. He would need to find the source of the electrical short and correct it before he could restore power to the compound. The trouble most likely originated with the fence, he reasoned – the damned, power-hungry fence.

Tucco spat orders to his men, directing them to search for the source of the shorted circuit. The workers, cowed by the darkness, set off in pairs, the beams of their flashlights constantly moving.

Tucco moved to the entrance of the generator cage, cursing the blackened compound. His eyes scanned the vague movements around the compound's perimeter. A deep chill swept through him. He dropped his cigar and withdrew his huge revolver. Ghosts? *Damn.* The darkness was getting even to him.

A metal projectile sliced through the center of his chest and protruded from his back. The impact slammed him back against the bank of circuit breakers. Tucco legs moved in a macabre dance of death as 2,500 volts surged through his body.

Stony's eyes fixed on the darkened estate. The only light came from Wynett's house, a bright castle against the black jungle. He glanced across the field at what remained of the bonfire and saw the flickering silhouettes of workers lying lifeless around it. Even the mule lay on its side. His steel-set eyes scanned the fields. The stalks were alive with moving shapes, animated shadows moving stealthily through rows of sugarcane. *Gorgon's troops had arrived.*

Stony dropped to the ground and rolled next to a stack of cut sugarcane. He ripped off his red T-shirt and appraised the ghostlike figures stalking toward him.

He glanced at the front gate. Closed. Without power, he knew it couldn't be opened. He would have to cut his way into the compound. He thought about the families trapped within. Steady – *think!* Rigid military training forced him to remain absolutely still. To reveal himself now would be tantamount to a death sentence.

Sweet Jesus, I love you dearly, but I'd sell my soul to the devil for a rifle.

Two black boys crouching over a jar of fireflies spotted the figures racing across the lawn. To their little eyes, the shadow people were playing a game of hiding. The boys climbed onto the porch of Wynett's manor and sat down on the top step to watch.

"Mamma," one of the boys called into the house in American English. "They're playing in our yard."

Renee, a towel in her hand, stepped onto the porch and followed the boys' gazes across the lawn. "Who's playing, Myron?"

Her smile vanished. Wynett's housekeeper had forgotten how black the jungle could become. What happened?

As her eyes adjusted to the dimness she saw them, though not clearly – figures moving around the perimeter of the estate, taking up offensive positions. Something was terribly wrong. These were not Wynett's people. They were masters of stealth. She knew they must be responsible for the darkness that had overtaken the plantation. Dread ripped at Renee's heart. *Dear God, don't let them hurt my boys!*

"Git home, both of you," she hissed. "It's past bedtime. Go on. Git home. *Git!*"

The boys' playful grins vanished.

"*I said git home!*" Renee screamed.

The boys ran from the porch, crying and racing toward their little cottage.

"Do you intend to spend the rest of the evening deliberating your next move?" Wynett snapped, his tone irritated.

Colonel Martinelli ignored the old man's prodding and remained statue-like, staring at the ornately carved chess pieces.

Wynett groaned inwardly only half interested in the intellectual contest he knew he'd already won. *Another marathon match.* Dr. da Silva had lied to him. Henry Armstrong was no player.

Wynett stood up from the table, stretched, and stepped to the window of his elegantly appointed second-story sitting room. He relished the respite from the clammy South American heat. God, how he loved nights in the jungle.

He drew back the curtains and peered across the darkened compound from his second-floor window.

Bloody hell – another problem with the generator. He waited for the backup generator to take over. It didn't. He heard his men shouting at each other in the darkness, running to investigate.

He stiffened. Under the moonlight, he saw intruders emerging from the jungle, breaching the fence, stalking toward his house from different directions in several slack skirmish lines.

Wynett stood rooted by the sill and watched. His eyes grew cold and dark as he considered the ramifications. *The bastard intends to rob me.*

Wynett watched a roustabout lead his magnificent quarter horse across the barn's threshold, their silhouettes framed by a single lantern within. A shadow appeared from nowhere and brushed silently behind the worker. The horse bolted. The roustabout slumped to the ground. Five more figures filed quickly inside the barn.

The tanks. They had come to take Saint Vitus from him.

Below, his housekeeper stood on the veranda, watching the shadows move across the lawn. Wynett almost shouted down a warning to her, but thought better of it. He withdrew from the lighted window and backed into the safety of the room's corner.

"Stony?" Renee called from the porch.

Silence.

The figures broke into a run toward the house. *Jesus, save me!* Before she could move, a Teflon-tipped arrow pierced her larynx, slamming her into the screen door, ripping it from its hinges. Renee fell heavily onto the floor of the foyer, groping at the impossible flow of blood pumping from her throat. She tried to speak, cry out, but her vocal cords were shattered.

Choking, her back arched in agony, Renee stared helplessly as a man in black fatigues appeared in the doorway and entered Wynett's manor.

Stony sprinted across the lawn toward Wynett's manor twenty yards away. He moved carefully through a tight grove of birch trees, knowing that his life depended on his ability to remain unseen. A single thought consumed his senses: warn Colonel Martinelli and the others.

Do it now or die.

Stony sprinted toward the house, expecting a bullet in his back. None came. He flattened against the side of the manor, his eyes searching for the intruders. He saw no one. Exposed by the house's light, he crabbed along the wall and peered into Wynett's first-floor study. The room stood dark and empty.

Stony hauled his solid frame deftly through the open window and set down noiselessly inside the study. He moved swiftly to Wynett's desk and sat in front of the shortwave transceiver. He ignored the sweat pouring down his face as he put on the headphones. He heard it immediately, the high-pitched squeal of the jamming signal. *Damn Wynett and his paranoia!*

He slid the frequency dial first right then left. The squeal remained unchanged, evidence that its power for the signal came from the same isolated generator that supplied the house. He flung off the headset.

Two strides took him to Wynett's gun rack, a splendid oak cabinet that housed a classic collection of hunting shotguns and rifles. He pulled on the cabinet door and found the case locked, its beveled glass reinforced with steel rods. *Fuck me!*

Stony swept around, his eyes scanning the room for an improvised weapon. A table lamp ... a bronze paperweight ... a half-filled bottle of Scotch ... a mantel clock ... Then he saw it. Wynett's big-game Browning rifle hung trophy like over the mantel. He lifted the intimidating weapon from its mount. Cartridges? He returned to Wynett's utility cabinet and opened each drawer with a creak that to him sounded like a muffled scream. He paused, listening. Nothing. He rummaged through several boxes of shells until he found what he needed and scooped up a handful of huge cartridges.

The study's door groaned open. Stony's head jerked up. The intruder entered the study with practiced restraint. Stony slid a single cartridge into the gun's chamber and pulled back the hammer with an audible click. He lifted the huge weapon.

The door moved again, this time with bold force behind it. Stony caught the barest glimpse of a figure dressed in black fatigues, carrying an automatic rifle. Stony jerked the trigger of his Browning. The blast transformed the door into a blizzard of splinters. A blood-spattered wall beside the doorway was the only remaining evidence of the intruder.

The gunshot startled Martinelli from his chair, the Beretta appearing in his hand.

"Your weapon, sir, is useless," Wynett observed coolly from his secure spot in the corner. "Sit down and move your queen out of danger."

Martinelli flattened against the wall next to the window, his Beretta pointed down in a two-handed grip. He could see nothing outside. What had happened to the lights? Who had fired a rifle inside the house?

"Dr. Armstrong, you are about to meet a client of mine," Wynett said, his voice civilly calm. "I advise you to move away from the window and do not resist. I am telling you this so that you may possibly live."

"What weapons do you have up here?"

"Sit down," Wynett ordered, his voice curt. "Or they will cut you apart like a holiday pig."

Stony stared at Renee's corpse, her wide, glassy eyes gazing helplessly up at him, warning him. Years of training, the resources of an elite army – all of it failed to protect her. He turned away from her, feeling suddenly cold despite the heat, dull and empty in his head, tired, old, too old.

He swore bitterly and bounded up the steps two at a time to the house's second level.

Martinelli pointed his Beretta at Wynett. "Don't you fucking move."

"Intruders are in my laboratory," Wynett said. "They are taking what we have worked to produce. And neither you nor I can stop them."

"Gorgon," Martinelli spat.

Wynett's expression darkened. "How do you know that name—"

The bedroom door opened with a crash. Martinelli whipped around, his Beretta ready. Stony stood on the threshold, his muscles glistening like oiled ebony, his eyes ferreting the interior of the bedroom. He pointed the Browning at Wynett.

The colonel lowered his handgun. "What's happening? Where are the others?"

Stony stepped into the room, keeping the huge gun pointed at Wynett. "Dead. Ambushed."

The colonel sighed heavily. "Jesus Christ, he can't get the organism. *We have to do something!*"

"We can't get word out," Stony spat. "This fuck's got every channel jammed."

Wynett looked accusingly at Martinelli. "Who are you? CIA?"

136

They all heard it, a creak of the hallway floorboards. Martinelli signaled Stony with a nod. The commando captain needed no orders. Stony roared into the hallway, the gun braced on his hip. There were two of them dressed in black fatigues, messengers of death creeping down the corridor.

"It's suppertime," he hummed.

The first raider jerked his weapon. Stony squeezed the trigger and the Browning exploded. The blast from the huge gun at close quarters tore the first intruder in two. His upper torso disintegrated in a brisk shower of bone and red pulp, while his disembodied legs kicked briefly about the hallway.

A shot from the colonel's Beretta over Stony's shoulder put a bullet in the center of the second intruder's forehead. The raider jerked backward and spilled headlong down the hallway. Martinelli spun and pointed his Beretta down the opposite end of the hallway. Clear.

Stony raced down the corridor, discharging the spent cartridge as he ran and inserting another. There were two more men on the steps. His Browning blasted the first intruder in the chest, hurling him back against his comrade. Stony reloaded. Before the second man could rise, Stony's next cartridge tore his head clear off.

Wynett slammed the door of the sitting room, barricading himself inside. Martinelli whirled and pumped four rounds into the door. "You son of a bitch."

The colonel saw movement from the opposite end of the hallway an instant before a metal arrow hurtled toward his head. He sprang backward. The projectile whisked by his face and plunged into the bedroom's oak door with a solid thud. The colonel dropped and rolled into a darkened bedroom across the hallway, discharging two quick rounds as he moved.

From atop the staircase, Stony heard other men entering the living room below. Reloading, he saw the shadow of another intruder approach the bottom of the steps. Stony raised his rifle.

He never fired. With startling swiftness, a machete sliced neatly through Stony's right arm above the elbow. He spilled forward with a bloodcurdling howl, more from surprise than pain. The Browning clattered loudly down the steps. The shock of spontaneous amputation came an instant later.

In the hallway above, Colonel Martinelli flattened against the bedroom wall and moved toward the door, snapping the second magazine into his Beretta. Something cold and sharp pricked the back of his neck. He froze and screwed his eyes to the side. A feral-like woman dressed in black held a sighted crossbow cocked and ready to put an arrow through his throat. The crossbow was merely for stealth. For serious firepower, a Russian-made AK-47 automatic assault rifle hung from her shoulder.

"He will not let me kill you yet," Tarra said. "He wants to interrogate the military commander who set this trap for him."

At the base of the staircase, Stony stared at the giant looming above him. What he saw made him forget the arm wound draining away his life with each heartbeat. Gorgon stared down at him with cold, reptilian eyes, a machete in his right hand, a crossbow made of steel in his left.

Stony tried to lift his head but found it unbearably weighty. "Just like a dog to hit a man from behind."

Gorgon's features did not betray the slightest emotion. He lowered his crossbow until the Teflon-tipped arrowhead hovered a breath above Stony's left eye.

Stony didn't blink. "Like I said ... just like a dog—"

A loud snap ... the arrow pinned Stony's head to the hallway floorboards.

MADNESS

Sinope
Friday, 2130 hours

Jose the trapper rubbed the stubby barrel of his new Israeli Uzi and gave Williams a cheery wink of gratitude. Youngblood increased the chopper's throttle for takeoff. But the aircraft didn't move. Youngblood sat rigid, listening to his headset, then cut the engines to idle.

"Get this thing in the air," Marshall shouted over the engine's roar.

Youngblood screwed his head around and yelled something about another passenger. Marshall craned his neck and glimpsed a figure dressed in camouflage fatigues carrying a gear bag around the opposite side of the aircraft. He groaned. Two thuds on the compartment door. Williams slid it open, and Julie tossed her gear bag up to him.

"Out of the question," Marshall hollered.

She climbed aboard. Julie wasn't in the mood to argue with anyone, least of all with the major. Traveling with him at night through the Brazilian jungle wasn't her idea of a fun-filled evening in the tropics. She was about to step onto her first battlefield with the real enemy.

She took the seat beside Jose and strapped herself in. "I go where the virus goes."

The whine of the Black Hawk's engines drowned out Marshall's curses of protest. The helicopter lifted into the night sky, leaned windward and proceeded due west at treetop level.

Stonecutters Garden

Colonel Martinelli looked into Tarra's green eyes, trying to read his foe, trying to understand this strange woman who was a finger-jerk away from putting an arrow through his throat. He could see nothing in her eyes, not the smallest hint of emotion behind her steely features. Any resistance, he realized, would be suicidal. He let the Beretta slip from his hands. "Can I at least know your name?"

"I will ask the questions," said a man in the doorway.

Tarra's features softened – and became almost attractive – at the sight of an intimidating man dressed in black fatigues and armor padding. Martinelli's heart pounded savagely in the presence of pure evil. Gorgon, a crossbow at his side, scrutinized the colonel with eyes that looked like two dark holes, absorbing every detail, evaluating every conceivable threat.

"I am the man you so desperately wanted to meet, captain," Gorgon said. "Or is it colonel?"

Wynett removed a bulky pack from the closet's top shelf, opened it and unfolded a full-body environment suit, complete with air tanks and hood. An innocuous thermal container sat on the room's mahogany table. With his eyes fixed on the container, he began dressing.

Martinelli's furtive eyes swept around the bedroom, searching for any option that might keep him alive. *I am a dead man.* He had often imagined dying in battle a brave, willful soldier. He didn't feel courageous right now. Certainly not brave enough to die.

Gorgon signaled Tarra with a jerk of his head. She grabbed the colonel's arm and flung him cruelly back against the wall. He resisted, and she clubbed him on the side of his head with a heavy chain and cuffs, rendering him senseless. She had little difficulty shackling him to the room's water pipe.

Gorgon picked up Martinelli's Beretta with a look of admiration. "You are a fool to plot an ambush for me."

The colonel strained impotently against the chain. "Go to hell."

Gorgon pointed the Beretta at Martinelli. The colonel screwed his eyes shut, anticipating the inevitable end. The gun discharged with a sharp crack, followed by Martinelli's shriek of anguish. The slug shattered his right kneecap, almost amputating his leg at the knee.

Tarra grabbed Martinelli by the shirt and pulled him roughly upright. "We know about your base on that miserable airstrip in Sinope. We watched you and your men infiltrate this encampment. Now we will take your creation while you and your men die in this rotting jungle."

Martinelli wasn't looking at her. His gaze was riveted on Gorgon. His mind reeled with thoughts of Julie. All he could think about was his daughter trapped in the hangar, a sitting duck for this bastard.

"I wish to know everything about your paramilitary group and how you came to know my business," Gorgon said.

Martinelli said nothing. *Don't pass out.* Gorgon discharged a second round into the colonel's left knee, prompting another shriek from his prey. The giant laughed, a menacing rumble from deep within his chest. "I will put the next bullet into your groin."

Gasping, fighting the onset of shock, Martinelli pulled futilely on his wrist shackles and forced his mind to focus on Julie. *Don't black out now ... not now ....*

Gorgon said to Tarra, "Bring Wynett in here. We have business to finish."

She swung the Kalashnikov off her shoulder, charged into the hallway and crouched in a firing position in front of Wynett's door. Two short blasts from her assault rifle tore the oak planks from their hinges. She caught only a fleeting glimpse of Wynett, clad in a full-body environment suit, disappearing behind the door to the bathroom. Tarra assailed the opposite wall with a second, longer, burst.

JOSEPH MASSUCCI

"He is wearing an environment suit," she shouted over her shoulder.

Gorgon threw the Beretta against the wall with enough force to shatter plaster. "He intends to kill us with his creation."

Tarra emptied the Kalashnikov's thirty-round clip into the bedroom wall, producing a blizzard of plaster, wood splinters and shards of aluminum ductwork.

Wynett huddled inside the porcelain bathtub while the rounds tore apart the room around him. He fastened his environmental hood securely in place, inflated the suit, and then cradled the thermos canister in his arms.

"Gorgon," Wynett shouted, "I very much want you to meet a friend of mine."

Tarra replaced the clip of her assault rifle. "I need a grenade."

"Not safe – you will release the agent. We must leave here." Gorgon swung his crossbow around and discharged a steel arrow into Martinelli's chest. The arrow pierced his right lung, missing his heart by two inches. Gorgon hurried from the room and hastened down the hallway with Tarra at his heels, his spiked boots echoing on the hardwood floorboards.

They charged out onto the veranda, where two of his soldiers snapped sharply to attention. "Burn this house and everyone in it," Gorgon ordered, before sweeping off the porch toward the jungle.

Upstairs, Wynett waited a prudent thirty seconds before crawling from his bathroom sanctuary and walking stiffly into the spare bedroom where Martinelli lay dying. He ignored the colonel and watched through the window as Gorgon's soldiers fled through his fields of sugarcane, vanishing into the jungle.

He opened his revered canister and carefully withdrew a glass vial.

Martinelli raised his swooning head. "Don't do it," he said, his voice strained, his breath short. "Christ, you don't know what you stole...."

Wynett disregarded him. He shook the vial furiously, breaking up the frozen ball within, before opening it. Martinelli wheezed and sank back in despair into a pool of his blood. "It's too late ... you bloody fool, it's too late...."

Wynett hurled the vial through the open second-story window and watched it shatter onto the veranda at the feet of the two mercenaries. He smiled knowingly when one of the soldiers crushed the innocuous-looking shards of glass with his boot. The hot, humid ambient night air already melted the ice crystals. Wynett knew neither soldier would feel anything unusual at first, despite having ingested the most powerful neurotoxin in existence.

Colonel Martinelli experienced a short-lived euphoria that rapidly mounted to a feeling of dread. His mind grew numb, his senses dulled. A cacophony of strange noises assaulted his ears. Still stranger phantasms obscured his vision. His brain screamed. The sensations had nothing to do with his wounds. This was different. He felt as though an army of ants were swarming through secret tunnels beneath his skin. He drew in a deep breath and expelled a cry from the worst chest pain he had ever experienced. He tried to speak, but instead of words he expelled flecks of blood. His limbs began undulating, dancelike.

Wynett, rooted to the window, watched Gorgon's mercenaries struggling on their knees in deep agony. He found the sight thoroughly amusing, his throaty laughter fogging his face shield. "You will not cheat me, Mr. Gorgon. You cannot see my army, but they will find you. Wherever you hide in this jungle, my army will find you and kill you."

A shriek, long and terrifying, drowned out Wynett's glee. The Businessman drew back from the window and stared in mute surprise at Martinelli. The colonel's throat had swelled to six times its normal size.

Gorgon and Tarra whirled at the inhuman shrieks of agony coming from Wynett's manor. Gorgon saw no sign of the flames that should have consumed the house.

Tarra slid the Kalashnikov off her shoulder. "I will go back and finish him."

Gorgon grabbed her roughly by the arm. "No. You will die. I have what I came for."

Wynett watched his lab assistant mutate into an abomination. As the virus devoured its victim's nervous system, rapidly reproducing itself, Col. Anthony Martinelli lashed out at Wynett with a roar, trying to rip his arms from their sockets in a mad effort to tear the shackles and pipes from the wall. Wynett recoiled, awed by the beast before him. He hadn't considered this, hadn't considered this at all. The colonel's bucking became so severe that Wynett feared he would break the shackles and come tearing after him in a foaming rage. Homicidal aggression as a result of brain-cell destruction, he reasoned.

Wynett was so enamored with the macabre sight that he failed to notice the stuffy air inside his suit. At first he attributed it to his exhilaration. As the air became increasingly foul, he rechecked his tank, designed to deliver two hours of air with normal exertion. The gauge read slightly less than full, yet he could barely breathe.

He fumbled with the valve, felt something odd and strained around to look at it. A bullet had taken a hefty bite out of the valve, rendering the air tank inoperable. In a rush of panic, he realized he was suffocating inside a polyethylene coffin.

The bastard will not win this....

Wynett bolted from the bedroom, consumed with the singular if illogical thought of escaping the farm before exhausting the precious pocket of air inside his suit. The virus had a short life span, a matter of minutes, after which succeeding generations mutated into increasingly less volatile strains. Could the air outside his suit already be safe? He was loath to find out.

Without warning, his legs swept from under him. He spilled headlong down the second-floor hallway. He twisted around to see what had tripped him and cried out in revulsion. It was Stony, his good arm flailing in a spastic arc. The man was quite dead – the arrow through his head had seen to that – yet his corpse moved as if eager to avenge its master's death. Wynett didn't doubt that the thing would have pounced on him if the arrow had not effectively pinned its head to the floorboards.

Wynett clawed on hands and knees down the staircase to the living room where another monstrous nightmare awaited. There, in the center of the room, thrashing as though to rise, was his housekeeper, Renee, an arrow splitting her throat. Instead of her winning smile, she showed him a hideous rictus of death, her lips struggling to form her last words.

He looked away in revulsion.

Wynett stumbled blindly out of the house to flee this nightmare. Gone were Gorgon's stricken soldiers who collapsed just moments ago on the veranda. He looked for them, fearful they would come charging out of the night and drag him to hell with them. His vision blurred, his oxygen-starved mind evaporating. He shook his head to keep from fainting.

And then he saw it. A light. The lantern-lit barn. His destination, his salvation. He staggered toward it, arms outstretched, groping for the door. The sculpted shrubbery appeared to sway in a non-existent breeze, its branches straining to stop him. Wynett shrank past them, horrified.

He stumbled through the barn's doorway and fell heavily onto the straw-covered floor. He lifted his head. The view of the barn's floor was more shockingly gruesome than he could have imagined. Gorgon's soldiers used the barn as a morgue for the slain farmhands. Their carcasses refused to lie still. The victims of this massacre lay twisting and arching, straining as though to rise and launch a collective retaliation.

Wynett pulled himself into a sitting position with his back against the stone wall. He could go no farther. His hollow eyes stared vacantly at the corpses, watching their grotesque movements, trying to see through this trick of his oxygen-starved mind. Why would they not lie still?

The corpse of a young black man at his feet turned its barely attached head to look at him. Instead of the glassy stare of a dead man, he thought he saw real anger in those sallow eyes. The corpse's mouth split into an appalling sneer, revealing teeth that gnashed and snapped at him. Wynett screwed his eyes shut, blocking the terrible image from his mind.

Lie still!

The air inside his suit was gone. Blackness descended. *Either take your chances with the virus-contaminated air or suffocate.* He contemplated doing nothing, thus putting an end to this horror. But his survival instinct would not allow it. His gloved hands fumbled to release the seal, and he swung the hood off his head. He lay back, exhausted. Sweet air refreshed his lungs, lifting the mist from his oxygen-starved mind.

The illness came quickly. It started as a bitter taste in his mouth, and then his head began to ache, as though a dull metal drill were boring into his brain. Strange phantasms paraded before him. He sensed the organism at work inside his brain, devouring his mind, hollowing out his skull.

But he did not die.

The virus had indeed mutated. Instead of death, it carried the seeds of insanity.

Wynett's eyes, sunken and hollow, darted from one corpse to the next. He never believed in the soul. Yet as he watched the bodies' unnatural movements, he saw mere shells, soulless, driven by a powerful new life force. Saint Vitus. The organism could move what death had stilled.

A grin stretched his lips. The organism was worth considerably more than he dared dream. A hiss erupted from his throat and rose in pitch, finally turning to laughter born of madness.

Oh yes, Mr. Gorgon, you will pay the price.

THE BARN

Stonecutters Garden
Saturday, 0520 hours

The MiL-24 Hind assault gunship descended from a purple-rimmed sky like a huge reptilian bird, its belly-mounted spotlight probing the strange fog below. The Peruvian pilot, a seasoned captain named Juan Batavia, saw no activity on the barren plantation. What the hell happened down there? It would be daylight in 10 minutes, and his orders were to have the aircraft down and the troops deployed before dawn.

He didn't like this mission. He didn't like the way it had been hastily organized and executed. He hadn't been properly briefed, nor was there any explanation behind the order to fly without a forward weapons officer. The chopper had no authority to enter Brazilian airspace. He knew little about the three British commandos in the gunship's troop compartment or what they hoped to find on this bizarre compound in the middle of the Brazilian jungle. Colonel Grainger had given him only an altitude and a compass bearing. Nothing else. Captain Batavia wanted to finish this mission and return to Peru, fast.

The pilot set down the gunship between the house and the barn, its blades churning up a strange carpet of snow-like ash that covered the once-green lawn. He cut back the jet engines to ground-idle and disengaged the rotor. Visibility was zero. What if the ash affected the engines? The thought of spending even a single day in this jungle prison made him shudder.

Batavia powered off the troop compartment's red lights, an aid to night vision, and turned on the exterior spots. The main cabin door slid open and out jumped the three British special forces soldiers, each carrying an M16 automatic assault rifle. The powerful halogen lamps turned the fog into a white nether world. The pilot watched them vanish like wispy apparitions into the strange mist.

"Sweet Mary, mother of God, stay with me," he muttered.

Batavia opened the scrambled TAC channel to his Peruvian air base 400 miles northwest of the plantation. He spoke in Spanish into his helmet's mouthpiece: "Specter One to Father. They are down."

The sharp *whip-whip-whip* of a descending military helicopter roused Wynett from a sound slumber. He sat up slowly, unsure of his surroundings and with no memory of how he got there. His head felt like mud and his ears buzzed. He wasn't even sure who he was, nor did he especially care. His dark, scarlet eyes scanned the barn's body-strewn floor, his mind yielding only the tiniest bits of the previous evening. He stared into the corpses' bloated and twisted faces, visages seemingly carved from wood. Who were these people?

Then he remembered Henry Armstrong – no, he had another name, didn't he? A general or some other military title? It didn't matter. The image of his helpless lab assistant chained to a bedroom wall struck him as terribly amusing.

He laughed, and in a loud voice full of spirit, he began singing, "Somebody calls you, you answer quite slowly, the girl with kaleidoscope eyes...."

The three British commandos approached the barn, vigilant for any signs of life. They weren't interested in the house. A hyperspectral imaging scan of the plantation from a reconnaissance satellite detected a single entity inside the barn that radiated enough body heat to be classified as a living human being. There were no such heat signatures inside the house. Were they too late to take down Gorgon?

Special Forces Colonel Grainger almost missed the corpse stretched in front of the barn door, at first mistaking it for a thick, twisted tree trunk. The remains – shriveled, leathery, unrecognizable – sent a shivery rush of adrenaline through him. He had seen corpses before, many in deplorable conditions, but never one as unsettling as this. *What happened here?* The SAS commander decided to forgo a probe for the cause of death, which he knew would be futile.

Then he heard a deep baritone voice inside the barn – singing.

Grainger's first lieutenant came back from the barn door and reported, "It's bolted from the inside."

Grainger spotted an open window along the side of the barn. His assault rifle ready, he motioned the others to follow.

The singing stopped.

The barn's interior was dark, too dark to make out specifics. Grainger saw vague shapes spread over the floor, possibly men, but he couldn't be sure without more light and a closer inspection. He grabbed the window frame with his free hand and lifted a leg inside. The barn reeked of death. The smell of manure laced with decay caused his stomach to roll. He paused, straddling the windowsill, listening, straining to make sense of this gruesome warehouse of shapes and shadows.

Grainger heard movement, a shuffling among the straw. *Rats?* With stunning swiftness, a man dressed in a strange white suit rushed toward him, pointing something at him. The light was practically nil. Several moments of stunned silence passed before the British commando realized he was staring down the barrel of an AK-47 assault rifle.

The point-blank burst into the soldier's chest hurled him backward out the window, giving Wynett a clear shot at his two comrades squatting in the fog outside. Two more bursts from Wynett's weapon produced a line of plum-shaped holes across each soldier's chest. The commandos spilled backward, their rifles spraying indiscriminate rounds into the side of the barn.

Wynett discarded his empty rifle and retrieved Grainger's M16. He checked the clip, pulled back the bolt with a precision click and braced the stock solidly against his shoulder. God – how he loved the feel of an M16.

Captain Batavia heard muffled shots above his idling engines. The pilot strained to see what had become of the British colonel and his SAS soldiers, but he saw nothing beyond the swirling dust cloud created by the rotor's downdraft.

A shadow of a man appeared through the lamplit fog just beyond the cockpit door. *Thank God they're finished—*

But this wasn't Colonel Grainger. Nor was it one of the colonel's men. A bearded man wearing the remains of a peculiar white oversuit walked up to the gunship's cockpit door. The pilot felt an odd rush of emotions as he stared into the business end of a military assault rifle.

The bearded man roared at him, "You are not welcome in my home!"

Captain Batavia reached for the TAC controls. A burst of rounds from the rifle shattered the Plexiglas door and raked across the cockpit, tearing the pilot through his shoulder harness.

PLAGUE

The Jungle
Saturday, 0515 hours

Gloom.

An endless forest of dense, dark foliage grabbed and scratched at Marshall's group. Youngblood had inserted them into the jungle seven hours ago. They had hiked five miles since then, excellent time, considering the thick terrain. The air felt damp and rotten, the heat steamy even before sunup, the ground an unbroken carpet of dense, clinging, wicked-smelling humus. Marshall acknowledged an overpowering claustrophobia as they hacked their way beneath the dark, cathedral-like canopy of branches that blocked out every trace of moonlight. The sun was rising, but it would take hours before they noticed its light. Even at noon, only a dim half-light ever touched the jungle floor.

Jose ceased chopping the undergrowth with his machete and called back to Marshall, "Animals and birds gone. Insects too. We are alone."

Marshall brought the others to a halt with a raised hand. "Far enough."

Williams swung the Galil rifle off his shoulder and unfolded its metal stock. "It's too quiet around here, Joe."

"Tell me about it." Marshall marched past Jose and directed his high-powered lamp along the wall of overgrown vegetation. Instead of pervasive green, a vulgar tropical blight had destroyed the foliage ahead, leaving withered and white husks. He wiped away the perspiration rolling down his temples. He didn't need a botanist's degree or Julie Martinelli to point out the obvious – this damage was no natural infestation.

Marshall waved the sergeant forward and swept his light along the ruined foliage. "Ever see anything like this? Christ, all that's left is the shell of the plant." He directed the light at his map. "We're less than an eighth of a mile from Wynett's plantation."

Williams let out a grunt. "I think we just found our goddamned bug."

Marshall called back to Julie. "I need you up here *now*."

Julie stumbled to catch up with Marshall. She set down a briefcase-size package at her feet with a groan, relieving herself of the eighteen-pound box none of the men had offered to carry. Her legs had turned to rubber and her sweat-soaked clothes made her feel as though she had just been dragged from a river.

Marshall directed his lamp at the foliage. "What do you make of this?"

Julie approached what had once been a low-growing plant. Crouching, she touched the damaged flora and rubbed it into a fine white ash in her hand. "What the—" She opened her instrument package and quickly brought the unit to life. Its gridded amber screen displayed a waveform pattern spiked with jagged peaks, identifying the presence of airborne organisms. A sample of air, automatically fed into the unit's processor, classified each organism, its strength and the approximate area contaminated.

"A class T_4 pathogen – artificially engineered," she said, her drawn face bathed with the display's queer light. "One part per one hundred thousand cubic meters of air."

Marshall watched her, a finger on his lips. "Is it yours?"

"Yes."

"We have to be certain."

Julie's eyes refocused on the major. "This system gathers metabolic fingerprints with a microplate of ninety-six miniature wells, each filled with dye, nutrients and a different chemical. When exposed to a microbe, the wells turn various shades of violet. The computer identifies the microbe based on the color pattern."

"In English, please."

"This system is very accurate," she said. "I programmed it to look for Saint Vitus. And I just found it. The virus is alive and well and living in this South American rain forest."

"Son of a bitch," Williams spat. "And we walked right fucking into it."

"We're on the fringe of the infestation," Julie said, reading new information from the screen. "The organism's genetic fingerprint has changed. Saint Vitus has mutated."

"Mutated into what?" Marshall asked.

"Into something harmless, or at least let's pray that it has. The organism is genetically programmed to lose its toxicity after several generations of mutation. Otherwise we would have been dead about twenty yards back."

Marshall knelt beside Julie. "I need to know if we have a lethal environment here or not."

Julie fidgeted under pressure to interpret the data, her shirt clinging to her back like a filthy wet dishrag. "Statistically, there's a high probability we're safe. I just don't know enough about the organism. Major, I'll need a radio linkup with Detrick to interpret this data."

"Relay everything you get to Lieutenant Spangler as a Code Red. Williams, have you raised the hangar yet?"

The sergeant shook his head. "I can open a channel, but Spangler still won't answer. Youngblood should be there shortly."

"Fuckin' great."

Julie opened her backpack and unfolded a bright orange nonporous suit with a battery powered air supply.

"What do you think you're doing?" Marshall asked her.

"I'm going to find my father."

Peruvian Air Force Capt. Laszlo Valachi bit down savagely on his Cuban cigar. Something had gone wrong. His gunship pilot missed two radio check-ins. Eight years of active duty on this base suggested the British colonel had botched the mission and lost his gunship. *What terrorist is so damned important that Grainger would take such a risk?*

Valachi lifted the telephone receiver and secured an instant connection with his airfield's hangar. "Full alert," he instructed the officer on the other end.

Three minutes later, two Russian-made MIG-23s under his command rolled onto the runway.

Julie's heart skipped a beat as she emerged from the jungle into an incredible white world. Her eyes scanned Wynett's estate through the suit's face shield. She gasped. The estate was an abomination of decay. The effects of the organism were far more devastating than she dared imagine. Despite the clammy South American heat, the farm stood cold and dead beneath a layer of white ash that had transformed the regal grounds into a shimmering snowfield. Wynett's huge stone manor rose from the decay like a castle out of a Lewis Carroll story.

"A horse appeared," she whispered, "deathly pale, and its rider was called Plague, and Hades followed at his heels."

What have I done, dad?

Determined to find out, she crawled through a hole deliberately cut in the chain-link fence, careful not to rip her suit on the nail-like ends. She proceeded toward the house, her eyes scanning every direction. The morning sun had broken through the treetops, bathing the scene in an eerie glow. She saw no one. The white, crisp grass turned to a fine powder under her boots. She felt hot, nearly to the point of fainting.

Julie hated her army-issued full-body environment suit for not allowing the evaporation of perspiration. Its manufacturer assured comfort for prolonged wearing, unless temperatures rose above seventy-five degrees. The morning jungle already exceeded that by ten degrees, turning the inside of the positive-pressure suit into a sauna.

"Marshall," she said into the hands-free mic threaded inside her suit's hood. "The vegetation on the northern end of the plantation is devoid of pigment. I suspect that as the organism mutates, its nutritional requirements change. Maybe at one stage it feeds on chlorophyll. A breeze apparently carried the organism to the north. The epicenter of the dead zone appears to be the house."

Marshall touched the SEND button on his belt-mounted transceiver and spoke into the mini-mic clipped to his collar. "Do you see any troop activity?"

"No. I'm going to investigate."

"Negative. I want you to stay put."

"Sorry, major. I'm quite capable of taking care of myself."

Marshall turned off the mic and said to his gunnery sergeant, "I don't want her in there alone."

Williams released the safety of his Galil. "It's your call."

Marshall said to the old trapper, "You don't have to go."

Jose grinned and held up his Uzi. "She is my future daughter."

"Welcome to your first biological battlefield," Marshall said. The major swept around and led the way through the jungle toward Wynett's estate.

Julie rechecked her bio unit. The air samples registered in the normal range, yet the display indicated trace genetic patterns she couldn't identify. She longed for her workstation at Fort Detrick and an afternoon brainstorming session with her adviser, Dr. Nancy Shaw.

She snapped on her transceiver. "Marshall, are you listening?"

Marshall reached the edge of the plantation, and there he stopped, taken by the sight. He could see Julie at a distance approaching Wynett's grand manor, which rose from the fog like a medieval castle.

His earpiece crackled with Julie's voice. "Marshall?"

"I'm right here," he said. "Christ, what happened here?"

"What's the status of that radio relay?"

"Still no word from the hangar. Youngblood's almost there."

"Keep trying. I need to upload my data to Detrick for collation—" She suddenly cried out over the radio.

"What is it, Julie? What's wrong?"

No answer.

Marshall and Williams stooped through the hole in the fence and broke into a run across the field, their boots stirring up angry puffs of white ash as they ran. Jose trailed at a comfortable trot.

Julie stood statue-still, staring down at a corpse by her feet. Marshall spotted other carcasses strewn over the lawn, dozens at least, effectively covered and camouflaged by the powder-like ash.

Julie looked up quickly as they approached. "You're crazy!" she screamed. "You could get yourselves killed coming in here without suits."

Marshall ignored her and used his boot to turn over the badly decomposed body. It was a boy with negroid features, clutching a handful of smooth sticks that appeared to be part of a game. A graphite arrow had struck the boy's lower back and protruded from his chest. The arrow, fired from a high-powered compound bow, was designed to bring down large game. Quick and silent, it heightened the pleasure of killing.

"Gorgon," Williams spat.

Julie crouched beside the corpse and put a hand to her face shield over her mouth. Marshall noted her fascination. She probably had never seen a dead body outside a funeral parlor, let alone a decomposing child murdered with an arrow.

Williams squatted next to her. "Looks like he's been dead for weeks."

"No more than a few hours," Julie said.

Williams looked at her, puzzled. "Say what?"

"Radical hemorrhaging and dehydration is one of Saint Vitus' symptoms." Julie withdrew a folding plastic case with five culture containers on one side and a scalpel kit on the other. She removed a scalpel handle, inserted a blade, mindful of her airtight suit, and went to work on the boy's wrist.

"Is that necessary?" Marshall said.

"Very. I'll need to analyze tissue samples." Julie parted the boy's skin, excised a piece of the radial artery and sealed it in a culture container. She filled a second container with a sample of the ubiquitous white ash.

Marshall walked among the dead, gazing numbly at the decomposed faces frozen with looks of confusion and shock. Gorgon's raiders ruthlessly murdered Wynett's soldiers, workers and their families. He wondered if any managed to escape into the bush.

He spotted a giant dust cloud rising beyond the house and heard the whine of an idling helicopter engine. He jabbed a finger at Jose. "Stay with her."

The old trapper readily agreed, stepping next to his future daughter-in-law.

Marshall and Williams followed the outline of what once was a cobblestone walkway leading to the opposite side of the house. A grand sight greeted them – a MiL24 Hind-E, an advanced Russian gunship with Peruvian military markings, its twin turbo jet engines idling.

"A paramilitary unit," Williams said. "Not even Gorgon could get his hands on this kind of hardware."

Marshall grunted, his expression cold. Peru's militia wouldn't leave one of its more lethal military aircraft unattended. Its crew and passengers couldn't be far away.

Julie and Jose caught up with them and stared mutely at the military helicopter. Marshall glanced back at them. The gunship, cloaked in the ash's fog, must have appeared to them like a prehistoric mastodon, its scaly wings poised for flight.

"Dead men," Jose said, pointing toward the barn.

Marshall turned to see. The old trapper was right – several corpses in dark uniforms, relatively clean of ash, lay scattered in front of the barn. The gunship crew?

Marshall said to Julie, "You stay here."

"I'm searching the house." She began trudging toward Wynett's manor.

"Jose, you stay with her," Marshall ordered.

The old trapper nodded and followed her, while Marshall and Williams broke into a run across the lawn. The major motioned Williams to take the barn, while he explored the gunship.

Marshall's pulse quickened by the time he reached the aircraft. He was certified to fly a Sikorsky UH-60 Black Hawk gunship. The Hind was its Russian counterpart. The gunship touted four fixed 23mm cannons, 160 27mm unguided rockets, and a dozen laser-guided antitank missiles. This single aircraft could inflict more damage on a Contra stronghold than a regiment of troops with armor and artillery support.

Marshall stooped under the gunship's rotor blades and opened the shattered cockpit door. Inside, slumped against the controls, sat the slain pilot, a Peruvian officer. A half-dozen wounds produced a stream of blood that soaked the armored seat and gathered on the floor in a puddle. Several rounds had shattered the windscreen, but the flight control deck didn't appear damaged. The major saw no signs that the pilot had succumbed to a neurovirus, man-made or otherwise. Bullets had killed the pilot, not a bug. But bullets from whom?

Marshall yanked the unfortunate pilot from his seat, dumping him unceremoniously onto the ashen ground outside. He climbed into the pilot's seat, damp with blood, and activated the electrics and hydraulics. He throttled the jet engines and idled them at twenty-five percent. The ship could be airborne in seconds. The fuel gauge registered fifty percent. He gripped the control column firmly and felt the powerful aircraft growl under his gloved hand. Marshall had flown an older Hind-C captured in Afghanistan. This aircraft was similar, though quite improved.

Marshall switched on the ship's main tactical screen and summoned up the moving map of the upper continent. Everything displayed for his inspection – radar installation coordinates, airfields, villages, farms, mountains and roads.

Julie stepped up onto the veranda of Wynett's Tudor manor and moved slowly, hesitantly, toward its massive double oak doors. Jose followed two paces behind her, his tired eyes darting from one ash-covered shape to another. Julie felt an eerie foreboding as the house's heavy front doors swayed in the slight morning breeze, beckoning her inside. Absent were the familiar jungle sounds, which should have filled her ears even inside the suit. Her breathing accelerated, threatening hyperventilation. She tried to relax, but the sound of her heart thudded in her ears.

Against her better judgment she stepped inside.

The remains of a black woman sat upright on the floor, staring at her with twin sockets for eyes, a metal arrow jutting from her throat. Radical dehydration had aged the corpse a decade in just a few hours. Julie's heart pumped violently. *Is she laughing at me? Jesus, it looks like she is.* She turned quickly away, letting her rapid breathing fog the face shield to block her view.

Jose stood rooted in the foyer and blessed himself with the sign of the Lord's cross. "I wait outside."

"Jose, I need you with me—" But he was gone.

Damn it. She didn't want to be alone in this house of horrors. But something compelled her to continue, with or without Jose.

The house's lower level had become a battlefield. A numbness seized her. She passed the remains of a soldier in black fatigues heaped outside the study, its leather visage reminding her of a museum mummy. A bead of sweat rolled into her right eye, stinging it. She wrinkled her nose in discomfort and tried to knock it away, but couldn't reach beyond the face shield. She forced herself to continue, aware of her own labored breathing.

Julie entered the first-floor study. She imagined Wynett sitting here with his books, and reading world news on his computer. His elegant dining room still had dishes set out. Wynett was a neat and orderly man, or at least employed a staff to keep his estate that way. He had a taste for the expensive, affirmed by the original paintings and elegantly carved ivory figurines, which filled every wall and shelf space. The white ash covered everything like centuries-old dust, transforming the mansion into a mausoleum.

In the kitchen Julie opened a door revealing a flight of stone steps leading to a black cellar. She didn't descend. Her childhood imagination shifted into high gear with visions of ghouls waiting for her down there. The demons are upstairs now. She shook her head and shut the door.

Where was her father? She refused to accept the possibility she would find him here among this collection of monstrosities, refused to accept the possibility that her bug had killed him. With the suit as her shield, protecting her from every danger seen and unseen, Julie navigated the gore-covered steps to the house's second level. She reached the landing and paused, her eyes trying to assimilate the hallway's man-like shapes in the early-morning shadows. There were bodies everywhere. She passed several open doorways, each room eclipsed in darkness. Her fear grew so great that she felt a firm grip on her heart pulling her into hell. Pushing against it, she continued.

She gazed down at the twisted and shrunken face of a man who looked somehow familiar to her. An arrow, the same type of Teflon-tipped projectile that had slain the woman and boy, was buried midshaft through the corpse's eye. She gasped ... *Stony.* She stumbled backward. How? *Stony, what in God's good name happened here?*

Fighting off nausea, Julie raised a hand to her face shield and realized she was trembling, an uncontrollable shivering that threatened to cripple her with spasms. She dreaded the thought of what else she might find up here. She drew in a deep breath and proceeded down the hallway, her suit growing distressingly warmer.

She found nothing amiss in the first two bedrooms. The third, however, was a shattered wreck of bullet holes and wood splinters. Pieces of an elegant marble chessboard lay scattered among the fragmented plaster. Someone had put up one hell of a fight.

Then she saw it – the Beretta lying in the hallway. His handgun. She picked it up. Slowly, reluctantly, she lifted her eyes to the bedroom's drapery, rolling in the breeze, beckoning her attention.

Then Julie saw it.

The sight forced a muffled gasp from inside her hood. Chained to a water pipe beneath the window lay a twisted corpse of a man with distinctive peppery hair. She recognized his familiar beige khakis. Her father's dark eye sockets stared at her with a look of stern disapproval. *What have you done to me?*

CELLAR

Julie bolted out onto the veranda and nearly ran into Jose, who caught her by the shoulders. "You find?" he asked.

She just stared at Jose, who appeared as pale as she. She held her father's Beretta in her gloved hand awkwardly, unsure whether to keep it or throw it away as hard as she could.

He nodded when he saw the gun. He knew.

Without a word she raced off the veranda and across the lawn, struggling in her bulky suit to get far away from the house.

The sound of automatic gunfire startled Marshall from his evaluation of the Russian gunship. Through the chopper's shattered windscreen he saw Williams roll clear of a burst of erratic fire coming from the barn's window. The gunnery sergeant took up a defensive position against the side of the stone barn and returned several shots with his Galil.

Marshall jumped from the gunship and checked the breach of his Franchi shotgun with a commanding *clack* as he ran. He flattened himself against the barn's stone wall beside Williams. He saw no sign of the shooter.

Marshall surveyed the three slain soldiers in British SAS commando outfits sprawled beneath the barn's window, each riddled with enough rounds to assure a kill. The pieces began to fit. The Brits had followed Alpha here. Like Afghanistan, they had come to claim Gorgon for themselves.

"Did you see who fired?" Marshall asked.

"Yeah ... an old man with a neat white beard," Williams said.

"Wynett?"

"Fuck if I—

They heard laughter and singing inside the barn – disturbing hallmarks of someone possessed. Williams jerked his rifle toward the window. The laughter tapered off, as though the source was retreating down a long hallway. Where could he go?

Marshall stripped off his gear except his cartridge belt. "Watch my back."

He took a running leap through the barn's window and rolled into a deep shadow, bringing up his Franchi all in one fluid motion. Williams covered him from the window. Marshall methodically directed his shotgun at each indistinguishable shape, every manlike silhouette. The cavernous barn reminded him of a crypt, the humid air thick with death. He saw no movement. Bodies, a dozen of them, lay in untidy rows across the straw-covered floor, too badly decomposed for him to determine if Stony's commandos were among them.

Williams eased through the window behind him, his Galil ready.

Marshall moved cautiously through the shadows and felt something spongy under his right foot. He glanced down. His boot rested on the neck of a corpse whose head barely remained attached by a thin strand of sinew. He kept moving.

The hair on the back of Marshall's neck bristled when he heard the sound of stone scraping stone. His expression grim, he moved to the back of the barn, pointing his Franchi into every darkened crevice. He found an M16 assault rifle, its magazine clip missing, lying next to a crack of light between a slab of stone – a door.

He motioned Williams forward. "Help me move this."

The two men lifted the slab with an agonizing screech, unearthing a crimson emergency light source and a cool draft of mildewed air laced with the medicinal smell of formaldehyde. They set the slab roughly aside. A wooden staircase descended into a cellar.

Marshall stepped into the opening and descended without a sound. Williams followed. The air beneath the barn reeked of chemicals. They strained to see under the weak emergency lighting. They saw no one. The cellar reminded Marshall of Frankenstein's laboratory, its squat arches supporting a moss-dripping ceiling over a roomful of modern lab equipment. In the center of the room sat twin high-capacity fermentation units. Here, in the middle of the primordial Amazon jungle, was one of the better-equipped biological laboratories Marshall had seen outside a research center.

Williams let out a low whistle. "How did Wynett manage—"

They heard laughter again. A deep hysterical fit coming from behind the lab's only other door.

"I want him alive," Marshall said.

Nodding, Williams withdrew a single, special round from his munitions belt and slipped it into the Galil's chamber. The cartridge contained a nonlethal serum that could paralyze a bear for 10 minutes or a medium-size man for several hours. Marshall lay spread-eagle in front of the door, belly down, his shotgun pointed to give Williams a clear shot at the center of the door.

Marshall fired four quick shotgun blasts in a cross formation, shredding the door's planks. The tiny room beyond held glassware – a storage closet. Through the flying debris, Marshall saw a stocky, white-haired man huddled in the corner, holding a canister.

"He's got a grenade," Williams yelled.

"Move against me and I will kill us all," the man said to them. It was Wynett, wheezing heavily, his rimmed eyes crimson, the corners of his mouth twisted into a demented smile. "Are you American?"

Marshall remained motionless and waited. Wynett stood and stepped from the closet, his canister-filled hand raised. "I must know—"

"Major," Jose called from the top of the steps. "Julie gone. She run away."

Wynett glanced toward the steps.

Williams fired. The cartridge struck Wynett square in the chest. He grunted and doubled over. Marshall bolted forward and caught Wynett's palm in a viselike grip, holding the canister immobile. Wynett struggled momentarily until he lost consciousness.

Marshall called over his shoulder, "Thanks for the distraction, Jose."

The old trapper descended the cellar steps and stared curiously at the roomful of lab equipment.

Marshall pried the aluminum canister from Wynett's grip, "It's not a grenade."

The canister weighed only a few ounces and measured three-quarters of an inch in diameter and six inches long, obviously from Wynett's extensive collection of arms paraphernalia. Its metal safety pin was still in place. Marshall had seen similar devices used in covert operations that could fire compressed gas from an ampule inside.

"What's in it?" Williams asked.

"What we came here for," Marshall said.

Julie ran toward the farming cottages behind Wynett's manor. The row of bungalows had been spared contamination thanks to a northerly breeze that pushed the lethal cloud to the opposite end of the plantation. She tried to wipe the stinging mixture of tears and sweat from her eyes, but the face shield denied her gloved fingers access. Nauseous and afraid of shock, she breathed in deeply, filling her lungs with the air pumping into her suit. She didn't feel any better.

Julie couldn't face Marshall and the others right now. She couldn't wrap her head around the fact that her father was dead. She refused to believe it. She nearly convinced herself that the thing she had seen in the house was someone else. Inwardly, however, the truth was tearing her apart. He was gone, and part of her was dying with him. *Wait* ... maybe he wasn't dead. Maybe he was waiting for her inside one of these charming servant quarters, ready to scoop her up into his arms in a bear hug like he had always done when she was a girl. *You know I wouldn't leave you out here alone,* she could hear him say.

Julie climbed the steps of the first house. She entered the solidly built bungalow and surveyed the living room with its neatly appointed furniture. To her utter disappointment, no one was here – he wasn't here. She stood absolutely still, listening to the oppressive silence inside her suit, feeling the rush of another wave of grief.

She heard crying. Somewhere nearby a child was suppressing the urge to break into uncontrollable sobbing.

Julie returned to the porch and listened. The crying came again, louder – beneath her. She hurried down the steps and peered beneath the porch. In the meager half-light, she saw a black boy, no older than ten, huddled in the corner, defending himself with a pair of sharpened sticks. He looked like a curled-up puppy, terrified of a world where everything appeared large and menacing. He stared at her, shaking. A metal arrow protruded from his abdomen. How could he survive that wound?

"Jesus," she said. "Jesus ... Jesus ..." *I must look like a monster to him in this suit. An alien.*

She unfastened the snaps, removed her hood and shook the long, flowing hair from her face. The outside air rejuvenated her lungs. She wiped some moisture from her face before crawling to the child and offering her hand. The boy would not give up his sharp sticks.

"Mommy promised," he said in Americanized English. "Nothing would happen to us here."

Julie fought back the swell of emotion in her throat. Reaching forward, she took the sticks from him, then gripped his tiny hand. She held his hand tightly until he stopped crying. She stared and saw no life left behind those innocent, vacant eyes.

MASSACRE

Sinope, Brazil
0545 Hours

Youngblood banked his Black Hawk in a wide arc over the hangar before setting down on the airstrip's runway. He cut back the throttles to ground-idle and disengaged the rotor, letting the engines diminish to a growl. He saw no lights in or around the hangar, no activity of any kind. The sun was rising, but the thick enveloping trees surrounding the airstrip kept him in darkness.

The pilot grabbed a flashlight and stepped down from the cockpit. He stood motionless before the sagging hangar, ignoring the hard rain that began to fall. He waited and watched. The old hangar appeared deserted. This didn't look right. He didn't believe in ghosts. But, standing before the lifeless structure, he felt malicious spirits watching him.

Youngblood approached the bent doorway, his eyes roving. His right hand unbuttoned the leather strap of his .45's side holster. Stepping inside, he slipped quickly into the deep gloom beside the doorway and listened. He could hear nothing but rain popping onto the corrugated iron roof and the rumble of his chopper's engine. He couldn't see anything. His right hand slid the .45 out of its holster and held it ready at his side.

He switched on the flashlight and played its beam around. "Spangler?"

Alpha's equipment sat dark and useless. Their staging base had been powered down. Most likely the generator was out. The stacks of crated supplies likewise sat untouched. No one, not even jungle marauders, had intruded here. He swept the light beam across Spangler's communication console until he spotted a figure in a white technician's frock slumped facedown over the desk.

"Spangler?"

Youngblood bolted to him, grabbed Spangler by his shoulder and turned him over. Only it wasn't Spangler. A dark man with short, black hair and a closely cropped beard, grinning at him, brandished a wicked knife. Youngblood recoiled with a shout, his flashlight clattering to the floor, and lashed out blindly with his .45. The heavy handgun connected with the intruder's jaw, a blow that sent him sprawling with broken teeth. In the confused darkness, Youngblood heard a shuffling and banging of crates as the man scrambled away, spewing a string of Arabic curses. Youngblood discharged several rapid rounds at the vague figure retreating in the dimness. He heard a muted grunt as the intruder fell against the wall and collapsed in a heap of rotted planks.

Youngblood couldn't contain his rapid breathing. He scrambled for his flashlight and directed its beam across the floor, wary of others who might be hiding there. The light fell upon a body lying on its back, half concealed behind a stack of crates. He stepped closer, thrusting his handgun before him. This time it *was* Spangler. Half his blood volume had poured out a throat gash the size of his palm and formed an appalling pool around him.

Youngblood looked away in frustration. The colonel's orders were to protect the staging area and everyone in it. They all had fucked up, including him.

"I'm sorry, DOS."

Marshall kicked open the double barn doors, and he and Williams half carried, half dragged an unconscious Wynett into the yard. Jose followed, covering them with his Uzi.

"Where's Julie?" Marshall hollered.

"She run away," Jose said, pointing. "Something scare her."

"Damn it ... go find her—"

"Major," she called to him.

The men turned in unison. Julie raced across the lawn without her environment suit, leaving an ash cloud in her wake as she ran. When she reached them, Marshall noted her eyes and cheeks were flushed from crying. His heart almost stopped when he saw the colonel's prized Beretta in her hand. *God, no ...*

Her eyes drifted downward, spilling tears. "It was a massacre ... they ..." The words choked in her throat.

Marshall let out a long, weary sigh of regret. Williams looked away and shook his head. *Tony, your men were supposed to kick Gorgon's ass to hell.* The major made a silent oath to his friend to finish this ugly business and get Gorgon. He owed Tony. He owed Julie.

"Dad just bought a great house in the Canadian Rockies," Julie said, forcing a smile. "When this was over, he planned to ... we were going to..."

She couldn't continue. Marshall watched her heart sink under the weight of unbearable emotion. He touched her shoulder. "Julie—"

She jerked away. "I don't want to hear you say it." She glared at Marshall as though accusing him for her father's death.

"You have my word that I'll get Gorgon for this," Marshall said.

"I don't care about Gorgon. That was dad's business, and it got him killed. I just want him back in my life." She glared at him, her eyes full of anger. "Can you give him back to me?"

She glanced at Wynett slumped against Williams' arm. "You bastard!" She lunged at Wynett, hammering and kicking him, screaming obscenities at him. "You did this. *You did this!*"

Wynett stirred with groggy annoyance.

Marshall struggled to contain her, but she had more strength than he expected. "Julie, we need him ... we need answers...."

Julie would not stop hammering Wynett with her fists. Williams used his free hand to keep her from his prisoner to little effect.

Jose hurried to assist Williams and grabbed Wynett around his waist. The old trapper suddenly let out a grunt. He collapsed onto his knees, a Teflon arrow protruding from his side. Julie reeled back and stared at Jose, horrified. He returned her gaze with a look of regret until his eyes rolled up into his head. He dropped facedown onto the ash-covered lawn.

"Get down!" Marshall grabbed Julie and flung her to the ground. He whipped off his Franchi. "Where did that come from?"

Williams dropped Wynett and slid the Galil off his shoulder, his eyes scanning the brush beyond the harvested fields. Marshall spotted a man in black fatigues on the southern edge of the field holding a black crossbow, half-concealed by the healthy foliage.

"Do you see him?" Marshall said.

Williams' nodded. "Two more squatting in the brush. A thirty-yard shot."

The gunnery sergeant leveled his Galil sniper's rifle at the brush. The assassin raised his crossbow. Marshall knew his sergeant could hit a target at a thousand yards. At thirty yards he could drive a nail into a board.

Williams fired three rounds in quick succession. Before his rifle report faded, all three mercenaries lay dead, a perfectly centered shot through each man's chest.

Julie knelt beside the lifeless trapper. A halo of blood flowing from under his corpse turned the ash around him a dark red. Marshall watched her. He knew the arrow could have taken out any one of them. The poor man just got in the way.

"Forgive me, Jose," Julie whispered, barely forming the words. She closed her eyes, brought her hand up to her face. "I can't undo this terrible thing. I killed my father ... I killed you. God, I don't know what to do."

Marshall saw movement in the brush on the southern edge of the field, and more foliage movement to the east.

Williams saw it too. "Here they come, Joe."

"Get inside the chopper," Marshall ordered.

Julie held up her father's Beretta. "I know how to use this."

"Put that away," Marshall said. He handed her Wynett's canister. "Don't let this out of your sight."

She tucked the Beretta into one of her jumpsuit's deep pockets and took the cylinder. "What is it?"

"A gift from Wynett."

Marshall climbed into the cockpit. Williams wrestled Wynett's deadweight inside the gunship's troop compartment.

"Can he fly this thing?" Julie asked the sergeant as she climbed in after him.

Williams closed the door behind her. "We'll find out together."

Marshall grabbed the shoulder harness, too damaged to do him any good. He jammed his Franchi beside the pilot's seat and advanced the throttles to flight idle. He waited what seemed an eternity for the aircraft's turbo engines to power up to seventy-five percent before engaging the rotor clutch. Overhead, the ship's five massive rotor blades began to slice the air.

Through the shattered windscreen Marshall saw at least a dozen men dressed in black fatigues approaching the gunship in a tight skirmish line. He inched the throttles forward. As the rotor's velocity increased, he felt rather than heard brief power losses, no more than a fraction of a second each, yet persistent enough to give a seasoned pilot serious thoughts of finding another mode of transportation. *What the—?* He watched the tachometer dip slightly with each power interruption, aware that at high speeds a serious vibration could tear apart the aircraft.

Then he saw it. A bullet hole beside the altimeter. *Jesus ... how'd you miss this one?* Did the aircraft's electronics have enough redundant circuits to keep the bird airborne? If not, this would be a very short ride.

"Armed men approaching from the south and east," Williams said from the narrow passageway between the troop compartment and the cockpit.

"I see them."

The aircraft's threat alarm sounded twice. Marshall switched on the gunship's radar display and saw two dots representing approaching aircraft 40 miles to the east. Fighters approaching. "Christ, what else?" he muttered.

Marshall switched off the ship's radar, an acoustic beacon the fighter pilots could hone in on. The twin Lotarev turboshaft jet engines whipped the gunship's main rotor blades into a dish-like blur. As the engine's RPMs increased, the troublesome mechanical flutter became less noticeable. Marshall knew the problem hadn't gone away. It was lurking somewhere like a coiled snake, waiting to strike. He glanced out the windscreen. Men in black fatigues were charging the aircraft, their weapons blazing. A round ripped through the gunship's cockpit over his head.

Williams inched open the troop compartment door, raised his Galil and squeezed off a full clip in several seconds. The gunnery sergeant's report dropped four soldiers and scattered the others. "Get us out of here, Joe."

Marshall drew in a deep breath, released the brakes and pulled up on the collective control lever. The gunship shuttered, refusing to move.

"Lift, you son of a bitch," he hissed through clenched teeth.

He increased the throttle. The twin engines roared. *C'mon you f—*

The altimeter needle began to quiver.

FLIGHT

Stonecutters Garden

Peruvian Air Squadron Comdr. Alfonso de los Heros surveyed the green blur sweeping by below him. He dropped his MiG's nose, extended its flaps and eased the fighter to the dangerous edge of a stall. A mere 400 feet above the treetops, a mistake now could cost Peru one of its few high performance aircraft –not to mention one hell of a good pilot.

At two hundred knots, Commander de los Heros and his wing man had only seconds to complete a visual inspection of the plantation. But it was enough to give him an eyeful. If he didn't know better, de los Heros would swear he had just over flown a snowfield. How was that possible in the middle of a tropical jungle?

He shoved the stick forward and brought his aircraft up in a wide arc, preparing for a second run. "Dove One to Nest," he said in Spanish into his helmet mic. "The plantation is deserted. It is . . ." He paused, searching for the right word. ". . . devastated."

Inside the Peruvian air base hangar 400 miles to the west, Captain Valachi spat out a cigar bit and thundered into the open channel to the MiG pilots, "The gunship. Do you see my gunship?"

"Negative," the pilot responded.

Valachi smashed the unlit cigar into his desk. *Scavengers,* he surmised. Scavengers working for the drug czars killed the crew and stole his gunship. *The fucks will use my formidable weapon against me.* He loathed giving the order that would likely end his less-than-brilliant military career. What other choice did he have? Allowing the aircraft to escape would result in the deaths of untold numbers of soldiers and civilians. Destroy the gunship and he could blame its loss on the reckless Colonel Grainger, who had confiscated it on orders from the British Defense Council.

But first they had to find it.

"Locate the gunship," he said slowly and deliberately so there could be no misunderstanding. "And destroy it."

Marshall engaged the Hind's turbo booster and felt the kick of the G-force acceleration pressing him into the armored seat. The engines screamed at full throttle. The bird's wheels brushed the treetops, avoiding the MiGs' radar by hiding inside the ground clutter. One hundred seventy knots ... one hundred eighty ... one hundred ninety ...

His thick swirls of black hair were soaked with sweat, and his shoulders ached from the tension. His back muscles tightened as he visualized the two fighters riding his ass, each with enough air-to-air missiles to down a dozen choppers. He glanced at the outside mirror, watching for them, then scanned the forest below. There was nowhere to run, nowhere to hide.

"You've got this thing moving," Williams hooted, squatting behind the pilot's high-backed seat.

"She handles like a fucking tank," Marshall spat, his knuckles white from his overprotective grip on the pitch-control column.

"How's the fuel?" Williams asked.

"Half. Maybe enough to get us to Bolivia by way of the Rio Madeira River."

"A lot of bad neighborhoods between here and there. Are you sure about this?"

"Hell no."

"Blackjack 64, this is Odessa 72," Marshall's headset crackled. "What's your status? Over."

"Son of a bitch – it's Youngblood," Marshall called over his shoulder. He keyed in the hangar's frequency on the communications display and spoke deliberately into his helmet mic. "We're airborne. Can't tell you our position. Code nine-two. We've missed you. What's the story at the hangar? Over."

"Spangler's dead – our terrorist friends."

"*Jesus—*"

"I wouldn't advise returning there," Youngblood said. "I'm airborne, proceeding east. Let me give you a rendezvous point—"

A warning tone in his headphones overrode Youngblood's transmission. The Hind's threat display tracked a pair of red blips above and behind them, seven miles from their tail and closing rapidly – two fighters approaching at twice the gunship's speed had them targeted and locked. Marshall activated the auto weapons console, then hesitated. Fighter pilots in high-tech confrontations were notoriously trigger-happy. And there was no way he could out-duel them. When a fixed wing aircraft acquires a helicopter, the fixed wing aircraft always wins. *Steady.* Marshall slid a gloved finger over the countermeasure console.

The fighters grew in his outside mirror until he could see their distinctive Peruvian markings. At the last possible moment, they broke attack formation and roared past in a blur, shaking the gunship. A scouting sweep, Marshall concluded. They want their $30 million toy back.

"MiGs," Marshall warned Williams.

His headset crackled again. The MiG commander's voice filled his ears with angry, staccato Spanish.

Julie watched Wynett sleep fitfully on the floor of the troop compartment. She gave serious thought to opening the compartment's door and shoving him into the jungle. Or, better yet, wrapping one of the aircraft's rappelling cables around his neck and hanging the son of a bitch outside. If that meant a murder charge, she didn't give a damn.

Wynett began to stir. Julie grew rigid. His hands twitched spasmodically, and he uttered a few incoherent words as though wrestling with a bad dream.

"Williams," she called to the front.

Wynett's eyes suddenly fluttered open. He gazed up at the compartment's roof, dazed, then twisted his head around and looked at her with cold, dark eyes that terrified her.

"*Sergeant!*"

Wynett's voice when he spoke was deeper than she remembered at Detrick. "We have met before, have we not?"

Julie yanked the Beretta from the pocket of her khakis, pulled back the hammer and, with two trembling hands, pointed it at his head. "That's right, you son of a bitch. This gun belonged to my father. I'm sure he wouldn't mind if I used it to blow your fucking head off."

Peruvian Air Force Commander de los Heros opened the TAC channel to the gunship and said to Marshall in Spanish, "I have you targeted and locked. You will not be permitted to continue. You will climb to 10,000 feet and proceed on a heading of two-two-four. Over."

Marshall didn't understand a word. He keyed the mic and replied in English to the MiG commander, "I have a critical oil leak. I'm losing my drive train. Give me your base coordinates. Over."

"Ah, the Yankees have joined the Latin American drug trade," the pilot squawked in broken English over Marshall's headset. "Climb to 10,000 feet and proceed on two-two four. Deviate from this flight path – even for a moment – and I will shoot you down."

Marshall grinned. "Whatever you say, comrade."

The MiGs roared past, regrouped on the heading back to their base and quickly lost visual on him. Marshall pushed the control column right and eased up on the throttle, turning the gunship around gracefully until it matched the MiGs' heading. He knew they would monitor his compliance by radar, and he intended to show them what they wanted to see.

Marshall keyed the troop-compartment intercom. "Buckle in back there. This'll get bumpy."

Marshall brought the aircraft to a hover 800 feet above the treetops. He activated the ship's auto fire controls, keyed the mic again and said to the Peruvian pilot with as much panic as he could feign, "Mayday. Mayday. Losing power. Fires in both engines. I can't keep her in the air—"

He dipped the gunship's nose sharply and fired four wing mounted air-to-ground unguided missiles, then punched the countermeasure console to release several bundles of metal chaff. The jungle below erupted in a fireball. The radar signature would show the detonation, followed by scattered echoes of countless chaff foils, which he hoped the MiG pilots would interpret as fuselage debris.

Marshall dropped the collective and yanked the control column to the right, rolling the gunship around ninety degrees down hard and fast – faster than he intended. He gnashed his teeth against the G-forces and squeezed the control column. The aircraft shot away from the explosion at a right angle, low, diving for the jungle's ground cover. He pulled out of the dive and felt the treetops whipping the aircraft's undercarriage.

Back in the troop compartment, Julie felt as though she were riding a runaway elevator that had just plunged thirty floors. She lowered the Beretta. "I'm going to be sick..."

Doubling back, Commander de los Heros saw a huge, black column of smoke billowing from the jungle. He could not find the Hind – not on radar, infrared, visual. Nowhere. The MiGs roared past the fireball, while de los Heros made a visual sweep of the area. Had the Hind pilot told the truth about the engines? Something bothered him. He throttled and climbed, and ordered his wingman to begin a methodical search of the area.

Marshall activated the moving map display. Rivers, hills, jungle, villages – there wasn't much to choose from. They were approaching the foothills of the Serra dos Parecis Mountains. His mind raced, calculating coordinates and airspeed. His plan was uncomfortably thin: follow the Parecis mountains into Bolivia and rendezvous with Youngblood at the first clearing along the Rio Madeira River. Ten minutes. Marshall needed a precious 10 minutes to hide the aircraft in the protective folds of the Madeira river valley. The MiGs' radar would be useless in that terrain, forcing the pilots to mount a visual search for them. That tipped the odds slightly in his favor.

Marshall listened to the pilots' Spanish transmission, most likely reporting their position and describing the scorched jungle. *Take the bait, you sons of bitches ... swallow it whole.* The fighters would burn fuel rapidly while they swept the search area. He assumed their mission range didn't extend much beyond the plantation. Any moment now they would need to turn back to their base.

Marshall glanced from his watch to the display once more, then out at the terrain. He shifted uncomfortably in his seat, keenly aware the party would be over if the MiGs found them again.

The gunship's radar pinpointed their position in the Parecis highlands, a little more than 40 miles from the Bolivian border. Rolling valleys rose around them, offering cover and protection. Isolated by the Serra dos Parecis Mountains, the Madeira River valley served as a haven for drug-trafficking camps. A valley of thugs. He searched the tactical display for steep cliffs and deep canyons, any closed topography inaccessible to high-performance fighters. But the Parecis had none of that, no hiding places for choppers, just gently sloping river valleys and highlands.

"Terrific," he muttered.

As the hills rose higher around him, turbulence pummeled the aircraft. An updraft provided some free lift while a head-wind blowing across the valley buffeted the aircraft. He eased off the power, cutting the Hind's speed in half, and hugged the side of the valley, the best defensive position he could negotiate.

They came without warning. The MiGs roared over the valley in a search formation. Their sudden appearance startled Marshall, and he almost lost control of the column. *Did they see us?* He knew a fighter pilot's vision funneled to the bottom of the valley, perhaps missing a drab olive green chopper flying halfway up. One pilot might not spot them. But two? He watched the MiGs' thunder down the valley and disappear, his mind cold with uncertainty. *Did they see us?* He brought the gunship over the crest of a hill and into a wider valley and sank to the bottom.

Halfway down the hill, the forest suddenly gave way to a clearing, an encampment. Marshall brought the aircraft to a hover over the makeshift barracks and tents. A dozen men scattered beneath his rotors' downdraft. Did he dare set down here? Rounds from small arms and rifle fire struck the gunship's undercarriage. More men joined the fray, some carrying what looked like ground-to-air and antitank rockets.

His jaw tightened. This was no mining camp. *We're hovering over a fucking drug factory.*

Williams appeared behind the pilot's seat. "Jesus, Joe."

In the outside mirror Marshall saw the MiGs arcing back, regrouping in attack formation. *Shit.* He clenched the control column, lifted the collective pitch lever and increased the throttle. The gunship shot away from the encampment in a dead run down the valley. Marshall's stone-set eyes searched for a smaller side valley with deep terrain he could wrap snugly around them. But there was nothing on the display. *Nothing!*

He no longer had a plan. There was only the present moment and survival. The cat was on the mouse's tail, and he had to outrun it or be eaten.

The MiGs rapidly approached from the rear in attack formation. *Careful.*

Marshall saw spurts of flame as the MiGs launched four AA-8 infrared homing missiles. *Four of them.* They weren't taking any chances. They were determined to end the hunt right here. He had played his bluff hand and lost. The game was finished. The missiles shrieked over the encampment and headed straight for them.

Don't look at them, for chrissake. Move your ass!

He pushed the throttle full forward, broke hard to the right and pitched up while pulling on the collective. The turboshaft engines screamed in protest. The gunship turned ninety degrees and raced for its life at treetop level up the valley wall. They gained a precious second. The AA's swept around in a wide arc like burning arrows, homing in on his engines' exhaust.

Marshall's fingers jammed all eight countermeasure buttons. His console blared as radar-jamming circuits activated and load after load of flares and chaff decoys dropped behind the gunship like stardust. Would it buy them another precious seconds to run? *Give it to me....*

Whomp.

One of the missiles detonated in the chaff. Three more to go.

The valley crested above him, a ridge of solid rock. His full-throttled engines screamed – one hundred ninety knots, two-ten. A few more seconds. His knuckles blanched from his brutal grip on the control column, his eyes locked on the top ridge. Threat-warning tones screeching in his ears heralded the missiles' inevitable impact. There was no room left to maneuver. His life and the lives of the others depended on the gunship's ability to outrace three A-88 missiles to the top of a mountain.

"Joe..." Williams shouted.

The rocky peak swept beneath them in a blur. Marshall shoved the pitch control forward, bringing the nose of the chopper down into a steep dive into a wide river valley. His every muscle strained to get the gunship out of the missiles' way. He felt no fear, only numb movement.

The ridge behind them exploded. The concussion from the simultaneous detonation of three A-88s pounded his eardrums and threw him viciously against the flight console while his knuckles fought to keep a grip on the pitch column. He cursed the damaged shoulder harness. The Hind's speed dropped alarmingly.

The Hind's rudder pedals felt stiff and unresponsive. The hydraulics were going. Damage-control lights above the cockpit windshield warned of a half dozen system malfunctions. The chase was over. Marshall used the sudden decrease in power to maneuver the tail rotor and spin the ship around while skidding sideways down over the treetops. He wrestled with the cyclic, but as hard as he tried he couldn't keep the aircraft horizontal.

Marshall maneuvered the gunship into a desperate hover over the treetops that slapped the undercarriage, a living jungle that meant to devour them. He moved his hands and feet briskly, dancelike, working the column and pedals to steady the aircraft's angle. He could smell the engines burning – wires, hydraulics, turbines. Everything.

"Jesus Fucking Chr—"

FREE FALL

Williams jerked open the troop compartment door to vent the hot, acid-tasting smoke. He saw the MiGs disappear beyond the next ridge, most likely soaring in a huge arc to return in attack formation. They had one minute, maybe less.

Williams surveyed the thick treetops under the gunship's pendulum-like swinging and shouted into the cockpit, "No way you're gonna put her down here, Joe."

"The main rotor's going," Marshall replied over the intercom. "I can't keep it horizontal. Get the hell out of here."

Williams grabbed one of the gunship's two rappelling cables driven by a winch powerful enough to hoist trucks. He looked at Julie, then at Wynett, who sat Buddha-like with his dark eyes locked on him. "God help us," the sergeant muttered, then pointed to Julie. "You first."

"Sergeant, I can't—"

"*Now!* "

Julie slung the instrument case over her shoulder and let Williams fasten the winch harness under her arms.

"I'm lowering Wynett next," Williams said, leading her to the edge of the compartment. "If he gives you trouble, use your gun on him."

Julie's eyes locked on the swaying treetops below. "Tell me you're not serious."

"You don't have to do a thing," Williams assured her. "I'll feed the line from here."

Julie screwed her eyes shut, fighting back a panic blitz. Williams spun her around and pushed her out of the compartment. A yelp tore from her throat. The rapid descent felt like a freefall even though she knew Williams controlled the winch cable, though still much too fast, she thought. She kept her eyes closed while she plummeted through the branches that slapped and mauled her like claws.

Eighty feet beneath the treetops, Julie hit the ground with a solid thud. *Down.* She opened her eyes. The jungle's half-darkness enveloped her. She couldn't see the chopper through the great liana-festooned trees towering above, but she could hear the sputtering of its dying engines. She scrambled out of the harness, gave the cable two hard jerks and watched the line vanish up through the thick, leafy canopy.

A dreadful thought occurred to her: Suppose Wynett makes it down, but Marshall and Williams don't. The notion scared the hell out of her. I wouldn't just be stranded in the middle of the jungle ... I'd be stranded in the middle of the jungle with Wynett! If it came down to that, she decided, she would kill him quickly with her father's Beretta.

"You're taking too much *goddamn* time," Marshall shouted.

Williams felt the aircraft become increasingly unstable. *Way too much time for this sack of shit*, he thought as he finished fastening the winch's harness under Wynett's arms. "If you even say 'boo' to the lady down there, I'll kill you. Do you understand me, mother fucker?"

Wynett looked at him coolly. "I suggest we remain up here, sir. A much safer option—"

Williams gave his prisoner a powerful shove out of the gunship, activated the winch and watched Wynett plunge into the forest below. He slung his rifle and munitions pack over his shoulders and hollered to the front, "I'm outta here."

Williams grabbed the second rappelling cable, swung out of the compartment and pushed himself away from the aircraft. The gunship bucked angrily away as he slid downward, the cable burning his gloved hands. The aircraft hovered unevenly above the canopy, swinging and side-slipping, viciously dragging the sergeant through the treetops. Williams twisted and turned with his descent, kicking a path through the branches as he spun, protecting his face with his arm.

The gunship dipped sharply, dropping him 30 feet before the cord became hopelessly tangled in the branches, suspending him like a puppet 10 feet off the ground. Williams let himself drop. He landed heavily in the mulch and dissipated the impact in a controlled roll through the high, twisted stalks. He rose shakily onto his knees. He could hear the gunship fighting its losing battle to stay in the air.

"Sergeant," Julie called through the din.

He spotted her half concealed in the brush, pointing the Beretta at Wynett's head while he sat beside her. He sprinted to her.

Julie's frenzied eyes scanned the treetops. "Where is he? Why isn't he climbing down?"

"The chopper's too unstable," Williams said. "He'll come down the hard way."

"What's that supposed to mean?"

"Once he lets go of those controls, the ship goes down. He'll land that thing in the trees."

Marshall felt the mounting vibration in the pitch control column as the rotor blades lost their valiant battle to hold onto the sky. The main rotor torque gauge sank dangerously with the ship's loss of power.

The radar-lock warning siren screeched through the cockpit and he knew the MiGs were returning in an attack formation. The display showed four points of light moving rapidly toward him – four more missiles. Marshall, his face streaked with rivulets of perspiration, drew in a deep breath – possibly his last, he realized – and eased down on the collective.

Now!

The gunship dropped into trees, slamming him against the instrument panel. Marshall fumbled to extinguish the two Lotarev engines. The rotor blades struck the branches and shattered, hurling ribbons of steel through the jungle at 500 knots.

With its nose angled downward, the gunship rolled dangerously to port, flinging Marshall sideways against the cockpit door with a force that paralyzed his lungs and left his head reeling. He made a desperate grab at the back of his seat for support, his legs pushing him away from the windscreen. He was falling, too stunned to do anything but ride eighteen tons of metal down through the branches. He screwed his eyes shut and saw an image of his mashed and broken body, indistinguishable from the scattered metal when he hit the jungle floor.

But there was no impact.

The aircraft came to a jarring stop. Marshall's eyes blinked open with a start. Dazed, unable to comprehend why he was still alive, he stared at the jungle floor two stories beneath him.

"Joe!" The sound of Williams' voice startled his mind back to the present reality. "Get your ass down here!"

The branches split and groaned under the weight of the gunship. The aircraft sank downward, twisting and cracking through the branches.

Marshall seized his Franchi and kicked open the cockpit door. He grabbed blindly at the branches and half climbed, half slid to the ground, then rolled hard onto his right shoulder. The fall left him stunned.

Marshall was only vaguely aware of a terrible roar bearing down on them. Two hands reached under his arms, pulled him to his feet and pushed him forward. Marshall limped blindly through the jungle on two bruised legs that, mercifully, weren't broken.

"Keep moving," Williams shouted.

Marshall heard two pairs of AT-6 Spiral laser-homing missiles tear into the treetops and detonate. He glanced back. The twisted wreckage that had once been a Russian gunship turned onto its back like a dying dragonfly and tumbled onto the jungle floor. Hurricane-like winds shrieked through the trees and sucked the heated air from Marshall's lungs. The twin Lotarev engines exploded with an impossible concussion, turning the wreck into an angry fireball that rolled into a thick, black pillar of smoke. The MiGs roared overhead. Marshall and Williams raced out of the fireball's reach while burning fuel chased after them like a fast-flowing stream of lava.

THE FIERCE PEOPLE

Marshall followed Williams through a curtain of jungle to a slight clearing overgrown with creepers, parasitic orchids, vines and moss. The climate of the damp upper river valley left the air fetid, the heat oppressive and debilitating, the ground wet and clinging. He found Julie standing sentinel over Wynett, Beretta in hand.

She exhaled slowly as though she had been holding it since landing. "I was beginning to think you weren't coming."

Marshall brushed past her. "Put that gun away."

"Yes, sir." She added under her breath, "And it's nice to see you too."

Wynett watched Marshall with intense dark eyes. "Do you realize the danger you have placed us in, sir? Our situation is hopeless without a radio."

Julie glanced at Marshall. "No radio? How will you contact Youngblood?"

"We won't," Wynett said evenly. "Without a radio, we are effectively sequestered from the rest of the world. Any notion of simply marching out of this valley is absurd."

Marshall looked severely at him. "Cork it."

"Friggin' great." Julie wiggled the equipment pack off her shoulders with a groan and eased into a sitting position at the base of a liana tree. She felt the slightest tickle on the back of her neck and, reaching back, touched a bug the size of a locust with long, thin legs and an ugly bloodsucking snout. She sat up suddenly. The tree was crawling with the strange-looking insects.

"*Reduviidae,*" Wynett said. "The assassin bug. Don't let them sting you, my dear Julie. They carry Chagas disease."

Julie sprang to her feet, brushing her hands frantically over her body. Wynett laughed at her, his shoulders jiggling as if on springs.

A birdlike whistle startled everyone into silence. *Whooooo! Whooooo!* came the answering call.

Williams swung the Galil off his shoulder and directed it at the trampled path leading into their clearing.

"The natives call them the fierce people," Wynett said, his voice low. "They are soldiers of the drug cartel. They own these valleys."

Marshall looked at him. "Are you bullshitting me?"

"The Indians are terrified of them," he continued. "The value the drug lords put on their privacy is priceless. They are not after our wreckage. No doubt they believe we are a part of the militia that is at constant war with them. They will hunt us down until they find us – even combing the wreckage for our charred bodies. And when they find us here alive, within the week the authorities will fish our mutilated bodies out of the Rio Madeira River, just as they have done with eighty other bodies this year alone. The corpses typically have their throats slit, their faces disfigured and their fingerprints removed with acid to make them difficult to identify—"

"Shut up," Julie shouted. "*Shut up!*"

Marshall clamped a hand over Julie's mouth and tackled her down behind a barricade of moss-covered tree stumps. "Not a word." Julie nodded. He said to the others in a raspy whisper, "Stay absolutely quiet."

Marshall heard the squawks of handheld radios. The sergeant rolled next to him. "At least a dozen. Well-camouflaged with rifles."

"Fucking great," Julie groaned.

A long, undulating, sustained chorus of screams shot through the forest like a train whistle. *Whoo-hooo-hooo!*

Marshall raised his Franchi.

189

"Fire a single round, sir," Wynett said, "and you will kill us all. You must set your guns aside and put your hands on the back of your heads. That is our only chance."

Suddenly bullets hissed over their heads, men screaming, foliage rustling, everything blurring in a drone of confusion. *We're going to buy it,* Marshall realized. *We're going to buy it in the middle of this goddamn jungle.*

Faces and gun barrels pushed through the sea of vegetation, some of them firing rounds. Wynett put two fingers in his mouth and let out a deafening whistle, one long and one short. The whooping and shouting ceased for an awkward moment. Then laughter – the soldiers were laughing at them. Marshall stared bitterly into the deadly ends of gun barrels closing in around them, the foreign faces behind the weapons eager to use them. He reached for his SAS knife.

"Don't do it," said a voice in English with a thick Portuguese accent.

Marshall turned quickly. A dark, oily-faced officer pushed through the tight circle of soldiers toward them. The officer scrutinized each of them. He smirked when he spotted Wynett sitting among them.

"Ahhh," he said. "The good doctor. And he brings his friends."

"Good day, Colonel Perez," Wynett said. "Always a pleasure."

Williams slid a furtive hand down the length of his Galil.

The colonel's ferreting eyes leaped to the sergeant. "Touch the trigger, colored man, and my men will cut out your heart while you watch."

EXECUTIONER

A small but well-armed contingent of soldiers marched their prisoners through the gates of a hidden jungle encampment with a single barracks in desperate need of repair. A driving rain heralded their arrival, rinsing the mud off them. Marshall watched natives in loincloths hoist bales of coco leaves onto their shoulders and bind them to mules. The drug lords used the forest's indigenous people for the menial harvesting chores the same way Southern plantation owners used slaves to pick cotton. The civilized world had introduced commerce to the jungle, and business was thriving.

Marshall held no illusions about his fate. As the senior American military officer commanding an illegal operation in a sovereign state, he knew he was finished. If they had been apprehended by the *Borlo*, Brazil's secret military police, at least he could have anticipated spending the rest of his life alone in a dark concrete cell, slowly losing his eyesight. But they weren't in police custody. By morning he would be dead, his features erased with a knife.

As for the others, they would die too, he realized. There would be no prisoner exchange or daring rescue attempt, even if General Medlock knew of their whereabouts. The U.S. State Department would deny Alpha's existence. Inside the United States military establishment, Marshall and his group did not exist. Dr. Carl Wynett, Col. Anthony Martinelli and his commandos did not exist. Saint Vitus did not exist. They were on their own.

Marshall surveyed the wretched barracks and allowed his eyes to wander the length of a radio tower rising like a high-tech steeple from its corrugated iron roof. He stole a sideways glance at Williams, who acknowledged him with raised eyebrows. Julie and Wynett, sloshing through the mud with hands clasped behind their heads, didn't appear to notice the hardware that provided the only thin link to the civilized world. He knew that Julie only cared about the canister still hidden in a pocket of her khakis.

The barracks' interior was as dismal and rude as its exterior. The place reeked of rot, sweat and urine. Fungus seeped between cracks in the floorboards like sloppy mortar. An abomination of torn plaster, bare light fixtures and decomposing furnishings, the barracks housed men more repugnant than the jungle vermin it was built to keep out. Inside, Marshall counted five soldiers, all unwashed and unshaven, each toting an automatic rifle.

One of the guards, all hair and muscle, reminded Marshall of Blackbeard the pirate, complete with an eye patch. The brute whirled a large-gauge chain as though it were a pocket watch while scrutinizing each of them with his single good eye as they entered. His woolly beard shifted and his eye glistened when he saw Julie. He lumbered over and began thoroughly frisking her. She shot a frightened glance back at Marshall.

Blackbeard found Wynett's aluminum canister hidden in a buttoned pocket of her khakis and tossed it to the oily-faced colonel.

"You mustn't touch that," Julie said. "Please listen to me..."

The colonel considered the canister in his palm. Marshall stiffened, a reaction the colonel was quick to notice. "Tell me what this is?"

"Marshall, for God's sake," Julie shouted, "don't let him open it!"

Marshall struggled to keep his feet planted and his arms firmly at his sides. He couldn't do a damn thing.

"The container is mine," Wynett said, stepping forward. "I will tell you its secrets. But for a price."

The colonel smiled and nodded. "Always the deal maker, yes, Herr Wynett? Let's talk."

The colonel cocked his head. A guard pushed Julie curtly down the hallway, while two others marched Williams at gunpoint down a flight of narrow stone steps leading beneath the barracks.

Marshall tried to conceal the defeat in his eyes as they led Julie away, the corrupt laughter of her receding captors taunting him. He couldn't listen anymore. He dug his heels into the slippery floorboards and lunged at the guard closest to him, a man not much older than twenty. His hands clawed for the guard's rifle. He saw a blur of movement behind him and felt a cruel blow to his kidney. He fell to his knees, his vision darkening. Blackbeard's heavy chain wrapped itself around his neck and yanked him roughly backward. Marshall groped ineffectively at it before another hammer-like blow to his kidney knocked him insensible.

"I wish to know your name," said the colonel, stepping into Marshall's view. "I wish to know the names of the men I kill."

The chain around Marshall's neck slackened so he could breathe. "Fife," he gasped. "Bernard Fife. My friends call me Barney."

"American CIA?"

"Deputy sheriff of Mayberry."

The colonel nodded to Blackbeard, who tightened his death grip on the chain. Marshall barely managed a lame sucking noise deep in his throat. He saw the officer's lips move but could hear nothing before blackness enveloped him.

Julie waited alone in a small dim room that served as the soldiers' sleeping quarters. Filthy mattresses lay strewn across the floor. There were no windows, and only one entrance. She didn't wait long before Blackbeard joined her. He closed and bolted the door behind him and let his good eye follow her body's shapely contours.

"Listen to me very carefully," Julie implored him. "You must convince your commander not to open that canister. He doesn't know what he has. You must get him to return it to me so I can destroy it. The contents of that container will kill us all."

Blackbeard laughed – a deep, ugly rumble that made her wince – and leveled a lustful gaze at her. Julie doubted he understood a word of English. He stepped closer, breathing heavily, his hot, foul breath pouring over her. He unfastened his pants and let them drop to his ankles, revealing a scrotum that reminded her of a low-hanging wasps' nest.

Julie covered herself with crossed arms. *"Marshall!"*

Marshall thought he was dreaming. How else could he explain this subterranean nightmare of shadow and gloom out of a B horror movie? But this was no dream. The stench that assaulted his nostrils, a horrendous blend of rot and excretion, was more effective than smelling salts. He woke with a start, his senses clearing, and assessed his predicament. He sat naked to the waist, strapped in a sinister-looking chair in the barracks' sub-basement. The leather straps – one around each arm and leg, another around his forehead, another around his chest – immobilized him. He caught a glimpse of Williams in his peripheral vision sitting similarly strapped to a chair beside him. *What in God's glorious world is happening?*

The cellar's only light came from a harsh incandescent bulb dangling above them. Large brown puddles covered the floor, and he could hear a constant echo of dripping water. He saw a shadowy collection of cauldrons and ovens lurking beyond cobwebbed archways, and beyond them stacks of petroleum drums. Between an archway, a fiendish-looking hulk of a man with a long drooping mustache sat sharpening a wicked knife on a foot-driven whetstone. A dungeon, Marshall thought, a dungeon right out of the Dark Ages.

"Where's Julie?" Marshall asked.

"It's about time you woke up," Williams said. "Welcome to the party."

"Where is she?"

"They're not gonna waste her down here," Williams said, then let out a huff of nervous laughter. "They're not gonna waste her on a death of a thousand cuts."

"You're shitting me."

"See the drain under your chair?"

Marshall tried to look down, but the strap held his head upright. "No."

"Take my word for it. Genghis Khan over there intends to cut fine, razor incisions from our temples to our ankles. He's making the blade so sharp the incisions will hardly bleed. He'll cut us until we slowly bleed to death. A guard guaranteed we'll be aware of the pain until the very end."

Marshall watched the executioner silhouetted by the flurry of sparks from the whetstone. "Fun."

Wynett surveyed the squalid room, fascinated by the paint peeling down the mildewed walls in long sheets. Colonel Perez examined each piece of Alpha's gear laid out on the room's only table. He seemed particularly interested in Julie's instrumentation pack. Finally he faced Wynett and stared at him curiously, studying him.

Wynett didn't blink.

"You are a puzzle to me," the colonel said. "You are a well-respected farmer and a man of considerable property, yet you and your American friends steal a gunship belonging to Peru's military. As an officer of Brazil's elite militia, I have access to all military intelligence coming in and out of this country. I am not aware of an operation involving foreigners in our valleys."

Wynett gestured to the room's only other soldier, a guard, standing beside the door. "It isn't prudent to speak in front of him."

"He will stay," the colonel replied.

"As you wish. The gentlemen and the woman are part of a commando unit that illegally infiltrated your borders to kidnap me. I assume the gunship offered a way out of the jungle. I cannot be certain because I was insensible when they abducted me and commandeered the aircraft. I can assure you, sir, that neither I nor they have any interest in your drug camps."

The colonel gave no clue as to whether he believed the story.

"Now I must ask you for a favor, Colonel Perez," Wynett continued. "It is imperative that you deliver me to U.S. authorities. They will reward you quite generously, I promise you."

The colonel lit a cigar, its aroma revealing his fondness for all things Cuban. "Why are you so important to the Americans? Why would the U.S. military go to these lengths to retrieve you from our country?"

Wynett looked at the colonel. "Why not? It's bloody good fun." He couldn't contain his laughter.

The colonel searched his captive's eyes. "You are not well, my friend. What happened to you? You have become grossly unpredictable and unreliable."

Wynett only laughed harder. The colonel shook his head in disappointment and returned his attention to Julie's waterproof instrumentation pack. He brushed cigar ash from the controls and pressed several buttons until the unit came to life. Its gridded amber screen displayed a waveform pattern he obviously could not comprehend. "It is a transceiver? But much too sophisticated for voice communications. This device records and unscrambles our transmissions. Yes?"

Wynett shrugged. "I believe the system identifies metabolic fingerprints from air samples. You must ask the woman for specifics."

The colonel returned the case to the table, then retrieved Wynett's six-inch aluminum canister. "Such a curious container. You will tell me what is inside."

"I will tell you everything in exchange for transportation to the States. I must be in Virginia no later than thirty-six hours from now."

"I can arrange transit for you to Sao Paulo. That is all."

Wynett fixed his dark eyed on the colonel. "That is most unacceptable."

Frowning, Colonel Perez removed the canister's safety pin and, holding the trigger arm secure, thrust the cylinder beneath Wynett's nose. "Tell me what is inside or I will open it in your face."

Wynett drew in a deep breath and put his hands on his head as though expecting the ceiling to fall on him. "Sir, I should warn you that it is dangerous to hold that container in so careless a manner. If you release the handle, you will fill this room with gas."

Wynett swung his arms down from his head with surprising swiftness. The vicious impact struck the colonel's canister-filled hand, and the cylinder clattered to the floor, hissing and sputtering. The colonel looked at his prisoner, astonished. Wynett screwed his eyes shut.

There was no visible gas cloud, but Wynett knew that the acute odor accosting the colonel was unlike anything he had ever experienced. The guard reached for Wynett but never laid a hand on him. He doubled over, unconscious before he hit the floor.

Colonel Perez drew his sidearm, a Walther PPK fitted with a twelve-bore suppresser. Wynett knew the colonel's burning eyes could see nothing. He never fired his weapon. The colonel fell to his knees in a coughing fit that expelled pieces of his lungs while Wynett watched with a grin.

Blackbeard struck Julie with a wild brush of his hand, then grabbed her shirt and tore it from her back with one quick motion. She gasped when he ran his huge, callused hands down her back.

Enraged, she whirled slapped his face. "God damn you!"

Blackbeard's features darkened. He withdrew a handgun from his shoulder holster.

Julie struggled to recall an Israeli defensive *Krav Maga* technique or two her father had taught her years ago. *Fuck it.* She locked her hands in a double fist and struck the side of his head as though taking a home run-size swing at a hardball. "Asshole."

The brute stumbled backward with a grunt, his feet entangled in his loose pants. Julie lunged, throwing her full weight onto him. She grappled desperately for his handgun. The weapon fired. The bullet tore through the brute's leg. He howled and, together, they collapsed against the wall with an awful crash, their combined weight shattering the planks. They landed heavily in a heap together. Blackbeard looked in stunned disbelief at the splintered edge of a splintered board jutting through the right side of his chest. Julie pried the gun from his grip, then rolled off him.

Blackbeard slammed his palms against the wall and struggled to rise, but the board kept him impaled. He returned Julie's astonished stare with an eye that radiated dark waves of loathing. The handgun was a well-traveled .45, its safety off. She thrust it at him. He snarled at her, spewing blood between his broken teeth. He grabbed for her with flailing his arms.

Julie moved into the corner well beyond his reach and kept the gun pointed at him. "*Marshall!*"

The executioner lifted his considerable bulk from the stool and moved to his prisoners, directing a lecherous gaze first at Marshall, then at Williams. He appeared to derive erotic pleasure from running his hideously scarred thumb down the length of the knife's blade. He grinned.

The executioner touched his knife's razor tip to Williams' right temple. The sergeant inhaled sharply.

Marshall glared at the brute. "You fucking pig."

The executioner ran the tip of the blade lightly down the side of Williams' face and neck, stopping at the edge of his shoulder. Marshall saw the veins on Williams' temple stand out like branches while he strained helplessly against the straps, tense and resentful, sweat cascading down his ebony features. The brute stepped back to admire his handiwork with a perverse look of pleasure.

"Stings a little," Williams huffed, almost giddy. "Bastard didn't hurt me."

The executioner grinned, an amused look that told both men that the fun hadn't yet started. He turned his attention to Marshall, touching the ominous blade to the back of the major's right ear.

Marshall remained absolutely still and stared into the brute's dead eyes. The executioner jerked his hand. Marshall felt a warm, slow trickle down his neck. "The bastard cut me."

The brute grinned again, opened his palm and showed Marshall his right ear.

"Jeessssuuuus Christ—"

The cage door at the top of the steps creaked open, followed by descending footsteps. The executioner's face darkened and he swept his massive torso around to face the intruder. A figure, backlit by the corridor above, stole down the steps. It wasn't one of the barracks' soldiers.

The executioner tossed the major's ear into a puddle, grabbed his knife by the blade and prepared to throw it. The shadow on the steps assumed a half-crouch and raised a handgun with both hands. There came three sharp suppressed pops from a handgun. Three rounds struck the brute square in the chest, pushing him backward with a grunt. He didn't go down. Three rivulets of blood streamed down the front of his butcher's overalls. He staggered forward, the knife still raised. Three more rounds augmented the wounds on his chest. The executioner's massive head finally bowed in defeat and his bulk toppled, landing with a heavy splash on the mud floor.

The figure descended the remaining steps and moved into the ring of light beneath the chairs.

"I am in need of your assistance, major," Wynett said. "It is imperative that you escort me out of here and deliver me to your superiors."

FREQUENCY

"Wynett!" Marshall shouted. "For chrissake get these straps off us."

"I am prepared to make a trade with your government," Wynett said. "At stake is a major American city."

Marshall locked a hardened gaze on Wynett. "What are you talking about? What city?"

"I must be on United States soil no later than thirty-six hours from now or there will be no deal. I want your word as a soldier of honor that you will do everything in your power to deliver me to your superiors in that time frame. Otherwise I will leave you strapped here and take my chances with the Brazilian guerrilla militia."

"What city?" Marshall demanded.

"Jesus, Joe," Williams said. "Tell the crazy mother fucker what he wants to hear."

"Deal," Marshall spat. "I'll carry you home on my back, if I have to."

Wynett retrieved the executioner's formidable knife and used its keen blade to slit the straps binding Marshall to the chair. He similarly released Williams from his binds.

The sergeant jumped up and drove his boot into the chair, shattering it with a single, solid kick. Williams glanced at Marshall with a scowl. "Jesus, Joe. Your ear…"

Marshall retrieved his shirt and used it to mop the flow of blood running down his neck. "Fucking bastard."

"There are three soldiers upstairs," Wynett said.

"Where's your friend the colonel?" Marshall asked, pressing the bloody shirt against the side of his head.

"He was foolish enough to open my container."

"*He what?*"

"The colonel and his guard succumbed to *pois gratter,*" Wynett said, rolling the term around his tongue like a shot of fine whiskey, "a species of Mucuna plant. I synthesized a colorless crystalline compound that rapidly assaults the respiratory and central nervous system. On the skin it feels like slivers of glass. Inhaled, it causes excessive secretion to rapidly fill the lungs. A victim quickly drowns on his own mucus."

"So what makes you immune to *pois* whatever?" Williams asked, delicately touching the fine, deep cut on his face.

"*Pois gratter* is fatal only if inhaled. To the skin and eyes it is merely an irritant. I simply held my breath while in the room" – he held up the Walther – "and borrowed this from the good colonel after he succumbed."

Marshall reached for the Walther. "I'll need that to get you out of here."

Wynett relinquished the handgun but made no secret that he intended to keep the executioner's wicked-looking knife. Williams found a sturdy hatchet under the executioner's grindstone table and noted its razor-sharp blade. Marshall checked the Walther's magazine, snapped it back and charged the breech. Two rounds left.

"Let's go."

The major led the way up the stone steps to the barracks' main corridor. It stood empty. They passed the interrogation room, where Colonel Perez and his guard lay stretched grotesquely across the floor. Marshall saw that the two had not gone quietly to eternity. Williams spotted his Galil among their gear on the table and made a move to retrieve it.

"Leave it for now, sergeant," Wynett warned. "*Pois gratter* is a heavy compound and does not dissipate rapidly."

Williams grunted his disgust.

Electronically distorted voices reverberated from the end of the hallway.

"The radio," Wynett said to the major. "I suggest you contact your people and arrange a rendezvous."

"Where's Julie?"

"Under close guard, I suspect."

Marshall moved swiftly down the hallway and slid silently next to the only open door. Two soldiers sat with their backs to the door in front of the outpost's radio, one listening through headphones, the other thumbing through pages of a lewd magazine.

Marshall eased open the door with a crack. The magazine reader glanced back at him. Marshall smiled amiably. However, there was nothing amiable about the Walther he held steady in his hand. The soldier jumped to his feet. A dull crack from the suppressed handgun sent him looping backward. The second soldier, still wearing the headphones, whirled in his chair. Marshall didn't give him a chance to stand. The Walther's final round transformed his face into a spray of blood and shattered bone. His body flailed backward, ripping the headphone jack from the console.

"Well done, major," Wynett said.

The three slipped into the radio room. Williams searched the slain soldiers for weapons and cursed aloud when he found none.

A shot roared from the room next to them, followed by shouting that was unmistakably Julie. Marshall and Williams burst into the hallway. The sergeant, his knuckles pale from an overly tight grip on the hatchet, half ran, half leaped at the door, his right leg thrust before him like a battering ram. The heel of his boot connected solidly and the door burst inward.

Marshall spotted Julie crouching in the corner, still pointing a hand gun at Blackbeard, who lay at her feet, a shattered board jutting from his back, his pants kicked off. A large-caliber exit wound had taken off the back of his head, revealing a half-empty cranial cavity.

Marshall went to her and eased the gun from her grip. She looked up at him in shock, her distant eyes unfocused. At first she didn't appear to recognize him. Then she saw his wound. "Oh, my God ... your ear..."

Marshall covered the side of his head with the shirt he still carried. "Are you alright?"

Wynett thrust his head through the doorway. "Call your people, major."

Before Julie could answer, Marshall returned to the communications room and took a seat in front of the radio, a multicalibrated transceiver with satellite relay capabilities. He reset the frequency. Suddenly a voice, loud and with minimal distortion, began cracking orders in Portuguese through the speaker.

"Radio traffic between two helicopter pilots," Wynett said. "They work for the drug czar who owns this compound and many like it. They cannot be far."

As the exchange continued, Marshall watched the VU meters' needles bounce from vehicle to vehicle. "They're approaching from the northwest." He glanced at another meter. "Amplitude twenty decibels – maybe 60 miles out. They'll be here in 20 minutes." Marshall thrust a finger at the large wall map. "I need our coordinates."

Williams pinpointed the outpost's position and read off the longitude and latitude coordinates of the camp, while Marshall reset the transceiver to the hangar's frequency. When the digital readout indicated an open channel, he spoke slowly into the microphone: "Alpha eight-seven to Odessa seven-four. Factor nine-two. Code one-seven-zero-one. Post error. Position one-seven-zero, four-two-seven. Repeat. One seven-zero, four-two-seven. January Alpha one-nine-seven zero. January two-seven-zero-four. Repeat—"

A shrill howl blared from the speaker, pegging the VU meters. Marshall grimaced.

"What's wrong?" Julie demanded.

"Jamming," Wynett said. "Our drug lord friends are on to us. Did you get through to your pilot?"

Marshall's expression registered anything but certainty. "I don't know if he's even still out there to hear me."

"If you did reach Youngblood," Julie said, "he'll never find us here in the jungle. Especially at night."

Marshall looked hard at Julie. "He'll see us – I'm burning this dump to the ground."

CONFLAGRATION

Marshall watched from atop the steps while Williams dumped three barrels of stored aviation fuel across the muddy floor of the dungeon beneath the barracks. The fuel's thick fumes accosted Marshall. He raised a kerosene lantern and hollered down, "Get up here, sergeant."

Williams bounded up the steps two at a time. The major hurled the lantern down into the dungeon. The glass shattered, igniting the fuel with an audible *whump*. Both men scrambled outside and joined Julie and Wynett, who were huddled in the brush.

Marshall couldn't tear his eyes from the burning barracks. Mesmerized, he watched flames appear through the corrugated roof and spread fast, tearing apart the structure. The basement's remaining aviation fuel ignited and exploded, turning the structure into a grand fireball that roared high into the night. The burning compound would make a fine night beacon for an aircraft. By morning, Marshall figured that anyone sifting through the smoldering rubble would find nothing in the foundation crater but charred grit and twisted metal.

"Joe," Williams said, "I've never seen you so jittery."

Marshall glanced curiously at his sergeant. "Jittery? Anxious, maybe ... never jittery."

Williams indicated the major's hand. "What's with the shaking?"

Marshall stared. His right hand shook spasmodically as though he were scared shitless. Scowling, he adjusted the bandanna Julie had fashioned to cover his ear. *Jittery my ass.*

Marshall returned his gaze to the burning structure. The flames reminded him of Saint Vitus, a deadly and uncontainable killer that devoured a man the way this fire devoured the barracks. He loathed to think that Gorgon now possessed such a terrible weapon. Why hadn't Alpha killed the bastard in this godforsaken jungle and forever rid the world of him? Marshall glanced at Julie standing beside him. Her hardened expression and riveted stare told him that she must have shared similar sentiments.

Marshall heard the faint thumping of a chopper approaching from the south – low, just above the tree line. Although he could see nothing in the night, he recognized the telltale wisps of a Black Hawk, its rotors in whisper mode.

Julie clutched Marshall's arm, and he could feel the tension within her. Despite the hot jungle night, she was shaking. He put a strong arm around her shoulder and lifted her chin, searching those deep brown eyes for the self-assured woman he had grown fond of. He hardly recognized her. "I'm taking you home."

Julie responded with a forced smile.

Williams stepped out of the brush and began waving his arms at the sky, although there was nothing yet to see. A half a minute later, Youngblood's sleek, black helicopter descended from the night sky and set down a prudent distance from the conflagration.

"You really piss me off," said Youngblood, climbing down from the cockpit. "I've been chasing you all goddamn day. Now hustle your asses. I picked up two choppers on radar approaching from the north about 15 miles out."

"The major needs medical attention," Wynett said to the pilot.

Youngblood's boyish grin vanished when he saw Wynett. Then his eyes bounced across each of their solemn faces, finally stopping on Marshall's hastily bandaged ear. "Sweet Mother…"

Wynett attempted to help Julie into the chopper's passenger compartment, but she pushed him away. "Don't you ever touch me."

Williams yanked Wynett roughly away as Julie slung her instrument package over her shoulder and climbed into the chopper. Williams and Wynett followed.

Marshall climbed into the cockpit next to Youngblood and strapped himself in.

"Jesus, major," Youngblood said, "what happened back there? Where's Colonel Martinelli? Where's Stony and his men?"

"They're not coming," Marshall said. "Now get us out of this damn jungle, cowboy."

PART THREE

Lucy

MAYDAY

The Caribbean Sea
Twelve miles off the coast of St. Martin
Saturday, April 30, 1445 hours

The coastline of the Virgin Islands sank beneath the wing of the twin-engine Cessna seaplane banking into a clear Caribbean sky. Neither of the two passengers noticed the view. Tarra withdrew an Uzi from her leather rucksack and gripped the weapon firmly, drawing strength from its sleek power. She checked the clip, drove it home with a precision snap and screwed on a fourteen-bore suppresser.

Gorgon grinned at her preoccupation with the weapon. The gun seemed to calm her. She was afraid of nothing, yet loathed flying, and her uncustomary uneasiness amused him. He couldn't resist taunting her with anxious looks during the plane's occasional sudden loss of altitude during the ascent. *My poor Tarra*, his hooded eyes mocked her. He touched her chin with playful fingers. "I found the one experience that frightens you. Yes?"

She slapped at his hand scornfully.

"Put your thoughts elsewhere," he advised her. "Think of pleasant things. Think of the tanker."

Gorgon, amused, settled back into his seat and kept his eyes fixed on her.

Seven hours. That's how long it took the seaplane to cover 1,200 miles of open sea before reaching the intercoastal waterway of South Carolina. The cabin's transponder chimed, signaling that they were in range of their target.

"We are landing?" Tarra asked, her voice eager.

She is anxious to be rid of this plane, Gorgon thought, even if it means trading it for a raft on the open sea. He said nothing and moved to the cabin's electronics rack to activate a modified Doppler radar unit. The size of the tanker 10,000 feet below them made it impossible to miss, even if the seaplane had inadvertently strayed miles from the shipping lanes. He fine-tuned the scan and relayed the ship's coordinates to his pilot. The aircraft banked awkwardly to intercept it, dipping steeply to port and spilling Tarra hard against the bulkhead. She cushioned the impact with her Uzi.

Gorgon frowned at her. "Put that away."

He picked up the microphone, flipped the low-powered radio to TRANSMIT and adjusted the directional antenna on the aircraft's underbelly. When he spoke his voice was cold and serious, his English flawless. "Mayday, mayday, mayday. Charleston, Charleston, this is Cessna four-seven-nine-two. We are 31 degrees north latitude and 82 degrees west longitude. Two on board. Engine fire. Oil pressure zero. Losing altitude. Attempting a water landing. Repeat. I will attempt a water landing. Mayday, mayday, mayday...."

The radio had only enough power to broadcast the Coast Guard distress call 30 miles in a single direction. But that was far enough. Tonight he needed only one unlucky tanker to intercept his transmission.

Central Virginia
Twenty-five thousand feet

Reluctantly, and with great effort, Marshall dragged himself from the thick fog of an exhausted sleep. He recalled with more than passing irony that they were returning home aboard the same C-141 Starlifter that had taken them to Sinope. Only tonight the huge aircraft bore little resemblance to a flying command center. There was no team left to command, no operation to monitor. The cargo compartment carried only a single quarantine trailer in which they all sat.

After Youngblood reached a neutral air base in Kingston, Jamaica, a crew of American army medical officers ushered them into a retrofitted isolation trailer, a cozy compartment with padded high-backed chairs. A surgeon stitched what was left of Marshall's right ear and gave him something to ease the throbbing.

Once aloft, Marshall and the others spent the afternoon debriefing on a four-hour conference call patched directly to General Medlock at the Pentagon. Finally, the team indulged in long-overdue sleep. Marshall conditioned himself to function capably for days without adequate sleep, as long as he could doze for at least 20 minutes twice a day. Marshall agreed with Charles Lindbergh that any sleep at all adds to wakened strength, whether it was minutes or even seconds. Julie wasn't as fortunate. Marshall knew she hadn't slept or ate since leaving Brazil, and that she couldn't wait to be back on United States soil. Restless and agitated, she had lost touch with her body's needs.

"We'll be landing in about 30 minutes, people," the pilot's serious-sounding voice informed them over the aircraft's intercom. "You'll find garments for each of you in the lockers. Please put them on at this time."

Marshall opened his eyes and found it difficult to focus them. He watched Julie open one of the lockers and sort through the suits. Her expression registered bewilderment. He pulled himself from his seat and, stretching his arms, joined her. These weren't civilian clothing, nor were they standard army gear. The locker was full of white coveralls and masks – biological isolation suits. Sizes for everybody. Someone wanted to make damn sure they didn't introduce any strange pathogens stateside.

"The army isn't taking any chances," Julie said. "They're treating us as though we have the plague."

Williams, reclining in his high-back seat, kept his eyes shut. "Come again?"

She held up a face mask. "They want us to wear these environment suits when we land. Just like the first astronauts coming back from the moon."

Williams' eyes fluttered open. "Gimme a break. I feel fine."

"We are okay, aren't we?" Marshall asked, exploring a locker.

Julie didn't respond. She seemed to be mulling over the situation, processing the data. Marshall didn't push her for an answer. They had all been exposed to a mutated strain of Saint Vitus. Did the Pentagon know something they didn't?

"Our bodies are fouled," Wynett offered from his seat in the corner of the trailer. "The abomination has made a home inside our bodies."

Youngblood, reclining next to him, stirred irritably and readjusted the cowboy hat over his eyes.

Williams snapped his seat upright. "You're full of shit, Wynett. I feel fucking fine."

Wynett smiled darkly, his face bathed in the trailer's eerie half-light. "No symptoms yet, sergeant. But the virus is exploring our bodies, adapting as it propagates. Your people are aware of this and will monitor us very closely. We are offering them a rare opportunity to study the effects of the organism on humans. They will learn much from our autopsies."

Marshall slammed the locker shut and instructed Julie, "Give Wynett another sedative so I don't have to hear his voice."

"He's already ingested the max," she said. "His mental state is extremely unstable. He'll go in and out of delusions. One moment he'll seem normal, the next..." She shrugged.

Marshall tried the door handle at the rear of the trailer. It wouldn't budge. He grabbed the intercom mic and said to the cockpit, "What's with this locked door, Jack?"

"Relax, Joe," the pilot's metallic voice blared over the trailer's intercom. "We'll be on the ground in a few minutes. Then you can ask the brass all the questions you want."

Marshall didn't like what he was hearing. The pilot was stalling until he could hand them over. But to whom, and for what purpose?

"Tell Medlock we're not putting on environment suits," Marshall said into the mic. "Jack, we're not infected. This bug works fast. We would all be dead by now if it was still dangerous." He appealed to Julie. "Tell him."

"No one's said you're infected, Joe," replied the pilot's disembodied voice. "Washington just wants to be careful."

Marshall was too tired to argue. He knew that once they were on the ground, all of them would be wearing those suits.

RESCUE

The U.S. Eastern Seaboard
Twenty-two miles off the coast of Charleston
S.C. 2213 hours

A man aboard a small watercraft in the night might have mistaken the 80,000 deadweight-ton crude-oil tanker *Lucy* for a moving mountain. The tanker was traveling from Venezuela with cargo for Universal Oil Company's refinery in Yorktown when Capt. Sergio Carlucci, master of *Lucy*, received a radio message from a distressed plane. The call alerted him that a single-engine aircraft with two persons on board had gone down in these waters. A routine call to the Coast Guard only added to the puzzle. The ship's radio officer couldn't send or receive any other transmission, nor could he locate the source of the problem. Captain Carlucci, a quiet, religious man with a strong sense of duty to aid his fellow man whenever possible, ordered his engines cut to a crawl and posted his nineteen-man crew as lookouts.

A pair of high-power binoculars to his eyes, Carlucci surveyed the dark shallow swells. He saw nothing but blackness. The night was calm, perhaps too much so. His usually confident manner tonight was restless and apprehensive, his hopes of finding someone alive out there diminishing with each passing minute. He stood by the rail, legs apart, and hid from the rest of his crew the deep lines of doubt etched around his fifty-nine-year-old eyes. Darkness had placed a black shroud over their chances of finding survivors. At least the weather was in their favor – clear skies with only light trade winds and calm seas.

Unfortunately, the moonless night reduced the already slim chance of finding a lifeboat or wreckage. A pity. Life was so precious. A few minutes more, Carlucci decided, and he would have no choice but to order the engines back to eighteen knots—

"I hear it!" shouted a port-side lookout, *Lucy's* first officer Francesco Amorosi. The young officer stood stiffly at the rail, listening.

Captain Carlucci appeared quickly at his side. Both men stood staring into the darkness, breathless, neither uttering a sound. Then Carlucci heard it too, a distant whistle piercing the night like a frantic bird cry.

A minute later Carlucci was on the bridge five stories above the deck turning the rudder hard over to port, initiating an emergency maneuver called the Williamson Turn, named after its developer, Comdr. John A. Williamson of the U.S. Naval Reserve. When the ship swung sixty degrees from its initial heading, Carlucci shifted to full rudder in the opposite direction until the tanker returned to its reverse heading. The length of two football fields, *Lucy* would have passed whoever was out there by some distance. The Williamson Turn allowed the vessel to reverse direction and head back along its original path, a critical procedure to locate a person who had fallen overboard. Carlucci handled the controls himself, refusing to let anyone else perform the precision turn. The former Italian naval officer completed the maneuver flawlessly, then ordered the engines cut to dead slow ahead-stop speed.

Carlucci, his gray-flecked hair glistening with sweat, raised the handheld radio to his lips but, like the vessel's ship-to-shore radio, he could neither receive nor send messages. Cursing, the captain retrieved a bullhorn from storage, stormed out onto the superstructure's "wing" – an outdoor deck off the bridge that offered him a view of the ship's fore and aft upper decks – and called down to first officer Amorosi in Italian: "I want all deck searchlights directed into the water. Divide the men and position them on each side of the ship. And pray to God while you hurry. We will not get a second chance."

The crew on *Lucy's* port side spotted something on the fringe of the searchlights – a rubber dinghy with two men on board wearing fluorescent orange life jackets, waving their arms. Carlucci piloted the vessel with its 600,000 barrels of crude oil to approach them, and made the maneuver look easy. In less than 20 minutes, the crew had passed a line with a safety strap to the dinghy and brought both men aboard. The rescue went smoothly, by the book. Once completed, the fully laden oil tanker swung slowly around in the Atlantic and resumed its original course and speed north toward the Chesapeake Bay.

Carlucci watched the rescue from the wheelhouse wing deck. He nodded agreeably when he saw that both men could walk without assistance. They must not have been in the water long. Good. Very good. "Bring them up to the bridge," he called down to Amorosi through the bullhorn. "I will have my steward standing by with hot coffee while the medic examines them."

Captain Carlucci was pleasantly surprised when the door to the wheelhouse opened and he discovered that one of the lives he had helped save tonight was a woman. Four of his officers gathered to greet the survivors, and there were handshakes all around. The two guests remained mostly cold and detached – understandable, considering what they had just been through, Carlucci thought. He could not deduce their nationality. He watched the woman while the ship's medic tried to examine her for injuries. She remained uncooperative and reacted with irritation to his probing. Carlucci found her dark, closely cropped hair and penetrating green eyes on an otherwise attractive face chilling.

Her companion, an intimidating man with dark features, appeared interested only in the bridge's instrumentation, which his probing eyes surveyed meticulously. While the steward served coffee to the guests on the bridge, Carlucci stood detached, regarding the two curiously. Both wore oilskin jackets beneath their life vests and carried shoulder bags as though they had expected a water landing. Neither appeared particularly fazed by the crash, an experience that would have stricken most men with nervous shock.

"I apologize for inconveniencing you, captain," Gorgon said in perfect, though accented English, a language all foreign officers on American petroleum company ships were required to speak.

"Nonsense," Carlucci said. "It is my duty." He said to his communications officer, "Are you able to use the radio?"

The officer shook his head. "Still no luck, sir."

"Then use the MariSat transceiver to contact the Coast Guard through the Houston office. Inform them of the rescue."

"Your radios will not work," Gorgon said. "A seaplane circling your ship at four miles is equipped with very powerful radio jamming gear. This same aircraft brought us here so we could intercept you." Gorgon withdrew a Ruger Mark 1 with suppressor from inside his jacket and pointed it at the captain's head. He drew back the hammer. "I am taking command of your vessel."

The radio officer reacted first. As he reached for the telephone receiver on the main console to alert the crew, a burst from Tarra's suppressed Uzi tore his heart in two before he could depress the call button.

The chief steward made a dash for the door, sidestepping Gorgon. The terrorist lashed out and grabbed the steward's head, breaking his neck with a swift, hard pull backward.

The two remaining officers on the bridge watched in horror as Tarra swung her weapon around and executed each of them with a brief, suppressed burst. Not a single round damaged the bridge's instruments. She watched with alluring eyes until the last of her victims stopped kicking and lay still in a widening pool of blood. Gorgon discharged a single round into the back of each's head to be certain. Tarra had effectively cleared *Lucy's* bridge sparing only Carlucci, whose kind, fatherly eyes, glazed in shock, stared helplessly and asked why.

He soon had his answer. Tarra peered into the hood of the ship's JRC radar display, set the range for 40 miles and adjusted the antenna beam for a narrow eastern scan. She moved the cursor over one of the phosphorescent signatures in the southwest quadrant and touched the identification button. The smaller vessel's transponder affirmed its identity.

"I have them," she announced. "Bearing one-eight-seven. Range, twenty-six kilometers. They are on a crossing course on our starboard."

Gorgon noted the ship's compass heading and instructed Carlucci, "You will alter your course seven degrees to starboard to intercept that vessel."

When the captain did not move, Tarra said, "I will do it."

"*No!*" Gorgon's deep voice reverberated off the bridge's stark walls like a gun blast. He riveted his steel eyes on Carlucci. "You will do it."

Carlucci could hardly form the words. "Put away your weapons. This ship carries a highly volatile cargo. A catastrophe will benefit no one."

"I am well aware of what you carry," Gorgon said. "Cooperate, and I will need no weapon. Cross me, and I will destroy your hundred-million-dollar ship and its cargo, and I will kill your unimpressive crew."

"For God's sake, why? Who are you? What do you want?"

"You need only know," Gorgon said, "that I am the man who has taken your ship. And I will have your full cooperation as well."

QUARANTINE

Fort Detrick
Saturday, 2243 hours

Julie, stuffed into a pair of bulky environmental overalls, slid next to Marshall on the wraparound sofa as the quarantine trailer eased back into the loading dock of one of Fort Detrick's bunker-like buildings. She liked the way he felt so close to her – strong and full of confidence – even if she had to feel him through a thick layer of nonporous material.

Marshall didn't notice her. His eyes were fixed on his left hand, suddenly prone to spastic fits of trembling, as though the limb had a mind of its own. The fingertips of his right hand were numb most of the time and his mouth felt insatiably dry. He tried to put it out of his mind and focus on where they were going. He thought it strange that no one had discussed the eventual destination of the survivors of Alpha. Their handling was quick and methodical, like a shipment of machine parts.

Marshall moved to the narrow window at the rear of the trailer, their only outside view. He didn't like what he saw. The faceless structure looked disturbingly like a prison. An armed contingent of soldiers oversaw their arrival under a forest of intense carbon-vapor lamps mounted on high stands. Technicians in white coats draped a polyurethane fabric sheet over the trailer. *They don't even want us breathing the air,* Marshall thought.

Marshall adjusted the black bandana Julie provided to cover the bandages over the right side of his head. He wore it like a headband. "What is this place?"

Julie joined him at the window. "The Slammer."

"Come again?"

"They're putting us in the army's biological receiving lab, 83,000 square feet devoted to studying bacterial pathology. Casualties of a biological war are supposed to be brought here for observation and quarantine."

"You know a great deal about this facility, young lady," Wynett said, his alert eyes watching her closely.

Julie ignored him and explained to the others: "I spent two days of my internship here participating in a crisis exercise. I was role-playing a patient."

"Welcome to the real world," Youngblood snorted, squeezing next to Julie for a glimpse out the narrow window. The pilot wasn't interested in the building. Marshall saw him staring at the Bell-Ranger helicopter sitting under the spotlights on Detrick's helipad. It had the military markings of a VIP aircraft, the sort usually equipped with advanced telecommunications equipment intended for a mobile command vehicle.

"Nice," Youngblood said. His eyes remained fixed on the chopper until it disappeared from his view.

Williams squeezed next to him for a look. "Quarantine, my ass. We're fucking prisoners."

"You are correct, sergeant," Wynett said, adjusting the strap of his face shield before putting it on. He looked like a fat scuba diver in his environment suit. "When you surrendered your weapons and stepped into this compartment, you ceased to be a soldier. Your war is over. Now you are a lab specimen."

Williams appealed to the major. "Say the word and I'll kick a hole right through this glass. We'll be out of here in thirty seconds."

"Spare us your heroics, sergeant," Wynett said, adjusting the mask over his face. "Violate the integrity of this trailer and you will risk spreading a plague that could very well ravage your country."

Williams turned to the old man and barked, "Since when did you care about spreading—"

"That's enough," Marshall snapped. "For now we do exactly as we're told." But he could well understand the others' claustrophobic frustration. He too loathed confinement of any kind, especially hospitals. But what other choice did they have?

The trailer gave a sudden jerk as it came in contact with the receiving dock, and there followed the sound of a heavy crash door grinding shut behind them, sealing them inside the fortress-like quarantine building.

"Please exit the vehicle and proceed into the building," a metallic female voice blared with enough volume to penetrate the trailer's aluminum skin. "Do not remove any personal possessions from the trailer. Do not attempt to breach the quarantine area."

Julie draped the instrumentation package over her shoulder. "This goes where I go. Technically, it's not personal." She slid on her face mask.

Marshall likewise snapped the mask over his solid features before pulling back the exit handle. The door opened easily, and he felt a distinct draft of air flow past him.

"Negative pressure to prevent stray organisms from escaping," Julie noted, her voice muffled by the face shield.

"I'll sleep better tonight knowing that." Marshall waved them forward.

The group proceeded single file onto the receiving dock. Their respirators concealed the smell of the dock's heavy oils, which sat in smeared puddles over the cracked concrete floor. They filed through a lone door into a receiving room outfitted with a tiny refrigerator and a table, token hospitality for the center's arriving guests.

The door closed automatically behind them. They could hear a high-pressure shower flooding the loading area, rinsing the trailer and their footprints with industrial-strength disinfectant and bleach. A second door opened into the complex.

"You are now in quarantine," the female voice informed them through the ubiquitous intercom system. "Please leave your suits in this room and proceed inside."

Williams yanked off his mask with a protesting snap. "Thank you."

The others peeled off their environment suits and tossed them unceremoniously in a pile in front of the refrigerator. Wynett chose to keep his suit and mask on. Julie led the way into the complex's L-shaped corridor, a sterile place with white walls and fluorescent lighting. Somewhere far off a telephone rang. She proceeded down the longer of the two hallways, with the others following. After what she'd been through in Brazil, Julie seemed more comfortable, more confident, back in her scientific environment, Marshall noted.

The facility resembled a clinic with its stark, sterile walls. A pervasive smell of antiseptics and closed doors with clipboard holders hanging outside completed the picture. Marshall thought he smelled alcohol, until he realized that the air itself was sanitized, the environment controlled down to the last drop of moisture and air pressure. He hated hospitals.

Julie opened one of the hallway's doors, passed inside and snapped on the switch, filling the room with harsh fluorescent light. She set her instrumentation case on a surgical table, then opened one of the room's many cabinets and surveyed the well-stocked medical supplies.

She returned to the hallway just as Williams emerged from the room next door. "There's a dentist's chair in here," the sergeant said.

"I think this is a goddamn CAT-scanning unit," Youngblood said, closing another door behind him.

"It's a magnetic resonator," Julie corrected him, then gestured to the doorways down the hallway. "The other rooms are biochemical labs, and there's also an X-ray area."

"Where's the staff of doctors and nurses?" Marshall asked.

"There aren't any," she said. "This center is completely isolated from the biosphere. There's no need for anybody to risk coming down here with us, even wearing an environment suit. All examinations are done remotely. There are fifteen private quarters in here, a kitchen, lounge, dining room, laundry, even a gym."

Farther down the corridor, a telephone began ringing again. Marshall cocked his head at Williams. "Check that out."

Williams nodded and moved briskly down the hallway.

The others continued their tour. "So how long do we have to stay in here?" Marshall asked.

"At least twenty-four days," Julie said.

"Say what?"

"Twenty-four days is the incubation period for most viruses. We could be here longer. Unfortunately, St. Vitus is a complete mystery. Some tests can take months."

"You mean the rest of our lives," he spat, and then wondered how long that might be.

"Joe, remember what we're dealing with," Julie said.

"I know ... I know," Marshall said. "I'm tired and frustrated." He shook his head. "I always thought my final battle would be against al Qaeda – not microbes. This creature of yours stays locked up, even if it means burying us in here with it."

Wynett removed his mask and ran a hand through his tousled mane of white hair. "While you people contemplate your bleak fates, will someone please direct me to a shower. I wish to turn in."

"Joe, the phone's for you," Williams called down the hallway. "It's General Medlock. And he doesn't sound happy."

"He never sounds happy." Marshall thrust a finger at Wynett. "Consider yourself my prisoner. You don't eat, you don't sleep, you don't take a crap without asking my permission first. You got that?"

Wynett responded with a throaty chuckle and headed down the corridor.

Marshall said to Julie, "See if you can get some of this equipment up and running. I want blood tests started tonight so we know what we're dealing with."

"Joe," Williams hollered, "answer the goddamn phone."

Marshall stormed down the hallway to find the telephone.

While the others ventured off to find quarters, Julie slipped into the corridor's last room – her favorite lab. The room was filled with refrigerator-size equipment covered with plastic dust covers. She found the light switch and grinned with satisfaction when the overhead lights blinked on.

She pulled the plastic cover off a Sun workstation, powered it on and rolled a chair in front of its monitor. Despite the center's seventy-four-degree ambient temperature, she felt chilly. She longed for her favorite mug filled with flavored coffee and cream. Maybe she could persuade Marshall to brew some for her while she established a communications hookup with her Stanford adviser. She put the machine in a terminal emulation mode and logged on to Stanford's network. *Just like home.*

She sent a quick message to her adviser, Dr. Nancy Shaw: U THERE?

Julie was surprised when a message beeped back almost immediately: I HEARD YOU WERE BACK IN TOWN. WHAT'S UP?

Julie looked at her watch and frowned. She typed: YOU'RE AT THE OFFICE LATE.

I DON'T SLEEP MUCH THESE DAYS. GENERAL MEDLOCK SAID YOU WERE COMING IN, AND I KNEW YOU WOULD LOG ON AND CHECK YOUR MAIL. NEED ANYTHING?

I MIGHT AFTER I GET SETTLED. ANYTHING GOING ON?

I LEFT A FEW NOTES IN YOUR E-MAIL IN-BASKET. NOTHING URGENT.

THANKS. I'LL LOOK AT THEM TOMORROW.

I'LL BE HERE FOR A WHILE, IF YOU WANT TO CHAT.

Julie smiled and typed, THANKS. THERE'S A GREAT DEAL I'D LIKE TO TALK ABOUT. BUT NOT RIGHT NOW. TOMORROW. SEE YA....

Julie logged off the network and requested Detrick's mainframe environment.

PASSWORD?

She typed APRIL to log on to the army's mainframe and requested access to the lab's programs.

*****RESTRICTED ACCESS DENIED*****
*****RESTRICTED ACCESS DENIED*****
*****RESTRICTED ACCESS DENIED*****

"Oh, you bastards." Someone anticipated she would want to look at those files and wasn't about to oblige her curiosity.

Her fingers performed a well-choreographed dance over the keyboard as she disassembled the master user ID file into its native code. The army's security measures were competent, but not nearly clever enough to keep her from simply rewriting the code so the program would authorize her password. She had yet to find a computer she couldn't "crack route" to the deepest level of the computer's operating system. Detrick's archaic computing network was no exception, and once she cracked into the system's server, she would have the access permissions of the center's highest-ranking officer.

She reassembled the machine language, uploaded it and repeated her request.

RESTRICTED ACCESS. ENTER USED ID

She typed in ZJCM01.

PASSWORD?

She again entered APRIL.

The computer hardly blinked as it checked her authorization, found nothing wrong with it, then obediently displayed a list of options. She highlighted the first item on the menu: FORT DETRICK'S BIOLOGICAL RECEIVING LAB.

The computer complied, showing her the Slammer's layout from its electronic security system all the way down to the last penny nail. Julie grinned. *Let's see what else we can do.*

MASTER

Lucy
U.S. Eastern Seaboard off Charleston, S.C.

Lucy's first officer Francesco Amorosi didn't like the way Carlucci summoned him to the bridge. The captain's intercom message, brief and unbecomingly curt, smacked of trouble. Had he fucked up? Hardly. The rescue had gone superbly well under his direction, and he already had visions of a company commendation and his picture on the employee website. And maybe a bonus, too. Nothing less for a hero. Still, something about the captain's summons bothered him. It wasn't like Carlucci to get a bug up his ass and bark orders at his men like a boot-camp sergeant, especially after saving lives. He should be sharing the crew's jubilation. What was his problem?

Amorosi entered the wheelhouse and found the main lights switched off, forcing him to grope about in the glow of the ship's multicolored instrumentation. As he reached for the main light switch, something cold and hard touched the back of his neck, something made of steel. Startled, he raised his arms in an gesture of capitulation. The twenty-seven-year-old seaman didn't need much imagination to visualize someone with a gun standing behind him, just a finger-jerk away from blowing off his head. What was going on? Robberies, though common while anchored off of Africa, were rare in these waters. He knew better than to resist. He had no intention of giving his life to protect someone else's cargo.

"Are you First Officer Francesco Amorosi?" asked a deep, sonorous voice behind him.

Amorosi kept his gazed fixed forward. As his eyes adjusted to the dimness he saw another figure standing between two of the ship's radar consoles. Captain Carlucci. The poor man didn't look well. Now Amorosi understood the captain's curt radio message – a warning made under duress. His eyes begged the captain for an explanation, a reassuring signal that all would be well. But Carlucci's eyes remained downcast, helpless. The man appeared deeply ashamed by what was happening to his ship and crew. Amorosi's hands began shaking.

"Are you Amorosi?" the deep voice hissed, its owner's lips close to the young mate's ear. "I will not ask you again."

The young officer drew in his breath sharply and screwed shut his eyes, expecting the worst. He nodded.

"Good," Gorgon said.

Amorosi winced when the cold metal jabbed the back of his neck and pushed him forward. He walked several paces between the consoles, his legs moving automatically, the gun barrel boring into his neck. Spent shells on the floor felt like rocks under his feet. The gunman ordered both men out onto the bridge's port wing deck.

The air was cold and windy, the night black. Amorosi, in the lead, saw several figures huddled against the chest-high metal wall. He could smell a peculiar stench in the chilly night air, a smell that reminded him of sawdust. Some primordial instinct told him that this was the smell of death. He heard a woman's voice, a throaty moan combined with long, heavy breaths, as though she were enjoying some deep satisfaction. His mind couldn't comprehend the contradiction of sight and sound and smell.

A woman rose from the shadows, stepped into the wheel-house glow and directed a pair of haunting green eyes at Amorosi. Despite the dimness, he recognized the woman from the sea rescue, now standing naked to the waist, rubbing bloodsoaked fingertips over her ample bosom.

"He is yours," Gorgon said to her.

Tarra smiled in appreciation and took Amorosi's trembling hand into hers. Her touch felt wet, warm, soft, reassuring. His breathing eased. He didn't want her to feel the convulsive fear that had tied his bowels into knots. She led him into the shadows at the end of the deck that swallowed them, and Captain Carlucci heard a sucking sound that suggested deep, lustful kissing. What was it? Suddenly, Amorosi let out a shriek – a hideous sound.

Carlucci cursed in his native Italian and forced himself to move to help the young man, but Gorgon launched a huge hand, blocking his way.

"Why do this?" the captain implored.

Gorgon put a finger to his lips, and they both listened to the young mate's anguished whimpering. Amorosi's tortured cries grew muffled as though he were being roughly gagged. And then came a silence, far more unsettling than any shriek.

Carlucci shivered as Gorgon put a bearlike paw on his shoulder and led him forward. The captain looked past the silent figures sitting with their backs against the wall. In the corner sat Tarra, rubbing her hands seductively over Amorosi's naked chest. Gorgon ordered her away, then pressed a flashlight into Carlucci's hands.

"See what she has done," Gorgon said, gesturing to the line of motionless figures.

Carlucci began shivering uncontrollably. He held no illusions that he too would sit here among these corpses if he didn't do exactly as the beast ordered. Cursing his lack of courage, he knelt before the figures and switched on the flashlight. He couldn't keep the beam still. He probed each face with the light and recognized his steward, radio officer, ship's medic and chief engineer. All of them were dead, of course. Carlucci crawled on hands and knees for a closer look at the fifth man. At first he didn't recognize him. Amorosi's blood-soaked cheeks were bloated as though he had been forced to eat something he had violently resisted. A strange appendage still protruded from his mouth.

"My ... God ..."

Amorosi's lifeless eyes stared vacantly back at the captain in solemn resignation, warning him that any resistance simply wasn't worth risking a similar fate. Carlucci bowed his head, deeply ashamed. Forgive me, my son, for letting you die at the hands of these barbarians. Would he vomit or pass out? He feared he would do both, and in no particular order.

"I am showing you this for a reason," Gorgon said. "Disobey my instructions, and the rest of your crew will sit here among them."

Carlucci rose unsteadily to his feet and, fighting the urge to retch, turned away from his tortured group of comrades, his face a white plaster. "Why ... murder him ... and torture him?"

Tarra cocked her head questioningly. "Torture? Your mate shared with me an experience any man would give his life to enjoy."

Carlucci directed his rage-filled eyes at the woman. "For the love of God, you fed him his own testicles."

She ran her tongue over her lips. "He would tell you how much he enjoyed it ... if he could still talk." She giggled hideously.

Carlucci threw up all over himself. Half-digested beans dripped down the front of his shirt and smelled of vomit. He collapsed onto both knees until the contents of his stomach had emptied onto the rubber mat between his legs. He noticed another odor – he had urinated in his pants.

A large hand rested solidly on his shoulder. "Tarra has a peculiar lust for men," Gorgon said, his voice oddly apologetic. "At the age of eight years, four men raped her and left her for dead in the desert. The incident aroused her hunger for coitus – she obsesses on it as few women do – and she satisfies her contempt for men in this perverse way. Never again will she be used by a man. Do not let her see your love for this ship or it will anger her. She is very jealous."

Carlucci looked at him over his shoulder, unable to respond.

"Meanwhile, you still are *Lucy's* captain," Gorgon said. "I need a man sufficiently skilled to handle this vessel. Only her true master will know how this ship behaves under all circumstances. You will keep normal radio contact with the owners of this vessel and proceed without incident to your destination in Yorktown. Do exactly as I say and you will live and prosper from our acquaintance. Disobey me, and I will let her kill you – in her own way. Do we have an agreement?"

A wave of total helplessness washed over Carlucci. His fear of these monsters crippled him more than anything in his life. "But you killed my officers ... my first mate...."

"Tarra will be your first mate, and I will provide you with a new crew. In exactly 20 minutes I want you to stop all engines and stand by. Will you carry out those simple instructions for me, captain?"

Carlucci, shivering spasmodically, nodded.

"Good. Captain Sergio Carlucci, you will now take charge of the bridge."

An hour after Gorgon and Tarra had come aboard, only Captain Carlucci knew that *Lucy* had been hijacked. If the remaining crew of sixteen suspected anything, none came forward with their suspicions.

On Gorgon's command, Carlucci stopped all engines and ran out the cargo boom.

Carlucci dismissed the barrage of inevitable questions from the ship's officer of the deck that followed. And then they waited. A fifty-foot tramp steamer slipped alongside in the moonless night and offloaded three truck-size pallets. Seventeen minutes later, *Lucy* resumed her original heading and speed, with fifteen of Gorgon's soldiers aboard and their very special cargo.

MERCENARIES

Quarantine

Marshall slipped inside a closet-size room off the quarantine center's recreation area and sat at a tiny desk with a reading lamp and an archaic push-button telephone. The door closed with a solid click behind him, causing a pressure change in his ears. The room was a soundproof anechoic chamber.

Marshall picked up the phone's receiver and said, "What the hell's going on, sir?"

He heard only the low static of a poor connection, as though Medlock had hung up on him. Finally the general's voice, chillingly terse, said, "Know one thing, mister: you don't talk to me like I'm one of your goddamn grunts."

Marshall pictured Medlock's vulture face and clenched beak on the other end ready to chomp off his head in a single bite. The major breathed a sigh of apology. "Sir, it's been a bad week. And it isn't helping matters that you have us locked up with a raving psychotic. Williams and I need to be at Fort Bragg."

"I can't allow that, major," Medlock said, tempering his tone only slightly. "You'll stay in quarantine for at least three weeks. And sorry about the arrangements. Under the circumstances it's not possible to stow Wynett anyplace else. Besides, we need your help interrogating him."

"Sir, what about Gorgon? As I explained this afternoon, I believe he's planning an assault on the U.S. mainland with at least five tanks of the organism—"

"Slow down, Joe. It's being handled."

"Handled? What's being handled? Who's handling what?"

"We're flying a special op team to our staging area at Oceana."

"Sir, let me mobilize Team 6."

"I must be speaking Arabic," Medlock grunted. "Didn't I make myself clear about your quarantine?"

"Put Major Warren in charge of the team. He knows the drill. I can feed him intelligence—"

"Negative. The situation is being handled."

Marshall could barely contain his anger. "Sir, don't write us off. Hell, nobody's even examined us yet. I owe Colonel Martinelli—"

"You're taking this way too personally, mister. I'm sorry for the loss of the colonel. But be thankful you're alive, for chrissake. Meanwhile, you're still part of Alpha. You can help me a great deal by getting Wynett to talk. I need every goddamn piece of information you can get from him."

"General, he's extremely unreliable. One minute he's complete rational—"

He heard a click, and then another voice came on the line. "Major, this is Commander Frank Haake of the State Department. I need to ask you some very specific questions about Operation Containment. Just give me five seconds to make sure this machine is recording everything."

Marshall sank back wearily in his cheap fabric chair. The absolute silence inside the soundproof room was unsettling. He couldn't remember ever feeling so powerless.

Lucy

Gorgon's fifteen soldiers, their faces blackened, swept through *Lucy* with expedient precision, leaving a trail of corpses in their wake. Four mercenary soldiers split off from the main assault group and descended deep into the bowels of the tanker. With paramilitary shotguns braced in front of them, they marched methodically through the engine room, control room, boiler room and lower pump room. They checked behind every pipe and conduit large enough to conceal a man. Their weapons and cartridges were carefully chosen to protect the machinery and pipes from damage.

Lucy's crew never had a chance to offer even token resistance. Seaman Dinelli, the ship's chief engineer, reacted instinctively to the sight of the death squad storming into his boiler area. The Italian officer's fist closed around the only weapon he could find – an eleven-pound steel wrench. An ear-splitting blast from a shotgun tore off his wrench-toting arm at the elbow, while a second blast blew the pale look of shock from his face ... and every other feature.

One of Dinelli's maintenance men, a young Filipino, grabbed the intercom mic, opened a channel to the bridge and shouted in poor English, "Captain, there are guns ... men in the boiler—" A blast from a shotgun tore into the back of his head.

The three remaining crewmen in the engine room, their hands raised in unmistakable gestures of surrender, stared helplessly at the row of shotgun barrels pointed at them. A series of rapid blasts transformed them into a heap of butchered corpses. Blood drizzled like rain through the grated catwalks beneath them.

The assault, quick and methodical, was far easier than Gorgon's elaborate scheme called for. Only one of Carlucci's crewmen remained alive. But not by coincidence. The lone survivor – a young crewman named Palombini – was led outside to the ship's upper deck, where he sat under close guard in the chilled night air. Gorgon walked out to meet him. Tarra strolled at his side, as did a slumped Captain Carlucci, his eyes downcast.

Gorgon towered over the young crewman who had lost four fingers on his right hand in the brief battle to take the ship. Palombini cradled his bloodied hand in his lap, his face red from shock.

Gorgon said to him in English, "Your injuries are unfortunate for a man so young. Tell me how much you loathe me for what I have done to you."

Palombini sat huddled on deck, trembling, his pleading eyes darting to his captain.

"He is a good man with a family," Carlucci said. "He operates the ship's cargo pumps, a job very important to us."

Gorgon shook his head. "I do not need him. I brought him here so that you can watch the death of your last crewman."

"For the love of God—"

Gorgon signaled Tarra with a jerk of his head. She drove the barrel of her Uzi into the young crewman's forehead and squeezed off a single round. Palombini let out an animal-like yelp and spilled backward, blood spouting from both his mutilated hand and his head wound. Tarra knelt down and kissed his still trembling lips.

Carlucci collapsed onto his knees and wept openly, his fists clenched in frustration and despair. "Dear God, tell me what to do? *What should I do?*"

Gorgon towered over him, a smirk stretching his stark features. "I am your god now. From this moment, you will gaze at my face with absolute reverence."

INTERROGATION

Quarantine 2255 hours

Julie didn't hear Youngblood slip into the room behind her, but she spotted his reflection on the computer screen as he approached. He gently placed his strong hands on her shoulders and began massaging the muscles at the base of her neck with deep, sensual movements. His probing fingertips felt very good, but his closeness made her uncomfortable. When she pulled away, he spun the chair around and squatted in front of her. Julie's eyes widened when he leaned forward and planted a perfect kiss on her lips.

"I'm sorry," Youngblood drawled, taking her hands into his. "That wasn't planned. Ever since I met you I've wanted to do that. God, you're beautiful ... and smart, very smart."

Julie was speechless. Not that she didn't find Youngblood attractive. She just couldn't picture them together. No, that wasn't it, was it? She couldn't picture herself with any man, especially a good-looking one she had to work with. Relationships always got in the way of her work. The truth was she didn't know how to respond to Youngblood's affections, or anyone else's for that matter. Besides, this wasn't the time or place for romance. *But there you go rationalizing again.*

"Julie," Youngblood said, his tone gentle, "what I'm trying to say is that when we get out of here I'd like to take you out to dinner, or to a show, or ... hell, anywhere you like. Just name it. But if you're involved with someone else ... or just don't want to

. . ." His voice trailed off and he gave her a sad, though thoroughly charming smile.

"Is there a problem?" Marshall's curt voice boomed from the doorway.

Julie and Youngblood whipped around with a start. Something was wrong – Julie could see the tension lines on Marshall's face. For a hopeful instant she thought it might be jealousy.

"I want everyone in the lounge," Marshall said. When neither of them moved, he added, "*Now.*"

Youngblood rose stiffly from his squat in front of Julie. "Jesus, major, can't it wait till morning? It's been a long day and we're all spent. Maybe after a good night's sleep—"

"Get your ass to the lounge, mister," Marshall said, his voice as frigid as Arctic rock.

"Yes, sir," Youngblood snapped.

Julie grinned. Yes, perhaps he was jealous. Interesting.

"And as for you," Marshall said, riveting a hard military stare at her, "I want you to draw blood samples from everyone and find a way to test them. By morning I want to see the results."

"Hey ... I'm a civilian..."

But Marshall was gone, the sound of his boots echoing heavily down the corridor, sending a not-too-subtle warning for everybody to hustle their asses.

Everyone gathered in the center's lounge, a congenial study area with several overstuffed sofas and deep chairs, a wet bar and two circular tables suited for meals or card games. The room could have passed for a lounge in a university student union.

Marshall directed Julie to one of the tables, where she laid out a medical pouch containing a syringe kit and blood specimen vials.

"Oh, Jesus," Youngblood said when he saw the needles. "I hope you've done this before."

"Only once." She replied with professional detachment while attaching an eighteen-gauge needle to the first syringe. "On a hamster. And I'm sorry to say it died in the process."

"I need to build up some iron in my blood." Youngblood stooped before a knee-high refrigerator behind the wet bar and opened it. "Helloooo. Can I interest anybody in a cold beer? I also have blush and white wine ... and diet Cokes."

"A blush sounds perfect," Julie said.

"You got it," Youngblood said, grabbing a chilled zinfandel.

Wynett sank comfortably into an overstuffed chair that meant to swallow him and said to the chopper pilot, "What is the chance of securing a Scotch and water?"

"For you, none." Youngblood opened the wet bar's lower cabinet and inspected a row of hard liquor. "But someone did think of everything."

"Negative on the liquor," Marshall said. "Alcohol is off limits."

"I'll have a Coke, hotshot," Williams said.

"Major," Wynett said, "surely you are not pretending to be on duty? There is a time to make war and a time to recharge. I believe it is now time to indulge our vices."

Marshall ignored him. "The Army's gone to a lot of trouble to make this prison comfortable for us. Maybe too comfortable. Forget booze. We're not sacrificing our edge over a couple of beers."

"What edge?" Youngblood snorted.

"People, let's just get this over with so I can turn in," Julie said. "Who's first?" She waved a syringe at Youngblood. "You flyboy?"

In bold macho fashion, Youngblood seat himself at her table and rolled up his sleeve. "Hurt me, baby."

"Make a fist," Julie instructed.

Youngblood created an impressive muscle for her. She wrapped a rubber tourniquet around his arm above the elbow and searched for a suitable vein to tap. Two minutes later she had three vials full of his blood, which she labeled and secured in the carrying case.

"Who's next?"

Again nobody volunteered, so Marshall volunteered Williams. When the gunnery sergeant made no effort to move from his chair, Julie brought her syringe and tourniquet to him.

Youngblood, flexing and unflexing his needle-pricked arm, said to Marshall, "So what did Medlock have to say?"

Marshall settled his weight against a table and folded his arms over his chest. "General Medlock isn't going to let us out of here for at least several weeks. Meanwhile he's going after Gorgon with a special ops team, though he won't say how or when. I want to convince Medlock there's nothing wrong with us. The sooner we get a clean bill of health, the sooner we get out of here."

"Spare us your military bravado, major," Wynett scoffed. "You are in denial. You are not going anywhere. Your war is over. Now please. I wish to return to my quarters, preferably with a bottle of Seagram's and a cache of ice. I would very much like to fall into a deep sleep with both those items under my arms."

Marshall dragged a chair from beneath the table, spun it around in front of the old man and sat astride it. "The Joint Chiefs need to know Gorgon's plans for those tanks you brewed up. And you're going to tell them everything."

"Major, I don't see the point belaboring—"

Marshall lunged forward, spilling his chair, and grabbed the front of Wynett's shirt into his fists, popping two buttons. His heart raced with rage. Everyone looked mutely at him.

"Listen to me, you *fuck*," Marshall hissed, his anger barely in check. "I've had a very bad week, thanks to you."

Wynett remained arrogantly composed. "You still don't understand, do you, major?"

"Understand what?"

"Gorgon owes me ten million American dollars."

Marshall's grip on him tightened and his teeth clenched. "Don't give me your insanity bullshit."

"I fully intend to secure payment from him or reclaim my merchandise. I don't want your muddled interference."

Marshall suddenly saw Wynett as he truly was: a madman. He released his shirt.

"I am a realist, major," Wynett said, "not a fool driven by misplaced notions of honor, God and patriotic duty. I have no intentions of writing Mr. Gorgon from my books. I cannot stay in business if I give away what I labor to produce."

"You're not going getting a nickel out of anyone."

"I disagree, major. Your superiors will provide whatever I request. They will even take me to Gorgon under military escort, if I decide that will serve my interests. I am deliberating my options."

"Your only options will be a firing squad or a noose," Marshall said.

"There will be no charges filed against me. Not now. Not ever. Considering what I know and the short time left before Gorgon reaches your shores, your superiors will need to act very quickly. I will tell them Gorgon's plans for a price: twenty million American dollars and no charges against me. The deal is nonnegotiable."

Marshall, glaring at the old man, said nothing. It took all his military training to resist the urge to hammer the old man to a pulp.

Julie knelt next to Wynett's chair with her syringe kit. "Roll up your sleeve."

Wynett ignored her and kept his eyes locked on the major's. Julie helped herself to his arm and wrapped the rubber tourniquet above his elbow. Wynett's eyes fluttered briefly when she inserted the needle into his vein. Three minutes later Julie retreated to the table with his blood specimen and sat watching Wynett closely. Almost immediately he began to perspire as though the climate-controlled room had suddenly become too warm for him.

"I believe you are next, major," Wynett said. "Though I doubt Miss Julie will draw anything but idiocy from those veins of yours...."

The color drained noticeably from Wynett face. He placed a hand over the spot where Julie had pricked as though it pained him. He stared at her, his fingers clutching his forearm. When he spoke his words sounded slightly slurred. "What have you given me, Miss Julie?"

Marshall glanced questioningly at her.

"A sedative," she said. "If you want specifics, it's scopolamine."

Wynett huffed, his eyes assuming an inward look. "My dear Julie, I am disappointed. I would have preferred datura stramonium, a far more effective sedative and much more interesting to the patient, though I have seen it used only by a remote tribe in Brazil. Take my word ... it is worth the trouble to obtain it."

"Sorry, but scopolamine is all I had. It's a proven method of loosening tongues."

"You mean making the subject ramble. You'll have to ... do ... better...."

Wynett's eyes rolled back into his head and his jaw slackened. He appeared deathly ill, and for a moment Marshall feared he was in cardiac arrest. "Is he okay?"

"I think so," she said. "He may pass out."

"How long?"

"I think I gave him too much. He can go under at any moment. He'll fight you. And you'll have no way of knowing if his information is accurate."

"Next time, check with me before you try anything crazy." Marshall, willing to take anything right now, expecting nothing, knelt before Wynett's chair. He ran his fingers through his waves of hair. His fingers were wet from sweating. "Okay, Wynett. Tell me all about it."

Wynett rolled his head in euphoric rhythm. "You may have stumbled onto something, Miss Julie, though it is not as pleasant as Scotch." Then he frowned. "Bastard ... stole my merchandise...."

Williams squatted next to Marshall and whispered, "He's hung up on this deal with Gorgon. Go with it."

Marshall looked hard at the old man. "What will he do with your merchandise?"

"Bastard ... stole it from me..."

"Yes, yes. Is your merchandise worth the price?"

Wynett's eyes suddenly opened, and he appeared alert. "Oh, yes. I gave him quality merchandise."

"How much does he have?"

Wynett smirked. "Five."

"Five? Five tanks?"

"Yes. Twenty-five liters."

"Twenty-five liters of Saint Vitus?"

"Yes."

"How will he deploy it?"

Wynett's eyes drifted shut and he appeared troubled. "Several ways ... missiles..."

"Missiles? He has Scud missiles?"

Wynett shook his head. "No, sir. Even the improved Scud-D surface-to-surface launcher could not adequately deploy a viral warhead...."

"What then?"

"Procyon computer-guided, independently targeted warheads..."

"Jesus. How did he get his hands on those?"

Wynett smiled. "From me."

Julie looked questioningly at Marshall and mouthed 'What's a Procyon?'

Marshall shook his head. "Later."

"First he must harness the creature," Wynett said. "Operation Harness ..."

"Tell me about Operation Harness," Marshall probed.

"Distribution ... law of supply and demand ... addiction ... you are addicted to it and he knows it."

"Addicted?" Marshall looked at Julie for an answer. She shrugged. "Are you saying the virus is addictive?" He asked anyway, realizing how stupid his question sounded.

Wynett slurred, "You will gladly welcome him inside your country because you are addicted...."

"You're not making any sense."

"Trojan Horse ... you will welcome him and the creature inside ... and then he will be free to strike ..." Wynett's head began rolling from side to side and his speech became notably more slurred. "Sweet crude ... sweet crude ... sweet crude ..."

"Sweet crude? Do you mean high-quality oil?"

"No one will stop him ... you will welcome him inside ... you are addicted to it ... you need it ... addicts, all of you."

"Wynett—"

"So secret ... floating city ... floating bomb ... no one can touch him ... too dangerous...."

Marshall drilled him with an icy stare. "I need to know where Gorgon is taking the virus."

Wynett exhaled silly staccatos of laughter. "Pay me first...."

"Negative."

"... grand lady ... she sits in the heavens ... adorned with jewels ... on a bloody river..." Wynett laughed deliciously, seemingly taunting the major's discomfiture.

Marshall appealed to Julie. "What's he babbling about?"

"He's fighting you."

"I can see that."

"He wrote it for his son ... inspired by the child's drawing ..." Wynett's head rolled forward onto his chest, where it remained, unmoving. He was out cold.

Marshall rose stiffly to his feet. The interrogation was over. He felt suddenly tired. *Who wrote what for his son?* "Anyone have a clue what he's talking about?"

"Could be babble," Julie offered, "or maybe he's talking in code."

Marshall, succumbing to his exhaustion, shook his head. With Wynett out, he knew there was nothing more he could do. Besides, they were all tired. And he needed time to sort out the old man's rambling. He turned to Julie. "What about the blood analysis? How long before you know what we're dealing with?"

"I'll put the specimens in the pathology lab's PCR unit and let it run through the night. We should know something by morning."

Marshall nodded.

"There is one unfinished piece of business before I can get started," she said.

"Name it."

She held up a fresh syringe. "I need your blood."

LONELY HEARTS

Fort Detrick

General Medlock pushed back from the conference table and considered everything he and his task force had just listened to on the table's 360-degree speaker. The general's solid military demeanor cracked long enough to allow a smile. He felt almost giddy.

Wynett's interrogation had gone surprisingly well ... better, in fact, than he had dared to hope. The fidelity of the quarantine center's hidden microphones surprised even him, leaving the bizarre impression that he had been sitting with the group two floors below. Putting Wynett in quarantine with Marshall was a masterstroke. The general stood, stretched the cramps from his legs and moved to a rack of audio gear at the opposite end of the conference room. He squeezed the technician's shoulder, silently thanking him for the audio hookup's excellent sound quality.

"I want you to send a copy of that recording over to my office for analysis," Medlock said.

"Yes, sir."

General Medlock turned to Dr. Nancy Shaw sitting at her computer terminal, and noted the solemn frown pasted on her face. He placed his hands on her shoulders. She shrugged them off in disgust.

"I just want you to know how much I appreciate what you're doing for me," Medlock said.

"Don't make this any worse by bullshitting me, general," she said, her eyes glaring. Her blunt features were stone serious, chiseled from seventeen years of skirmishes in academia politics. "I'm not one of your grunts, nor did I volunteer to be here. I fully intend to file a complaint with the State Department at my first opportunity."

Medlock snorted. *Civilians.* "Exercise whatever rights you think you need to, ma'am. But I know you'll feel differently after shaking hands with the president for your help during this crisis."

"I don't like spying on people, especially one of my most gifted students. Why don't you just level with them? Why manipulate your own people like this?"

"Because I'm out of time. Small groups will draw on extraordinary powers of problem-solving when they're backed against a wall. Marshall's a very resourceful man. Martinelli's injection was brilliant. I'm counting on them to find out what a military interrogation team may not. Bonding is a powerful motivator, and I will exploit it to the fullest."

"That's psy-ops bullshit, general."

"Considering the lives at risk here, I'll use every available resource in whatever ways I see fit under Section 3 of the Homeland Security Act. And that includes your services. Are you clear on that point or do I have to get an executive order?"

"Yes, sir, general. Unfortunately, very clear."

Medlock's birdlike features broke into a self-righteous grin. "Good. I want you to use your database to unravel Wynett's babbling. Draw correlations. See if it means anything. Get me something."

Medlock didn't wait for her acknowledgment. He returned to the conference table, where the members of his task force were dissecting each part of Wynett's interview. "Okay, people. What's it all mean? Higgins?"

Maj. Samuel Higgins, BERT's logistics officer, cleared his throat as he stood. He worked best on his feet, pacing. "We agree that Wynett's reference to sweet crude means a lighter grade of crude oil, which has little or no sulfur."

"So how's Gorgon going to use it?" Medlock asked curtly.

Higgins raised his arms as though the answer were obvious. "Wynett told us. 'Floating city ... floating bomb.' Gorgon may be smuggling the virus into this country aboard an oil tanker."

Heads around the table nodded in agreement.

"What about those goddamn Procyons?" Medlock asked. "Jesus, that sucks. Can he launch them from a tanker?"

Dr. Theodore Gruber, BERT's science consultant, nodded. "That wouldn't be a problem. Even the smallest tanker has a deck wide enough to accommodate the launch platform and its control station."

Lieutenant Hernandez slapped his palm hard against the table. "The name of the ship. Find out the name of the ship and we've got him."

"Lucy," Dr. Shaw said matter-of-factly from her workstation. "Gorgon's tanker is named *Lucy.*"

All eyes turned to her. Medlock stood. "Where in hell did you come up with that?"

"The song," she said, pointing to her screen. "That's what Wynett was raving about. He was teasing them, alluding to the Beatles' song 'Lucy in the Sky With Diamonds.' He was telling them, yet hiding it from them. Not very bright, actually."

Medlock turned to the others for validation. He counted two nods, the rest blank stares. "A song about drugs written by addicts?" the general said, making his way around the table to her workstation.

Medlock leaned over her shoulder and stared at her Macintosh screen ... a Google search. His eyes scanned the list of links of her keyword search. One of her open desktop windows showed the crimson back cover of the Beatles' *Sgt. Pepper's* album, complete with lyrics. Some of the highlighted words on one of the songs seemed to suggest bits of Wynett's ravings. Another window displayed an oil tanker registry – the seventeenth name on the list, flying a Liberian flag, was *Lucy.*

Medlock place a hand on her shoulder and squeezed. "Doc, send Martinelli a message. Get her to talk about the interview with Wynett and see what else she knows. See if she's filed any notes on her computer. Will you do that for me?"

She shuddered visibly. "Please don't touch me."

Medlock gave her shoulder a final squeeze, then returned to the conference table to address the group. "In one hour I want every piece of information you can find on that tanker – engineering blueprints, schematics, everything."

"What about Wynett's offer?" Lieutenant Hernandez said. "Are you going to negotiate?"

"Negative," Medlock said. "But I do think it's time I talked with this son of a bitch myself."

Dr. Shaw stared at her computer, her eyes unable to focus on the screen. She didn't feel well ... this business was eating her up inside. Spying on Julie was too easy. She simply shared her computer session, which allowed her to open any file on Julie's personal storage disk for General Medlock's inspection – even her personal email.

"Sorry, honey," she said to the screen.

DESTINY

The U.S. Eastern Seaboard
Sunday, May 1, 0603 hours

Capt. Sergio Carlucci moved among the mélange of crates and steel containers Gorgon's soldiers had stacked in the ship's lower pumping room. The inventory of armaments was as unconventional as it was extensive. He ran his fingers over an unopened crate's military symbols and serial numbers, speculating on the weapon stored within. How powerful? And for what purpose?

He watched two mercenaries assembling a curious piece of military hardware that reminded him of a Gatling gun, only much larger. The men worked quickly and with seasoned mastery, transforming unassuming pieces of metal into formidable weaponry. They will install that on the ship's upper deck, Carlucci figured, just like the other exotic killing machines they had brought aboard.

The mercenaries allowed him to watch. Gorgon wanted Carlucci to see the extent of his considerable firepower, a strong persuasion against resisting.

Besides, Carlucci still was *Lucy's* master. His orders were to operate the ship normally, or as routinely as seventeen highly trained killers would allow. To do that he needed access to the lower decks. The captain intended to use this privilege to investigate the extent of Gorgon's hold on his vessel, probing for weaknesses. So far he found none. He had to think like a terrorist, not an old ship's captain.

Carlucci slipped into the pump room's maintenance shop. He spotted the cylinders immediately. At first he mistook them for beer kegs – they were the same relative size and shape. Five in all and arranged neatly against the far wall, these were no ordinary containers. He knelt before the first and ran his hand down its gunmetal gray surface. It was unlike anything he had ever seen before, capped with a very sophisticated valve mechanism. Were they bombs? If so, they resembled nothing he had ever seen during his sixteen years as a naval officer.

Carlucci stood and surveyed the rest of the workshop. On a bench sat six disassembled conical projectiles, each a meter high. He moved to them, sticking his nose to within inches of one, scrutinizing the integrated circuit boards inside. They were warheads, he realized, warheads for missiles.

Next to the workbench sat an open crate containing tube-like cylinders, each the size of a wine bottle. There were dozens of them in this single crate, and there were many crates. He tapped one of the cylinders with his pencil. Hollow. Empty tubes and warheads. How would they figure in Gorgon's plan? He looked again at the larger, keg-like tanks. Somehow they were the key.

Carlucci checked the bulkhead door. No one was coming.

His confidence rising, he returned to the larger tanks and probed the valve on the first, determined to learn Gorgon's secrets. The valve was made of a material more durable than steel. He tried to move what he thought must be the valve's lever. Frozen. Only someone intimately familiar with this mechanism – an engineer – could open these tanks.

The notion hit him with a rush of excitement. If these tanks were crucial to Gorgon's plan as he believed they were, opening them might render him impotent. Tampering also could get him killed, he realized. Was his life too high a price to pay to thwart Gorgon? He thought not. The last twelve hours had been worse than any nightmare. His men, all good seamen under his care, were dead on his watch. This moment offered him perhaps his only chance to avenge the deaths of his crew and stop the madness that had overtaken his ship. *Take it.*

A wrench lay on top of an oil drum. He seized it and considered the heavy steel tool. Did he have the courage to go through with it? Did he have the courage to die?

Captain Carlucci swept around, wrench in hand, and hovered over the first tank. His heart thrummed in time with the deep rumble of the ship's engine. His father once told him that conquerors and cowards feel exactly the same fear. Conquerors just respond to fear differently.

Carlucci raised the wrench high over his head. A hand, easily the size and strength of a bear's, caught his hand midair and held it tightly. Fear seized him. The solid, mechanized clicks of cocking shotguns drew his attention to the hatchway. Two soldiers stood inside the maintenance room, ready to fire.

Gorgon twisted the wrench from Carlucci's hand. The captain winced in agony.

"You are a fool," Gorgon said, tossing the wrench aside. "One more day. I need you alive only one more day."

Carlucci, wheezing with fear, straightened to his full height. "How many will die because of these? And for what reason?"

"Come," Gorgon grinned. "I will show you what role you are playing in the new world I will fashion."

Gorgon and Carlucci rode the tiny service elevator up to the superstucture's master deck, one level below the bridge. They entered the captain's quarters. Behind a glass partition, four of Gorgon's men hovered over a conference table layered with charts, maps and diagrams.

Gorgon led Carlucci to the head of the table so he could see everything. The captain gazed down at a marine chart scribed with a detailed route into the Chesapeake Bay, ending in the York River at West Point. Another blueprint provided a comprehensive schematic of a refinery. A third sheet diagrammed the refinery's off-loading dock. Still another drawing, detailed a product pipeline network starting at Yorktown and leading to major population centers throughout the east-southeastern United States. Circled in red were New York, Philadelphia, Baltimore/Washington, Richmond, Atlanta and Jacksonville.

On the table sat one of the tube-shaped cylinders Carlucci saw in the crate in the maintenance shop. This one was open, its top unscrewed and sitting to one side. Inside was a thermal vessel, capped with a small valve. Next to the cylinder sat an orange object made of polyurethane with ribbed sides.

"The tanks you were about to treat so irreverently," Gorgon said, "hold an organism created by the United States military. If you had succeeded in opening the tank, we all would be dead. I have enough and more of the organism to kill every man, woman and child in North America and in every ally nation in the United Nations."

Carlucci shook his head. "Even if this . . .this . . . weapon is what you say, you cannot use it. The movement of this tanker is severely restricted by maritime law. And she is s1ow."

Gorgon laughed wickedly. "The voyage of this tanker is only the means, captain, not the end. Tonight you will dock and off-load your cargo as scheduled." He drew the pipeline schematic to him. "Look at this diagram. Yorktown represents the beginning of a major distribution network for transporting refined crude throughout the north and southeast United States. No doubt you are aware how such a pipeline system works, captain?"

Carlucci remained silent, offering nothing that might help him.

"Refined products," Gorgon explained, "are sent to distribution terminals throughout the country through a pipeline network such as this one. To isolate one product from the next – a higher octane gasoline from a lower octane product – a cylindrical separator known as a 'pig' is put into the pipe ahead of each product."

He picked up the orange, ribbed object. "This pig rides ahead of the product, pushed by the pressure of the liquid behind. When it arrives at a distribution terminal, an operator diverts the incoming product to the appropriate storage tank. The pig is recovered in a simple relief valve."

Gorgon picked up the cylinder from the table and handled it reverently, as though it were a precious artifact. "One of these cylinders will be placed inside each of these pigs. Each cylinder will carry one quart of my organism. Tonight I will put seventy-four of these containers into the pipeline system at Yorktown. These containers will open automatically and release their contents the moment they are removed from the relief valve. No other intervention is required. The contents of each container will contaminate at least 700 square miles. Within twenty-four hours, the Lion will have his victory."

Carlucci's eyes shifted to the charts, but he was unable to focus on them. His mind spun in the aftermath of Gorgon's insanely brilliant revelations. Madness. Evil. Genius. Could this monster by stopped?

At that moment he knew what he had to do, he understood his destiny. He spent his career as a seaman protecting the ships and crews under his command. Today he must outwit this monstrous adversary and develop a plan to destroy this ship and sink her. Millions of lives were at stake.

A scheme began to form in his head, and he began to tremble in anticipation. The ship's closed-loop inert-gas system pumped carbon monoxide from the exhaust of the huge diesel engine into the cargo tanks, replacing the oxygen. The system minimized the chance of accidental combustion. That was the key. Turn it off, and the cargo's gas could ignite with a single spark. Gorgon would be dead, and with him this horror he carried with him. Would he be allowed near the pump-room controls? And, if so, how would he introduce that spark?

For a long moment there was silence. Suddenly Gorgon shattered the quiet with laughter that sent tremors of dread to the core of Carlucci's soul.

"As you have observed, captain," Gorgon said, "the new world order begins on your watch."

PROGNOSIS

Quarantine
0918 hours

"Christ, I don't believe this."

The results from the pathology lab's Polymerase Chain Re-action unit weren't what Julie expected to see. Each of their DNA sequences contained thousands of mutant genes. Without a doubt, a significant biological change had taken place in their systems. The question became one of survival – how much time did they have?

"Looks like you're having a bad morning," came a deep voice from the doorway. "I can come back."

Julie spun away from the screen. It was Williams. "Sergeant ... you startled me. Come in ... please."

Williams, dressed in a T-shirt, shorts and running shoes soaked from a hard workout in the center's weight room, closed the pathology lab's door behind him and approached her workstation. His eyes, fixed on the monitor, seemed to be searching for some encouraging news among the columns of numbers scrolling down the screen. She knew that nothing he saw would make any sense to him.

"Thought I'd drop by in case you needed anything."

"You mean in case I could tell you something," she said.

Williams plopped his huge frame into the cheap molded chair next to her. "Now that you mention it."

For the briefest moment she considered lying to him, telling him what he wanted to hear – that she could find nothing unusual in his blood. But lying to her friends would only make a bad situation worse. *Deal with this.* Besides, he would know soon enough.

"I might know something this afternoon," she said slowly, "after I run more tests."

"You're stalling." His congenial grin vanished, and he looked at her very serious. "How bad is it?"

She sighed and shook her head. Here goes. "You and Joe can forget about Gorgon. The army will never let us out of here. The good news is we can all look forward to a hefty medical disability."

"How long do we have?"

"I can't tell you that." She pressed a finger to the screen. "Do you see these numbers?"

Williams leaned toward her display. "What do they mean?"

"I'm still running tests to find correlations from the tissue and plant samples I took from the plantation. It'll take weeks to sift through the data. What's fascinating about Saint Vitus is the clever way it adapts to its environment. The organism catalyzes its own replication in simple chemical systems without the help of enzymes. That's why it spreads so fast. It brings together two molecular building blocks to create its own template molecule and accelerates their coupling to form a second template. The new molecule makes copies of itself by promoting this reaction between its two building blocks while they're bound to the template. It's really quite remarkable."

Williams wore the confused look of a third-grader mistakenly stuck in a calculus class. "Haven't a clue what you just said."

She smiled apologetically. "Sorry. What I'm getting at is each generation of Saint Vitus is less toxic than the one before. Man built artificial toxicity into the organism, while nature gives it up in exchange for adaptability."

"Is that supposed to be good news?"

"Yes. That's why we're still alive." Julie rolled her chair in front of the lab's electron-scanning microscope. She clicked on the postcard-size display.

Williams followed and peered over her shoulder at the display's luminous circles of life.

"I can show you slides of each of our blood cells," she said. "There are abnormalities with the same genetic fingerprint in mine, yours and Joe's cell cytoplasm. Youngblood's sample shows no deformation because he didn't come in direct contact with the organism on the plantation. He's the only healthy one among us. That suggests Saint Vitus isn't airborne contagious once it infests the host. Wynett's the worst. His blood shows evidence of gross malignancy, which isn't surprising, considering the length of time he was exposed. I'd like to see a magnetic resonator image of him. He most likely has tumors in advanced stages in his brain."

Williams let out a long, weary sigh. "After putting my ass on the line so many times, I'm gonna buy it from a goddamn germ."

"It's too early to start planning your funeral, sergeant. The toxicity could take a long time to break down our immune systems."

Williams' brow furrowed. "Did you see Joe's hand this morning? The trembling's gotten worse."

Julie looked hard at him. "Sergeant, I don't know what this synthetic aberration in a mutated state will do to us or how long it will take before we see more symptoms – it's a total black box. And there's something else I can't figure. I found a gene I can't identify imbedded in the infected cells. I suspect it has something to do with a mutated version of Saint Vitus, but I won't be sure without more testing. If I can talk the army into giving me time on one of its Crays, I might be able to identify the enzymes and see what Saint Vitus is up to."

Williams sank back into his chair. "When the brass gets wind of what you've found, they'll bury us in here."

"They already have. I'm going to need the medical opinion of a highly specialized team, something on the order of the NIH's Recombinant DNA Advisory Committee. I'll consult with my adviser, Dr. Shaw."

"When are you gonna tell Joe?"

Julie turned away from him. "None of this will matter to him. He doesn't have any feelings."

"Jesus, Julie. He feels a great deal more than you're likely to ever know. Except he's programmed not to show it." He emphasized the word programmed as though it would mean something special to her. "After fifteen years in the service, he's forgotten how to show his feelings. It would do him a world of good if you could bring him out of his suit of armor before he dies in there. All he knows is you'd rather talk to this computer instead of him. He needs to know you trust him."

She looked at him, hurt. "This is very difficult work. I need to find the precise shape of the virus. To do that I need to crystalline the protein, then take a long series of X-ray pictures. Processing these photos through a computer will give me a three-dimensional image."

Williams rolled his eyes. "There you go, making excuses."

"What's your point, sergeant?"

"Don't have a point." Williams was on his feet, heading for the door. "You've got work to do and I need a shower." He opened the lab's door, turned and added, "With any luck, you'll live long enough to find out what you're missing – about Joe, that is."

USAMRIID
Fort Derrick

General Medlock's hand remained frozen around a polystyrene cup half filled with cold, black coffee. It had been a long night. He needed sleep, and his drawn expression showed it.

He had removed himself from the discussion around the conference room table to mentally devour several pages of statistics on crude oil tankers contracted to U.S. oil companies. On one of the pages an analyst had highlighted the name *Lucy*, an eighty-thousand-deadweight-ton oil tanker currently working for Universal Oil Marine Transport Company in Houston. That translated to six hundred thousand barrels of crude oil.

Maj. Samuel Higgins, BERT's logistics officer, was on his feet, listing the technical issues of the crisis on an electronic "chalkboard" that could print hard copies of anything written on it with a washable marker. "*Lucy* loads medium-gravity crude from Universal's oil fields in Venezuela. She has a cruising radius of 17,000 nautical miles. Her route takes her across the Caribbean, up the United States' Eastern Seaboard to the Chesapeake Bay, where she'll dock at her company's refinery in Yorktown."

"It fits." Medlock grunted.

"*Lucy's* perfect, sir," said Lieutenant Hernandez, a young officer with baby-smooth features. "She's small by tanker standards, which means she won't need special port handling. Fully laden and retro-fitted with armaments, she'd pose one hell of a threat if he intends to use her to gain entry to this country. At the very least he can threaten a first-class oil spill if we try to intercept her – that's if Gorgon doesn't release the bug first. That bastard's got himself a floating fortress."

Medlock stared over his coffee cup at the lieutenant with eyes cast in steel. "You're having too much fun, Hernandez. You sound like you want to be on that goddamn ship with him."

The young lieutenant stiffened. "Sir, I was only pointing out—"

"Forget it," Medlock said. "It's been a long night."

"Where the hell is *Lucy's* schedule?" Major Higgins said. "We need to find out where she picks up a river pilot." He thrust his marker at Lieutenant Hernandez. "Find out *Lucy's* present location and which pilot station she uses. Monitor any change in her routine radio messages. I want to know if she's done anything out of the ordinary."

Lieutenant Hernandez punched a preprogrammed button on his cell phone and relayed the major's instructions to his staff.

"Let's ask Universal to take a look," Major Higgins suggested. "One of their choppers can drop in for a surprise inspection."

"Negative," Medlock said. "Keep those corporate pricks out of this. When we find out where she picks up a pilot, we'll put in our own man. Though I'd bet Gorgon won't allow a pilot anywhere near the vessel."

"He won't have a choice if he wants to stay discreet," Higgins said.

The phone in front of Hernandez rang. Thirty seconds later the lieutenant relayed to the group: *"Lucy's* last routine message came three hours ago over the MariSat channel. She's approaching the Chesapeake Bay. She'll arrive at the pilot station offshore of Cape Henry this afternoon. She's scheduled to dock at the company's Yorktown refinery at 1830 hours tonight. And so far there's been nothing unusual about her voyage. Let me take this to a Code Red, sir."

Medlock shut his report with a snap. "We'll stay orange until we get more facts. Make a call to the joint chiefs and brief them. Meanwhile let's try to get a man aboard on a recon. Find an enlisted seaman who can pilot that tanker upriver and get him wired. If they won't let him aboard, that'll at least tell us what we need to know."

Dr. Theodore Gruber, BERT's science consultant, cleared his throat apologetically while running his fingers through his surviving wisps of white hair that always drifted up and outward. Slouched in a bland blue blazer and gray slacks that looked like he'd just awakened wearing them – and he probably had – Gruber was an MIT engineering professor, who last year headed Raytheon's new technology program.

"Excuse me, gentlemen," Gruber said. "I believe this Gorgon fellow has made a serious blunder."

All eyes shifted to Gruber, who had been sitting undistracted scribbling on a yellow legal pad full of calculations.

Medlock said, "What have you got, Ted?"

"A Procyon missile," Gruber said, still making copious notes on the pad in front of him, "is designed to deliver an explosive warhead with a maximum range of 950 nautical miles. Let's assume he's using a conventional warhead canister that jettisons on reentry and spins to the ground while dispersing its contents

– the only way a bacterial and chemical agent can disperse from a warhead."

"What's your point?" Medlock spat, impatient.

Gruber slid back his chair, walked slightly stooped to the head of the table and took the black marker from Major Higgins. He wiped off several of Higgins's notes on the board to make room for his crude sketch of the slope of a missile path from a sphere he labeled 'tanker.' "As designed, the missiles' trajectory is far too steep for the Gorgon's warhead, and upon reentry it would be traveling much too fast to disperse a viral agent."

Medlock leaned back thoughtfully in his chair, touching his fingertips together. "Ted, are you saying his warheads won't work?"

"Not unless he's reengineered the boosters to reduce the trajectory and speed – and that would take a team of engineers and technicians. It's a gamble, to be sure. And to complicate matters for him, a storm front is moving across the northeast seaboard from the west, and he's riding straight into it. Dispersing an airborne toxin in thirty-knot winds would be ineffectual. No, he must have something else planned. Perhaps he is taking the neurotoxin inland for a larger attack."

"That's why I'm not going to let him reach that refinery," Medlock said. "The only question is how."

"I say our best option is a commando assault of the vessel," Major Higgins said. "Once on board, a team can neutralize the missiles by simply taking out the electronics truck. Then Gorgon's vulnerable to a full-scale assault."

Medlock nodded. Organizing a small, covert assault force intrigued him. At the very least it was the genesis of a solid plan. "Too many unanswered questions, too many risks," the general said. "If we're to have any chance at all, we need a recon of the tanker first. I want to know how many men Gorgon has on board, where he keeps the tanks and what they look like. That's going to take time."

"Perhaps there's a shortcut," Gruber said, wiping his writing hand on a blue tie emblazoned with golden statistical symbols.

He looked directly at Dr. Shaw seated in the far corner of the room. "Would you kindly download and print out Julie Martinelli's collated data about the organism? I need to know if those poor bastards locked downstairs are still airborne contagious." Then he appealed to Medlock, his exhausted, academic features suspiciously enlivened. "I think it's time you cut a deal with this Carl Wynett."

The White House
Oval Office
1154 hours

The president and Senator Edward Baker were absorbed in a terse discussion about Al-Qaeda's nuclear capability when Michael Brennan was shown into the Oval Office. Director of the Central Intelligence Agency, Brennan didn't need an appointment to meet with his boss. He had access to the president twenty-four hours a day. Unassuming and sporting horn-rimmed glasses and a crew cut, Brennan looked more like a staff accountant than head of the world's most powerful intelligence organization.

The president and his guest turned in unison as Brennan entered the office. Their discussion ended abruptly.

"Excuse me, Mr. President, Senator Baker," Brennan began, uncharacteristically serious lines creasing his usually benign features.

The president gestured the CIA director into a blue high-backed chair beside him, inviting him into their circle of discussion. "What is it, Mike? I don't like it when you get that look on your face."

Senator Baker touched the president's arm. "Perhaps I should go."

The president looked at Brennan for affirmation. "What about it, Mike? Want him to leave?"

Brennan sat down stiffly on the proffered blue suede chair in front of the office's fireplace. "That's not necessary, sir. This also concerns the senator. In fact, his Fort Detrick's investigation triggered what I'm about to tell you."

Senator Baker looked suddenly pale.

"Whatever you say," the president conceded.

Deliberately, and with what seemed to the others glacially slow, Brennan removed his glasses and used a handkerchief to wipe each eye. Then he tucked the handkerchief inside his coat and cleared his throat.

"Mr. President ... a situation has developed that I think you should know about."

CONTAINMENT

Quarantine 1300 hours

Marshall knocked twice on the door and didn't wait for permission before slipping into her room. He found Julie sitting at the small circular table, her father's Beretta lying before her like a funeral wreath, her dark eyes glistening. Startled by his unexpected appearance, she quickly wiped away tears with the back of her hand and tucked back her hair with her fingers.

"You're not welcome here right now," she said, fumbling through her sweater pockets for a tissue. "Please respect my space."

"I knocked first."

She looked at him coldly while blowing her nose into a tissue. "Then you know I want to be alone."

"You're always alone." He closed the door quietly behind him and walked around her bed, slowly, his eyes drifting down to her father's Beretta. He took the weapon into his hand and felt his mentor's strength in its heavy, elegant metal. She didn't seem to mind. He sat down on her bed and contemplated the weapon, paying his respects to its owner. The gun was so much like her father. It was as though he were here with them, his strength and his soul residing within its metal.

"It reminds me of him," she said at last, tucking the spent tissue into her sweater pocket.

Marshall looked thoughtfully at her. He didn't tell her that those were his thoughts too.

"He once told me," she said, "that a gun gives a man a power only God should have. Still, I love it. It reminds me of who he was, what he was. I never touched his guns, but I can't let go of this one ... I can't let go of him."

Marshall considered the Beretta and realized the handsome handgun had no magazine clip. Useless. The Beretta was just like him: a custom-made, finely tuned weapon, unable to do its job.

He replaced the Beretta on the table in front of her. "I'll never forget him."

Despite her best effort to control herself, tears rolled freely down her cheeks. She was vulnerable now, and he had no idea how to comfort her.

"Joe," she said, her voice unsteady, "I ... made some terrible mistakes. I ..." She reached as though to touch him, kept her hand there, but dared go no further.

He wrapped her hand in his, hoping his touch would somehow give her strength and make her feel safe. It was all he could offer.

"I miss him so much," she said. "I don't know how I can live without him in my life."

"You're every bit your father's daughter and you'll find a way," Marshall said firmly. "You're the strongest woman I know."

Julie smiled wanly. "I've been thinking about how everything has changed since he died. How I've changed. Without him I have no compass, no one to guide me."

"You don't need anyone to guide you." He reached for her arm and pulled her tentatively toward him. She slid off the chair, as though waiting for his cue. He wrapped his arms around her, burying his head in her hair.

Julie, sobbing, pressed her face into his muscular neck. She wept openly. "Oh, Joe. I've treated you terribly."

He pushed her gently away from him so he could look deeply into her moist brown eyes. She returned his gaze, unable to speak. He felt an overwhelming rush of compassion and desire, of sorrow coupled with a profound awareness of her frail vulnerabilities and insecurities. Unsure, he leaned forward and kissed her lips lightly. They felt wonderful. When he drew away, she looked at him. He knew it was right – no, perfect – to be with her in this moment despite the horrors surrounding – and within – each of them.

This time she kissed him, a long, deep, lingering kiss that set new boundaries. She kissed him again, and this time there was a painful urgency in her kiss. She was hungry for him. A great exhilaration within obliterated her every fear and regret.

She pushed him down on the bed with firm insistence, then took her time exploring his strong contours as she removed each item of his clothing. She smiled as she ran her hands admiringly over his muscular chest, then brushed a finger playfully over his face, seemingly delighted to feel his week-old sandpaper beard.

Marshall watched her, intently, his excitement building with every electric touch of her hands. She kept him prone, slowly but deliberately increasing the excitement now throbbing between her slim fingers. Unable to hold his enthusiasm, he sat up and pushed her back onto the bed to undress her. And he, too, was pleased by what he saw. Her body was absolutely perfect.

He pulled her, finally, into his arms, though awkwardly, new lovers that they were. Pressed against him, she felt indescribably warm and wonderful. The clumsiness passed, and quickly, naturally, they became one.

"You feel so good," she sighed.

Marshall ran his hands down the graceful curves of her back. "So do you," he whispered, then locked her in another deep kiss. They explored each other's mouths, letting go completely, giving themselves to each other.

Marshall rolled her onto her back and mounted her. She let out a gasp of surprise as his member slipped deeply inside.

USAMRIID 1330 hours

General Medlock pushed his way into the small interrogation room and looked questioningly at Lieutenant Hernandez. "He'll only talk to you," the lieutenant said.

"Then get your men out of here," Medlock snapped.

The lieutenant dispatched his staff quickly from the room, and Medlock secured the door behind him. The general dragged a folding chair across the concrete floor with a screech and sat down in front of Wynett. "So start talking."

"I regret that this meeting must be a short one," Wynett said. "Simply stated, I sold Abdul Banna the armaments to defend the ship and I know how he will use them. You are in a very dangerous situation, general. I do not envy you. An explosion on any of the tanker's decks will effect the release of the organism you wish to contain. A mistake now could cost millions of lives. If you are to have any chance at all, you must take immediate action. Which means, sir, you are at a negotiating disadvantage."

"What's that supposed to mean?"

"It means, general, that in exchange for my information in any quantity and quality I choose to give, you will give me exactly what I want."

"And that is?"

"I need a super cutter to escort me to the oil tanker *Lucy* while she still is on the Chesapeake Bay. Once underway, I will supply you with information that will allow your men to board the vessel and disable the Procyon missiles. That is all I can offer you. How you take down Gorgon and his men will be up to you."

Medlock scowled. "That's insane. Why the hell would you want to meet Gorgon now?"

"We have unfinished business."

"Maybe you want to team up with him again. Maybe he needs you with him before he can carry out his attack. Maybe you're manipulating us with bullshit just to get out of here."

"That is the first risk you must take. General, time is short and I need to ask you one question."

"No one's stopping you."

"Am I dying?"

Medlock shrugged. "Ask a doctor."

"Sir, you must be candid with me if we are to continue doing business. I am certain that you know the results of Miss Martinelli's blood tests. I am simply asking you to share them with me."

General Medlock let his breath out in a long sigh. "Yeah, you're dying." He waited for him to react. When he didn't, he added, "Brain tumors."

Wynett nodded, and his eyes grew distant and reflective. "I suspected as much from the headaches. What a fine tomb *Lucy* will make."

The White House Situation Room
1415 hours

General Medlock marched to the foot of the elongated table and stood almost at attention across from the president of the United States, who sat somberly amidst the warriors summoned for battle against two of the world's most evil men. A pessimistic mood hung over the room like a noxious cloud of smoke.

Medlock quickly scanned the room. Around the table sat the director of the CIA, the chairman of the joint chiefs and the national security adviser – the men and women who embodied the president's mantle of power. In the corner lurked an ashen-faced Senator Baker, conspicuously avoiding the general's glare. There were no aides present.

The president quickly drew the general into their circle of discussion. "I'm not pleased with the way this situation has been handled," he began. "I understand you've been managing this disaster ever since the organism was stolen from Detrick. What I can't understand is how you allowed matters to come to this. I'm appalled that bin Laden's terror group penetrated United States territory under our noses, carrying with them this ... this ... scourge of yours." The president almost spat in disgust.

General Medlock frowned. Saint Vitus wasn't *his*. "Sir—"

"I want this stopped immediately," the president said, glaring at the general as though Gorgon were coming after him personally. "If you can't do it, damn it, then I'll get somebody who can. That organism must not be released, not by a missile, not by any means. My God, this can precipitate a plague like we haven't seen since the Middle Ages." He grew rigid, a hand on his forehead as though struggling to contain his rage. When his anger quelled, he continued, though strained. "I am prepared to do whatever it takes to save our nation, crush Al-Qaeda and send a message to terrorists everywhere. We will not be castrated with our own knife nor become the brunt of international outrage over this ... abomination."

"Sir—"

The president raised a hand, his face drawn and bitter. "I don't want an explanation, general. I want you to carry out a single directive."

"Yes, sir."

"After considering every option, we have only one choice" – the room was silent, all eyes on the president – "a tactical thermonuclear warhead."

There it was. The phrase floated in the air like the very plague the solution was meant to stop. No one dared move, no one dared breathe it in for fear of infection. Medlock was the first to react, his lips parting in a bleak, wintery smile.

The president looked at him, astonished. "Did I say something funny, general?"

"Sir, a nuclear detonation over the ship is not—"

"For the past three-quarters of an hour," the president said, "we have been debating every option to resolve this crisis, from effecting an assassination of bin Laden to doing absolutely nothing. The joint chiefs are at Code Red and I'm standing by to address Congress. bin Laden believes Allah has given him another chance. We've considered every available scenario, and each hypothetical response poses a risk that his terrorists will launch those missiles. Except one. A low-yield tactical nuclear detonation in U.S. waters, however abhorrent, is preferable to the release of the organism. A point-one-megaton nuclear warhead is just large enough to vaporize the ship, while evaporating most of the crude oil and scattering the remains over a two-mile area. If we detonate before the tanker reaches the Chesapeake Bay, the impact on civilian areas will be minimal. Drastic? Yes. Effective? One hundred percent."

"The fallout—"

"We'll evacuate. The radiation will dissipate out to sea, unlike your monster that breeds and spreads."

"Sir, what you're suggesting poses unacceptable risks, not to mention the scandal of nuking our own waters."

The president's gaze circled the room. He seemed to be debating whether to share with the general an ugly secret. "The U.N. weapons inspection team in Afghanistan," the president said slowly, "has hard evidence that bin Laden is ready to test a primitive nuclear device. We will fabricate evidence that this maniac smuggled a small-yield nuclear device into U.S. waters aboard the tanker and detonated it prematurely. I'm told that no scientific investigation team will be able to discern the difference. Yes, a lot of folks will want my ass. But I'm sure the American people will stand behind me when I launch a retaliation that will finally kill that monster."

General Medlock planted his hands palm-down on the table's mirror like mahogany surface and leaned forward. "With all due respect, sir, let me offer you another option. We don't believe Gorgon intends to launch the Procyons. We believe the missiles are merely a backup threat to camouflage a larger operation, most likely to smuggle the virus inland. A Special Forces team is standing by in Oceana to carry out a covert assault on the tanker. We have a chance to deal with this quietly and effectively. No one need know this organism or bin Laden's terrorist plot ever existed."

The president listened to the general, warily, as though hoping to hear another way out of this crisis. But in the end he shook his head. "The organism is a great threat to the American people. The bastard's smirking at us, for chrissake. He knows this country – any country – is entirely vulnerable to this sort of attack. We've got a fleet of warships and attack aircraft standing by at Oceana ready to sink that tanker, yet we can't use them. *We can't use them.* This is worse than nuclear blackmail. No, general. I wish there was another way out of this, but every minute we allow that tanker to continue, we risk more lives. There simply isn't time to consider other options."

"Then allow a compromise, sir," Medlock said, "one that won't undermine your option."

"What is it?"

"Stand by with your nuclear option. The moment something goes wrong with my plan, we nuke the ship, special-op team and all. We can accept the sacrifice in the interest of saving a lot more lives. You can have it both ways."

The president scowled, indicating that he didn't like the general's proposal. Medlock knew he wanted guarantees, which only the nuclear option provided. Too much was at stake – perhaps even the president's own life.

"I can't risk that, general," the president said.

"Sir, my commandos are the best. The elite from every Special Forces unit – SEALS, Delta, Green Berets. We're ready to move. The name of the operation is Maximum Containment."

The president turned his back on the group, and for a full minute said nothing. The silence was frightening. Then he turned, riveted an acute glare at Medlock and said, "Can you guarantee me one hundred percent that the organism will not be released during your assault?"

Medlock drew in a deep breath and told the president what he wanted to hear. "With your nuclear backup, sir, the guarantee is one-hundred percent."

"Then you have my authority to act. And God damn your soul if you're wrong."

DEPARTURE

Quarantine 1700 hours

"He's gone," Julie whispered into Marshall ear.

Marshall woke from the deepest sleep he had enjoyed in a month, with no idea where he was and no memory of how he had gotten here. Dream-soaked images of Julie swirled through his mind. Had he just heard her voice, or was he still asleep? Then the events of the afternoon came flooding back, and he realized that he was in her bed. He smiled. His desire for her stirred again when he smelled her flowing sweetness and he opened his eyes to see her standing over him. He wrestled her down onto the bed, rolled on top of her and drove his semi-tough member between her legs. She was fully clothed in an abrasive jumpsuit.

"Did you hear what I just said?" Julie said, pushing him off her. "Wynett's gone."

"*What?*" Marshall fumbled in the dimness for his chronometer on the table. The luminous dial said he had been asleep for more than three hours. He switched on the lamp. "Gone? What do you mean *gone?*"

Julie swung her legs over the edge of the bed. "We searched the whole friggin' center, and the son of a bitch isn't here. Williams and Youngblood are going through every room again."

Marshall pulled on his jockey briefs with a snap and stormed out of her room and down the hallway, his bare feet slapping the sterile linoleum. His mind was racing. Gone? How could he be *gone?*

He found Williams sitting cross-armed at one of the lounge's tables, a look of profound frustration etched across his features. The remains of a penny-poker game and empty Coke cans littered the table, while Dan Fogelberg's "Part of the Plan" blared from a portable audio player.

"Going to church in your Sunday best, Joe?" Williams snorted at the major charging through the lounge half naked.

Marshall jabbed the player's off button. "So where is he?"

"Hell if I know," Williams said. "But he ain't in here."

"Did you check the pathology lab thoroughly?" Marshall asked. "He's nutty enough to lock himself inside a goddamn freezer."

"He ain't here," Williams repeated, his voice raised in uncharacteristic impatience.

Youngblood strode into the lounge and dumped himself into a chair across from Williams. "You're not going to believe what I just saw." The pilot stared at Marshall's perspiring chest and briefs, then watched with a scowl as Julie tossed the major a pair of khaki pants and a long-sleeved shirt.

"What am I not going to believe?" Marshall asked.

"Medlock's people pulled Wynett out of here," Youngblood said.

Marshall stepped into the khakis. "How do you know that?"

Youngblood cocked his thumb in the general direction of the center's communications room. "I saw it on the outside monitors. A bunch of officers whisked Wynett out onto the helipad and loaded him onto a troop transport. It's recorded in case you'd like to see for yourself."

"Don't look now, ladies," Marshall said, buttoning his shirt, "but I think we've just been conned."

"What's that supposed to mean?" Julie asked.

"We're not contagious, and Medlock knows it."

Marshall stormed down the corridor, slipped inside the phone room, lifted the receiver and waited an impatient thirty seconds for someone to answer. A woman finally said, "How can I help you?"

"Talk to me. What the hell's going on up there?"

"This is Sergeant McGinnis. I'm filling in for Lieutenant Lowe, who isn't available. What can I do for you?"

"Where are they taking Wynett?"

Her youthful voice dropped a full octave. "I'm sorry, major. I'm not authorized to give you any information. I have strict instructions."

"Let me speak to someone whose nose isn't buried six inches past the brass' sphincter."

"I'm sorry, sir." Her tone had taken on the dull, mechanical quality of an answering machine.

He threw down the receiver. "This is bullshit."

"Meet me in the computer lab in two minutes," Julie hollered down the hallway. "And dress for a chilly night."

Marshall scrambled out of the telephone room. "Say what?"

"I'm getting us out of here," Julie said, then disappeared into her computer lab.

Marshall, his adrenaline pumping, turned to the others and said, "You heard the lady. Move your asses and grab a jacket."

Marshall hustled back to his quarters and grabbed his boots and a pair of wool socks from his closet before joining the others in the computer lab. He found Williams strapping his wicked black-blade serrated knife to his right ankle, while Julie sat in front of her computer holding her mug half-filled with cold coffee. Beside the terminal lay her father's Beretta.

Marshall slid his chair next to Julie's and stomped on his boot. "So tell me your little secret. How are you getting us out of here?"

"While you were on the phone," she said, "I found a message waiting for me in my inbox."

"What's it say?"

Youngblood and Williams pressed behind them while Julie jabbed the keyboard's PF2 key to access her incoming electronic mail. At the top of the list was a message from a Dr. N. Shaw.

"Who's N. Shaw?" Marshall asked.

"Nancy's my Stanford adviser." Julie pressed the PF1 key to view the note:

JULIE

I'M SORRY I DIDN'T TELL YOU BEFORE THAT I'M HERE AT DETRICK TWO FLOORS ABOVE YOU. I'M UNDER A STRICT GAG ORDER. THERE'S A TASK FORCE UP HERE LISTENING AND WATCHING EVERYTHING YOU SAY AND DO. WYNETT HAS INSISTED ON MEETING GORGON'S HIJACKED OIL TANKER, WHICH WILL REACH THE CHESAPEAKE BAY IN ABOUT TWO HOURS. A COVERT ASSAULT TEAM WILL BOARD AND ATTEMPT TO STOP HIM. THEY'RE CALLING THE OPERATION MAXIMUM CONTAIN-MENT. ALL HELL'S BREAKING LOOSE UP HERE WHILE MEDLOCK GETS READY TO FLY TO HIS COMMAND HANG-AR AT ANDREWS AIRFIELD. I'M NOT SURE WHERE THE TROOPS ARE STAGING.

THE GENERAL DOESN'T WANT YOU INVOLVED. I WANT-ED YOU TO KNOW WHAT'S GOING ON – I'M TIRED OF ALL THE SECRETS AND ALL THE BULLSHIT. MY JOB HERE IS FINISHED ANYWAY ... AND I'M GLAD. SORRY I HAD TO BE SO SNEAKY. PLEASE HIT PF4 NOW TO DELETE THIS NOTE.

NANCY

"We're in a goddamned fishbowl," Youngblood said.

Marshall put a finger to his lips, signaling each of them to remain quiet. He whispered into Julie's ear, "Get me out of here."

She grabbed her legal pad, scribbled a note and showed it to him. *Any idea where they're taking Wynett?*

Marshall snatched her pad of paper and pen and scribbled, *Probably Oceana. That's three hours by car.* He thought a moment, then finished, *That's IF we can find a car and drive out of here.*

"Let's follow Wynett in a chopper," Youngblood whispered.

Marshall raised his eyebrows, intrigued.

Youngblood grabbed the pad of paper from Marshall and wrote, *There's a chopper on the helipad.*

Marshall laughed out loud when he read Youngblood's note. "You've been hanging out with Wynett too long."

Youngblood grabbed the pad from Marshall and wrote, *I don't think we have another option.*

"I think it's a splendid idea," Julie said, forgoing writing on the pad. "They're treating Wynett like a goddamn VIP. I'm not letting him get away scot-free. Besides, we're plumb out of time." She typed a command into her computer, slid back in her chair and bit her lower lip. They all watched the word WAIT appear briefly in the lower left corner of the screen before disappearing.

Marshall said, "What are you up to?"

Julie raised her hand to silence him. Marshall listened but heard nothing. They sat there for ten seconds waiting for something to happen ... twenty.... Nothing did.

Youngblood shook his head. "All dressed up and nowhere—"

"*Quiet!*" Marshall shouted.

More silence. Youngblood, smirking, stepped into the hall-way and mocked, "No one here 'cept us ghosts...." He stopped, his jaw dropping. "Well, I'll be the south end of a northbound horse."

Marshall stood. "What is it?"

Julie, too, was on her feet, her expression hopeful.

"The crash door" – Youngblood looked at the major, his face wide-eyed and boyish – "is open."

Marshall bolted into the hallway. Youngblood was right. The electronically controlled door leading into the receiving-dock area stood ajar. He could hear the muted sound of a larger mechanical door moving beyond it – the service-bay door to the outside.

"*Yes,*" Williams said, his fist raised in victory.

Marshall swept Julie into a bear hug before she could dash from the lab. "You're beautiful."

"Oh really?" She laughed, hugging his neck. "A simple shell program I put together last night in case of an emergency."

Suddenly the center's emergency red lights began flashing and the alarms erupted in a deafening cacophony of sound. Their congratulatory grins disappeared. A metallic, emotionless voice boomed over the intercom: "*Quarantine has been breached.*

Do not attempt to leave quarantine. Repeat. Do not attempt to leave quarantine."

"We're screwed if those doors shut," Julie shouted.

The four of them sprinted down the hallway.

"Quarantine has been breached. Do not attempt to leave quarantine."

Marshall burst into the receiving room and entered the center's cavernous loading dock. The quarantine trailer was gone. A loud, staccato buzzer and spinning yellow light warned them to stand clear of the great steel service-bay door rolling shut. "A fail-safe routine," Julie shouted over the din. "The security program is compensating for the failure my command introduced into the system. It's sealing the building."

"Everybody out," Marshall hollered.

Williams and Youngblood bolted across the loading dock.

Marshall grabbed Julie around the waist and tackled her back into the center. "Sorry, babe," he said. "I want you safe in here." He planted an impeccable kiss on her lips and snatched the Beretta from her. "I'll see you tonight."

Before she could protest, he sprinted into the receiving room and slammed the steel door behind him, locking her inside with a mechanical click.

He heard Julie driving her boot against the metal door from the other side. *"Marshall!"*

The service-bay door had less than four feet to go before it sealed him inside. Williams, peering beneath from the outside, beckoned him to hurry. "Get your ass out here, Joe."

Marshall jumped down onto the concrete floor and raced toward the massive door as it rolled closed. He flattened onto his buttocks as though sliding for home plate and pushed his legs under the door. His upper torso wouldn't clear. He felt the door's crushing weight begin to press down on him. He couldn't stop it.

Two pairs of hands grabbed him by his legs and yanked him cruelly out into the chilly May night. The heavy service-bay door closed behind him with a pneumatic *thud.*

GANCICLOVIR

Youngblood blew on his hands and rubbed them together. "I wish I had my bomber jacket."

"I wish I had a bomber," Marshall said. The major grabbed Williams' hand and pulled himself to his feet.

The VIP command helicopter sat idling on the campus helipad. Marshall led the way to the helipad where a uniformed security officer stood rigid by the open compartment door, watching them approach with a hand on his holstered .45. Marshall pegged him as a reckless jock who would eat a urinal deodorant cake on a dare.

Marshall ducked under the rotor blades and tucked Martinelli's empty Beretta under the guard's chin. "Don't take this personally, but we need your ride." The guard stared wide-eyed while Youngblood relieved him of his sidearm.

"Now walk away from here," Marshall ordered. "Slowly."

The young guard turned and dashed off in the general direction of USAMRIID main building.

Youngblood opened the cockpit door and said to the pilot, "New orders. You're wanted inside."

The helicopter pilot pulled off his flight helmet and roared at Youngblood, "Who the fuck are you?"

Youngblood offered him his best Georgian grin. "Don't shoot me. I'm just the messenger."

"My ass." The pilot reached for his radio.

Youngblood pointed the guard's .45 at the pilot's head. "One way or another, in ten seconds you're gonna be out of my life."

The pilot's sharp features turned notably pale under the low light of the flight deck's multicolored instrumentation. He scrambled out of the cockpit.

Youngblood strapped himself into the pilot's seat, engaged the rotor clutch and throttled the turboshaft engines for takeoff.

Marshall and Williams climbed into the troop compartment, an airborne combat communications center loaded with racks of electronics. Williams secured the compartment door behind them. An academic-looking gentleman with wireframe glasses and thin wispy hair sat buckled into a seat, a briefcase full of papers spread out on the table before him.

"Good God ... you're Major Joseph Marshall." The man slid a handful of papers into his worn shoulder bag and clutched it to his chest. "I suppose you want me to leave."

Marshall let him see his Beretta. "Depends. Who are you?"

"Dr. Theodore Gruber, BERT's science consultant."

Marshall flashed him a congenial grin and took a seat across from him. "We're on the same team. I need you to bring me up to speed on this situation real fast."

The helicopter gave a shudder as it lifted off the helipad.

Gruber sprang to his feet and shouted, "Are you *insane?* This vehicle is General Medlock's communications link to the command hangar at Andrews Airfield. You're jeopardizing this entire operation."

"Nothing's in jeopardy," Marshall said. He indicated the electronics behind him. "You have my permission to keep the flow of information moving, if that's your job. Meanwhile, I want you to get on the LINK II and inform all parties that Major Joseph Marshall and Gunnery M.Sg. J. C. Williams are part of Maximum Containment on special assignment. And then you can start by telling me how many assault troops are staging at Oceana."

"Two hundred," Williams said, sifting through Gruber's paperwork. "It's all here."

General Medlock emerged from USAMRIID's main entrance in time to see his helicopter bank to the east, gather speed and disappear into the dusk. His chopper pilot rushed up to meet him. "A couple of assholes in civilian clothes commandeered my aircraft at gunpoint."

Medlock passed a weary hand over his grim features. "Marshall just earned himself a felony court martial. I'll see he gets life for this stunt." Then he recalled Julie's prognosis and realized Marshall had nothing to lose. And certainly nothing to fear from a general. He let out a sigh. *I'm out of time.* Hell, maybe Marshall and his sergeant are just what I need tonight – *ha, a couple of kamikaze commandos.*

He leveled a frightening glare at the pilot. "Get my goddamn car."

Marshall made his way to the flight deck and asked Youngblood, "Where's Wynett's chopper now?"

"He's 30 miles ahead of us," Youngblood said, watching the radar. "We'll be in Oceana in about 25 minutes."

Marshall nodded and started to withdraw when Youngblood hollered back, "Can I ask you a question?"

"No."

He asked anyway, "What's Julie like?"

Marshall dismissed him with a scowl and headed aft.

"So don't tell me," he said to himself, then muttered, "I'll find out for myself."

Quarantine

Julie sat behind the quarantine center's communications console and watched Marshall's helicopter take off on the security monitors. She was barely able to control her anger. "You son of a bitch."

Marshall had taken away her last chance to stop this nightmare. Her Catholic upbringing poured guilt and shame into her heart for creating a monster that was about to kill a lot of innocent people. She no longer dreamed of being infected. Now she dreamt of starting a fire in a forest that spread to every corner of the world.

Ever since leaving South America, Julie accepted the possibility that there might indeed be a God – or at least she allowed for the possibility of divine intervention in her life. She accepted the notion that a God, or some reasonable facsimile, had allowed her to live long enough to undo this terrible wrong she had committed. Stopping Gorgon would have been her atonement. Now she was trapped in quarantine, unable to act on her reparation. Maybe the Almighty intended to make her an example to the rest of the world. See what happens, my children, when mere mortals meddle with creation. Julie Martinelli, the Creator. Come see what she's done.

Damn you, Marshall, for leaving me behind!

"Julie, are you there?" Marshall's voice blared over the UHF band.

Her trembling fingers set the broadcast channel to all frequencies. She slid the headset over her ears and pressed the transmit button. "Joe?"

Marshall's voice filled her headset. "Set your frequency on one-two-nine. There's a scramble channel on the console. Find it and turn it on so we're in sync."

Julie did as he instructed, and a hideously garbled noise filled her ears. She heard three sharp sync tones, then Marshall's voice came in loud and clear.

"Better?" he said.

"I'm furious with you right now."

"If you want to rip me a new one, it'll have to wait."

"You had no right to leave me out of this."

"There's nothing you can do out here. I need you safe and sound where you can do me some good."

"There's no such thing as safe and sound. We're dying, you son of a bitch." Her words came out in a sob.

There was a pause from the chopper, then, "No one gets off this planet alive. Stay on this channel. I need you." The LED readout indicated that Marshall had ceased transmitting.

"Bastard." Julie spun away from the console and nearly shouted out loud at the sight of a woman standing in the doorway holding a hefty stack of papers.

"Thought you might want some company." It was her Stanford mentor Nancy Shaw.

Julie whipped around to compose herself and managed, "Nancy ... how'd you get in here?"

"I eavesdropped on your last conversation and figured out what was going on," she said. "I came in through the emergency door before the center auto-sealed itself. So I'm stuck in here with you."

Julie peered past her academic adviser into the cinderblock corridor. It was empty.

"Don't worry," Shaw said. "I'm the only one who bothered to listen in. Everybody else was either getting ready for the showdown or making plans to get upwind of Dodge. Anyway, I figured Marshall wouldn't take you with him."

"Bastard doesn't give a damn about me."

"Cut the crap and save the self-pity for your analyst. He did you a big favor. You're each right where you belong. If he didn't give a damn about you, he'd have brought you along and let you kill yourself."

Julie frowned at her. "Why did you come down here? I may be contagious."

"You're not, and the Brass knows it. It's all in here." Shaw lifted a stack of printouts the size of the D.C. telephone directory. "Here are the numbers you wanted run through the Cray. I did it on General Medlock's orders. Knock yourself out."

"Nancy, I'm scared shitless."

Shaw looked at her sympathetically. "After what you've been through, I'd be surprised if you weren't."

Julie struggled to lift her left hand, which seemed terribly weighty, and showed the doctor her trembling fingers bent unnaturally at right angles.

Shaw bit her lower lip.

"It feels so strange," Julie said, "like it no longer belongs to me."

The general's personal white Lincoln Mark VII skidded to a stop in front of him. General Medlock, his neck veins throbbing, climbed into the backseat and yelled at his driver, "Get me to Andrews Airfield as fast as you can drive this thing."

Marshall searched the chopper's armament cabinet, found a 9mm magazine and pushed it into the handle of the empty Beretta. He grabbed a leather pilot's jacket from a locker and slipped it over his shirt. Williams did likewise.

Marshall sat down next to Gruber and snatched the shoulder bag he still clutched to his chest. "I need every piece of information you've dug up about Gorgon's movements in the last forty-eight hours."

"It's all right in front of you," Gruber said.

Marshall sifted through Gruber's satchel and found a map of Virginia detailing the tanker's route approaching the Chesapeake Bay. He spread it on the chart table before him and noted a dotted line plotting the tanker's projected course up the York River to a refinery just north of Yorktown. Marshall followed its route with a quivering finger.

"It's getting worse, isn't it?" Gruber asked, watching the major's hand.

Marshall glanced up at him. "What's getting worse?"

"Your viral affliction. It's affecting your motor coordination. I think I understand what this is all about. You want to kill Gorgon before Saint Vitus kills you. A noble exchange. But you're denying the fact that you can't possibly be effective in your condition." He shook his head. "You're a terrible threat to the success of this operation, son. Your malady and recklessness are about to get people killed."

Williams thrust a finger at the old man and shouted, "I feel fucking fine."

The pencil in Marshall's hand suddenly snapped, though he wasn't aware that he'd put any pressure on it. "Not another word about it." He hid his trembling hand in the pocket of his jacket. "Sergeant, I want you to monitor all voice communication. Find out what's going on."

"Yes, sir." Williams put on a pair of headphones and plugged them into the navy's LINK II combat information system.

"If Gorgon wanted to launch his missiles," Marshall said to Gruber, "he would have done so already. He could have struck dozens of targets along the coast hours ago and been halfway back to Afghanistan by now. Why is he boxing himself in? Why does he need to dock that tanker?"

"Because he intends to take Saint Vitus inland," Gruber said. "He needs the threat of those missiles. But there's a seventy-percent probability that something's gone wrong with his launch system. We're running the logistics – weight ratios, payloads, trajectory, thrust, weather, everything. In any event, the assault team's first priority will be to take out those warheads. There's no margin for error in that regard."

"What if he starts pumping crude oil into the bay?" Williams offered. "You're going to piss off a lot of watermen."

"An environmental mess is the least of our problems." Gruber said. "We haven't even factored that into our equation."

"Where's the ship now?" Marshall asked.

Without much thought, Gruber said, "Thirty-two miles from the mouth of the Chesapeake Bay." He looked at his watch and twisted uncomfortably in his seat.

"What's your problem with the time?" the major asked.

"The president won't allow the tanker to reach the bay."

"Not a whole lot he can do about it," Marshall said tonelessly.

Gruber looked timidly at the major, anxiety written all over his face. "Yes, there is."

Quarantine

Julie sat at her computer workstation, her legs tucked beneath her, making notes with her good hand on the stack of printouts her adviser had given her.

Nancy Shaw sat across from her, watching her pupil over a hot cup of freshly brewed chamomile tea.

"Here's something I didn't expect to see," Julie said, circling a group of numbers on the printout. "Another virus is coupled with Saint Vitus."

"Coincidence?"

Julie shook her head. "It's too prolific, too consistent. It's in every single one of our infected cells."

"Could be part of the mutation," Shaw said, sipping her tea. "You could be looking at a new variation of St. Vitus, several generations removed."

"Not this virus," Julie said. "I've been able to track the pattern of St. Vitus' mutations. This other virus hasn't changed a bit. And I think I can identify it."

"Man-made?"

"Nope." Julie looked up at her. "It's a friggin' mouse tumor virus."

Shaw scowled. "A mouse-tumor virus? Are you certain?"

Julie flipped through her printout. "It was gene-spliced – Saint Vitus introduced it into our systems."

Shaw set down her tea mug before her suddenly shaking hands could spill it. "Do you know what you're saying, dear?"

"I think I'm saying that Dr. French was one clever son-of-a-bitch virus creator." Julie looked hard at Shaw. "Find me six cc's of the antiviral ganciclovir."

OCEANA

Andrews Air Force Base
1805 hours

General Medlock's driver negotiated a turn onto a frontage road that took the Lincoln around the far side of Andrews' number-three runway. Every 500 feet a soldier with an automatic rifle waved the general's vehicle quickly past. Medlock stared at the dashboard's digital clock – eight-zero-five. Wynett would be on his way to the tanker by now.

The car stopped abruptly in front of a brightly lit hangar, the area thick with activity. A tall, lanky officer minus a jacket, his sleeves rolled up to his elbows, opened the passenger door. "Sir, Wynett took off 17 minutes ago. We're taking him as far as the entrance of Chesapeake Bay at Cape Henry where the tanker is scheduled to pick up a river pilot. If he doesn't get aboard, he comes right back here."

"What about Option Two?"

"Already initiated."

Option Two rolled out of the hangar and taxied toward the runway – an F-15 Strike Eagle bomber, followed by an EF11 Raven for jamming support. Medlock noted the F-15's unconventional payload, two tactical nuclear glide bombs hanging from each wing. His eyes took on a distant look of resignation. "All those good men I'm sending out there. Jesus Christ, what's happening to us?"

"Marshall's chopper is landing at Oceana. Say the word and we'll have him shot on the spot."

Medlock climbed out of the car and watched the F-15 roar off the runway and vanish into the last light of day.

"Sir," the officer pressed, "what about Marshall?"

Medlock shook his head. "Get him on that tanker. He's the best goddamn chance we have."

Oceana Naval Air Station
Virginia

The skids of Medlock's command helicopter had barely touched down when Williams and Marshall stormed out of the troop compartment and raced across the tarmac. Special Forces Commander Alexander Stern met them halfway, holding a drawn .45 at his side.

"Christ, Joe," Stern said, "I never thought I'd be taking your ass into custody at gunpoint."

Commander Stern was a commando's commando – tough, mean and highly skilled. Large framed and eager to show off an all-muscle body, he didn't let his age of forty-seven years keep him from participating in every op under his charge. One hell of a tactical planner, he also was one hell of a soldier. "How in Christ did you manage to get yourself into this mess, Joe?"

Marshall spotted the drawn .45 in Stern's hand and the dangerous squint in his eyes that said he was ready to use it on him. "Al, I need your help."

"Damn right you do, pal. I have orders to arrest you on sight ... or put a bullet into your fat head if you resist. I don't need this right now."

Marshall matched Stern's rock-steady eyes. "I need to be part of this op. I'm asking you as a friend."

Stern thrust the .45 at Marshall's forehead and drew back the hammer with a dangerous click. "Not a fucking chance. Jesus, Joe, don't make me use this."

"Commander," yelled a first lieutenant running across the tarmac with a handheld ComSat transceiver. "It's Medlock at Andrews. Says he has a priority-one directive for you."

Stern never took his eyes off Marshall as he grabbed the transceiver from the lieutenant and put it to his ear. "Stern here." His face remained frozen while he listened, and Marshall watched him slowly lower the .45, reseat the hammer and slip it into his side holster. "Yes, sir." He thrust the transceiver back into the lieutenant's hands, and an uncharacteristic grin broke his solemn features. "You're in. Medlock's orders. Don't ask me how or why. We gotta go."

Marshall let out a long sigh as he walked Stern back to the hangar. He felt his adrenaline flowing. "How many men do we have here?"

"Two Delta squads from Bragg and every SEAL within 500 miles," Stern said. "We're putting thirty SEALs on the tanker in the first assault. Forty Delta troops are standing by in Sea Stallions. We have regular ground troops waiting in Yorktown in the unlikely event the bastard makes it that far upriver. General Medlock wants you and your sergeant on the tanker with the first assault."

Marshall nodded. "I need a Franchi and my sergeant needs a Galil."

Commander Stern checked his clipboard. "I'm putting you on launch number nine. Lieutenant Greenberg on the dock will get you whatever you need. Get your asses moving. You're shoving off in five minutes."

Stern turned and hustled back toward the hangar.

"Congratulations, major," Gruber said, appearing at Marshall's side. "Looks like you got your wish. If you manage to get on board the tanker, it's imperative that you immediately sever the power cable between the launch vehicle and the missile pallet. Do that and you'll kick the son of a bitch in the balls. He won't be able to target those missiles."

"But he can still fire them?" Marshall asked.

"Yes, the missile platform has a redundant launch system that can fire manually," Gruber said. "A bullet in the platform's motherboard will disable the entire missile pallet."

"Got it." Marshall extended his hand to Gruber. "And thank you."

Gruber took his proffered hand and frowned, his faced paling notably. Marshall realized that instead of a firm handshake, Gruber could feel the tremor of a very ill man.

"Good luck, major," Gruber said. "I know you'll do what you have to do. Don't let that bastard kill any more people."

Cape Henry
United States Eastern Seaboard

Lt. Cmdr. Thomas Lee tightened his grip on a pair of high-powered binoculars to steady his view against the even rolling of the cutter's deck. Three weeks past his twentieth anniversary in the service of the United States Navy, the wizened veteran was a tall man whose heavy oilskin breaker gave his substantial frame the gray, rocky appearance of Mt. Rainier.

Lee's keen hazel eyes, buried beneath twin outcrops of gray brows, peered through the night binoculars with a laser-like intensity that could find any object in the roughest seas, day or night. He spotted *Lucy* six miles off his starboard bow. Locating something as large as an oil tanker hardly required psychic abilities. Would getting the old man aboard be as easy?

Commander Lee lowered the binoculars, his lips drooped in a half-frown. His cutter looked more like a pleasure craft than an armed navy vessel, a disguise which worked well in drug-trafficking patrols off Miami. But at close range, any good seaman would spot the ruse, and that bothered the hell out of him.

Lee became aware of someone approaching from behind. He half-turned and saw Wynett, dressed in an orange one-piece survival suit, staring vacantly in the direction of the tanker.

"She still isn't answering us," Lee said. "Nor has she stopped. Did you consider a strong possibility they won't let you aboard?"

Wynett, his distant eyes narrowing, shook his head. "I will meet with him."

Lucy

"Approaching vessel," Tarra said, her eyes buried in the ship's radar hood.

Captain Carlucci whirled at the news.

Tarra narrowed the tracking beam on the bridge's radar display to a west-northwest scan. "Range, five-point-three kilometers, bearing three-two-seven ... on an interception course." She pressed the headset to her ear. "The river pilot is requesting permission to board."

"I can see him," Gorgon said, scanning the rising swells through a pair of night binoculars. The dusk's gray half-light was rapidly yielding to a blackness that swallowed the bay. "Let him board and bring him directly to me." Gorgon lowered his binoculars and said in a low voice as though to himself, "A horse appeared, deathly pale, and its rider was called Death, and Hell followed at his heels."

"What does that mean?" Tarra said.

Gorgon shook his head. "The journey we began at the settlement of Kumar is almost at an end."

Oceana Naval Air Station
2009 hours

Marshall and Williams climbed down into the rubber Zodiac launch beside Lieutenant Greenberg, a seasoned Special Forces officer who would be their pilot and navigator.

"Commander Stern just radioed me about you gents," Greenberg said.

Marshall regarded the slightly short, slightly stocky, slightly aging Navy SEAL. Despite Greenberg's disarming, fatherly smile, Marshall didn't doubt he knew at least a half dozen ways to break a man's neck with his hands. "What did Stern tell you about us?"

"Says you're the best," Greenberg said, shaking first Marshall's, then Williams' hand. "Glad to be on your team tonight."

Clad in black rubber wet suits, hoods and taut slipper-like boots, Marshall went to work, only vaguely aware of the other teams along the dock also loading and readying their launches. The staging area was dark. He could hear the sounds of men working, but saw little. Marshall smeared black camouflage paint onto his face, obscuring the boundaries between wet suit and flesh, then tugged on a pair of skintight leather gloves. He clamped a miniature transceiver to his SAS belt, put the headphone over his good ear, adjusted its tiny microphone over his mouth and switched on the belt unit. Williams did likewise.

"A lot of gents in Washington will no doubt be monitoring everything we say tonight," Greenberg warned the two. He grinned. "So be careful who you hurl your curses at."

A soldier on the dock passed down munitions satchels and a pair of weapons – a Franchi paramilitary shotgun and an Israeli Galil sniper's rifle. He also gave each of them a pair of image-intensifying goggles and a tiny waterproof notebook, detailing *Lucy's* deck plan. Marshall slipped on the goggles and focused them. The world once again became visible in an eerie green-yellow glow.

"Let's go."

Lucy

Captain Carlucci met a very winded and exhausted-looking Wynett at the top of *Lucy's* gangway. Wynett seated himself heavily on a pipe, unable to breathe. He looked ghastly. His face was beaten, his skin the pallor of death, his bloodshot eyes deep-sunk in hollowed sockets, his lips bloodless. Carlucci thought the old man might pass out.

Wynett struggled to focus his eyes on the sea captain standing over him and wheezed, "Requesting permission to board, captain."

Carlucci's suspicious eyes moved from Wynett to the disguised cutter racing away from the tanker, then back to Wynett. "You are not a pilot, are you?"

Wynett, struggling to take a breath, put a spasming hand on his forehead. "No, sir. My business is with the man who commandeered your vessel."

Carlucci looked curiously at him. "Then am I to understand the American military knows about this murderous madman?"

"You are correct, sir."

Carlucci nodded. "Then God has heard my prayers tonight."

STRIKE EAGLE

2010 hours

Cmdr. Buzz Hayes eased his F-15 Strike Eagle into a gentle bank that would circumscribe another forty-five-mile arc around *Lucy*. Hayes reduced power to his twin turbine engines to conserve fuel. The night promised a long wait.

His bombardier, a young lieutenant named Pete Booker, once again checked the position of each armament switch on the aircraft's newly retrofitted tactical bombing system, not unlike the conventional air-to-ground bombing unit he had trained on. He noted the time in his kneeboard log – a regular tactical exercise. He glanced at the three-dimensional computer image of *Lucy* on his heads-up display, then moved the cursor over the ship's radar image and pressed a key to retarget and lock the tanker on the auto-tracking system. Piece of cake. The length of a football field – and slow – *Lucy* was a ridiculously easy target to track.

An alert tone blared in Lieutenant Booker's headset, and data flashed across the bottom of the VDI display. New orders. He mentally decoded the display information and felt every muscle in his body involuntarily tighten.

This was no exercise.

Shit – that's fucking Newport News down there! Somebody had made one hell of a mistake. Didn't they? Or was he about to become the first bombardier since Nagasaki to launch a nuclear attack? He shifted his eyes to the infinite blackness outside the canopy. "Jesus," he said into his helmet mic.

Commander Hayes let out a nervous huff. "You're not likely to get his help tonight." Then the pilot's voice hardened. "You got a problem, lieutenant?"

"Negative."

The bombardier opened the scrambled UHF channel to the command hangar. He heard the voice scrambler beep, then said, "Hawk One to Father. Request voice confirmation."

The radio was silent for several seconds, and then a voice responded, "Stand by to attack target at coordinates two-six-four and one-seven-nine. Repeat. Stand by to attack target at coordinates two-six-four, one-seven-nine."

Jesus, this is really happening, Booker thought. Another tone sounded in his headset as the orange AUTOPILOT DISCONNECT light blinked on. He felt the aircraft roll as Hayes began the bomb run. One button, the bombardier mused. That was all that stood between him and a bona fide nuclear hell. For the first time in his military career his hands were trembling ... trembling during a *fucking* mission! One button. Why me, Jesus? Why am I the one? *Because this is what you trained for!* He thought of his wife and four-year-old daughter probably asleep in their home in Virginia. He would press one button, and two minutes later a low-yield tactical nuclear bomb would transform the tanker not far from them into a thick, stinking cloud of hydrocarbons.

The White House Situation Room

"What the hell's happening out there, general?" the president said into the phone's receiver.

"My troops will rendezvous with the ship in approximately four minutes," Medlock said from the hangar at Andrews Airfield.

"I'm taking a terrible risk with your plan," the president said. "I don't want that tanker on the bay."

"Four minutes, Mr. President," Medlock said slowly and deliberately. "In four minutes my men will be on board that tanker and finish this business."

Quarantine

Dr. Nancy Shaw inserted the syringe into the permeable tip of the bottle and withdrew 10 milligrams of the antiviral ganciclovir. "Give me your arm."

Julie reached for the syringe with a trembling hand. "I'm perfectly capable of giving myself a shot."

"Give me your arm," Shaw insisted.

Julie acquiesced.

"This is twice the normal dose," Shaw said, pulling, the syringe out of her arm and pressing a cotton ball hard into the inside of her arm, just above her left elbow. "We'll give it 10 minutes, then take another blood sample."

Julie nodded and let her thoughts drift to Marshall. Where was he now? What was he doing? She didn't try to push him from her mind. Quite the contrary. She drew newfound strength from the mental image of him out there to destroy the virus.

The mouth of the Chesapeake Bay
2017 hours

The Zodiac rubber water raft skimmed smartly across the bay in complete darkness. Marshall peered through his night goggles at the ocean swells, but he could see nothing. Those aboard the tanker would be equally blind. For the moment they didn't need to see. An Air Force AWAC plane circling 20,000 feet above acted as their eyes, feeding the tanker's position to the teams' GPS units. Lieutenant Greenberg's gaze darted continuously from the compass to the receiver, which indicated the tanker was only fifty yards to port. There were no ship lights to act as beacons.

Nine other Zodiacs with three-man crews approached the tanker from different headings. The plan called for the troops to rendezvous on the ship and disable the missile pallet. How they managed that serendipitous feat once on board would depend entirely on their opportunities. There had been no elaborate setup, no training for this mission, little planning. There simply hadn't been time. Medlock was gambling that the tanker was too large for Gorgon's men to patrol every foot of bulwark. He figured that ten teams – thirty men – would tip the odds for success in their favor. There were a lot of crossed fingers tonight in Washington.

Marshall had too much time during the short crossing to contemplate what could go wrong. What if Gorgon saw them approaching? What if only one of the teams managed to get on board? What if the missiles fired? What if the virus was released? What if ... what if ... ? He shook his head, forcing his mind to focus exactly where it needed to be – on revenge.

A shape the size of a large island appeared before them. *Lucy*. She looked gigantic. Her deck and anti-collision lights were out, making her virtually invisible. Marshall watched the massive ship approach, tapping a knuckle thoughtfully on his lips. Williams, sitting motionless at his side, kept his night goggles focused on the tanker. The breeze decreased as the huge wall of the tanker loomed up over them, shielding them as they maneuvered along its side. No one said a word.

All Marshall could think about was Julie. Thank God she was safe. He found it difficult to stop the flow of feelings between his brain and his heart. The sensations were new to him. He couldn't rid her from his mind. He closed his eyes and grew rigid, forcing himself to once again become a machine. But he couldn't. Something was different this time, he realized belatedly. Julie. She was with him – a part of him.

Marshall's eyes flared open when Lieutenant Greenberg let the craft bounce purposefully off the tanker's hull, which now towered over them like a great cliff. The lieutenant adjusted the muffled outboard motor to match the ship's speed. They worked quickly to secure the launch. Despite the rolling water, *Lucy* moved slowly and evenly, her fully loaded cargo tanks stabilizing the ship deep in the water. Had anyone seen them approach? The element of surprise was their most potent weapon.

Marshall could barely make out the ship's bulwark on the forward bow just 15 feet above them. "Can you secure a line to that anchor aperture?"

Greenberg squinted upward. "Piece of cake."

"Watch that rail," Marshall ordered his sergeant. "If you see anything that looks like a head, put a bullet through it."

Williams swung his Galil sniper rifle off his shoulder and scanned the bulwark above through the weapon's night scope.

Lucy

Wynett followed Carlucci across the deck sluggishly, his gait impaired. A soldier in black fatigues and carrying a Kalashnikov fell in behind them. Wynett felt neither fear nor intimidation, only a fatigue at the core of his soul. *Lucy* was everything he had expected and like nothing he had imagined. Her vast size astounded him, and he could feel her solidness beneath his feet. With a road of pipes stretching the length of the vessel to the superstructure, she looked more like an industrial facility than a ship.

Wynett had no memory of walking the lengthy deck, entering the superstructure or climbing the narrow stairwells to the bridge deck. Only after he entered the wheelhouse did his attention return to the pressing reality.

Lucy's bridge was crowded with soldiers in black fatigues. The wheelhouse reeked of death, as though an animal had died, rotting inside the walls where nobody could reach it.

Gorgon peeled away from the chart table and loomed over Wynett, his hands arrogantly on his hips. Carlucci moved into the corner and watched. Gorgon's face turned to stone. *"You."* His eyes narrowed. "I would not have believed you capable of this."

Wynett betrayed no emotion.

Tarra peeled away from the main console and shrieked when she saw Wynett. She grabbed Gorgon's arm. "The missiles. You must launch the missiles now and finish this. Then let me kill him."

"Give this up," Carlucci said, making his way forward. "I implore you in the name of sanity to surrender this vessel."

Two of Gorgon's men pushed Carlucci back with their weapons. That didn't deter him. "It is madness to continue." He appealed to Tarra. "Tell him. Make him listen."

Gorgon roared at Wynett, "I demand to know why you came here."

Wynett said soberly, "To collect my money ... ten million American dollars. I delivered to you the most effective weapon of mass killing ever devised and you gave me nothing in return. I am here to collect my fee per our agreement."

Gorgon's head flew back and out came an ugly laughter that boomed off the wheelhouse's metal walls. "You are truly mad."

"The United States militia must know who we are and what we carry," Tarra shouted. "They will not let us proceed."

Gorgon's face darkened, and when he spoke to Wynett there was cold contempt in his voice. "In Tampico you saw how I deal with treachery. Before I kill you, you will tell me what the American military intelligence knows about my plan."

Wynett's eyes fluttered, and he looked every bit the old, dying man he was. "They know we are having bloody good fun."

Gorgon gave a quick, irritated jerk of his head, and three of his soldiers surrounded Wynett, their weapons pointed at his chest. The old man did not react with the slightest alarm.

Beep ... beep ... beep ...

Tarra returned to the ship's radar console and peered into the unit. "Small watercraft approaching from different directions. Maybe ten. Their range extends to thirty meters."

"What is this trap?" Gorgon demanded.

Wynett said nothing, offering only a knowing grin.

Gorgon whirled to Tarra, "Alert the deck. Prepare for a boarding assault."

Gorgon moved to the bridge's window but could see nothing but blackness beyond the ship's forward bow. When he spoke, his tone was subdued. "No navy on earth can undo the seeds I have sown. Soon the world we once knew will change. No one can stop that. No one can stop me."

ASSAULT

Marshall twisted through the narrow opening between the anchor aperture and the massive chain and lay face down on *Lucy's* forward deck. Williams followed and slid beside him. The deck felt cold, much colder than the ambient air temperature suggested. Neither man moved. The quiet, broken only by the churning river sweeping past the ship's sides, felt eerie.

Marshall scanned the deck through his image-intensifying goggles. He could see vague shapes and protrusions across the deck. And men. Gorgon's troops were strategically stationed, some manning the ship's armaments, some patrolling, some scanning the bay through night binoculars. The terrorists appeared hyper-vigilant, expectant. Marshall counted seven on the forecastle, nearly invisible in their black uniforms.

Marshall screwed his neck around. His eyes widened. One of Gorgon's soldiers stood at the bulwark mere feet behind him scanning the bay forward of the ship, his silhouette a shade blacker than the night. Williams saw him too. Marshall withdrew the Beretta from his back holster, but his trembling hand couldn't keep the gun still.

Williams reached for his ankle and unsheathed his black serrated knife. The sentry spun at the slight sound. Williams' knife vanished in a blur of hand movement. The soldier grabbed the base of his throat with a gargled grunt and collapsed against the rail.

Commander Alexander Stern steadied his balance in the small, swaying Zodiac and lifted onto his shoulder what looked to the uninitiated like a miniature bazooka. He took an inordinately long three seconds to sight the tanker's bulwark, aimed high to compensate for the rising and falling swells, then pulled the trigger. There came a sharp puff, and the thin nylon cord unraveled quickly as it spiraled upward. The four-pronged rubber grappling hook flew over the rail and landed with a muted thud on *Lucy's* steel deck. Stern yanked the cord until the hook caught on the bulwark. He listened. Not a sound from above.

Don't think about it, he told himself. *Just act.*

Stern covered the fifteen-foot climb in eight seconds. His two commandos followed him, M-24 assault rifles strapped to their backs.

Stern swung his legs over the bulwark and landed in a half crouch on the ship's darkened deck. He could see only vague shapes rising from the tanker's open deck. There simply wasn't enough light for the goggles to amplify. His two men crouched at his side and unfolded the stocks of their automatic rifles. *How many other teams made it on board?* Stern made a quick sweep of the deck through his rifle's night scope, searching for the missile platform. Where the fuck was it? There were too many unrecognizable shapes – pipes, hatches, valves...

Movement caught Stern's eye – man-sized shapes at ten yards. He swung his rifle toward them. He never had the chance to fire. A dozen rounds tore into Stern and his two men.

He felt only a cold numbness as he died.

Marshall spotted several of Gorgon's soldiers running aft. Gunshots ripped through the night. Marshall grimaced. Gorgon's soldiers were launching a counterattack of fire at the troops storming *Lucy's* side. *Poor bastards don't stand a chance.* The port and starboard 30mm chain cannons began firing at the Zodiac rafts on the bay, filling the night with their awful pounding. A massacre.

"What are you waiting for?" Marshall hissed at his sergeant. Williams raised the Galil with its flash-suppressed muzzle and sighted the starboard 30mm chain-cannon operator through the infrared laser-assisted scope. He positioned the laser beam on the soldier's chest halfway between his heart and throat and fired a single, suppressed round. A plum-size wound blossomed beneath the laser marker. The terrorist looped backward over the bulwark and disappeared into the bay. His huge gun fell silent. The gunnery sergeant placed his scope's beam similarly on the port cannon operator and fired. The mercenary crumpled to the deck, his cannon silenced.

Williams continued a cold, calculated sweep of the upper deck. Expertly, methodically, he fired. He took out a third terrorist running with an AK-47 braced on his hip. The soldier flew against a wall of pipes and dropped. Williams dropped a fourth soldier. A fifth. A sixth. Each went down without a sound, the well-placed round inflicting too much damage to warrant even a cry of protest from the target.

In the first minute of the assault, Williams had secured *Lucy's* forward deck.

"Radio them," Tarra shouted at him. "Tell them you will release the plague if they do not call off the attack. They will listen."

Gorgon remained rooted before the wheelhouse window, listening to the mounting gunfire in the night. He had no intention of bartering with his enemy. No deals, no terms, no communication, no change in plan. He stood at the window, watching the muzzle flashes on deck.

"They will not let us pass," she shouted. "We must aban-don—"

Gorgon whirled and struck Tarra's face with a wild brush of his hand. Her head flew back, but she remained upright, absorbing the blow.

Wynett chuckled. "You are no different than an ordinary man."

Gorgon thrust a finger at Tarra. "You talk of treachery. I have no intention of joining Allah in his paradise." He stepped to the main console and lifted the phone off its cradle. "Mr. Balla – begin Unharness."

Four of Gorgon's soldiers drew back a tarpaulin that concealed a platform the size of a small trailer. The pallet carried nine computer-guided Procyon missiles mounted on a hydraulic launch vehicle. A smaller, armored truck containing the electronic control equipment sat next to the platform, attached by way of a thick power cable.

Captain Carlucci moved to the wheelhouse window and spotted the men preparing the weapons platform. He recognized the missiles' conical-shaped warheads, the same projectiles he had seen in the pump room's workshop with the odd-looking tanks. The enormity of what Gorgon intended to do suddenly became clear to him. The missiles would carry the organism inland.

"No, no, *noooo!*" The guards pushed Carlucci back. "You must not do this."

"Remain at your post," Gorgon ordered him. He depressed the transmit button and said into the intercom, "Target one and two for Norfolk."

From the missiles' launch vehicle, a woman's voice barren of emotion crackled back, "Positioning."

Carlucci returned to the window and stared, unblinking, while the twenty-three-foot missile pallet began rising on hydraulic legs. When the platform reached an angle of sixty-seven degrees, the hydraulic pistons stopped, the warheads positioned.

"Arm one and two," Gorgon said.

"One and two arming," the woman's voice crackled. A pause, then, "Launch ready."

"Launch on my order."

Tarra giggled wickedly.

Carlucci drew in a deep breath and held it.

"Launch!"

Carlucci charged out onto the wing deck just as the solid-rocket boosters on two Procyon missiles ignited. The brilliance of their tails, as bright as the sun, burned his retinas. He threw up a hand to protect his eyes. The missiles burst from the launch platform with a terrible shriek and roared into the night, leaving a fiery tail in their wake. A noxious blanket of smoke covered the deck like a death shroud.

Carlucci couldn't move. He stood there, silent, watching, listening to the fading thunder. "May God have mercy on all those in its path."

Marshall and Williams covered their ears against the auditory assault of the missile blast's pressure wave. The decks lit with the brilliance of day as the twin Procyons roared away into the night like twin giant magnesium flares.

"Jesus, Joe," Williams said.

Marshall gritted his jaw in frustration. "We're too late."

Andrews Airfield

The communications officer spun away from the radio console and said to Medlock, "The AWAC reports two missile launches. Trajectory northwest. First possible target is Norfolk."

The hangar grew somberly quiet. No one moved. Every eye remained fixed on the general.

Medlock's jaw tightened, "Inform the president. Tell him to order Option Two."

The communications officer spun back to his console to carry out the order.

General Medlock, suddenly weary, his shoulders hunched in defeat, swept around and walked briskly across the hanger, opened the door and vanished into the night.

Quarantine

Julie didn't realize Nancy Shaw had slipped into the room behind her until her mentor put a hand on her shoulder and said softly, "I just heard it on the secured channel."

Julie whipped around, panic swelling inside her. "Joe? Is he ...?"

"No, the missiles. Gorgon just fired two of them."

Julie turned away and shook her head. When she spoke, her words were barely audible. "Please forgive me."

White House Situation Room

The president's aide set down the phone receiver. "Gorgon launched two Procyon missiles. General Medlock advises Option Two."

A grim-faced president accepted the inevitable news with a shallow nod. "Proceed, Mr. Nicholas."

F-15 Strike Eagle

The bomber's heads-up display flashed *Go*. The bombardier would receive no further authorization. Lieutenant Booker depressed his console's AUTOFIX button to download *Lucy's* current position into the glide-bomb's onboard computer while simultaneously arming it. He touched an orange switch labeled WEAPON RELEASE.

"God, forgive us our trespasses," he muttered, the only prayer fragment he could think of at the moment before depressing the switch.

The orange weapon release lamp flared as the nineteen-hundred pound tactical nuclear bomb disengaged from the hydraulic wing launcher and disappeared into the bomber's slipstream.

DOWN RANGE

Chesapeake Bay
Off the coast of Norfolk

Lt. Cmdr. Thomas Lee stood alone on his vessel's quarter-deck, staring into the blackness. He wondered whether the eccentric old man he'd delivered to the terrorist-held tanker had just thrown away what was left of his ailing life. Most likely, he conceded. Either the old man had astonishing nerve or he was a bloody fool—

The deck's loudspeaker roared, "Incoming projectile bearing zero-two-two ... airspeed five hundred twenty-two knots. Estimated impact approximately 3,000 feet off our starboard." The announcement's metallic quality couldn't mask the distress in the pilot's voice.

Commander Lee whirled and looked skyward, east southeast. He spotted the bogey immediately – overlapping globules of light hurtling through the veil of clouds off his starboard beam. He stiffened, his face bone-tight. *A goddamn missile.*

Lee thrust the radio to his lips and exploded, "Full speed ... hard left rudder ... *move your ass!"*

Commander Lee braced himself on the rail while the vessel swept around. His keen eyes never left the rapidly descending bogey. He could see two distinct tails. *Christ, two of them!* He saw a small flash as the warheads separated and spiraled toward the bay. It would be close, he knew, damn close. He watched the twin tails of fire hurtle downward until they reached sea level where they disappeared in the eternal blackness of the Bay. Lee braced himself for the shattering concussion. But there was no detonation, no explosion, no great eruption of water. Only a strange wind, warmer than the night air, that swept over the deck and quickly dissipated.

"Haley Alpha Two to Andrews," Lee said over the secure naval channel to Medlock's command center at Andrews. "Two missiles down 37 degrees north latitude and 76 degrees west longitude. Impact approximately 3,000 feet on my starboard—"

The radio fell from Lee's grip and shattered onto the deck. He turned toward the pilothouse but was unable to focus his eyes. A bizarre sensation rippled through Lee's extremities as though his veins were curling like snakes beneath his skin. In a panic he dug his fingernails deep into his flesh and pulled back the skin of his forearm as though peeling a fruit.

He tried to call for help, but he had no control over his voice, no motor control of his extremities. *Jesus help me.* A paralyzing fear gripped him. He knew he was dying and hadn't a clue why.

Lee's legs buckled and he collapsed in a convulsive fit. His extremities pounded the deck viciously again and again and again, mashing his limbs into a paste. He couldn't utter a sound. His mouth and eyes remained open long after the back of his head had smashed to pulp against the steel deck.

Lucy

"Mr. Gorgon," Wynett said, his tone mocking, "there is something you should know about your missiles."

Gorgon turned to him with dark, questioning eyes.

Carlucci noted the terrorist's uncertain expression and asked Wynett, "The missiles? There is a problem?"

"The missiles obey my command," Gorgon said, his voice icy.

Wynett could not contain his giddy laughter. "I would have been delighted to explain to you the fundamentals of Procyon aerodynamics, but you left my estate in such haste."

Gorgon towered over the old man. "What is this nonsense?"

"A Procyon," he said, "has a maximum range of 950 nautical miles. That poses a problem for your special warhead. To achieve that range, the missile's steep trajectory and high speed would prevent the virus from dispersing. To disperse the agent effectively, the missile must not reach an apogee of more than six thousand meters or exceed a velocity of nine hundred seventy kilometers per hour. So you see, I was forced to make radical recalibrations to the boosters."

Carlucci looked at him, puzzled. "I do not understand."

"The range," Gorgon demanded. "Tell me its range."

"Twenty miles," Wynett wheezed. "You must move this tanker very close to your target. Washington is out of the question, I'm afraid. And now your vessel is on a collision path with Saint Vitus. Pray that the wind disperses the virus before we reach the vicinity of the missiles' impact."

He thrust a finger at Carlucci. "I want the engine ahead full."

Carlucci implored Gorgon, "This is madness—"

"Do it!" Gorgon roared. "Or die where you stand."

"Kill him," Tarra said. "I will pilot this ship."

Captain Carlucci raised his hand in defeat and moved to the ship's main console, his heart swollen with foreboding. Increasing the ship's speed was a simple task. If not him, then someone else – Gorgon's lieutenant Tarra – could easily do it. You cannot die now, he reminded himself. *You must scuttle this ship.*

Carlucci pushed the engine lever forward to full speed.

Gorgon said to Tarra, "Twenty miles will be enough. My seven remaining warheads will obliterate the eastern seaboard."

Oceana

Dr. Gruber heard the news of the missile's scuttle from the AWAC aircraft. Seconds later he had computed the logistics. He slammed his hand hard onto the desk and yelled, "His missiles have no range."

All eyes in the staging hanger turned toward him.

Gruber lifted the receiver of the emergency telephone tied directly to Medlock's handheld unit and waited several impatient seconds for the general to answer.

Andrews Airfield

General Medlock stood at the edge of the runway without his overcoat, listening to the night. So far he'd heard nothing. No sonic boom, no distant thunder. How would a nuclear detonation 100 miles away sound? Would he feel its heated wind?

Medlock's portable phone began ringing. He raised it to his ear. "Medlock."

"Gorgon's Procyons can't reach land," Gruber blurted. "At least not yet. They fell eight miles short of Norfolk where the wind will carry the virus out to sea. At eighteen knots the missiles will be in range of land in about 20 minutes. Your commandos must take out that missile pallet now—"

"Jesus fucking Christ," Medlock spat. "We're already a minute and a half into the drop."

Medlock pressed a button on his phone and secured a scrambled channel to the White House Situation Room.

There was a click in Gruber's ear. Medlock was gone. A solemn-faced Gruber replaced the receiver. Poor bastards. A *fucking* minute and a half too late.

The F-15 pilot and bombardier both saw the message flash across their respective heads-up displays: ABORT in large, red letters, accompanied by a high-pitched warning screech in their headsets.

"Jesus, are you copying this?" Commander Hayes said to his bombardier.

Lieutenant Booker didn't respond. He depressed the ABORT button on his weapons console with a trembling finger and prayed the prototype system would function as designed.

The bombardier wondered, almost giddily, if he was the first person in history to disarm a nuclear weapon falling toward its target.

Two thousand feet above *Lucy*, the bomb's trigger mechanism jerked back into its safety position, rendering the device inoperable, while the foot-long plutonium canister jettisoned and parachuted for immediate recovery. A second and a half later, thirty-six pounds of high-yield plastic explosives detonated.

The shell of the tactical nuclear bomb disintegrated in a spectacular fireball over *Lucy*.

Gorgon listened to the growing firefight on the ship's forward deck. "They are using the darkness to infiltrate my ship." He spun away from the pilothouse window. "The lights. I want every deck light on."

Tarra slid from her stool in front of the radar hood and appealed to him. "Lights will show them the way to the missiles—"

Gorgon, sneering, pushed her viciously aside and threw a bank of switches on the main console. On the ship's upper deck, powerful sodium-arc lamps atop the loading arms and crow's nest flared, lighting *Lucy's* deck with the brilliance of day.

A harsh light washed over Marshall and Williams like a huge consuming wave, burning their retinas. The lights blinded Williams as he fired. The suppressed round hit wide of its mark by two inches, piercing the terrorist's right lung. The thug went down with a wail in front of his comrade, who watched him thrash and gurgle to death.

"I'm blind," Williams shouted, shaking his head to rid himself of the painful afterimage.

Marshall cursed and tore off his night goggles. "Clear me space around the weapon's truck." The major leaped over the anchor mounting and sprinted aft, crouching behind the network of pipes as he made his way to the missiles' armored electronics vehicle, the brains of the Procyon system.

Williams lifted his Galil and struggled to sight the armed sentry standing next to the truck's rear door. As the figure came into focus, he fired. The bullet tore the mercenary's heart in two. He fell back against the truck with an audible *whomp.*

Gorgon watched through his binoculars as a lone commando ran aft toward the missiles. He saw other soldiers in black wet suits climbing over the bulwarks to take his ship.

Gorgon said into his transceiver, "Officer of the deck, there are intruders on board, middeck, moving aft. Defend the Procyons."

When Gorgon received no acknowledgment, he replaced the binoculars to his eyes and realized his folly. His officer of the deck was dead, as were all his troops stationed forward. The intruders had breached his forward defenses and were killing his men as they moved aft. He realized at that moment that *Lucy* had reached the end of her voyage.

"Arm and fire the remaining missiles," Gorgon said into his transceiver. "I order you to launch all missiles at once. I repeat. Launch the Procyons."

"Sloppy, Mr. Gorgon," Wynett scoffed. "Very sloppy."

Gorgon fixed Wynett with a baleful stare and said to Tarra, "Put these men into the tank. See that they have an interesting death."

Inside the armored electronics truck, a woman with alluring features acknowledged Gorgon's order to fire. She released the missiles' safety, keyed in the new launch sequence code and watched the green status lights flare to active. The seven remaining independent pre-targeted missiles armed automatically and waited for her command to launch. She glanced at the radar. The display was clouded with blotches of green. Jammed. She grinned. She no longer needed—

A frightful blast rocked the vehicle and the rear door blew off its hinges. She spun in her chair in surprise. Her eyes caught only a glimpse of the silhouetted figure standing outside the rear doorway, holding a paramilitary shotgun.

Her hand shot to the MISSILE LAUNCH button.

The shotgun blast hit her chest. She tore backward out of the chair, her hands grasping and clawing at the air. The commando pumped three more rounds into the vehicle's instrumentation, creating a blizzard of electrical sparks, smoke and glass.

Marshall spun away from the rear door and pointed his Franchi at the thick electrical cable that fed power and instructions to the missile platform behind the truck. A dark figure appeared from the front of the vehicle and pointed a Kalashnikov at his head. The right half of the terrorist's skull disintegrated in a thick red storm that blew in the direction of the exiting bullet from Williams' rifle. Nearly headless, the terrorist jerked to attention, blood pumping from his hollow skull, before dropping.

Marshall discharged a shotgun blast at the electrical cable, severing it with a coarse hiss of sparks that sounded like an angry sea snake. One more target, he thought. Destroy the pallet's onboard computer, and Gorgon would be impotent. Two more soldiers materialized from behind the missile platform and charged him. Marshall's Franchi blast tore off the gun-toting arm of the first soldier, who went down with a shriek. The second mercenary, wielding a Kalashnikov, fired a wild burst at Marshall. Bullets ricocheted off the side of the armored truck.

Marshall dove to the deck and rolled under the vehicle, its high axle offering him enough room to maneuver. The mercenary kept the major pinned under the vehicle with a series of short bursts while another soldier, a technician, leaped to the missile platform. The second soldier went to work on the Procyons' keypad, manually resuming the launch sequence.

"The missiles are still operable," Marshall yelled into his transceiver. "Two men are at the platform ... can you get them?"

Williams leveled his Galil at the missile pallet. The control vehicle blocked his targets. "Joe," the sergeant said, "move that damn truck out of my way."

Gorgon's technician, a slim soldier with glasses, leaned into the missile platform's opened electronics bay and rerouted the cable on the manual launch system. The standby light on the keyboard blinked from red to green. He now had control of the missiles. He keyed a series of protocol commands into the platform's onboard computer to begin the manual launch sequence. There was no way to hasten the process. Eagerness would be foolhardy, he knew. A single wrong entry would lock up the system, forcing him to reboot the onboard computer and start the procedure again.

Another sound more alarming than gunfire roared across the sky – an approaching jet – taking precious concentration away from his work. He keyed in the final command and watched impatiently as the lengthy instruction code downloaded.

The twin-engine blast nearly deafened him. The technician reeled backward in alarm as an AV-A8 Harrier jet descended from the sky in front of the ship, its engine exhaust bringing the aircraft to a hover over the forward deck as though it were a helicopter. The technician, shielding his face from the jet's powerful downdraft, glanced at the keyboard. The LAUNCH READY light remained stubbornly red. His string of curses were lost in the roar.

Slowly and with incredible precision, the jet began creeping aft.

The Harrier's superheated exhaust washed over the technician like a hurricane from hell. The terrorist took refuge behind a tower of deck valves and huddled, hands cupped over his ears. The Harrier pilot was damned good, he thought. The missiles couldn't launch, not without bringing the jet crashing down on the ship's deck. When the missiles were ready, he needed touch only one key to launch.

One key.

But he couldn't. Not while the Harrier remained airborne.

Inside the Harrier, Youngblood moved the jet forward and brought it to a hover 200 feet above the missile platform. He saw two of the terrorists scatter from beneath the aircraft's exhaust. Grinning, he pirouetted the aircraft around and maneuvered it to match the ship's roll and forward speed, creating a metal ceiling over the missiles.

"I figured you might need some help," Youngblood said over the scrambled LINK II frequency.

Marshall, lying on his back under the semitrailer, pressed the headpiece to his good ear. "Youngblood? You crazy son of a bitch—"

"At your service. Our navy brethren at Oceana kindly loaned me this outstanding piece of hardware for the evening. I promised to return it in one piece."

Several rounds raked off the Harrier's starboard wing. Youngblood's boyish grin vanished. He gripped the stick hard and nudged the throttles forward to gain altitude. A sheen of sweat soaked his brow and began to seep down his forehead and nose.

"Get a move on, major, and disable that pallet. They're not going to let me stay up here all night."

Williams used the drain-tank pipes as cover to move closer to the missile's control vehicle. He saw four of Gorgon's men scatter among the network of pipes, working their way forward to defend the missiles. He couldn't get a clear shot at any of them without rupturing a pipe, nor could he target the missile pallet. That fucking truck ...

Another wave of SEALs, clad in black rubber wet suits, climbed over the ship's bulwarks and unfolded the collapsible stocks of their M-24 automatic rifles. "That's right, join the party," Williams muttered.

Gorgon's soldiers leveraged their positions among the ubiquitous pipes and divided their fire between the boarding assault troops and the Harrier.

"Joe," Williams radioed to Marshall, "move that damn truck!"

Marshall rolled from under the truck and shielded his ears against the jet's downdraft. *Fuckin' A...* A vicious volley of fire ricocheted off the truck's armor skin while the remains of Gorgon's army jockeyed between the pipes, moving fearlessly toward the missile pallet.

Marshall dove through the truck's driver-side window. Two of Gorgon's men moved around the side of the vehicle, their automatic weapons raised and ready. The first soldier flung open the driver's door and stared mutely down the barrel of a military shotgun. Marshall fired. The close-range blast tore off the soldier's head and lobbed it across the deck like a football on a touchdown pass. His spastic torso flailed back into the arms of the second mercenary. A simultaneous round from Williams' rifle transfixed the second mercenary's chest, and the two terrorists, arm in arm, dropped together in a macabre dance.

Marshall slid into the driver's seat and brought the engine to life. He slammed it into first gear. His foot jammed the throttle as he released the clutch. The armored truck lurched forward with a shriek of protest and began rolling clumsily along *Lucy's* upper deck, exposing the missile platform.

Williams, lying spread eagle on the deck, sighted the missile pallet and waited for one of Gorgon's men to appear. "Go for it, assholes, and I'll blow your mother fuckin' heads off."

Marshall sent the truck hurtling aft toward the superstructure, the huge wheels skidding over the metal deck. *Is this all this bucket can do?* He revved the engine and drove the truck through pockets of firing soldiers, scattering them.

A lone mercenary, a large man with dark features, stood defiantly in the center of the deck firing his automatic weapon. Marshall saw the muzzle flashes and heard the bullets ricochet off the truck's armored hood. The windshield shattered in a hail of glass pellets that shot past his face like BBs. *Fuck you.* Marshall ignored his stinging forehead and concentrated on the confounded look in the terrorist's eyes only a few feet in front of him.

The impact flung the mercenary under the truck's huge front wheels. The tires bounced and skidded over supple flesh, tearing skin from bones, mashing limbs and crushing his skull nearly flat. Marshall, grinning, felt hardly a bump.

The truck smashed through pipes and conduits, and left in its wake clouds of vapor erupting from the ship's damaged closed-loop inert gas system. The ship's superstructure rose up before him. *I'm outta here.*

Marshall opened the driver's door, jumped clear of the truck and rolled hard against the steel wall of the boat deck. Stunned, he watched the truck careen and crash into the ship's pumping conduits like a ball shot from a cannon. The truck flipped onto its side and smashed headlong into the superstructure.

THE TANK

Tarra and two of her soldiers escorted Carlucci and Wynett across the ship's upper port deck to one of the forward storage tanks. She spun the toggle dogs and lifted the hatch, releasing a heavy waft of petroleum vapors.

"Be careful," she said, "you might slip." She broke into that peculiar laugh Carlucci could no longer stand. Tarra's features hardened and she jerked her head. Her mercenaries prodded the prisoners into the narrow opening.

Carlucci climbed first, hand over hand, down 40 feet of narrow ladder to the bottom of the gloomy compartment. The rungs were slippery and left his hands muddy. The only light shone down from the open portal above. He could see vague patterns of elaborate pipes and valves, countless beams and struts, nooks, crannies, and crevices, and the gray walls of the great metal tank rising high above him. The fumes were unbearably intense. He held his breath before expelling a coughing fit. There was no escaping it.

Wynett followed and was heaving terribly by the time he reached the bottom. The hatch banged shut overhead, and the toggle latches creaked as they locked. The two stood in absolute blackness, listening to the ship's deep rumble. There were no other ship sounds except for an occasional scuffle of boots on the steelwork high overhead.

"A cargo tank, I assume," Wynett offered.

"A slop tank," Carlucci corrected him, then shuddered when his disembodied voice boomed back from the darkness. "When the cargo compartments are cleaned," he said in a muted voice,

316

"the remaining sludge is pumped into this tank until it can be disposed of safely."

"A delightful place to die," Wynett said.

"This tank has been flushed and cleaned," Carlucci said. "Otherwise we would have succumbed by now." The captain turned around, tried to acquire his bearings, couldn't, and squatted on the slippery floor. Carlucci heard Wynett scuffle into a sitting position against the steel wall.

"I suggest you make yourself comfortable, captain," Wynett said. "We are not going anywhere."

Tarra sat before the pumping room's computer-controlled station governing the flow of crude oil in and out of the ship's massive storage tanks. She activated a series of switches and brought the ship's cargo pumps to life. The schematic's valve indicator on the port-side slop tank blinked from red to green. She giggled.

Deep inside the ship, a hydraulic valve opened and crude oil from the number-seven cargo tank began flowing into her makeshift prison.

Carlucci felt the floor vibrate. He heard movement – a sloshing sound – as though something living was slithering down the walls. But this was no serpent. He knew the sound – medium-gravity crude oil spilling onto the tank's steel floor.

Carlucci stared into the unspeakable darkness. The agonizingly slow flow rate would take hours to fill the compartment. Tarra took perverse pleasure in a slow, tortured death, he thought. "Holy Mary mother of God..."

"Mr. Gorgon is frightened," Wynett rasped, not a trace of panic in his voice. "Or he would not be killing us."

Quarantine

Julie didn't dare believe what she was seeing, didn't dare believe the demon had been exorcised. Twenty minutes had passed since Nancy Shaw gave her the injection of ganciclovir. During that time she watched her twisted fingers relax to normal and, despite some residual numbness, her hand once again felt like her own. *Incredible.*

Shaw slipped into the room. "Your blood tests are normal."

Her mentor's words flowed over Julie with dreamlike buoyancy. In fact, the entire room had taken on an aura of unreality. Did she dare believe?

"Did you hear what I said?" Shaw persisted, gripping her shoulder.

Julie spun around and looked at her, and then her eyes fell to the summary printout in Shaw's hand. The meticulous rows of numbers would no doubt prove that St. Vitus could be defeated.

Shaw, her eyes ringed with deep lines of concern, stooped in front of Julie's chair. "How do you feel, dear?"

Julie, unable to express how she felt, managed only, "Fine."

"Fine? Just fine? You've come back from the dead and you're just fine?"

Julie broke down and wrapped her arms around Shaw's neck, holding her tight. Her mentor scrambled to keep from spilling backward. "Hey," she laughed. "I'm glad to see you too."

Streams of tears rolled from Julie's eyes. She pulled back from Shaw and, embarrassed, said, "I'm so friggin' stupid."

Shaw frowned at her student. "Stupid? I think not. Reckless maybe, but not stupid."

"No. I mean about the ganciclovir. It was right in front of me all the time, but I didn't see it. Jeez, I'm so dense. I even dreamed about it, for chrissake."

Shaw nodded thoughtfully. "You saw what you thought you were supposed to see and didn't consider any other possibility. I'm still half in the dark. Tell me how you figured this one out."

Julie leaned back in her chair, blew her nose in a tissue and stuffed it into the pocket of her sweater. She drew in a deep breath and felt good – as though a creature with deep claws and sharp teeth had just been wrenched off her back. "Ingeniously simple. Dr. French wanted to broaden the safety margin of his experiment, so he spliced another gene into Saint Vitus – a suicide switch. He used a mouse-tumor virus to make Saint Vitus sensitive to the antibiotic ganciclovir. It acts as a switch to inactivate Saint Vitus. French intended to turn off the experiment with the antibiotic if something went wrong."

"So why didn't he use it to save himself?"

"He had no way of knowing how potent the first generation of Saint Vitus would be or how quickly it would spread through the nervous system. He never had a chance. But as the virus mutates, its toxicity decreases and spreads much more slowly through the host's system, though it's still inevitably fatal."

"What about Joe and his sergeant?"

Julie stood suddenly. "The son of a bitch thinks he's incurable," she said. "He's likely to get himself killed on that tanker."

Julie bolted from the room. Shaw ran after her down the hallway to the communications room.

"If you're thinking of calling him," Shaw said, "you'll never get access to the channel, not now, not during the operation."

Julie sat down at the communications console and punched into the LINK II network. "I'm calling General Medlock. He's got to patch me through to him."

Lucy

Carlucci stood at the top of the tank's ladder and pushed feebly on the hatch's lever. Frozen. He would die in here, he realized. Refusing to succumb, he looped an arm through the top rung and held his wrist tightly, locking his arms together like a safety pin. The air inside the compartment was too foul to breathe. He was dying, and he knew it. In a few seconds he would black out. Then his body would fall from the ladder and plunge into a rising lake of oil below.

He withdrew a pair of steel pliers from his coat pocket and began pounding the hatch with them. His actions were desperate, frantic. What else could he do with the remainder of his life? The sound of metal against metal reverberated loudly in his ears.

He paused, breathing the last of the air trapped inside the hatch cover. He no longer heard Wynett's groans below him. The poor bastard most likely was already dead. Carlucci didn't fear death. Not now, not after watching his men perish so violently. As the blackness of eternity enveloped him, Carlucci shook his head in frustration, defeated. His inability to stop Gorgon and the abomination he intended to unleash weighed on his soul. His life would end, while the monster lived. And he couldn't do a damn thing about it.

Carlucci began choking. Still he managed to reach up and pound the hatch one last time. His lungs ached ... he could not take in another breath. As death came for him, he began to tremble. Yes, he was frightened. His arm began slipping from the rung. Let it end now. He heard the gurgle of crude below, accompanied by another sound – a strange creaking as though the ship's seams were coming apart. What was it?

An intense white light washed over him, and with it came a cold draft of night air that roused his sensibilities. The heavy hatch above him opened and banged onto the deck. He gazed up into the deck's bright sodium-arc lights and felt his retinas ache.

A face broke the circle of light above – a soldier, his face painted with black camouflage. This wasn't one of Gorgon's men. The soldier was a Navy SEAL.

"Well, prick my ass!" the soldier said in a flat, Texas drawl. He grabbed both of Carlucci's wrists and hauled him out of the tank with a single pull.

"You don't look like a terrorist," the Navy SEAL said. "Who the fuck are you?"

Carlucci rose to his knees and took in great lungfuls of the crisp night air. His head pounded while the deck seemed to spin around him. "I am the ship's captain ... he put us in the tank to kill us...."

"Us? Who's us?"

"The bridge," Carlucci gasped, pointing, "I must get to the ship's bridge and stop this vessel."

Youngblood felt rather than heard the Harrier's systems fail. The arms fire from the terrorists below had crippled his aircraft. The stick's vibration grew worse. He gripped it harder, flexing his arm muscles until they ached from the tension. He ascended another 100 feet, giving himself precious room to maneuver if he had to.

"Hold on tight, boys and girls," he said to himself.

Both crimson engine-fire warning lights glared at him like the eyes of a raging night beast, while the cockpit's alarm sirens wailed in his ears. The rpm, hydraulic and oil readouts all told him to eject his ass out of there – fast.

Youngblood ignored them all. He felt remarkably alive, pushing the Harrier's flying envelope further than any other pilot could have done. He took in all the readouts at once. Saw everything. He focused only on tweaking extraordinary performance out of the Harrier to maintain its position over the missile pallet. He knew that once he moved the aircraft, the missiles could launch. He vowed not to let that happen.

"Oh, what fun it is to fly ..." The aircraft dipped as it momentarily lost power in both engines. He jammed the throttles forward, raising the aircraft several more feet. "... in a one-horse open sleigh."

The terrorist missile technician knew the Harrier was in serious trouble, knew it had sustained too much damage from ground fire to remain airborne much longer. But how long? He could hear the choking sound of its turbo engines struggling to maintain their revolutions. Yet the aircraft hung there, stubbornly, like an annoying wasp over a picnic plate. The Harrier would have to maneuver out of the missile's way in the next seconds if it were to set down safely. And when that happened, he would charge the platform and launch the missiles. *One button.*

But the Harrier wouldn't move. He gritted his teeth. How much longer? Seconds, no more.

Suddenly the Harrier dropped. The technician's eyes opened impossibly wide – the only indication his brain registered what was happening. He had no time to move. A cry caught in his throat as the Harrier dropped straight down onto the missile pallet and blasted across the deck, killing him instantly.

"I'm outta here."

Youngblood grabbed the eject lever on the side of his seat an instant before the awful concussion. Too late. The Harrier's engines exploded. Countless pieces of turbine blades traveling at the speed of sound sliced through the cockpit, ripping the flight deck to ribbons. Sparks and fire replaced the flying glass.

An instant later, Youngblood's remains were indistinguishable from the Harrier's shattered instrumentation.

Marshall watched the Harrier go down. Its wreckage tumbled across the deck like a flaming Ferris wheel and burst through the ship's bulwark. A tremendous fireball lit the black Virginia sky. The tangled Harrier and missile platform fused into a single mass of metal, cartwheeling grotesquely into the Chesapeake Bay.

He saw no sign that Youngblood had ejected. All that remained was an orange-white fireball that leaped high into the night before morphing into a thick, black cloud that dissipated quickly into the night. Darkness once again descended as though the Harrier and the missiles had never existed.

Marshall pressed his back hard into the metal wall of the ship's boat deck and wiped a mixture of sweat and soot from his face. He touched his mouthpiece and said slowly and without emotion to all military channels, "Harrier down. Missile pallet destroyed. Missile capability negated. Repeat. Missiles negated."

Andrews Airfield

Marshall had barely finished when General Medlock opened a channel to Oceana and said, "I want the air assault to begin immediately. Repeat. Mobilize full air assault."

Gorgon entered *Lucy's* pumping room and stepped to the main console. He knew a larger assault force would try to take the ship now that his missiles had been destroyed. He ignored the myriad switches and gauges that controlled the ship's cargo movements and fingered a toggle lever his technicians had installed under the main console. He engaged it.

Instead of flowing through the off-loading lines, light crude and condensate from the top of the number-four cargo tank began spewing across *Lucy's* upper deck like an open fire hydrant. The retrofit was performed merely as a precaution, a remote contingency. Now it would buy him the time he needed to finish his business.

Gorgon withdrew his Ruger and used it to shatter the pump-room window. He discharged a single round at the deck.

A holocaust.

The fuel ignited, and twenty-foot flames turned *Lucy's* deck into Dante's Inferno. Gorgon's eyes widened with glee while he watched the ocean of fire engulf the remains of his army and the assault infidels. No one could escape it. He laughed as burning men dove headlong over the bulwarks and into the bay.

And then there was nothing but flames.

CAPTAIN'S BRIDGE

Williams charge from the wall of flames and slammed his back against the steel wall next to Marshall.

"You okay?" Marshall huffed.

Williams, wincing, touched his smoldering vest with cracked and callused fingers. "Son of a bitch is gonna blow this ship right out of the water. When it goes, we go with it."

Marshall grimaced. Gorgon's defenses were impeccable. No one could survive this firestorm, much less set down more troops in the middle of it. "What about the others?"

"I saw a handful go over the side." Williams gestured toward the area where the Harrier had gone down. "Why did Youngblood do it?"

Marshall, his eyes set in stone, methodically slid more cartridges into his Franchi. "He gave us a way to finish this business." He chambered the last round, then shifted his severe gaze to Williams. "I'm not leaving this boat till I see that bastard's blackened corpse."

"What are we waiting for?"

Marshall and Williams slipped into the superstructure through the upper deck side hatch. The ship's interior, dark and cool and quiet, offered a welcome respite from the flames outside. Marshall crouched in the hallway and listened. Nothing. The boat deck quarters appeared deserted, the lights out.

Marshall pulled a notebook from his SAS belt and consulted the general arrangement plan of the ship's superstructure. The floor plan showed the wheelhouse four decks above them. "There's a staircase halfway down this hallway," he said.

Marshall attached a light to the barrel rail of his Franchi, and then moved down the corridor, pointing his weapon into every darkened quarter. They came upon the bodies of two SEALs. The major swept his light along the corpses riddled from automatic fire.

"Poor bastards were ambushed," Williams said.

Marshall motioned the sergeant into a steep, narrow staircase leading up to the next deck. The steps above him appeared empty.

Marshall ascended the first flight, and then continued up to the officer's deck, while Williams covered the stairwell behind. The major heard no troop movement, only the pounding of his heart. As he made his way up to the captain's deck, a silhouetted figure appeared on the lightless landing directly above him. Marshall dropped to one knee and fired. The figure vaulted into the hallway as the wall at the top of the stairwell exploded with buckshot. A man began shouting in a heavily accented voice that reverberated throughout the superstructure. Marshall leaped up the steps two at a time and charged into the hallway. An older man sat on the floor, his hands clutching his right leg.

"*Don't shoot,*" the man pleaded, raising his hands against the shotgun.

Marshall jammed the barrel of his Franchi into the old man's throat. He saw a strange, quiet dignity to this man, even in the middle of the chaos. He wore a badly looted seaman's uniform, not the black khaki fatigues worn by Gorgon's soldiers, and his gray hair, weathered features, accent and generous paunch didn't fit the terrorists' profile.

"Who the hell are you?" Marshall shouted.

"My name is Sergio Carlucci," he said. "I am *Lucy's* master, a prisoner on my own ship. Please. I am trying to stop this ship."

Marshall pulled Carlucci to his feet and frisked him for a weapon. Finding none, he prodded him back out of reach.

"You're going to get yourself killed." Marshall quickly inspected Carlucci's wound. Three inches to the left and the shot would have hit an artery. "Put something over that wound."

Carlucci kept his eyes on the major while he withdrew a grease-covered handkerchief from his jacket pocket and tied it around his shin.

"How many of Gorgon's men are on the bridge?" Marshall said, motioning upward.

"None. Those who remain went below. Most likely to the engine room."

Marshall helped Carlucci into the stairwell and prodded him up the steps. "Show me your bridge."

Carlucci tripped his way up to the navigation bridge. The three of them entered the wheelhouse, lit up like day by the blazing deck below.

"Stop the engine," Marshall ordered.

Carlucci moved to the helm and took the ship off autopilot, shut down the engine and released the anchor. Nothing happened. The ship's readouts indicated that the massive diesel engine still turned at full power, pushing the massive ship up the York River at eighteen knots.

While the captain worked, Marshall rifled through the scattered piles of maps and photographs on the chart table. Williams guarded the doorway. There were dozens of grainy photo images and technical drawings of docks, buildings and odd bits of heavy equipment. Marshall scanned a marine map of the York River from Yorktown to West Point, scribbled with checkpoints, headings, logarithmic speeds and times. Someone marked a comprehensive route for the ship that ended at a refinery on the outskirts of Yorktown.

"He intended to use a pipeline to send his weapon inland," Carlucci said.

"Why is this ship still moving?" Marshall demanded.

Carlucci repositioned every switch and tried the routine again. The ship would not respond. He could not stop *Lucy*.

Carlucci spread his arms palms-up in a helpless gesture. "He has taken over the engine control room and has locked the guidance system. He is letting the computers steer the ship to Yorktown. The system works off the ship's gyrocompasses – the repeaters are tied into the ship's steering system. But it is only meant for deep seas, never in closed navigational waters. What he is doing is very dangerous. I cannot disengage it from here."

Marshall moved to the captain's side and pointed his Franchi at the main console. "Maybe this will."

"No," Carlucci said, pushing aside the barrel of Marshall's shotgun. "He does not need the bridge. He controls everything from below."

"What about his escape? How does he intend to get off this ship?"

Carlucci shrugged. "There is an emergency door in the engine room, just above the waterline. Perhaps he is already off this ship."

Marshall heard choppers approaching and moved to the window. Two C-1 Sea Stallions maneuvered into holding patterns a prudent fifty yards forward of the ship, one port, one starboard, waiting to deploy troops. They just hung there. Setting down in a sheer sea of flame the size of a football field was out of the question.

"What the *fuck* do they think they're gonna do?" Williams said.

An Apache AH-64 gunship descended from the night sky and swooped down like a hawk in front of the ship's superstructure.

"Get down." Marshall tackled Carlucci to the floor just as the gunship opened fire with its 30mm chain-fed cannon. The wheelhouse's windscreens shattered in an appalling blizzard of flying glass while the consoles exploded in sparks and metal. Carlucci watched with wide eyes while the rounds tore apart his bridge. The gunship moved on, directing fire from one window to another, methodically clearing the ship's quarters with 20-round bursts of 30mm high-explosive dual-purpose rounds.

"Stop firing at the bridge," Marshall yelled into his transceiver. "The navigation bridge is secure. Cease fire. Repeat. Cease fire."

A metallic voice squawked into Marshall's ear. "Stay the hell put, major. I'll relay your position to the assault force commander. *Stay the hell put.*"

"The organism is stashed somewhere below deck," Marshall yelled. "An explosion will rupture those tanks."

Carlucci grabbed Marshall's arm. "He keeps tanks in a maintenance shop on the bottom deck, a place where he assembled the warheads for his missiles. I have seen them."

Marshall jumped to his feet. "Show me."

The communications officer at Andrews Airfield spun away from the radio console. "Marshall's inside the superstructure. The bridge is secure."

There was an outburst of victorious hoots and hollers from the men in General Medlock's command hangar. The officer pressed a palm against his headphones as more information poured into his ear. "The upper deck's on fire, sir," he said. "The choppers report a twenty-foot wall of flame the length of the ship, though the source doesn't appear to be the cargo tanks. The ship's still moving at eighteen knots."

Another aide thrust a portable phone at the general. "It's the president, sir."

"Jesus." The room fell silent as the general accepted the phone. "Medlock here."

"Give me an update," the president said.

"*Lucy's* upper deck and superstructure are secure, sir."

"Congratulations, general," the president said. "Is the ship anchored?"

"Sir, the ship's upper deck is ablaze. Deploying troops will take time."

"Goddamn it, I want that ship stopped now. Get that organism back into military hands. That was our deal."

"Yes, sir," Medlock said after the line had gone dead. He shoved the phone back to his aide.

Medlock's jaw tightened. What the hell is that son of a bitch Marshall doing? If he's in command of the bridge, why is the fucking ship still moving?

"Sir," the communications officer said, "the op commander on the number-one Sea Stallion says he can rappel some of his

328

men onto the starboard bridge wing deck and get them inside the superstructure."

Medlock slid his finger along the ship's diagram to the wing deck next to the wheelhouse and nodded. "Tell him to get his men down onto that ship."

Major Higgins, BERT's logistical officer, beckoned the general to his chart table. "Sir, the ship is eight miles from the Coleman Memorial Bridge at Gloucester Point," he said, his finger thrust solidly on the lower right-hand corner of the nautical chart. "It's a swing span, opens at right angles. The tanker's draft is 42 feet, which won't take it much past that bridge. We'll need to alert the bridge operator to open the bridge."

Medlock's eyes swept the large general arrangement blueprint of *Lucy*, searching for a solution, seeing nothing but problems. Every minute brought the tanker closer to more people. Fuck you, Gorgon. *Fuck you!*

"The drawbridge stays closed," Medlock ordered. "The tanker isn't getting past it."

Marshall led Carlucci and Williams down the narrow staircases, around one landing after another, until they reached the superstructure's boat deck. The lights on the ship's lower decks were out, and to descend further meant proceeding in total darkness. He ruled out using the tiny service elevator, which could take them directly to the engine room. Too exposed.

"Feels like we're walking into an ambush," Williams said.

Marshall retrieved the ship's schematics and looked for another way down. There wasn't any. Gorgon could easily cover every access to the engine room. A large bead of sweat rolled into Marshall's eye.

"In here," Carlucci said, leading the way into the third-deck pump room.

Unlike the sophisticated high-tech station on the ship's upper deck, the pump room was all muscle, boasting a labyrinth of valves and pipes that extended deep into the ship. Carlucci opened a tall tool locker and retrieved a wrench the size of a baseball bat and an equally long flashlight. Marshall and Williams followed him to the port bulkhead, where he knelt down and went to work. Carlucci fitted the wrench's huge teeth over one of several lug bolts embedded in the wall and, grunting, twisted it loose. The captain winced with each flex of his arm. Marshall took the wrench from him and forced his shaking hands to remove the remaining bolts. The three of them lifted a three-foot steel plate off the wall and set it roughly to one side.

Marshall thrust his head into the opening and could sense rather than see the depth of the crawlspace, which dropped several stories below them. Carlucci squeezed in beside him and played the beam of his flashlight off the steel braces that supported the ship's outer hull.

"I'm afraid to ask what you have in mind," Marshall said.

"There are six meters of space between the dual hulls," Carlucci said.

"Yeah, so?"

"We climb down."

CRAWLSPACE

Carlucci descended hand over hand down an uneven row of rusted footholds embedded in the side of the number-seven cargo tank. Marshall and Williams followed without the benefit of the captain's flashlight. The space between the hulls offered little breadth, but it was deep, extending four stories below them like a cavern fissure. The dank and heavy air lacked a pervasive petroleum odor, Marshall noted, evidence of the effective closed-loop inert ventilation system. Still, he was keenly aware that if a cargo tank erupted, they would be cremated beneath the world's largest oil pit.

At the bottom, Carlucci moved to the next section of cross struts and directed his flashlight's beam on a service aperture whose tiny, twisted ladder delved still deeper into the ship.

Carlucci sat at the edge of the hole. With the flashlight in one hand and the massive wrench in the other, he began descending into the blackness. Marshall swung the Franchi over his shoulder and followed. The ladder took them into a cramped area just large enough for the two of them. Williams watched from the ladder above.

Marshall, feeling a distinct claustrophobic squeeze, asked, "Where to, skipper?"

Carlucci handed Marshall the flashlight. Kneeling, the captain went to work with his wrench on the first of a dozen floor bolts. As Carlucci loosened the bolts, Marshall expected a sudden surge of river water to shoot up through the hull like a geyser. However, the wrench echoed hollowly against the steel plate, suggesting another void beneath. The captain made quick work of loosening the bolts, and the two wrestled the steel plate to one side. A waft of chilled, rusty air rose up to greet them.

Carlucci reclaimed his flashlight, lowered himself through the new opening and splashed down into a foot of bilge water. There wasn't enough clearance to stand upright. Marshall followed and, crouching in the bilge, surveyed the area illuminated by Carlucci's light. The air was musty and foul. A vast, unholy cavern supported by steel cross-beams and struts stretched ahead and behind them as far as the light would reach.

Marshall heard the massive ship groan heavily above them. "Where in hell are we?"

"The ship has two hulls," Carlucci said. "We are standing between them. This space runs the length of the ship along the keel."

Williams lowered himself down beside the two. "I've been in some hellholes before ... but—"

"This way," Carlucci ordered, trudging aft, taking the light with him.

Gorgon, dressed in a rubber wet suit, set a rucksack carefully on the maintenance shop's workbench. The bag held a brick-size, high-yield plastic explosive with a layer of electronics embedded into its top.

Tarra finished her inspection of the row of Saint Vitus cylinders stacked against the far bulkhead. "Will this work?" she asked. "What if the tanks do not rupture?"

"In seven minutes there will be a very large hole in this ship's hull," Gorgon said, examining the timer on top of the brick of explosives. "There is enough force in this bag to rupture the tanks and unleash my eager creatures along the river."

Gorgon activated the device and watched the tiny panel of blinking red timing lights begin counting down to detonation in seven minutes. He lifted the bag of explosives and set it with care behind the row of tanks. "It is almost finished." He noted the foreboding stamped on Tarra's features. "Your Allah is pleased. Still you are troubled?"

"There is too much activity on the river," she said. "Someone will see us. And will we have enough time to get far enough from the explosion to avoid contamination?"

Gorgon scoffed at her concerns. "The engine room's emergency door is well hidden. No one will see us leave. In seven minutes we will be upwind, watching the death of this vessel from shore." He grinned. "Come. Let us begin our new lives together."

Gorgon turned and slipped through the hatchway, leaving Tarra to lock the bulkhead hatch behind them.

Carlucci played his light along the silted panels at the end of the crawlspace searching for a set of latches. Marshall and Williams waited in the bilge behind him. The captain found what he was looking for and began beating back the six toggle dogs with the tip of his huge wrench.

Gorgon heard the echo of metal striking metal through the floor beneath him.

"They are coming for us," Tarra hissed.

Gorgon scanned the floor of the pump room and spotted the manhole cover. "There."

Tarra swung the Uzi off her shoulder. "I will finish them." Gorgon raised a firm hand. "Do not fire a weapon in here. A ricochet will rupture a pipe."

She withdrew a wicked-looking knife. "Go. I will join you at the emergency outlet."

Gorgon swept around and vanished, moving briskly between the boilers on the way to the engine room.

He stopped suddenly. A dark figure detached itself from the boiler and blocked his path. At first Gorgon did not recognize the man in the half-light. A special op soldier? The tousled intruder, slicked with crude oil and barely able to support himself, held a Kalashnikov pointed at him.

"Greetings, Mr. Gorgon," Wynett said. "You and I have a $20 million business deal to finish. Although I'm sure we can work out other arrangements."

Carlucci drove his hand upward and pushed the manhole cover aside with a clang. Marshall and Williams followed him up through the hole into the ship's lower pump room. Countless rows of pipes lined the walls and ceiling. The major felt the steel under his feet resonate from the massive three-story diesel engine in the next compartment throbbing at full power.

Carlucci pointed. "The maintenance locker is through that service hatch. That is where he keeps the tanks. I have seen them."

Marshall squatted next to the locked hatch to the maintenance shop and threw back the four toggle locks. Williams covered him, his rifle aimed at the center of the hatchway. Marshall kicked open the hatch, his shotgun raised. The room appeared empty.

The three sprinted inside. Marshall dashed to the row of tanks and spotted the satchel with the red timing lights. The readout indicated four and a half minutes until detonation. "The son of a bitch rigged the tanks to explode."

Williams joined him. "Jesus, he's stashed Armageddon in here."

Marshall probed the bag with his spasming hand. "There's no way to disarm this thing in time ... even if we knew how."

"I'll get it out of here." Williams grabbed the bag's handle and lifted it carefully. Marshall noted that Williams' hands were also trembling. *How the fuck are we going to do this?*

Tarra pounced on Williams' back and drove her knife into the vulnerable spot between his shoulder blades. Williams grunted in surprise, dropped to his knees and sent her sprawling over his shoulder. Marshall whipped around. Tarra sprang up and rammed her shoulder into Marshall's chest, slamming him hard onto the deck. She dove on him, tigerlike in her ferocity, her wicked blade angled toward his throat.

Marshall grabbed Tarra's knife-wielding hand with both of his and pushed back with all his strength. The effort wasn't enough against her brute force. The blade sank toward his neck. Suddenly Tarra's head jerked sideways with a sickening crack. Her knife hand grew limp. There came a whisk, followed by another bone-shattering crack. Again her head jerked unnaturally. Marshall flung Tarra off him. Carlucci swung his huge wrench a third time like a baseball bat, producing another crack as it connected with her skull.

Marshall grabbed his Franchi and discharged two blasts into Tarra's chest at close range. She fell back against the metal wall with a screech, then flopped around in a pool of her blood, struggling to rise. A third shotgun blast into her face finally stilled her.

"I can't breathe," Williams said.

Marshall joined Carlucci at the sergeant's side. Williams rose onto his knees, laboring to draw a breath.

"How bad are you hurt?" Marshall asked.

Williams shrugged off his jacket, revealing an SAS tactical assault vest. "She knocked the goddamn wind out of me." He slipped off the vest and inspected the damaged cartridge pocket. "Damn. The bitch trashed my only detonator."

Marshall, grinning, slapped the sergeant's arm.

Williams grabbed the explosive satchel and huffed, "Gotta go." He bolted into the outer pump room and charged the open manhole in the deck.

Carlucci ran after him. "No! You will never make it out in time. An explosion will rupture the cargo tanks and the hulls. She will drop her cargo as she sinks."

Williams whipped around, looking desperately for a way out.

"Through the engine room," Carlucci shouted, pointing to the service hatchway. "There is an emergency door on the aft hull just above the waterline. Quickly!"

Williams rushed into the boiler room and froze. Time stopped for the gunnery sergeant. Gorgon stood before him like Satan himself, staring, his lips pressed together in frustration. Something was wrong, Williams noted. Gorgon didn't move. The terrorist's eyes shifted to the satchel in Williams' hand, producing ever-deepening creases of apprehension on his forehead. Still, he made no move.

"Do not fear him, sergeant," Wynett said, stepping from the shadows of the number-one boiler.

Williams' eyes darted to the old man wielding an assault rifle pointed at both of them. Wynett's features spasmed abnormally as though something living were burrowing beneath his skin. Williams winced. How could the old man still be alive, he wondered?

"You will find Mr. Gorgon a docile fellow," he said, "when he has an automatic rifle pointed at his back."

RUPTURE

The York River at Gloucester Point

Simon Goski, the Coleman Memorial Bridge's second-shift operator, scowled at the man wearing a raincoat standing in the doorway of the drawbridge's pilothouse. The stranger's lips were moving but the distorted oldie blaring from the room's cheap radio masked his words. The portly bridge operator looked past the man and saw an armed soldier on the roadway outside directing the arrival of a camouflaged military transport truck large enough to hold two dozen troops. He watched several unmarked cars skidding to a halt on the bridge outside the pilothouse window. What the hell was going on?

The man in the raincoat didn't ask permission to turn off the radio – he just did it. "Simon Goski, my name is Timothy O'Connor." He flashed an ID. "CIA. During the next hour you'll do exactly as I say."

Goski gawked at the ID inside a leather wallet and read every word three times.

"Mr. Goski, I need your absolute cooperation," O'Conner said.

The drawbridge operator pushed back his chair with a raw screech as he rose and pressed past the CIA man. For the moment, his sole interest was the bridge's radar, an ancient machine that still used vacuum tubes. "Not till I open the bridge," Goski said. "There's a oil tanker headin' straight for us. And her captain won't answer his fuckin' radio."

"Mr. Goski," the CIA agent said, his voice firm, "please take your hands off those controls or these soldiers will take you into custody. Do you understand?"

Goski, baffled by the man's tone, let his tree-trunk arms fall to his sides. No – he didn't understand any of this. But this much sank in – do as you're told and don't ask questions.

Goski peered through the pilothouse window into the night. He couldn't see anything, not even the river. But he knew the tanker was out there, moving steadily toward them. *This is bullshit.*

"Mr. Goski," O'Conner said, "no matter what happens in the next hour, no matter what instruction you may receive to the contrary, this bridge will stay closed."

Williams lifted the rucksack to show Wynett the electronic detonator blinking inside. "One of us better get this thing off the ship – fast."

Wynett understood the situation immediately. He sold Gorgon several of these explosive devices cleverly engineered to take longer to disarm than the detonating timer would allow. "Up to mischief, Mr. Gorgon?" he said. "I see you intend to punch a very large hole in this ship and blow the organism into the slipstream. A frantic move, I should think, one that will vastly limit your effective range. I am disappointed that after so much planning – so much hardware procurement – you would resort to desperate means to complete your mission. Anything but failure, yes?"

Gorgon said nothing, his intense eyes locked on Wynett's, studying him.

"Take it, Mr. Gorgon," Wynett said, his voice dropping a chilled octave. "Take that bag from the sergeant or I will empty this magazine into your back."

Gorgon didn't move, his eyes never wavering.

"Mr. Gorgon," Wynett said, "I will give you only three seconds to comply before I open fire."

Gorgon's jaw tightened as he reached for the satchel's leather handle.

"It's all yours, pal," Williams said, placing the bag's full weight in Gorgon's hand. He slid the Galil off his shoulder.

"No, sergeant," Wynett said. "I forbid you to touch your weapon."

Williams disregarded him. "Screw you, old man."

Wynett discharged a single round into the boiler beside Williams and saw it ricochet into the engine room, absorbed by machinery. "The next time I will hollow out your head."

The sergeant let the Galil drop to his side. "I hear ya."

"Well, I'll be damned," Marshall said, slipping through the bulkhead hatch behind Williams. Carlucci watched from within the hatchway.

Marshall and Gorgon exchanged icy stares. "I'm taking you down right here," Marshall said, raising his Franchi. "I'm going to enjoy this. Let's call it a debt I owe to a good friend."

"I will not allow that, major," Wynett said. "Mr. Gorgon and I are about to complete our business. He will satisfy his debt to me by holding that bag when it detonates. I am offering him a very generous deal. Mr. Gorgon will become a martyr for his cause – a notion I know he loathes."

"Wynett," Marshall said, taking a cautious step forward, "the explosion will release the virus. You'll be letting this asshole fulfill his contract."

"My tanks are constructed of one-inch-thick Belfast steel," Wynett said. "They can withstand forty thousand pounds of pressure per square inch. An explosion between these boilers will not be sufficient to blast through two steel bulkhead walls and rupture my tanks."

Wynett glanced into the satchel. The pattern of blinking lights had changed, indicating the device's microprocessor had begun its final sequence. "Only a few seconds more until we all become martyrs—"

Gorgon swung the dangling satchel upward, catching Wynett hard on the jaw. It had all his strength behind it. The old man's teeth cracked, and he collapsed onto both knees with a grunt. Gorgon vanished into the engine room.

The satchel landed at Williams' feet. "Sheeeee-iitttt."

"No fucking way." Marshall pointed his Franchi. But Gorgon had vanished.

Williams pushed Marshall aside, grabbed the satchel and hurled it with all his strength across the engine room.

Gorgon dashed between the heavy machinery and paused. His eyes sought and found the emergency door above the waterline two catwalks overhead – his only way out. He watched the explosives bag fly overhead and land with a dull thud on the second-story catwalk.

Gorgon dropped facedown into a metal trough between the generators and waited. For a heart-stopping moment nothing happened.

The plastic detonated.

A terrible blast ripped out the heart of the engine room. The great upheaval shattered the catwalks and pipes, and hurled them missile-like through the control room's huge glass window, smashing the computerized instruments within. The twin ten-ton generators rent from their stools and pitched sideways, cutting power throughout the ship against the diminuendo of machinery screaming to a halt.

The damage was spectacular and extensive. The blast tore a gaping hole the size of a truck in *Lucy's* aft hull. Tens of thousands of gallons of river water roared into the engine room with the ferocity of a raging waterfall, cascading over the ruined machinery. Amber emergency lights blinked on, illuminating the room with a dim, bloodlike glow.

Stunned, his hearing numbed, Gorgon ignored the blood trickling from a dozen lacerations and pushed himself off the grated deck into a sitting position. He owed his life to the shield of the massive generators. His eyes focused on the gunmetal gray of a military shotgun barrel pointed at his head. The barrel was shaking – its owner could hardly use his weapon effectively.

He glanced up at the major and grinned. *This man is too ill to fight.*

"Stand up," Marshall demanded.

Williams, his Galil leveled, maneuvered carefully to cover Marshall.

Gorgon rose to his feet with a smirk. *I will take them both out.*

An earsplitting crack from a Kalashnikov tore the Franchi from Marshall's hand and twisted its barrel. Gorgon whirled.

"*Christ,*" Marshall shouted at Wynett, "you nearly took off my fingers."

"He is not your prisoner," Wynett said.

Gorgon let them see his amused look of contempt – *thank you Herr Wynett, my willing pawn.*

Wynett touched the red-hot muzzle to the back of Williams' ear. "Sergeant, please discard your weapon into the water."

Williams winced. "Shit." He flung his Galil into the water, where it disappeared into the boiling surge.

"Wynett, for chrissake," Marshall said. "Let me deal with him."

Wynett redirected his Kalashnikov at Marshall with an amazingly steady hand. "I am growing weary of you, major. I saved your life once so that you could deliver me to your people. You served my needs admirably, and I am grateful for your help. However, I will kill you and your sergeant if you do not do exactly as I tell you."

Cold river water foamed around their knees. Marshall gritted his teeth in frustration. He didn't trust Wynett to finish this. Still, he knew the next burst would kill them both while allowing Gorgon a chance to escape. Maybe the old man would kill the bastard. But Marshall knew the chances of that happening were slim.

Wynett circled Gorgon before jabbing him viciously in the back with the barrel of the Kalashnikov. "Mr. Gorgon, I wish to introduce you to some acquaintances of mine."

Gorgon, his stony features betraying nothing, led the way back through the boiler area. Marshall withdrew the Beretta from his back holster and directed it at the two as they marched between the boilers. He couldn't stop his hand's grotesque shaking movements while watching them disappear through the bulkhead hatchway – *useless!*

"Whatever we're gonna do, Joe," Williams said, "it's gotta happen right now."

Marshall lowered the Beretta. "Christ, I can't. I'm losing it."

Carlucci moved to the twisted railing and made a quick damage assessment of the ship's drive train. The incoming water was pushing the ship down by the stern. He hollered to the others, "This vessel is a runaway. The ship's momentum will take her far upriver where she will ram a bridge pylon."

"So let it ram a pylon," Marshall said, struggling to put away his Beretta.

"She will rupture her hulls. I will try to reengage the rudder manually from the bridge."

Carlucci scanned the damaged catwalk above. All that remained were twisted pieces of steel hanging precariously over the flooded compartment. "I am a good climber. I will scale the hull to reach the stairwell."

"You'll never do it," Marshall said. "Use the way we came in."

"There is no time," Carlucci said. "The crawlspace will flood. I will use the stairwell."

Carlucci charged into the cold surge, fighting the strong current of river water pouring into the engine room. What at first appeared to the captain as a quick swim quickly proved unmanageable as he fought the buffeting rapids swelling between the machinery. Twice he found himself submerged and thought he would drown, but each time his head broke the surface as he continued his desperate struggle to reach the hull.

The ship began listing, spilling tools, barrels and gear toward the rear bulkhead. The unstoppable flow of water swept

Carlucci against the hull, where he grabbed the first steel brace and pulled himself out of the water. He began hoisting himself up the side of the engine room's hull.

Williams put a hand on the ear of his headpiece in response to an incoming message. "Joe, you're not going to believe this."

"What is it?"

"It's Julie ... she's tied into the LINK Two."

Marshall fumbled with his headset. "My unit's dead. What's she saying?"

"Saint Vitus."

"What about it?"

The sergeant looked curiously at Marshall. "Says she's found an antidote."

Wynett forced Gorgon into the maintenance shop and bolted the hatch behind them. There was no other way out.

Gorgon stared at Tarra's mutilated corpse heaped against the bulkhead and grimaced. *Stupid bitch – you let them in here.* He faced Wynett, his expression arrogant. "So you intend that we both drown in here. Your lack of creativity disappoints me."

"Drown, Mr. Gorgon?" Wynett said. "I have a much better deal—"

Gorgon lashed out at him with a sudden sweep of his hand. He grabbed the barrel of the Kalashnikov and twisted it from Wynett's grip with maniacal fury. *A child has a better grip,* he thought.

The old man, disarmed, stared at the terrorist, his mouth agape. Gorgon, his eyes cold and dark, skillfully maneuvered the weapon around in his hands and discharged a quick burst into Wynett's abdomen. The blast pushed Wynett back against the row of virus tanks, toppling them all with a crash. A long, weary sigh poured from the old man's lungs. Gorgon, savoring the sight of his rival's agony, raked another burst across Wynett's legs. The old man didn't seem to feel anything.

The terrorist laughed wickedly. "Now we do business my way."

Wynett, gasping, hugged one of the virus tanks and twisted the valve's regulating element. "Mr. Gorgon," he spat, blood foaming down his chin. "It is my pleasure to introduce you to Saint Vitus, your comrade in arms."

Gorgon, sneering, emptied the clip directly into Wynett's head.

In the strange stillness that followed, Gorgon heard a snake-like hiss while the tank's contents emptied into the compartment.

INFECTED

Marshall tore off his broken ComSat headset. "Give me your earpiece."

Williams relinquished his miniature transceiver to the major, who fumbled to put it on. He said into the mouthpiece, "This is Marshall in *Lucy's* engine room. Who's on this channel?"

"This is Major Higgins," came a static-laden voice – the reception deep inside the ship was poor at best. "I'm with General Medlock at Andrews Airfield. We need to know the status of those tanks. Are they secure? Has Gorgon been eliminated?"

"Negative on both counts," Marshall said. "We will proceed—"

"*Joe!*" – it was Julie – "you must leave the ship immediately."

Marshall pressed the headset to his ear. "Where the hell are you?"

"I'm in a helicopter on my way to Yorktown. I'll meet you there. Joe, the virus need not be lethal. An injection of ganciclovir destroys the infected cells. It works ... I've tried it. But you can't delay the treatment. Get off that ship now."

Marshall stared at his trembling hands that felt as though a strong electrical current were flowing through them, paralyzing them. The pain was getting worse, and he knew his condition was deteriorating rapidly. "I can't do that ... I'm not finished here."

"I don't want to lose you, Joe," Julie said. "Get off that ship and meet me in Yorktown."

"Do what she says, major." It was Higgins again. "We have troops aboard. They'll handle this now."

"An explosion caused heavy damage to the engine room," Marshall said. "All accesses are blocked. The sergeant and I are the only ones who can finish this."

"Joe," Julie said, "please listen to me—"

"Sorry, honey. I need to go." Marshall turned down the volume of his transceiver and said to Williams, "Let's find him."

Carlucci crawled his way up the damaged stairwell, negotiating the broken steps that turned the steep stairwell into a scrap yard of twisted metal. Climbing past it, he rushed headlong up the three remaining flights to *Lucy's* bridge and stormed into the wheelhouse. He found a contingent of American commandos huddled over the ship's controls, trying to make sense of the shattered readouts. The overhead fluorescent lights were out, but it hardly mattered. The number-four center tank unleashed a mountainous fireball on deck that rolled into black clouds high over the ship.

"Hold it right there," hollered one of the Special Forces soldiers with the name Captain Frank Elliott stitched onto his shirt. "Keep your hands where I can see them or you're a dead man."

Carlucci, his hands raised, moved cautiously forward. The acrid haze from the inferno on deck stung his eyes terribly, forcing tears that flowed freely down his cheeks. "I am Captain Sergio Carlucci. *Lucy* is my ship. He took her from me."

Elliott frisked Carlucci while another soldier, a sergeant, covered him with an automatic rifle. Satisfied Carlucci wasn't a threat, Elliott led him to the helm and pushed the other soldiers aside. Introductions were disregarded. "We have a situation here," Elliott said. "There's a swing bridge a half mile upriver. It's not going to open. If you're who you say you are, then stop this ship right now or you're going to have one hell of a mess to clean up."

Carlucci stepped to the helm. He saw the Coleman Memorial Bridge beyond the bow, a dark steel giant blocking their path. "Holy Mary – what have they done?" He appealed to Elliott. "Radio and tell them to open that bridge."

Elliott shook his head. "The orders are to keep the bridge closed. My job is to stop this ship."

Carlucci scanned the instrumentation. The damage was substantial, the equipment useless. He turned the pilot wheel full left, then full right. No response. The explosion in the engine room had severed the links to the rudder's hydraulic arms.

"There is one chance," Carlucci said. "I can try to move the rudder manually and scuttle her in the shallows along the bank. We must take our chances and pray the hulls hold together."

"Whatever you're going to do, captain," Elliott said, "make it quick."

Carlucci knelt beside a floor panel and uncovered the ship's emergency steering assembly, which bypassed the rudder's hydraulics. "Tell your men to evacuate the ship," Carlucci ordered, tossing the panel aside. "There is nothing more they can do up here."

Elliott ordered his men off the bridge. Some of the commandos raced out onto the wing deck to the outside stairs. Others bolted down the damaged stairwell.

Carlucci inserted a special rod into a floor pipe and began pumping it back and forth as though it were a horizontal slot machine, manually moving the ship's rudder. The effort quickly proved too much for him, and he began to swoon.

Elliott, the last to leave the bridge, glanced back at Carlucci. "Are you okay?"

"I cannot do this," Carlucci said.

Elliott returned to the captain's side.

"Tell me what to do," Elliott said, taking over the strenuous pumping.

Under Carlucci's direction, Elliott managed to move *Lucy* ten degrees to port. The slight change in course wasn't enough, though, not by a large margin.

Lucy's forecastle slipped between the bridge's pylons, and the swing bridge passed over her forward deck like a dark beast of prey. The crow's nest was the first casualty, sheared off with a great crash. As *Lucy* continued her journey under the span, the bridge cut down the ship's loading booms like a sickle chopping weeds, then headed for the ship's superstructure.

Carlucci and Elliott, absorbed in the business of manually moving the ship's rudder, never saw the steel beast waiting for them. *Lucy's* superstructure struck the Coleman Memorial Bridge at fourteen knots. The impact was devastating. An endless tearing and screeching of metal howled through the night. The wheelhouse collapsed. The superstructure and funnel disintegrated in a tangle of metal, lurched backward, then slowly, ponderously, tumbled in a mammoth heap into the York River behind the ship.

Captain Sergio Carlucci and Special Forces Captain Elliott were dead long before the labyrinth of mangled steel settled on the riverbed 75 feet below the surface. Nothing even remotely resembling human remains would ever be distinguishable from the wreck.

Marshall felt the shock of the collision viciously jar the entire length of the vessel. He and the sergeant braced themselves in the knee-deep water in the ship's lower pump room. *Lucy* was listing dangerously aft.

"In here." Williams pressed his back against the bulkhead hatch and pushed it open. The amber emergency lights inside the compartment offered little illumination. Marshall entered first, scanning the dimness and listening. Williams slipped in behind him.

"So where are they?" Williams asked.

"Maintenance," Marshall said, pointing to another hatch.

Marshall found Carlucci's huge flashlight and played its beam along the forward bulkhead. All he could see were pipes. And a lone hatch. The major heard a curious noise above the roar of incoming water – a groan of metal and the cracking of a hatch seal. Suddenly the hatch to the maintenance area burst open with enough force to bend its steel hinges.

Marshall stared mutely at the hulking form beyond the transom. "God almighty," he gasped, his unsteady light beam creating a circus effect.

Gorgon's face, bloated beyond recognition, had become a mask of mutated fury. Saint Vitus had created a beast – a maniacal, cold-blooded beast.

Gorgon's distended eyes stared at Marshall with something resembling a mix of rage and determination. The major withdrew his Beretta, unable to imagine that this transformed aberration had once been human. "Sweet J—"

Gorgon stooped through the transom and pushed himself into the pump room. From deep in his throat came a series of guttural moans that bespoke excruciating pain. It was the sound of a dying animal. Every muscle, every strand of sinew in his body, was alive and bloated with unnatural strength.

Williams grabbed Carlucci's baseball-size wrench from the floor. "Sweet Mother," he said, "the area must be infected." He glanced at Marshall. "I don't want to end up like him."

Marshall directed the Beretta at Gorgon but couldn't keep his hand steady. "I can't pull the trigger."

"Damn it, Joe, send that bastard to hell," Williams shouted. "*Do it!*"

Gorgon never took his eyes off Marshall. He walked slowly, spastically, toward him, his undulating, twisted legs reminding the major of a lifelong cripple who suddenly, miraculously, could walk. A massive hand unfurled from a stub of flesh that had once been an arm and reached for him. Marshall stepped backward. Gorgon's lips parted and out came a low, guttural noise that sounded like "*Martyr.*"

Marshall dropped the flashlight and fought to steady the Beretta with both hands. He let Gorgon move within reach before discharging three rounds into his chest in rapid succession. Gorgon went down with a hideous growl.

"*Yes,*" Williams shouted. "See you in hell, *fuckhead!*"

Marshall raised the volume of his transceiver and shouted into the mouthpiece, "Julie?"

"I'm right here."

"At least one virus tank ruptured in the ship's lower pump room. Gorgon became infected. I just dropped what was left of him. Jesus, we're breathing the same air."

There came a crackle of fading static in his ear, then he barely heard Julie say, "Joe, water is an ideal growth medium ... organism. If the virus spreads past the bulkheads ... devastate the Eastern Seaboard. You've got ... contain ..."

"I'm losing the signal. Tell me what you want me to do."

In the Bell-Ranger helicopter whipping over West Point at one hundred and fifty knots, Julie grabbed the young lieutenant's arm and jerked him toward her. "I need the tanker's pumping schematics."

"And I need you to prepare for a landing at Yorktown in five minutes," the lieutenant said.

"Give me that *fucking* chart!"

The lieutenant, scowling, pulled the chart out of a file folder. Julie snatched it out of his hands and flattened it over the chart table. She ran her finger over the pumping diagram, trying to match the schematic with the ship's compartments. *Goddamn, it's too complicated.* Her finger traced the intricate network of pipes until she located the pump room on the tanker's lower deck.

"Joe," she shouted into her headset, "flood that compartment with crude oil – and do it quickly."

"Repeat that," Marshall said. "I don't understand what you want me to do." He felt the angle of the deck increase, spilling aft everything not fastened to the deck. Cold water surged around his ankles.

"Crude oil is extremely toxic," Julie said. "It will kill the organism. Find the offloading lines. Most of the oil movement is controlled by automatic hydraulic butterfly valves. Look for a circular hand-operated valve to the emergency flow inspection line. It's manual. Open it to start the flow ... rupture the line..."

"Which line?" Marshall asked. "Say again. There are dozens of pipes."

"Just open that valve ... rupture every friggin' pipe in that compartment."

"What's she saying?" Williams said.

Marshall's eyes scanned the labyrinth of pipes lining the walls and ceiling. "She wants us to flood the compartment with oil to kill the organism."

"Say what?"

"Look for a circular valve." Marshall retrieved the flashlight and moved its beam along the pipes until he spotted a single manual valve on the far wall. "There. Open that valve. I'll find a way to rupture the pipe beyond it."

Williams sprang for the valve. But he didn't make it. Something beneath the water caught his ankle and yanked him to the floor. Gorgon sprang up from the water with an unsettling cry. His arm lashed out like a cobra, catching the sergeant's back as he scrambled to his feet. The blow drove Williams headlong into the bulkhead wall where he fell into a squatting position, stunned by the ferocity of Gorgon's unnatural strength. A single, well-placed blow would have broken his back.

Marshall whirled. "What the fuck—?" He leveled the Beretta with both hands and discharged the last two rounds into Gorgon's back. Astonishingly Gorgon remained erect.

Marshall's spasming fingers felt his SAS belt for another magazine. He didn't have a spare.

The deck's dangerous angle continued to rise, filling the compartment with water at an uncontrollable rate. *Lucy* was going down.

Williams crawled to the valve on hands and knees. Gorgon watched him, his muscles rippling as though he were struggling to control his extremities. Williams grabbed the valve wheel and pulled himself up. Flexing his back muscles into tight ropes, he began turning. There came a sharp hiss as crude oil flowed into the inspection line.

Gorgon lunged and rammed his tentacle-like arm against Williams' neck with brutal force that would have killed him had he not driven the gunnery sergeant's head into a crevice between two exposed pipes, protecting the bones in his neck. Williams struggled to fill his lungs with air. Trapped, unable to push Gorgon away, he could only stare into the monster's bloated, rage-filled eyes only a breath away from his.

"Break those ... fucking pipes," Williams gasped.

Marshall stormed into the maintenance shop and grabbed Wynett's Kalashnikov. He checked the clip, found it empty and, cursing, threw it aside. He looked at Tarra's undulating corpse. Pursing his lips, he knelt down and felt through her munitions belt, opening one pocket, then another, letting the contents spill. There were spare Uzi magazines, detonator fuses, chokes, cartridges. He found what he needed in a side pocket – a concussion grenade. He slipped it into his palm, then sloshed through the knee-deep water back into the pump room.

The major charged Gorgon and rammed him with his shoulder. It had all his strength behind it. Gorgon's grip on Williams only tightened. The gunnery sergeant flexed every muscle in an unsuccessful attempt to push the monster away. "Get this thing off me..."

Marshall found Carlucci's huge wrench, lifted it onto his shoulder and, charging forward, swung it with both hands into Gorgon's back. The weighty steel connected with a dull thud, caving in the pulpy flesh.

Gorgon flew away from Williams and reeled down the sloping deck, stumbling back into a deep swell of oil and river water. His throat opened with a moan, allowing thick, foul water to pour into his lungs.

Williams searched four feet of water for the open manhole in the deck. All he could see was black. "The crawlspace is flooding," he yelled to the major.

Marshall fought his way to the pipes on the forward bulkhead and jammed the grenade behind the valve wheel on the inspection line. "I'm right behind you."

The sergeant dove headfirst into the water toward the manhole.

Marshall pulled the grenade's pin and dove after him.

Gorgon struggled to rise, his squidlike fingers working themselves into fists, his unearthly eyes darting about the compartment. Long after his mind should have welcomed a merciful death, Gorgon remained aware of his predicament. Saint Vitus made sure of that. The virus needed its host conscious, needed the enzymes only cognizant brain activity would produce.

The grenade detonated with an earsplitting blast, shattering the pipes. A volcanic eruption of flame and crude oil blasted through the compartment. The full brunt of the explosion struck Gorgon solidly in his upper torso, hurling him though the open hatch into the flooded engine room. His fingers stretched helplessly outward.

What remained of his body smashed headlong against an unyielding boiler.

SUNKEN

Marshall and Williams swam through the flooded crawlspace between the ship's hulls, a dense, black tunnel filled with oil suspended like gooey smoke. The cold water transformed Marshall's limbs into weighty planks of lumber. His lungs ached. He could hear the muffled groans and screeching of metal as the ship's frame buckled under the pressure of the imploding river. Had the crawlspace already flooded from one end of the ship to the other, he wondered? If so, they were about to become entombed between the rusted hulls of a sunken tanker.

Twenty yards farther down Marshall and Williams surfaced in a black cavern and gasped great lungfuls of air that reeked of oil and river water. The atmosphere was thick and foul, nearly devoid of oxygen. Williams clawed up the steel plates and, coughing, cracked open a green phosphorescent light stick. The illuminated compartment reminded Marshall of the inside of a municipal sewer.

"Christ, Joe," Williams huffed, "we were exposed to that bug. Why didn't we turn into a monster like that asshole?"

"Sergeant," he said, crawling up beside him, "we'll discuss it later over a case of cold Heineken." Muffled thunder and earthquake-like tremors pounded the steel panels beneath them. Marshall stood. "The cargo tanks are going."

The two men pushed on, hunched beneath the great support beams of the steepening cavern between the hulls. Thirty yards farther, the light's green glow played off the forward bow.

"We might not get to that beer," Williams said. "A fucking dead end."

Marshall took the light from Williams and directed its glow on the riveted steel plates overhead. He found what he was looking for – another access cover similar to the one Carlucci had used to get them into the lower pump room. He passed the light to Williams.

"What do you have in mind?" the sergeant asked.

Marshall didn't answer – he didn't know where this hatch would lead to. He withdrew the empty Beretta and used the butt of the handgun like a hammer to pound open the latches while the rapidly rising water filling the compartment rushed around his waist. His lower extremities felt as though they were encased in ice.

Williams looked into the blackness behind. "We're out of time, Joe."

Marshall knocked open the last of the six latches, tucked the Beretta in his back holster and placed both hands on the access cover. He struggled to maintain his balance in the swift water that swirled around his head and shoulders. The area would be flooded in seconds. He could feel his legs slipping while his feet scrambled for support against a cross-beam. *Fuck me.* He applied brute pressure against the cover until it yielded with a reluctant screech.

Marshall's legs gave out, and the strong current swept him hard against the hull, stunning him. *"Jesus Christ."*

Williams' grabbed his leg and pushed him forward. "You first."

Marshall ran his trembling fingers along the steel plates, feeling his way aft. The rushing water flooded the last air pocket between the hulls. *Where in hell is that access?* He felt Williams' strong persistent hand pushing on his leg. Then he saw it – a dim light ahead, a shade lighter than the cold, inky blackness smothering them.

Marshall found the manhole and pulled himself up through the opening. His head broke the surface and he inhaled heated air between fits off coughing. They were in the frame webbing between the forward peak ballast tank and the ship's outer hull.

Williams surfaced beside him and gazed upward. A storm of fire ringed the world above. They stared up into the mouth of an active volcano fueled by the two forward crude compartments. "Is there no way outta this hell hole?"

Marshall scanned the high, narrow space and saw *Lucy's* 25,000-pound beams swaying in slow, undulating curves. "Maybe 75 feet of scaffolding to the top." He grabbed the first beam and pulled himself up. "Don't stop to smell any roses."

"Aye, sir."

They began climbing quickly up the web of steel beams that held the ship's hulls together. Marshall heard the grotesque shrieks of steel twisting and bending against the powerful forces tearing the ship apart. *Lucy* was surrendering to the immutable laws of physics. With frightful groans, she was making her final voyage to the bottom of the river.

The two commandos reached the top of the scaffolding and found a steel grating blocking their access to the ship's main deck. Marshall saw a frightful blaze beyond consuming what was left of *Lucy's* decks. The heat radiating through the opening felt like an open blast furnace. Where there wasn't fire, thick black smoke rolled across the deck.

Marshall drove his shoulder against the grating but the searing heat forced him back.

Williams glanced down at the rising water rushing toward them. "Fuck this." The sergeant braced his back against a horizontal support beam and, with steely determination, jammed his feet against the grating. Marshall could smell the stench of rubber burning off his wetsuit's soles.

Williams took in a deep breath and, with a single swift kick, knocked out the steel grid with a crash. Water roared over the bulwark and cascaded down what little of *Lucy's* deck still remained above water, allaying some heat, while sweeping everything not welded to the ship into a boiling surge of smoldering, sizzled debris.

Marshall gripped Williams' shoulder. "You'll join Julie and me tonight for a late supper?"

Williams smiled. "I'm looking forward to that Heineken."

The major's expression turned grim. "If things go bad ... tell her..."

Williams squeezed his hand, "You'll tell her."

The sergeant let go and rolled through the opening. Marshall heard him holler back, "I've got an appetite for baby back ribs," before vanishing through a wall of black smoke.

Marshall rolled out onto the deck after him. He grabbed a boot he first mistook for Williams'. It was the remains of a man consumed by fire. All that remained were a set of leg bones thrust into boots, a charred spinal column, a skull fused to the bulwark.

The deck's listing increased, threatening to dump him into a raging cauldron of boiling oil. Marshall caught a fleeting glimpse of Williams making his way toward the rail. The firestorm made it impossible to determine direction with any degree of certainty.

River water poured over the bulwark, but it did little to extinguish the flames. The burning crude simply lifted off the deck and swelled atop the waves, creating a fiery prison around him.

"Williams—" Marshall shouted. A wall of water crashed down on him.

The deck vanished under his feet, leaving him thrashing in a powerful whirlpool that threatened to pull him down with the tanker. Marshall felt himself spiraling downward inside the angry current. He clawed and kicked through the liquid blackness, fighting the angry vortex. His lungs burned with the intensity of the inferno above him.

His head broke the surface and he sucked in what air he could. He couldn't get enough. The insatiable fire had devoured all the life-giving oxygen on the surface of the river.

Flotsam from the wreck swirled around him. *Lucy* was gone. All that remained to mark her grave were flames and rolling black smoke. He looked up. Even the sky was on fire – hydrocarbon vapors flared with unearthly combustions.

Marshall felt his convulsing limbs tighten. To his horror he realized he could no longer move his arms. His muscles broke into uncontrollable spasms.

"Williams," he shouted. Foul water poured down his throat. He felt himself sinking. He raised his rigid arms as far as he could. *"Williams!"*

He could no longer cry out. Blackness. He sank through the cold, blackness ... sinking ... sinking ... sinking....

GRAVEYARD

An empty oil drum spun past Williams. He threw himself over its top and used his weight to keep the flotsam stable. The right side of his face and shoulder ached in ways he'd never experienced, and he could taste blood.

He ignored his injuries and looked desperately across the field of water debris for a glimpse of the major. "Joe?" No answer. "Joe ... goddamn you!"

Williams began kicking in circles, negotiating the columns of fire in search of his comrade. But he was gone.

He ran a hand over his head and muttered, "Goddamnit, Joe."

Williams heard the sound of approaching choppers. Suddenly, one of the Sea Stallions roared directly overhead. A second chopper appeared, then a third, their powerful spotlights sweeping the river as though it were a great stage. The rotors' downdraft whipped the water into ferocious swells.

Williams kicked and pushed the drum toward the riverbank several hundred feet away. A spotlight followed him to shore where he discarded the oil drum and stumbled up onto the rock-strewn bank like a drunkard. The night's brisk wind felt like steel whips on his exposed skin. He collapsed on the bank, paralyzed by the chill.

The sergeant touched his bleeding face and shoulder. His vest felt like a charred rag. He scooped up a handful of mud and pressed it against the side of his face. The pain intensified. He began shaking uncontrollably.

"Fuck you, Gorgon," he muttered. "Fuck your miserable soul."

The shriek of a whistle cut through the night, and suddenly there were soldiers everywhere, sliding down the embankment with their weapons drawn. Amid the frantic shouting Williams heard the unsettling clicks of rifle bolts being pulled back.

The lead soldier yelled at him, "Put your hands where I can see them."

Williams' arms were in spasm. He couldn't comply. The contingent of soldiers formed a tight circle around him, pointing a dozen gun barrels at his head. A chopper's spotlight blinded him.

"Identify yourself," one of the soldiers roared, his voice bordering on hysteria. He pointed a .45 with both hands. A weekend warrior ready to shoot anyone they thought might be a terrorist, Williams thought.

Williams, his trembling now a deep, unyielding spasm, said to the lieutenant in an unsteady voice, "Get me the fuck out of here."

Another voice – a female's – shouted, "Let me through ... *goddamnit, let me through!*"

It was Julie.

She broke through the circle of soldiers and knelt beside him. "It's the sergeant," she hollered back to someone he couldn't see.

Julie shouted at the solider with the pistol, "This man is a U.S. commando. He has third-degree burns. Get a stretcher down here fast." The lieutenant holstered his .45 and bolted up the bank.

Williams watched her prepare a syringe from her medical kit. She was crying as she pushed the needle into his arm. She managed to ask the question he dreaded to answer.

"Where is he?"

Williams grabbed her hand. "I'm sorry ... he wanted me to tell you that he loved you."

Julie touched the sergeant's arm to steady herself. She appeared ready to pass out. She averted her eyes to the river's enormous graveyard of heavy black smoke and roaring columns of fire. "Why did you have to leave me too?" she whispered to the night. Julie put a hand over her face while the sobs poured out of her. "Why? Why ... ?"

"We have another one," a soldier hollered from the riverbank.

Julie whirled. Williams lifted himself onto his elbows and watched several soldiers splash knee-deep into the river to retrieve what he first thought was a piece of wreckage. As they pulled it ashore, he could see a quivering manlike mass attached to a watertight case with military markings, one of Gorgon's munitions containers used to transport missiles.

Julie scrambled down the bank on hands and knees, dragging the medical kit behind her.

"He's one of ours," a soldier shouted.

Julie slid beside him. "Oh, my God!"

Marshall was writhing and undulating, yet he managed to hold the case in a death grip. It took three soldiers to pry him off the unlikely raft.

"Thank God ... thank God!" Julie cried over and over as she prepared a syringe.

Marshall never felt the needle pierce his arm. Julie hovered over him like an angel, nestling his head in her lap, her face, cast in gold by the fiery river, a mask of divine strength.

She smiled at him and ran her fingers through his matted hair. "You're safe with me now. You're safe with me now."

Marshall tried to return her smile but failed pathetically. He couldn't stop staring up at Julie. He did feel safe with her, a wonderfully contented sensation he'd never felt before. A brisk wind whipped over him. He couldn't feel the chill. He couldn't feel much of anything. Just safe.

He closed his eyes and let his mind and soul drift in the warmth surrounding him.

NEPTUNE SPEAR

Abbottabad, Pakistan
Monday, May 2, 0059 hours (local time)

Navy Seal Assault Commander Eric "Buzz" Hauser was the first commando from Razor 1 to rappel from the Stealth Hawk chopper. The even purr of the helicopter's stealth rotors stirred the quiet night, its downdraft pouring into the courtyard like a tropical storm. Hauser saw movement in the compound beneath the chopper – a white bed sheet whipping from a drying line. A folding chair picked up by the rotors' air blast flew against the white cement building with a bang. But no defenders. *Hustle your ass.*

Hauser moved quickly to the back of the roof and jumped down onto the building's terrace. He sensed his fellow assaulters behind him, matching his movements, storming down the building's terrace, weapons ready. They made no sound.

Twenty seconds after landing, the Neptune Spear team were inside the house, charging down the third-story hallway. A woman appeared from a doorway. One of his wives? – Hauser couldn't be sure. An intense white strobe from one of the commandos flashed into her eyes. She cried out and stumbled, blinded.

Another commando grabbed her arm and pushed her to the floor, while Hauser and the others continued down the hallway one behind the other, their weapons raised.

A head emerged from an open hallway door. The bearded man stared mutely at the approaching assaulters, and then closed himself inside the room with a bang. There was no mistaking the face of the man he had just seen. Hauser touched his inter-squad radio and shouted, "Geronimo, Geronimo, Geronimo," informing the others that he had identified their target.

The stairwell lights at the end of the hallway flared on, followed by the sound of someone rushing up the stairs. Hauser heard a pair of suppressed shots followed by the garbled gasps of a dying resident.

He ignored the skirmish, focusing instead on his target. He reached the bedroom door, his assault partner behind him.

"Let's do it," his partner said.

Hauser kicked open the door, and the pair moved inside the bedroom. Their weapons' lights swept a short hallway and then lit up the bedchamber. The room smelled musty, like ancient linen. They illuminated a bearded man and a woman standing next to a charpoy. The woman shouted at them, but Hauser didn't understand a word. The bearded man stood behind her, silent and staring, his hands disarmingly at his sides.

Osama bin Laden – The Lion.

"Gorgon says go fuck yourself," Hauser said.

bin Laden shoved the woman toward the pair and dove across the bed, a hand reaching for an AK-47 assault rifle leaning against the headboard. The woman screamed.

Hauser and his partner aimed past the woman, their green laser beads converging on the man's chest.

"No, no, no!" the woman shouted in Arabic.

The two commandos fired four suppressed shots in the same instant, the reports sounding as one.

The first round pounded the mattress just to the left of his face. A second round grazed the woman's thigh.

bin Laden never touched his rifle. The third bullet struck dead center of his chest. The final entered his skull, spilling brain matter across the tussled sheets.

EPILOGUE:
FORT DETRICK
QUARANTINE CENTER

Monday, May 2, 0700 hours

Marshall sat slouched in one of the quarantine center's overstuffed chairs, his feet up, sipping his third cup of black coffee this morning. The mug in his hand was rock steady. He ignored the throbbing ear beneath a thick gauze patch, and ran his fingers absently through clumps of matted hair that felt like mesh wire. Three shampoos with dishwashing detergent – the best oil solvent for hair – had done a number on his dome.

"I'll have it shaved," he said to Williams.

The gunnery sergeant, lying across the lounge's sofa, winced when he touched the layer of bandages covering the right side of his face and shoulder. "You'd look goooooood with a bald pate."

Julie let out a throaty chuckle from her chair beside the major.

Marshall knew the gunnery sergeant was in considerable pain. He also knew Williams would never let on that his injuries were anything but minor. The sergeant no doubt would insist on returning to active duty while most men with burns as severe as his would still be on their backs in a trauma unit.

Julie sat with her legs tucked beneath her, making notes on a thick stack of printouts. She had moved from her chair next to Marshall only once during the night when summoned to participate in the debriefing call with the joint chiefs.

"Morning people." It was General Medlock.

Marshall turned his stiff neck and saw the general grinning from the doorway of the quarantine center's lounge, his arms outstretched like a proud papa. He appeared genuinely happy to see them. He carried a well-traveled copy of the morning's *Washington Post*.

"Well, well," Julie said. "So you've ventured into the lair of the cursed plague people. Aren't you afraid you'll catch your death?"

Medlock smiled. "I'm on my way to the White House to meet a very happy president. He'd like to give each of you the Congressional Medal of Honor. But you understand why he can't go public with this incident for national security reasons. You're all under an indefinite gag order. He says he'll make it up to you some way. Meanwhile" – he waved the morning's paper – "I wanted you to see this."

He held up the front page. The headline read:

U.S. forces kill Osama bin Laden;
'JUSTICE HAS BEEN DONE'

"Oh my God," Julie said.

"*What!?*" Marshall sat up, stunned, and finally broke into a broad smile. "Congratulations, general."

Williams extended his hand. "Let me see that."

Medlock passed the newspaper to the sergeant.

"I'll take the travel section," Julie said, setting aside her printouts. "I'm taking Joe home to the Colorado Rockies."

"Unless," Marshall said to the general, "you're having us committed to a military hospital."

"You're free to leave anytime you'd like," Medlock said.

Williams turned to an inside page and let out a huff of laughter. "I'll be damned. There wasn't room on the front page for this story. Get a load of the headline: 'Tanker sinks; its oil still trapped on board.' There's not a word in here about Gorgon or a terrorist plot. Listen to this shit: 'The crippled oil tanker *Lucy* sank in the York River near Yorktown about nine forty-five p.m. yesterday with much of its 17 million gallons of crude still on board, offering hope that an environmental disaster could be averted. Authorities gathered at the site throughout the night to inspect the tanker submerged in 70 feet of water to determine how badly its double hull had been damaged. The inspection will determine if the ship's oil tanks will remain watertight so rescuers can eventually pump out the crude. The number of dead crewmen from the explosion aboard *Lucy* last night still has not been determined and no survivors have been found. Some reports speculate the initial explosion occurred while crew members, none U.S. nationals, were cleaning an empty oil tank. The tanker was on a routine trip from Venezuela to a refinery in Yorktown. Early speculation suggests that the low river level from the lack of spring rain may have played a role.'"

Marshall raised his arm in victory. "Equally nice work with the media, general."

Medlock accepted the accolade with raised eyebrows. "The media would have my ass if they knew the inspection team is a special army underwater salvage squad. Julie, have you figured out why these men are still alive after that virus tank ruptured?"

Julie picked up her mug and thoughtfully sipped the creamy brew. "We built up an extraordinary immunity to Saint Vitus. Our exposure to a mutated strain on Wynett's plantation produced remarkable antibodies in our systems. It'll take months to sift through this first round of data from the Crays to construct a model of our long-term health profile. But it doesn't appear the antibodies will affect the quality of our lives." She set down her mug, then jumped up from her chair and plopped into Marshall's lap, slipping her arms around his neck. "I don't care if we're on our deathbeds, I'm holding you to your promise of a lobster dinner tonight."

Marshall pulled her closer. He planted a lingering kiss on her lips, then looked deep into her eyes. "I wouldn't have it any other way." He shot a glance at Williams. "You're joining us, of course."

Medlock frowned. "This man needs a hospital."

"It's the Yankees and the Tigers," Williams said, scanning the sports page. "I'll have the place to myself and there's plenty of cold Heineken in the fridge. I'm not moving from in front of that TV."

Medlock chuckled at the sergeant's resilience. "Suit yourselves." Then his expression turned serious. "I'm truly sorry for not trusting you. Thank God you are more stubborn than I am and did what you believed was right. I salute you all."

"Hindsight's twenty-twenty," Marshall said. "By the way, Colonel Martinelli mentioned something about a reward for taking down Gorgon."

Medlock nodded. "You and the sergeant can retire comfortably tomorrow if you like."

Before Marshall could respond, the general turned and was gone.

Marshall heard his spit-polished shoes knocking briskly down the sterile corridor on their way out of the center and into the bright Spring sunshine.

"We are launching a new initiative that will give us the capacity to respond faster and more effectively to bioterrorism or an infectious disease – a plan that will counter threats at home, and strengthen public health abroad."

—President Barack Obama

"While the United States debates the development of a massive defensive effort against nuclear attack ... the fact remains that this nation is almost entirely defenseless against chemical, biological and toxic weapons of mass destruction. Some of these weapons may already be secreted within our borders; others could be synthesized by our enemies within a matter of hours, or days at the most."

—Defense Consultants
Joseph D. Douglass, Jr.
and Neil C. Livingstone